Gray springing forward, and dashing the contents of his glass in the landlord's face, seized him by the neck, and fairly choked the words down his throat.—p. 57.

THE BEAUTIFUL SPY.

AN EXCITING STORY

OF

ARMY AND HIGH LIFE IN NEW YORK IN 1776.

BY CHARLES BURDETT,

AUTHOR OF "THREE PER CENT A MONTH," "SECOND MARRIAGE," "MARION DESMOND," ETC., ETC.

PHILADELPHIA:

JOHN E. POTTER AND COMPANY,

617 SANSOM ST.

PRESS OF JOHN E. POTTER & COMPANY
PHILADELPHIA

TO

WILLIAM CURTIS NOYES, Esq.,

This Book

IS RESPECTFULLY DEDICATED,

AS A MARK OF HIGH PERSONAL REGARD AND ESTEEM, AND IN GRATEFUL APPRECIATION OF PAST KINDNESS,

BY HIS ATTACHED FRIEND,

THE AUTHOR.

CONTENTS.

APPENDIX.

I.

II.

INTRODUCTION.

In the latter part of the month of May, 1776, the city of New York was garrisoned by about thirteen thousand troops, regulars and militia, under the command of Major-General George Washington, comprising men from every section of the country this side of North Carolina, and as far north as New Hampshire.

His head-quarters were established at what was then known as Richmond Hill, and which is more fully described in the succeeding chapters, now familiar to present residents as the country seat of Col. Burr, and after his purchase and occupancy, named Burr's Hill.

The second in command was that gallant and tried old soldier, General Putnam, whose feats in the wolf's den have become as household words with every schoolboy in the country. He had established his head-quarters at the house well known as No. 1 Broadway, on the corner of Battery Place, built many years before by Major Kennedy for his private residence, and in later days familiar to New Yorkers as the residence of two mayors.

General Putnam's aid at this period was Major Aaron Burr, who had sought the post in preference to a similar position in the military family of the Commander-in-Chief, where he was confined exclusively to the duties of an amanuensis, which did not suit his ardent, active military spirit, and General Putnam was glad to avail himself of the services of one who had proved himself as eminent with the pen, as with the sword.

In the month of May, General Washington was summoned to Philadelphia to attend upon Congress, then in session, and General Putnam was left in chief command, with instructions to fortify the city at every point to repel a threatened invasion, as Admiral Howe, with his fleet, and an army of some thirty thousand regulars and Hessians, had left the waters of Virginia under the command of Lord Howe, and it was presumed that the next point of attack would be the city of New York—which supposition was fully borne out by subsequent events, as recorded in history.

On the last day of May, and, of course, during the absence of General Washington, General Putnam was one day the recipient—through a boat from Staten Island (then occupied by the British), bearing a flag of truce—of a letter from Major Moncrieffe of the British army, who with his regiment was encamped on the island, in which he set forth that the chances and hazards of war had compelled him to leave his only child, a daughter just past fifteen, Margaret Moncrieffe, alone and unprotected at the house of a widow lady near the town of Elizabeth, and with entire strangers; and as he could not foresee what the perils of war might bring forth in a day or an hour, and as the locality where she resided might soon become the field of active operations, he was loath to leave her there if it could be possibly avoided. He therefore implored the general, as a soldier and a gentleman, to afford to his child that which he could not—a shelter and a home until such time as he could place her in a position of greater security.

General Putnam promptly replied, that the request would be cheerfully granted, and that in in his own home, in the bosom of his family, she would be at least assured of hospitable treatment. The young girl was sent for on the following day (the first of June), and from that time remained an inmate of General Putnam's family, until detected in communicating with the enemy, when she was sent off to King's Bridge, then Gen. Mifflin's head-quarters.

Miss Margaret Moncrieffe, the heroine of the book, though really only a child in years, for she had just passed her fifteenth summer, was, in all that belongs to woman of feeling, heart or passion, fully developed, and history has recorded that a most romantic attachment sprang up between herself and Major Burr, the handsome, gallant and accomplished aid—on her part with all the fervor of her passionate nature, on his, with more caution and prudence; and that his love for her was not a supreme and reigning passion, may be assumed from the well known circumstance, that it was he who having detected her in imparting secret information to Governor Tryon, then on board the flag ship, Duchess of Gordon, lying opposite Staten Island, gave such information as caused her removal to a place where she would find other and less dangerous occupation.

It was during General Washington's absence that a plot was concocted by Governor Tryon, aided by Matthews, a well known Tory, then mayor of the city, who was residing at Flatbush, to capture General Washington, hoping thus to terminate the war by one bold blow. Margaret Moncrieffe contributed materially to the possible success of their plans, in which the Tory residents of the city, together with many Provincials who had been bought over, had joined, by conveying secretly to Governor Tryon information as to the location and strength of the various fortifications on the island; but fuller details of the plot will be found elsewhere.

The pages which follow are derived from these two incidents—the mutual attachment of Aaron Burr and Margaret Moncrieffe, and the infamous plot of Tryon and Matthews. Every name is historically correct, save two or three introduced to fill up the story. Every incident is historical—the dress and appearance of the principal conspirators are described as accurately as could be derived from the authorities consulted, and save the *main incident*, that Aaron Burr was seduced from his allegiance to his country, or his devotion to her cause, by Margaret Moncrieffe, the author claims that he has woven a fiction founded entirely on facts.

Without this explanation, he would never present it for public praise or censure. With it, which is but simple justice to the best abused and most maligned man who ever filled a high and honorable station, the work must abide the decision which the public may award.

MARGARET MONCRIEFFE.

CHAPTER I.

GENERAL PUTNAM AND AARON BURR.

It was a pleasant morning on the 31st day of May, 1776—not exactly morning, for the sun had passed the meridian nearly an hour—General Putnam was seated in the apartment on the lower floor of his head-quarters, at No. 1 Broadway, which he had appropriated as an office for the transaction of all his official business—the reception of reports, the issuing of orders, and all the details which belong to the position of Commander-in-Chief of the troops which then garrisoned the city of New York, some thirteen thousand in number.

He held his position by reason of the absence of General Washington, who had been summoned by the Congress, then in session in Philadelphia, to consult with the members of that august body (alas! how sadly and woefully changed), with reference to the suspected movements of the British fleet, under Admiral Howe, which convoyed transports containing an army of some twenty thousand regulars and Hessians, under the command of Lord Howe, and which had recently left the waters of Virginia. It was supposed that their next point of attack would be the city of New York, and orders had been given to fortify the island at every accessible point.

General Putnam was seated, or rather lounging on a hair-covered mahogany sofa, elaborately carved, and studded with brass nails—then, no doubt, thought to be a superb piece of furniture—and was holding in his hand an open letter which he had just perused.

At a large oval table which stood in the centre of the room, and which was covered with papers lying about in disorder and confusion, was seated a young man, dressed in the blue and buff uniform of the day, such as was worn by the regular troops (when they had any to wear). His sword lay on the floor beside him, and his chapeau had been placed on the other side. He could not have been more than twenty or twenty-one years of age, for his countenance was almost boyish. His face was oval, with a broad, expanded forehead, white as snow, where it had been covered by his hat—his complexion pale, but not sallow, though somewhat bronzed by exposure—his nose was beautifully shaped, and of just proportion to his face—his mouth closely cut, and evincing a spirit of determination and perseverance, fully borne out by the history of his after years, while his chin was small and delicate as a woman's. His eyes were of a dark hazel, so dark, no sign of a pupil could be seen, and the expression of them, when he chose, was wonderful—they could be likened only to those of a snake, for their fascination was irresistible. But the great charm lay in his smile, which no one could resist—so sweet, so mild, so speaking. In figure he was about the medium height—his form as perfect as that of any sculptured model, and there was a grace, an ease, a quiet dignity in all his movements, which spoke one born to achieve greatness.

Such, in brief, was Major Aaron Burr, at the age of twenty, and who, at that early age, occupied the high and honorable position of Aid to General Putnam, by whom he was treated as a son, and to whom he gave his unlimited confidence. He was engaged in making out some orders previously dictated by the general, when his labors were interrupted by the latter, who, starting from the sofa, said, "There, major, read that—that is the letter just brought by the truce-boat from Staten Island; what on earth can I do with it?"

Major Burr, laying down his pen, perused the letter, and looking up in the general's face, said in his low, soft, musical voice, for which, elsewhere than on the field of battle, he was so famed, "I see only one course; Major Moncrieffe appeals to you as a soldier and gentleman; as such, you can make but one reply."

"Well, I suppose that's so; write, then, that Gen

eral Putnam will gladly accede to Major Moncrieffe's request, and will to-morrow dispatch a squad of men to escort his daughter to the city, and that in his quarters, and with his family, she will find a home and welcome, until the position or circumstances of her father might enable him to reclaim her."

The letter was written, signed, formally sealed, and addressed, and was handed to the orderly with directions to have it sent out to the British truce-boat, then lying off and on, a few hundred yards from the shore.

The letter which had led to this conversation, had been brought on that morning by a boat from Staten Island, bearing a flag of truce, which was met a few hundred yards from the shore (for of course an enemy's boat was not allowed to come within hailing distance of land), by one from the Provincial general.

It was from Major Moncrieffe, of the British army, whose regiment was then encamped on Staten Island, preferring a very singular request. The writer stated that the chances of war had necessitated a separation from his only child, Margaret, a motherless daughter, who had accompanied him from England. She was now alone and unprotected at the farmhouse of one widow Adams, near Elizabeth, and he implored General Putnam, as a soldier, a gentleman, and a father, to grant shelter and protection to his child. She was, he said, scarce past fifteen, utterly inexperienced, and required that care and attention which he could not now bestow upon her; and he promised, if his request was complied with, to relieve the general from the responsibility at the earliest possible moment.

"How am I to get her here, major?" asked the general, taking up the letter of Major Moncrieffe. "He writes that she is at the house of one Mrs. Adams, near Elizabeth. Do you know anything about the place?"

"Everything, general. Mr. Adams, the father, now dead, used to oversee my uncle's farm near Newark, and, since his death, the widow moved with her daughter, to the place on which they now reside, which belongs to us, and which she occupies rent free as long as she lives. She has a nephew—a bold, dashing young fellow, who ran away from home to follow me through the route to Quebec, and who is now a sergeant in McDougall's regiment."

"I wish he was in a better place," growled the general, "for that regiment was notorious for its utter lack of discipline, its general inefficiency, and the turbulent disposition of the men.

"Well, as you know the place and the people, suppose you go over to-morrow and bring this young lady hither. I wonder what she is like."

"The letter says she is a mere child, and inexperienced. She won't give you much trouble, I fancy. I will take a squad of picked men, and go after her to-morrow, for I shall be glad again to see the good old lady and her daughter."

"Pretty, eh?" said the general, with a comical look, to which Major Burr replied, laughing,

"Oh, yes, very pretty, general, and a terrible little patriot."

"So much the better. I wish we had more men like her. But consider that arranged. Now do you go on and finish up those orders. I will take a ride around the works, and see how they advance. I want to have everything finished before General Washington's return, which can't be delayed many days longer;" and seizing his chapeau, he directed the orderly to have his horse brought to the door, and rode off to inspect the works, for he never trusted to others to do that which he could best do himself.

In the evening, at the tea-table, the general informed his wife and daughters of the intended accession to their family circle, to which, of course, no opposition was offered; and Major Burr having made all his preparations for the morrow's journey—for it was something of a journey in those days, even to Elizabeth—retired early, and left the family to discuss, in anticipation, the possible merits or demerits of the new comer.

CHAPTER II.

MARGARET MONCRIEFFE.

The town of Elizabeth, in the month of June, 1776, was very different in its character and population from the Elizabeth City of the present day. A few scattering log-huts embedded in woods; hundreds of acres of uncleared lands, covered with stately trees, and here and there a small farmhouse, afforded the only evidences of the existence of the town of Elizabeth, as it was then called, whose limits, however, extended for a circuit of many miles around.

At the extreme end of the township, and on the side nearest to the Staten Island shore, there stood, at the time of which I write, a small farmhouse, as it was then called, though at the present time it would scarcely be dignified with the name of cottage. It was a low, one-story dwelling, built of hewn stone, with a wing extending some thirty feet, which was formed of rough-hewn logs, and plastered with mud.

The farm on which it was located, had evidently been cultivated for a long time, for the house was surrounded with appliances of comparative comfort and indications of civilization rarely found in that vicinity at that period of our country's history.

A large orchard of apple-trees fronted the house, and in the rear it was bounded by a forest of maple and chestnut, then, of course, in full leaf, and which contrasted beautifully with the snow-white house; for the homestead, though built of stone, had been white-washed, presenting an appearance as attractive to the eye as it was gratifying to the taste.

It was, perhaps, an hour before noon, on one of the most sultry days, early in June of the memorable year 1776. Everything about the dwelling was as quiet as though it contained nothing human. There was scarcely air enough stirring to ruffle the leaves on the trees, and the sun, nearly at meridian, poured down his rays with an intensity almost overpowering.

At this hour, the quiet of the place was disturbed by the tramping of approaching horsemen, and, as the sound reached the house, one of the inmates appeared at the door of the wing, which was appropriated to culinary purposes.

"My sakes!" exclaimed the party who, on hearing the sound of horses' hoofs, had approached the door; "I wonder if it's more of them marciless cow-boys?"

"I guess not," was the reply which came from the lips of a young girl, who, with sleeves rolled above her elbows, was hard at work in the suds of the wash-tub "Colonel Malcolm's men have given them such a fright they won't be around here soon again, I guess."

"Massy sakes! who on airth be they?" exclaimed the first speaker, as she gazed down the road which fronted the house, and pointed in the direction toward which she was looking; and as she spoke, she shaded her eyes with her hand, as if to aid her vision, rendered indistinct by age.

"Why, mother, can't you see?" and the speaker, who had left the wash-tub and joined her mother in the doorway, peered out in the direction whence the sounds approached. "Don't you see they are Continentallers? Some scouting-party, I'm sure; and, oh dear me! they've caught me in a nice fix. Mother, you go and get something ready for them to eat;" and, as she spoke, she unpinned her dress, which had been tucked up around her waist, and smoothing it down, turned to go again into the kitchen, where she had been occupied, and, pausing an instant in front of a small glass which hung between the windows, smoothed down the glossy hair which floated in luxuriant masses over her face and neck, and, with a smile and blush at her own vanity, so natural to her sex, she retired to an inner room to prepare herself for a reception of the approaching visitors.

"Why, Patsy!" exclaimed the elder of the twain, as her daughter left her side; but Patsy either did not or would not hear her mother, and she was left alone to receive those whose coming had already been heralded by the sound of their horses' feet.

The party consisted of nine horsemen; and at the head, mounted on a large, powerfully-built and spirited charger, rode the leader—a young, beardless man, who, to judge from his appearance, had scarcely more than passed his teens. He was dressed in the blue and buff Continental uniform, as were his followers; but there was so little difference in the attire of the party, it would have been difficult to select the leader, but for the straps across his shoulder, denoting that he was entitled to wear epaulettes, and the air of command which seemed to sit upon him as naturally as if born to it. As the party approached the house, the old lady went out to the fence which surrounded it, and, with a low courtesy, said:

"Won't you halt, gentlemen, and have something to eat after your hot ride?"

The leader of the party drew up his horse at this salutation, and, dismounting, threw the reins to one of his companions. Approaching the hostess with a courtly bow, he said:

"This, I believe, is farmer Adams' house?"

"Of course it is. Why, bless me!" and she peered earnestly into the face of the speaker, with an expression of mingled doubt and pleasure; "sure you ain't little Burr?"

"As sure as you are Mrs. Adams," replied the party addressed, and he extended his hand, which was warmly grasped by the delighted old lady, who, turning toward the house, exclaimed, at the top of her shrill voice:

"Patsy, come down here; it's little Burr. Why, Aaron, where did you come from? We heard as you was killed there at Quebec, and Patsy has been crying ever so much about you; come in, Aaron. But what on airth be you doing with all these men?"

"I will tell you when we get inside, my good old friend," said Major Burr, for he it was. "We have had a hot and dusty ride, and my men are terribly hungry and thirsty, too."

"I'll take care of them, I'll warrant you. Tell 'em to come in." And turning to his men, he gave the sign to dismount, which was promptly and gladly obeyed, for theirs, indeed, had been a hot and dusty ride, and fastening their horses to the fence in front of the house, they awaited his further orders.

"Why on airth don't you ask 'em in, Aaron?" exclaimed the old lady, whose ideas of hospitality recognized no distinction in rank.

Major Burr smiled, and turning to his followers, beckoned to one of them, who approached, and with a military salute, stood awaiting his orders.

"Keep one man on guard—take the rest in, and our kind landlady here will give you something to eat and drink." Then addressing Mrs. Adams, who had looked with wondering eyes upon the youthful hero, he said, "Come, where's Patsy? I haven't had a kiss since I left her, eighteen months ago. Ah, Patsy!" he exclaimed, as the young girl entered the room, smiling and blushing, "how do you do?" and seizing one hand, he clasped her waist with the other, and before she had time to resist, had she felt so inclined, which is exceedingly doubtful, the young soldier had imprinted a hearty kiss upon a pair of as pretty, and rosy lips as New Jersey could boast of at that time.

"Why, Aaron, I am ashamed of you," said the blushing girl, struggling to release herself from his embrace, "before all these men!"

"You shall take it back, Patsy, as soon as we are alone," and he smiled wickedly. "Let your mother take care of my men, and do you get something for me; I am hot, tired, and hungry."

"Your men, Aaron!" said Patsy, opening her large blue eyes with a stare of astonishment, as she gazed upon the youthful speaker.

"Yes, Patsy, my men. But come, what do you suppose brought me here?" and as he spoke, a crimson blush illuminated the beautiful face of the young girl, for his words recalled pleasant memories.

Perhaps she thought he came wooing, for he had often told her how much he loved her, and she, poor fool, had believed him. She had heard of his gallant exploits with Arnold—had read, with flushed cheeks and beating heart, the high commendations officially bestowed upon him, and as he stood there before her, bronzed, weather-worn, yet bearing himself so gallantly, her heart beat high with the hope which her lips dare not express.

"I am sure I don't know, Aaron," she murmured. "I beg pardon," she interrupted, as she remembered that he was now Major Burr, and the leader of the party.

"No, Aaron always, and always the same Aaron," he said, raising her hand to his lips, and imprinting a kiss on it, at the same time fastening upon her a glance which brought the crimson tide again to her face. "I have come to relieve you of the presence of—let me see, what is her name," and he drew from his pocket a letter, which, having opened, he glanced over hastily. "Margaret Moncrieffe," he continued, refolding the letter, and replacing it in his pocket. "I have come for her by order from General Putnam."

"Surely you are not going to take her prisoner?"

"Oh, no," he replied, laughingly; "we don't make war upon, nor prisoners of, women."

"She isn't a woman, Aaron—she is only a child. But"——

"Well, go on," he said, seeing that she hesitated.

"No matter; judge for yourself. Come, take a seat

in the parlor, and I will find something for you to eat and drink."

"But where is Miss Moncrieffe? I must hurry her off, for it is necessary I should be in the city to-night."

"She is somewhere about—I suppose under the trees, reading. She spends half her time out of doors, reading, or firing at a mark, and I can tell you, Aaron, she is a desperate shot."

"She won't bring me down, Patsy," said the young major, gallantly, "for your image will be between us;" and again the warm blood mantled her brow and cheeks, and her eyes fairly glistened with happiness. "While you are getting some refreshments, I will seek her out. Where do you suppose she is?"

"In the small grove," and she pointed to the spot named, which was distant, perhaps, two hundred feet from the house.

Unbuckling the heavy horseman's sword, which had, during this brief conversation, been dangling about his heels, he laid it on the table, and, with a graceful bow and smile, left the room, and strode off toward the grove, which he well knew, for with it were associated memories of a character so pleasant as not to be easily effaced, for it was in that grove he had told his boyish love to the blushing, happy girl whom he had just left, and had received an avowal of her own in return.

CHAPTER III.

LOVE AT FIRST SIGHT.

As he approached the well remembered spot, he observed the object of his search, half reclining on the green sward, leaning against a tree, and deeply engaged in the perusal of a book which she held in her hand.

"Miss Moncrieffe," he said, approaching the young lady, who, pausing in the perusal of her book, dropped it by her side, and fixed upon the intruder a gaze of the most unbounded astonishment.

"I suppose it is me you mean, for my name is Moncrieffe, though I don't know why you call me Miss. Are you looking for me?"

"I am ordered to seek Miss Moncrieffe, and convey her to New York," he replied, with a graceful bow and a military salute.

"Ordered to convey me to New York!" she exclaimed, throwing her book away; and springing up, she stood before him, with flushed cheeks and flashing eyes; "and who has presumed to order me to be conveyed to New York?"

Major Burr smiled with a singular expression, while he gazed upon the young Pythoness, as she stood glaring at him; then gracefully removing his hat, he felt in his pocket for the letter under which he was acting, and while thus engaged, she continued:

"If you have come to take me a prisoner, I tell you plainly I *won't* go, and you don't look like"——

"Young lady, don't give yourself any unnecessary alarm," said the major, a little haughtily, and as he spoke, he extended to her the letter for which he had been searching in his pockets. "You are at perfect liberty to stay or go with me, as you choose, but it is your father's wish"——

"My father!" she exclaimed, hurriedly interrupting him, and grasping the letter which the young officer held toward her. "Is he a prisoner?"

"He is not, Miss Moncrieffe. How soon he may be, the fate of war can alone determine."

"Then I don't care for anything;" and as she spoke, she opened the letter which the major had handed to her. A hasty glance showed her that it was a missive addressed to General Putnam by her father, in which he implored his protection for his daughter, until her father's circumstances should permit him to reclaim her; for as he was at present situated, he could afford her neither shelter nor protection, and the spot where she was then located might soon become the theatre of active hostilities.

"I beg your pardon, sir; I did not imagine such a state of things. General Putnam is very kind, and I am truly grateful to him. I am at your command, sir."

"Command me, Miss Moncrieffe," said Major Burr, with a smile, and one of those graceful bows which in after years made him so irresistible.

"Oh, for gracious sakes!" she exclaimed, half pettishly, and she half smiled, half pouted, "don't call me Miss Moncrieffe. My name is Margaret. Please to call me Margaret. I am not a young lady by some years. How old do you think I am?" she inquired archly, bending upon him a searching glance, but dropping her eyes as they met the flashing orbs of the young soldier fixed upon her with an expression of intense admiration.

She was tall—quite up to the standard fixed by that *arbiter elegantiorum*, Lord Chesterfield—with a form fully developed in all the glory of budding womanhood; large, lustrous eyes, a complexion so shaded between blonde and brunette, it was impossible to decide which predominated; hair black as the raven's wing, and presenting an *ensemble*, which a painter or sculptor would have been proud to embody as his ideal of perfection in womanhood and beauty.

And there she stood before a young officer scarcely out of his teens, awaiting, as did Helen before Paris, the judgment she had courted.

Perhaps she was shocked at the boldness of her own question; perhaps she was struck with the gallant bearing of the slender, graceful youth who stood before her; perhaps, a hundred things; but certain it is, the rich blood mantled her cheeks, and added, if possible, new lustre to charms almost perfect.

"You are young enough to make me wish you were older, and old enough to make me wish that I was older," was the gallant reply, and as it was uttered, a bright smile mantled her beautiful face, and raising her eyes to his own, she gave him a glance which sent the hot blood coursing through his veins with marvellous rapidity. She had understood and appreciated the compliment so delicately conveyed.

"Well, we won't talk about that," she said, with a bright smile, at the same time extending her hand, which was grasped with marvellous alacrity by the gallant officer. "Now, how much time can you give me to prepare for my journey?"

"Not very much of a journey, Miss Moncrieffe."

"I think your memory is very treacherous," she interrupted, with an arch look.

"Well, Miss Margaret, then; it is only a ride of about sixteen miles, and any of our horses can go that distance in a couple of hours; but it would be rather hard riding for a lady."

"I'll wager my pistols against yours, that Selim will do it in less time than that, and not draw a long breath."

"Pistols—Selim—I don't understand what you are talking about," exclaimed the major, really confounded by her words.

"Why, don't you carry pistols? I thought all the rebel officers—I beg your pardon," she interrupted, seeing that the countenance of the officer grew dark at the word—"you must not mind what I say—I am a foolish girl, and even my father says I am not more than half witted; I certainly did not mean to offend or insult."

"How about Selim?" said the major, his countenance again brightening as he met the gaze of those lustrous eyes, at once forgetting the slur she had cast upon him and the cause he had espoused.

"Oh, he is my pet horse; father brought him from England for my use, and oh, he is such a beauty!"

"I wonder if he is as handsome as his mistress," mentally exclaimed the young officer, as he gazed upon her glowing face; but he did not say so in as many words, though he looked it, and Margaret understood his thoughts, for she blushed and smiled at his expression.

"But come, Mr."—— and pausing, she looked inquiringly at him.

"I am called Major Burr in New York. Here, Patsy calls me *Aaron*."

"And are you the Aaron Burr who"——

"There, Miss Moncrieffe—Margaret, I mean," said the major, laughing, "that will do; I have not the time to receive or pay compliments now. I must be in New York to-night, and, if you consent to accept

General Putnam's invitation, you must be there also."

"I shall be ready—let me see—thirty minutes—will that do?" she said, after a momentary pause; "a soldier's daughter is not troubled with an excess of baggage, and what little I have, can be carried in my valise, strapped to my saddle."

"General Putnam has a pillion prepared for you, and"——

"General Putnam did not know Major Moncrieffe's daughter or he would not have taken that trouble, for which, however, I shall gladly thank him. But come, Major Burr, I am delaying you—I see you look impatient, and I won't detain you;" so saying, she moved toward the house, walking side by side with the young officer, who, as they conversed, gazed upon her with looks of undisguised admiration, and listened to her remarks with an appearance of the deepest interest.

"My father has been fortunate in providing a home for me in such an excellent family," she said; "for it has been very lonesome here, and I don't know what I should have done without Patsy. She is such a dear, good girl one can't help loving her; don't you think so, Major Burr?" and she gave him another glance of those large, liquid eyes, which brought the hot blood to his face, at which his companion smiled archly; for she thought she read in that blush a secret. The major, however, made no reply, and they walked on in silence.

As they approached the fence at which the horses of the escort were fastened, Margaret caught sight of the trooper on guard, and a singular expression crossed her face, which was not, however, observed by the major. When within two or three paces of him, she pointed to some object in another direction, and, as Major Burr turned his head to observe it, she looked full in the face of the sentry, and a glance full of meaning was exchanged between them unobserved. That glance, brief as it was, spoke volumes, and had it been noticed by the young officer, might have saved trouble, sorrow, and misery, and prevented the effusion of much precious blood.

"Now, then, major," she continued, as they entered the house, "I see Mrs. Adams has been preparing refreshments for you, and while you are enjoying her hospitality, I will pack up my small wardrobe and saddle Selim."

"One of my men will get your horse ready, Miss Moncrieffe."

"I would like to see one of your men attempt it," she said, with a merry laugh, and, as she spoke, she cast a hurried, but searching glance around the group of hardy troopers, who, with their heavy swords trailing on the floor, were standing around the table on which Mrs. Adams had placed the homely refreshments, so welcome to them after their hot and dusty ride "He does not know anybody but his mistress.

I take entire charge of him myself, and he follows me about like a dog."

While thus speaking they entered the best room, honored by the appellation of parlor, simply because it was not appropriated to culinary purposes; for the furniture was of the most ordinary and homely description — rush-bottomed chairs, with high, straight backs; a small, but very substantial mahogany table with two leaves, stood between the windows, which looked out upon the road, and above it was a small looking-glass in a plain gilt frame. Around the room were hung three or four coarse engravings on Scriptural subjects; while the white floor, scrubbed and cleaned until it was almost of the whiteness of snow, was destitute of a carpet.

On the table between the windows, Patsy had set forth the refreshments for the young officer, and, as he approached, drawing with him one of the high-backed chairs, he met her gaze fixed on him with an inquiring expression, as if she had intended to ask: "What do you think of her?"

If the major read her glance aright, he made no reply, but seated himself abstractedly, and for a few moments leaned his head upon his hands.

"Well, major—I mean Aaron," she hastily said, correcting herself, "you seem in low spirits."

"No Patsy," he said, raising his head, and looking affectionately on her open, ingenuous, and really hand some face, reading in that look the love which he felt she bore him; "I am tired, and, besides, I was thinking."

"What for your thoughts?" she asked, archly, as he commenced his repast.

"I dare not dispose of them, even to you, Margaret —I beg pardon, Patsy!"

"Already, Major Burr," said the young girl, half reproachfully, and he well knew what she meant by that word, for his awkward mistake had implied a sudden intimacy between the two thus strangely brought together, which justified such an appellation.

"On my word, no, Patsy," he replied, looking steadily in her face, and speaking with such an earnest, sincere warmth of manner, as convinced her of his truthfulness. "I *was* thinking of her, but not as I think of you."

Patsy's countenance brightened as she listened to this denial of her suspicions, for she believed every word he said, and drawing up a chair, she seated herself near him.

"When shall we see you again, Aaron?" she inquired.

"I dare not say, Patsy, for I cannot surmise, myself. General Washington has gone to Philadelphia to confer with Congress as to Howe's next movements; the fleet has sailed from Virginia, and the impression, I believe, is, that New York will be the next point of attack. We are making all preparations to meet him, and ever since I have been in the city, I have been on duty day and night, hastening the fortifications of the place. It was only by chance I was selected by General Putnam to escort this young lady to his quarters, as I happened to be in the house when her father's letter reached him."

"Is she going to reside with General Putnam?" asked Patsy, with an appearance of anxiety, which she could not conceal, and which was seemingly not justified by the simple assertion just made.

"Oh, yes; the general replied to her father, that he would cheerfully admit her as a member of his family, until he could have an opportunity of restoring her to him, or until he was in a position to receive her."

For an instant Patsy sat mute, and with her face leaning on her hand, then raising her eyes to those of her companion, she said, earnestly:

"You won't think meanly of me, Aaron, if I tell you what I am thinking of?"

"I never could think meanly of you, Patsy," was the reply, uttered quite as earnestly as had been the question.

"Then," and she lowered her tones, and approached her face near to his own, "I think you had better watch her very closely."

"Why—what do you mean?" inquired Major Burr, pausing between his mouthfuls. "She is only a child."

"Yes, but a forward and precocious child. She is shrewd, observing, and so devotedly attached to the cause in which her father is engaged, I really think she would scruple at nothing to forward its success."

"I thank you, Patsy, for your warning," said the young major, smiling; "but I am sure you are mistaken in your own thoughts," and he looked meaningly at her—so meaningly, that the blood mounted to her face, and her eyes fell beneath his ardent gaze.

Perhaps she was. Perhaps there lurked in her bosom the apprehension that the fascinations of the young and beautiful stranger, who would be thrown constantly into his society, might win from her the heart she now trusted, and believed was all her own. Perhaps there arose some latent fear, that once within the sphere of her attractions, he would forget the truthful girl to whom he had so often offered vows of enduring love. But if such was the case, no words passed her lips to confirm it, and seeing that she had been misconstrued, she at once changed the subject. In a few minutes, and before Major Burr had completed his repast, Miss Moncrieffe entered the room, bearing in one hand a small russet-covered valise, and in the other a pair of horseman's pistols, elegantly mounted, and which she placed on the table before him, saying, as she did so:

"There, major, are those not beauties?" and she looked at them almost affectionately. "My dear father carried them through two campaigns in India, and left them with me when he was ordered to join his regiment on Staten Island, and I have made good use of them, I promise you."

Major Burr took one of them up, and after examining it with the eye of a connoisseur, replied:

"They seem to be very superior weapons; can you really use them?"

"Ask Patsy," she said, laughingly, as she deposited her little valise on the floor at her feet, and she turned to the party named, as if seeking her reply.

"You will find very few who can use them with greater certainty than Miss Moncrieffe," replied Patsy; and as she spoke an expression of pain crossed her features, for she saw the gaze of Major Burr fastened upon the fair stranger with evident admiration. She was dressed in a long green riding-habit, which, fitting closely, set off her fine, full form to the greatest advantage, the long train being drawn around in front, and tucked inside of the broad leather belt which encircled her waist. Her hair had been drawn up, and was concealed by a cloth cap of the same color as her dress, and ornamented with a black ostrich feather, and which, being placed jauntily on one side of her head, gave an expression to her really beautiful face, which might well command the admiration of the young officer, who, as he looked, thought he had never seen anything half so beautiful.

Miss Moncrieffe noticed his look, and turning to Patsy, saw that the color had entirely left her face, which, as she gazed on Major Burr, bore an expression of absolute pain, and a flash of triumph rose to her eyes, but it passed away as quickly as it had come.

"Now, then, I will go and saddle Selim, and will be with you in a few moments, so make your adieux, major," and she smiled archly, turning from him to Patsy, whose color, now returned, covered face, and neck, and brow.

CHAPTER IV.

PREPARING FOR THE JOURNEY.

MARGARET left Major Burr and Patsy, and proceeded directly to the small shed, scarcely worth the name even of stable, where Selim was housed, and as she passed along the path which led to it, a singular expression was on her face. Perhaps it was one of triumph—perhaps of mere exultation—perhaps—but no matter what; it was an expression evidently called there by some extraordinary occasion, and it was well that he who was most connected with it had not observed it.

Selim, a noble, powerful bay horse, showing all the signs of blood and breeding, turned his head as he heard his young mistress enter the stable, and fastening his large eyes upon her with an expression almost human, neighed out his pleasure at the sight of the one to whom he was so strongly attached. Selim was indeed worthy of all her high praises, for in addition to the possession of great powers of endurance and high speed, he seemed endowed with even more than a horse's sagacity, and naturalists have placed that animal at the head of all others for intelligence and instinct —an instinct amounting sometimes almost to intellect.

"Selim, my good friend," she said, approaching and patting his neck, "it's no play-ride to-day; you are going among those who don't like anything that comes from dear old England, and I am afraid you won't fare so well as you do even here."

Selim rubbed his nose against her shoulder, as she was untying the halter which secured him in his stall, and testified his pleasure again at her presence by a low whinny. Perhaps he understood what she said.

"Yes, old friend," she continued, as she lifted down the cumbersome side-saddle of those days, and placed it on his ready back, "you'll have a long and hot ride to-day, and you won't have your mistress to take care of you when you get to the end of your journey. No matter; be a good fellow, and I'll come and see you, if I can't do any more."

The saddle was adjusted, the girths tightened to the regular mark, and the heavy military bridle, which formed a part of his trappings, placed in his mouth without resistance, for Selim was glad to have the little exercise which the occasional rides with his young mistress afforded.

As she led him out toward the fence, where the troopers' horses were picketed, she turned toward the house and looked through the open door of the kitchen, or rather that portion of the house devoted to kitchen uses; she perceived the troopers still standing around the table, and a glance in the other direction showed that the same man was on sentry whom she had first noticed, and between whom and herself such meaning glances had been exchanged.

Assured of this, she approached him boldly, and in authoritative tones commanded him to make her horse fast also; as he advanced to obey her mandate, she turned toward the house, so as to be able to perceive any one who might come out, and said to him, but without looking at him, "what are you doing here, Hickey, and wearing that uniform?"

"Can't you guess, Miss Margaret?" he replied, in low tones, at the same time taking hold of her horse's bridle, and leading him to a spot most remote from the horses which he was guarding, followed, however, by Margaret, who continued in the same strain:

"Does any one suspect you, or your purpose?"

"Not a soul. Governor Tryon knows all about it, but he's on board the Duchess of Gordon."

"Do you communicate with him?"

"We used to do so before old Putnam took command, and without any great trouble; but as soon as he came, he forbade all communication between the ships and the shore, and the ships have now gone down outside the bay."

"Can you send word to him now?"

"Oh, yes, we manage that," he replied with a meaning smile, "only there's a good deal more risk about it than there used to be. Where are you going, miss?"

"To New York, to live with General Putnam."

"In his house?"

"In his own house, with his family. Can you send word to Governor Tryon that I am there?"

"To be sure I can; and how glad he will be to hear it."

"Tell him I am ready to do anything he desires, to serve my country and her cause. You stupid fellow," she suddenly exclaimed, in a loud voice, as she saw a trooper emerge from the house to relieve the party with whom she was talking, so that he might enjoy the hospitality of Mrs. Adams, "don't you see how you have fastened that horse?"

"Where can I see you?" she added, in tones so low they only reached the ears for whom they were intended.

"I must manage that when I get to the city. Right opposite the general's quarters, there is"—— But the approach of the trooper checked the sentence, and he said in his usual voice, "I will fasten him better, miss," and he commenced fumbling about Selim's bridle, who, however, stood with his head turned, and eyes intently fastened upon his mistress, as if to ask why she permitted any one to do that which belonged only to her.

"Of course you don't know me, Hickey." A look

assured her that she was understood, for his relief was now too near for further words.

"That is a fine horse you have, miss," said the trooper—a tall, fresh-looking young man, standing over six feet in his stockings, and he gazed admiringly on Selim.

"He is, indeed," she said, turning upon him her brilliant eyes, and trying to read in that glance his character.

Whatever she might have read, she could find in his frank, open, sun-burnt countenance, no encouragement to hope she could bring him also within her power by the fascination of her charms, and she continued:

"He is a noble, brave beast, and I love him—don't I, Selim?" and, approaching him, she patted his arched neck, as he stooped to receive her welcome caress.

The young trooper gazed alternately at the maiden and at the horse, and upon each with looks of admiration, for each were worthy of it, and, turning to Margaret, said: "He looks to be high mettled."

"He is as gentle as a lamb, and as playful as a kitten, and minds me like a dog," and as she spoke, she gave him another friendly pat, and turned to go into the house, to await further directions of the young officer, in whose charge she was to remain until placed in a proper position of security.

She found Major Burr and Patsy as she had left them, still seated at the table, deeply engaged in earnest conversation; the cheeks of the young girl were flushed—her eyes beamed with a soft look, and there was every indication, at least on her part, that they had arrived at a mutual and pleasant understanding, though Margaret had too much tact to notice the change in her appearance; but, approaching the table, she took from it her pistols which she had placed there on her first entrance, and, opening the pans of the locks, examined them carefully, to see if they were properly primed; then, drawing forth the ramrods, she tried each barrel, to see if it was duly loaded.

"You are exceedingly particular, Miss Moncrieffe," said Major Burr, as he looked admiringly at the young and beautiful girl, thus cautiously providing against accident or design.

"I was always taught that a pistol would be useless unless loaded and primed," she said, quietly; and having satisfied herself that all was right, and, lifting her valise from the floor, she continued: "I will have this strapped on Selim, and then I shall be ready for you, major," and she moved gracefully away, bearing in one hand the loaded pistols, and in the other the valise.

Major Burr, with a gallantry and a grace peculiar to himself, and in which few could excel him, sprang forward to relieve her of the valise; but with a smile and a courtesy, she declined his aid, and again he was alone with Patsy.

"I don't like her, Aaron," said Patsy, turning to the major, as she followed with her eyes the retreating form of the graceful girl.

"I know that very well," he replied, with a quiet smile; "but there's no occasion for alarm, Patsy." And Patsy shook her head meaningly; for she had good cause to dread the fascinations of the beautiful and high-bred girl, as compared with her own humble but more substantial charms.

A few words of kindly greeting passed between Margaret and her hostess, as she thanked her courteously and gracefully for her kindness during the period she had been an inmate of her family. To Patsy she gave a warm embrace, and, as she imprinted on her forehead a farewell kiss, she drew from her finger and slipped on one of Patsy's, a beautiful turquoise ring.

"Keep that, Patsy, in remembrance of me; and perhaps the time may come when I shall be able to repay your kindness to me. Now, major, I will leave you to your adieux," and, with a quiet smile, she withdrew, and proceeded toward the place where Selim was picketed.

The valise was strapped on behind the saddle; the pistols were carefully placed in the holsters, and stepping lightly on the outstretched hand of the young trooper, who had paid her the compliment of admiring her horse, she sprang to the saddle, and, adjusting herself in the seat, turned her head toward the house and awaited the approach of the leader, who was to escort her to her new home.

A very few moments sufficed to pay his adieux to Mrs. Adams and Patsy, and, vaulting in the saddle with a light spring, the party was put in motion.

Major Burr and Margaret brought up the rear, the troopers riding about a hundred feet ahead of the main body, to keep a look-out ahead, and in this order they left the house, and were soon hidden from sight by the dense forests through which their road lay.

CHAPTER V.

THE ROYALISTS IN THE CITY.

BUT leaving the major and his fair and fascinating companion, let us turn to the city of New York, where events were daily transpiring which involved seriously the deepest interests of the Colonies, and which, if carried to consummation, might have terminated most disastrously for their cause and liberties.

The head-quarters of the commander-in-chief were at that period located at Richmond Hill, now far below the centre of our city's limits, though then so far removed from its resident population as to be deemed at a great distance from the city proper. The house selected for the head-quarters of General Washington was large and spacious, affording abundant room for his family and suite, and was in after years purchased by Major Burr, and occupied by him as his residence, the hill and pond which lay beneath being recognized as "Burr's Hill" and "Burr's Pond."

It was situated on an eminence commanding a view of the Hudson River and bay, for at that time there were no houses or other objects in the vicinity to obstruct the vision. The mansion was surrounded by noble trees; a carefully cultivated lawn stretching o.' one side as far as the road, which r n past the house and a beautiful garden, in a high st te of cultivation, skirting it on either side.

Across the road, and distant per aps two hundred yards southward, stood a small tw -story farm-house, occupied at that time as a taver , by a well-known Tory, named Corbie. It was the resort of all parties—Whig and Tory—for Whig and Tory alike, in those days, would frequent any place where refreshments could be procured, for there were very few allowed in the city at that time. There was one at the lower end of the city, known by the sign of the "Highlander," and standing at wh is now the corner of Broadway and Beaver stree directly opposite the then head-quarters of Gener Putnam, already named; but the house kept by Co bie, being furthest removed from the city proper, and hence less under the surveillance of the officers, rece ved much the larger share of custom; and it was surmised, as it was afterward well established, that within its walls was hatched many a conspiracy against our country and its liberties. The life-guard of the commander-in-chief, when not on actual duty at Richmond Hill, found this a very convenient place of resort, and many a Continental dollar found its way into the rapacious pocket of Corbie, in exchange for the Jamaica rum and other bibables which he kept on sale. Here Whig and Tory met, as it were, on neutral ground, and here were freely discussed the affairs of the two nations—no, of the parent and child—which then convulsed the world. Many, too, were the brawls, by day and by night, which the house had witnessed, and which were only suppressed by the approach of the guard, who were ordered thither when the discovery was made that some quarrel was going on. General Putnam, however, had put Corbie under heavy bonds, and thenceforward the house was much more peaceable, though none the less suspected.

It was on the night before the departure of Major Burr, with his escort, to bring to New York the daughter of the British soldier, who had been confided by him to the care and courtesy of the rough, blunt, but brave and honorable soldier, General Putnam—a charge cheerfully assumed, and which was most faithfully kept. The sky was overcast with heavy clouds, portending a thunder shower, or storm of long duration, and the inmates of the house gathered in the bar-room, or rather the room devoted to the reception of such guests as came there only to smoke their pipes or quaff their liquor.

There were several soldiers from the fortifications and various breastworks, which extended up from the Battery as far as Richmond Hill; there were some of the life-guardsmen, and there was a fair sprinkling of Tory residents from the vicinity; there, too, conspicuous among the motly throng, were three of the soldiers belonging to the Smallwood's Maryland battalion, noticeable especially for their showy scarlet uniform, trimmed with buff, and at that time they were almost the only corps in the city, out of the thousands by whom it was garrisoned, who could boast of a uniformity of dress or accoutrements.

There were, however, two or three persons present deserving more than a passing notice; and entitled justly to the first consideration, was the landlord, Corbie, whose name has been handed down to posterity as connected with the most infamous plot that ever was conceived by an enemy claiming to conduct an honorable warfare. He was a small, rosy-cheeked man, with a round face, a keen blue eye, and a nose which evidenced his familiar acquaintance with the contents of his larder and cellar. Although in the humble position of landlord of a wayside house, he was by nature and intellect fitted for much higher uses, and the choice of this man, by Governor Tryon, as the chief agent in a plot so desperate in its conception, and which, if successful. would have been productive of the most disastrous results, displayed on his part a just conception and a correct appreciation of character, for the man was really as shrewd and cunning as a fox; never taken by surprise under any circumstances, cool, brave, and determined, ready for any emergency, and so devoted a royalist, that he would have lost his right hand sooner than deny his allegiance to his sovereign. His keen, penetrating eye was ever wandering over his guests, and intuitively he seemed to read the character of each. There were the restless, nervous, homesick light horsemen from Connecticut, who, having volunteered cheerfully for the defence of the city, refused to perform any duty except such as might be discharged with the aid of their horses, and who were subsequently dismissed by the commander-in-chief, with the stinging remark, that "he did not care how soon they were discharged, since they declined to stand guard, work in the batteries, or perform any of a soldier's duty."

There were the gallant Jerseymen, commanded by the intrepid Morgan, who played such a conspicuous part in our country's history in after days, dressed in homespun, linsey-woolsey—in fact, anything which would cover them—and armed with their unerring rifles, with which they ever committed such fearful havoc as to render their name a terror to the foe, and their appearance a signal for flight to any equal numbers.

The South Carolinians, the Pennsylvanians, the hardy sons of New Hampshire, all were represented on that evening. Conspicuous among all, however, from the honorable position filled by them, and the confidence reposed in them, were the "life-guardsmen," appointed to protect the person of the commander-in-chief; tall, stalwart men, who had been well and severely tried, but who had never been found wanting; men who had earned by bravery and incorruptible fidelity, the glori ous privilege of protecting the life and person of the deliverer of his country.

Foremost among those, and especially noticeable from his commanding height and erect bearing, stood Thomas Hickey, a deserter from the Royalist army, but one who had so often proved himself brave and true, that he had been promoted to the high and honorable position of a "life-guardsman."

"Come, boys, another round; I'll stand treat for the company this time, and I don't want anybody to drink to my toast who don't choose," said a short, thick-set man, with a red face; a nose much redder than his face, and remarkable for his keen, light, restless blue eye, which was ever wandering around with an expression half-searching, half-suspicious.

He was an Englishman by birth, an Englishman in feeling, and thoroughly English in his attire. He was dressed in a drab fustian coat, knee-breeches of the same color, made of corduroy, and wore heavy top boots. It was Gilbert Forbes, the gunsmith, who had his shop on Broadway, near what is now called Maiden Lane, and being a perfect master of his trade, his shop was frequented by the better class of customers, without distinction of party or country.

"Come boys, one more round," and he turned to the landlord, Corbie, with whom he exchanged a significant glance, and the willing host placed upon his table glasses for the company, and proceeded to fill them according to the tastes and wishes of his guests.

"None of your infernal Tory toasts, Mister Forbes," said a tall, strapping young countryman, one of the Connecticut light horse, who had so promptly volunteered for the defence of the city, when rumors of an expected attack from the British reached their State, but who when required to mount guard, work on the batteries, or perform other military duties, declined, on the score that they were horsemen, and ought not be required to do duty of foot soldiers; "I won't stand any of them," he continued, straightening himself up, and glancing around to see how many friends he could count upon in case of trouble arising from his interference.

Forbes laid down his glass, which he held in his hand, and gazed on the speaker with looks of anything but friendly regard: "Look here, my young friend, you ain't master yet, and mayhap you won't be so soon as you expect; so it's best to keep a civil tongue in your head, or you may get it broke for your pains."

"Shut your own mouth, you infernal Tory," exclaimed one of Smallwood's men, advancing to the side of his Yankee friend; for though there was the most desperate sectional feeling existing among the motley array of Continental troops then occupying the city, on an occasion like the present, when trouble appeared to be at hand, North and South were forgotten, and the gallant southerner was as ready to fight for his Yankee comrade, as he would have been to fight with him, on the smallest provocation.

"Well, I'm in my own house, any how, and I will do as I choose, and I'd like to see the man who will interfere with me. I'll offer a toast, and you can drink it, or not," said Corbie, filling a glass for himself, and without waiting for any reply, he exclaimed; "Here's to the King and his cause, God bless"——

He had not time to finish his sentence, for Gray, the Connecticut farmer, sprung forward, and dashing the contents of his glass in the landlord's face, seized him by the neck, and fairly choked the words down his throat.

Forbes and the other Tories sprang to the assistance of their friend. Weapons which hitherto had been concealed, were now drawn forth, and a general and desperate affray seemed inevitable. At this juncture, the door of the tap-room was thrown open, and a tall, commanding-looking man, with a sergeant's chevron on his arm, and bearing a musket, entered, and advanced between the contending parties:

"Silence!" he exclaimed, in a voice of thunder, as he saw the position of affairs; "silence, and disperse, or I'll put every man in the guard-house."

"And who the devil are you?" exclaimed Forbes, glaring at the intruder.

"I am the sergeant of the guard, and if you don't cease from brawling, I'll march every man to the guard-house. Corbie!" and he turned to the landlord, who, released from the vice-like grasp of the young giant, was adjusting his rumpled shirt and cravat, "I shall report your house as disorderly, and have it shut up at once, if I hear any more of this again."

"I don't keep a disorderly house, Sergeant Drake, and you know it. I've got a right to speak my mind in my own house, I'm thinking."

"You shan't drink such an infernal Tory toast as that in my presence, if it was ten times your house," exclaimed Gray, the young Connecticut soldier, whose blood was now at fever heat.

"Come, disperse, and let's have no more words about it," said the sergeant. "You, Forbes, are always mixed up with some brawl, or doing something worse. Go home, and don't compel me to make you."

"I'd like to see you do it," said the gunsmith, sulkily.

"That is easily done," replied the sergeant, turning to the door, and advancing, as if about to give the order for the guard to advance; but he was interrupted by Corbie, who passed rapidly from behind the bar, and laid his hand upon the soldier's arm, gently.

"Please don't, Sergeant Drake; it's not my fault, and it will only hurt me, you know, without doing you any good," and he winked so significantly, that the color came to the sergeant's face, for the truth was, he had taken many a sly glass with Corbie, for which he was never required to pay.

"Well," he said, half hesitatingly, "I will pass this over, but—— Ah, Hickey!" he said, for the first time perceiving the life-guardsman, who had managed thus far to keep out of the sergeant's sight, "I was looking for you, but did not expect to find you here. I have left orders for you to report to Major Burr, at head-quarters, to-morrow at six o'clock."

Hickey's countenance fell as these words were uttered, and he turned from the speaker to Forbes and Corbie, as if to ask them what it meant. The sergeant was at that moment engaged in looking around among the inmates of the room, and did not perceive this movement; if he had, he would have noticed that glances full of meaning were exchanged between the trio.

"Very well, sir," replied the guardsman, touching his cap, for he was by these words under orders, and without a reply, except to bid the assemblage good night, he left the room, and proceeded to his barracks near the "Richmond Hill House."

"Sergeant, you had better take something; it won't do you any harm, and it's a nasty, wet night," said Corbie, going behind the bar, and while speaking he poured out a tumbler two-thirds full of Jamaica rum, which he handed to the sergeant, who tossed it off with a relish that showed he was well acquainted with the flavor of that liquor.

"Now, then, good night," he said, smacking his lips, and trailing his musket, he started for the door; but before he reached it, turned and said: "Now, boys, no more brawling nor quarrelling."

"Oh, no, of course not," chorused the party, Whigs and Tories, glad to have escaped thus easily from a night's sojourn in the guard-house.

"Come, boys, empty your glasses without the toast," said Corbie, as the door closed on the retreating form of the sergeant. "It's getting on to nine o'clock, and you've all got to be at quarters by that time, according to orders. Forbes," he said, turning to the gunsmith, "it's a miserable night. Do you stay here with me; you couldn't get through the lines in time, I'm sure."

"Thank'ee, Corbie, I will," replied Forbes, and he drained his glass, an example which was followed by the party, who strolled out, one by one, until at length the landlord and the gunsmith were alone.

"That was a narrow escape, Forbes," said the burly landlord, as he proceeded to close his house, locking and barring the doors and windows, a precaution rendered very necessary, for often parties of straggling Whigs, who had been caught outside of the lines after hours, would force an entrance into his house, and compel him to entertain them until morning, when they would depart, leaving the host to collect his reckoning as he could.

"The boat will be along before a great while, and if"——

"Never mind. Walls have ears; so keep mum, and wait for the signal. Matthews sent word that a dispatch for him was coming up to-night from Governor Tryon, and there ought to be some money with it."

CHAPTER VI.

THE ATTACK AND ITS RESULTS.

"You have seen hard service for your years, major," said Miss Moncrieffe, as they rode along, and the young girl looked at the beardless soldier by her side, with a patronizing air which would have become a matron of forty.

The major smiled as he interpreted her look, and retorted: "I think you, for your years, have a decided advantage over me."

"Ah! but I've never seen real service," she replied, archly.

"Would you be afraid?" he asked, earnestly.

"I am a soldier's daughter," she said, commencing with a smile, and closing with something of hauteur in her manner.

"Suppose the Cow-boys should attack us," he said willing to test her, and scanning her face as he spoke.

"I think I could make sure of one, perhaps two," and she pointed with the handle of her riding-whip to the holsters which contained her pistols. "If I should miss them both, I should trust to Providence and Selim's heels."

"I hope your courage won't be tested; but in case we should be attacked, please to observe what I say, for you are under my charge—you must fall to the rear; and if there are too many for us, you must make Selim show his heels, and ride directly back to Mrs. Adams."

"I'll have two shots at them any how, before I do start. But what would Patsy say if I was to leave you, and what message should I give her?" and she peered in his face with an expression which brought the blood to his cheeks.

"Never mind Patsy," he replied, resuming his composure, "I would rather speak to you than of her, a thousand times."

Again she fixed her searching eyes on him; but this time he not only met her glance unabashed, but returned it with such interest, it was now her turn to blush—for there was an intensity of admiration in his look which she could not fail to interpret. "I don't believe you, major," she said, at the same time touching Selim slightly with her whip, causing him to spring forward some yards ahead of her escort, who, however, quickly joined her, and for a few moments they rode in silence. During these few moments, both were revolving in their minds the words and looks of the past minute.

Margaret saw in the young officer, who had already earned such fame, one whom any woman might be proud to win. He was young, handsome, distinguished, and held already a high post of honor and confidence, and her heart acknowledged his vast superiority in everything pertaining to a gentleman and soldier, over any she had ever met. On his part, he saw a lovely, dashing, fearless girl, very beautiful, very fascinating, polished and refined in her manners, and well fitted by birth, manner, and education, young as she was, for any position. The contrast between the high-born girl by his side, and the truthful, but uneducated Patsy, was so great, Margaret could not but gain by the comparison. He thought what a wife she would make, and he determined, in forgetfulness of all he had said to Patsy, and heedless of the pangs which his faithlessness would cause her, to make the effort to win this paragon.

Strange to say, neither of them for a moment gave thought to the gulf which separated them. She, the daughter of a British officer—he, her father's enemy by choice and principle. It was a case of decided and most desperate love at first sight; and each, unknown to the other, had succumbed to the influence of the little blind God who rules the world.

"I was not jesting, Miss Moncrieffe," said the major after this brief silence, which led to such a momentous result, "when I spoke about the Cow-boys," and he spoke with deep earnestness.

"Nor was I, when I spoke about my pistols and

Selim," she said, smilingly. "You don't know what a girl can do until she is compelled to. I have smelled gunpowder before," she added, with a bright, merry laugh. "I practise with my pistols every day, and would shoot even with you for a wager."

"And I would not with you," said the major; "you would be sure to win in anything you undertake, and it is never allowed to bet on a certainty," and he bent on her an admiring and searching glance.

"Perhaps you would let me win," she said, archly, returning his glance with one so full of expression, it brought the blood to his face.

"I could not help myself, I am sure," he added, with deep earnestness; "you always win when you choose."

"Not always, I am afraid," she said, with a half sigh, and she glanced at him timidly; and as she caught his eye fixed intently on her, she averted her head, so that he could not discover the blush which crimsoned her cheeks, called there by her own words.

"With me you would be sure; for, although I am a soldier, I would surrender to you without an effort at resistance."

"Would you, indeed?" she said, turning to him, a bright sunny smile illumining her face, which, animated as it was, presented as lovely a picture as a lover or painter ever gazed upon.

"Upon my honor, Miss Margaret, as a soldier and a gentleman, I would."

"How am I to take you, major?" she added, half archly, though her countenance, as she spoke, wore an expression of earnestness, very little in unison with her light and trifling manner.

"In any manner you choose, only take me," he said, with a glance of the most profound admiration, and he fixed upon her a look which spoke the intensity of the feelings which animated him, for he was fairly trembling with emotion.

"There's my hand on that bargain," and the same bright smile which had conquered him, lighted up her beautiful face. "Henceforth you are my prisoner."

"Forever, and gladly;" and the delicate hand was seized by the impassioned and conquered soldier. "Yours ever, yours only, only keep me." And thus, in these few moments, and in such few words, were settled the destinies of two just entering upon life.

Major Burr, who had won imperishable renown by his coolness and bravery, on every occasion, when either had been called forth; who had passed waist-deep through the snow to attack the frowning fortress of Quebec; who, when the chance shot fired by a sailor, carried death and desolation into the ranks of the Americans; when a hasty retreat was ordered by the one who should have led them to a renewed attack with the certainty of success, refused to leave his beloved commander who lay cold in death, but staggered through the snow, bearing his precious burden on his youthful shoulders; he, the intrepid soldier, surrendered at the first summons of the enemy whom few have ever successfully resisted—Love.

Every thought, feeling, and emotion of which he was capable had, within the acquaintance of a few short hours, been surrendered to the fascination and beauty of one who well knew how to use both, and who, equally with himself, was conquered, though she was not so ready to surrender. And she, accustomed as she was to flattery and adulation—conscious of her own powers—she too yielded to the common enemy, even while she had claimed the victory and her prisoner, though she almost dreaded to acknowledge it.

Neither had spoken one word of love; but as between each other words were needless; for under the guise of playfulness there lurked a depth and strength of feeling of which each was conscious, and each felt that the other loved.

Poor Patsy! little did she dream how her destiny had been affected in the few hours which had intervened between the arrival and departure of him to whom every feeling of an earnest, honest, truthful woman's heart had been given—but not unsought.

When Major Burr released the tiny hand held out to him in consummation of his surrender, he looked long and earnestly in the glowing face of his lovely companion, and in the calm but truthful gaze with which she met his glance, he read their mutual happi ness; and not another word was spoken by either from that moment on the subject nearest and dearest to both their hearts.

"Now, Margaret," said the major (he felt familiar), "I was very earnest when I spoke of those rascally Cow-boys. If they have received information of my intended journey hither—and I should not be surprised if they had, for our city is full of villainous Tories and spies—they will surely attempt to intercept us."

"And for what earthly object, major?" asked Margaret, looking intently at him.

"To hang me; and as for you"——

"I understand," she said, anticipating his sentence, and biting her lips till the blood almost started from them. "But I will keep one of these," and she pointed to her pistols, "for my own use—the other they shall have."

Major Burr gazed upon the beautiful speaker with looks of the most intense affection, and wondered inwardly how one so young, so frail, so delicately brought up, could be so fearless; but her words and actions only endeared her more to him.

"Now, Margaret, remember my orders," and he emphasized the word. "I am your commander in this affair—you are mine in all else. Should those wretches attack us, do you remain in the rear, and if worsted, you must fly for your life."

"And leave you, Aaron?" she said, tenderly, and a tear moistened her eye. "I won't;" and the heroic spirit which animated her, spoke through her eyes, from which the tear departed almost as soon as it had come, at the thought of danger to him she loved. "Yes," she repeated, as Major Burr actually stared at her in astonishment at hearing such words, "I won't—commander or no commander—I won't leave you."

"Disobedience of orders is punishable with death, Margaret," he said, smilingly.

"And desertion, too," she added, looking archly at him; "would you subject me to that?"

"Then you enlist with me?"

Whatever answer she might have made, was cut short by the sudden halting of the two troopers ahead, and this movement having been caught by the quick eye of the young soldier, he left Margeret's side and galloped to the front.

"What is it?" he inquired of Graham, one of the two who had ridden on as the advance guard.

"I think I saw some one moving in the woods yonder," and he pointed to a spot where the roads diverged, one leading to Ramapo, and the other to Orange.

"I will ride on and see," said the major; and as he spoke he drew the reins tighter, and was in the act of putting spurs to his horse, when a flash and a report, heard and seen almost simultaneously, proceeded from the spot toward which the trooper had pointed.

By this time the other men had galloped up to the spot where their leader stood, and awaited his orders.

"I am badly hurt," said Graham; and as he spoke, he leaned on one side and slid from his horse, falling heavily to the ground.

'You are hit, major," said Hickey, addressing his commander, as he saw the blood streaming down his buff breeches.

"Not much, I think. It won't do to give them a chance for another shot. Draw your pistols, men, and forward!" and with one glance to the rear to see if Margaret had obeyed his directions, he galloped forward, pistol in hand.

As they neared the woods whence the firing had proceeded, another volley was discharged, and Hickey with a muttered curse, exclaimed:

"Curse 'em, I've got it too; go in boys, kill the cursed cowards!" And the party dashed to the edge of the woods; from which there rushed, in a compact body, a dozen or fourteen rough looking ruffians, dressed in every variety of costume, and each armed with a musket or fowling-piece.

As the small party of Continentals caught the sight, they discharged their pistols with such effect that five of them dropped to the earth; then throwing away their pistols, they drew their swords, and charged.

But the Cow-boys—for it was a party of these scourges—anticipating this movement, met them with a volley from their muskets and fowling-pieces, which, fortunately, did no damage except to maim one of the horses, so as to render him useless; but his rider dismounting, advanced as rapidly as he could on foot, sword in hand. For a few moments, a hand-to-hand fight occurred on the edge of the wood, the troopers using their heavy cavalry swords, and their assailants clubbing their muskets and fowling-pieces. Four of the Cow-boys were either sabred, or so injured as to be unable to do any further mischief, and the remainder finding themselves unequally matched, took refuge in the woods, where they knew the mounted men could not, or would not follow them.

Major Burr's men were intent upon putting to death all of their assailants who still lived, but he forbade this inhumanity, and ordering his men to dismount, directed them to examine into their condition.

Three were stone dead; four desperately wounded, either by pistol-ball or sabre, and the remainder, though slightly injured, were still unable to escape. "I hate leaving these infernal scoundrels here, they may do more mischief; but I must," said Major Burr, addressing his men, who stood about him awaiting his further orders.

As he spoke those words, a shot from the rear attracted his attention, and wheeling his horse quick as lightning, he plunged the spurs into his sides, and dashed forward. A loud scream from the quarter whence the shot had proceeded, sent every drop of blood to his heart; and with every pore reeking with perspiration, drawn forth by the agony caused by that sound, he dashed on; and as he turned the curve in the road, which had thus far hidden Margaret from his sight, he saw her struggling in the arms of one of the ruffians, two of whom had made a short detour of the woods, and had come upon her suddenly as she sat on her horse, listening anxiously to the sounds of the muskets and pistols, and the clashing of the sabres, as they struck the assailants' weapons.

Quick as thought, she levelled a pistol, which she had drawn from its holster at the moment of the first firing, and as one of them neared her, she discharged its contents full in his face. The ball struck him in the throat, and he fell to the earth with a groan and a curse. Before she could detach the other weapon from its holster, the second ruffian was upon her, and seizing her by the arm essayed to drag her from the saddle.

It was then, for the first time, she uttered any sound, and the wild scream of terror which issued from her lips, had been heard by her newly-won lover. Before he could reach the spot where this most unequal conflict was going on, Margaret, who had resisted with her utmost strength, aided by Selim, who reared, and pranced, and wheeled in his efforts to free his bridle from the hold of the ruffian who was assailing his young mistress—had been dragged from her seat, and the fellow was bearing her, struggling and screaming toward the woods.

But Major Burr had seen enough to arouse all his energy, and to inspire him with the courage of desperation, and spurring his horse forward, he caught the ruffian by the cravat, and being too near to use the blade of his sword, dashed the hilt into his eyes with a force that drove them from their sockets, and he fell senseless to the ground, his arm still clasping the waist of the now fainting girl. Springing from his horse, Major Burr, forgetting, in the intensity of his passion, that a helpless foe lay before him, brought down his sabre with a force which sent it crashing through his skull, and he rolled over, dead.

Releasing the almost inanimate form of Margaret, whose clothes were covered with the blood and brains of the dead ruffian, he strove, by every endearing epithet and caress, to recall her to consciousness. In a few moments his men came galloping to the spot, and seeing their commander seated on the greensward, holding the senseless form of their charge in his arms, their rage was unbounded.

"Your flask, any of you," he said, as they approached, and three or four rough apologies for flasks were handed him, by as many willing hands.

As he was unwilling that any one should be present when Margaret returned to consciousness, he directed his men to scour the road, as well in the rear as forward, and he would attend to the lady, an order which was most cheerfully obeyed; for every man was anxious to have another chance at these lawless ruffians, who were the terror only of the innocent and defenceless, and who never made an attack under equal circumstances.

A little rum poured down Margaret's throat, brought her to partial consciousness, and opening her eyes languidly, she met the gaze of Major Burr fixed on her with an intensity of anguish which went to her very soul, and feeble as she yet was from affright, she smiled on him, and gently pressed the hand which held her own.

"I am not hurt at all, Aaron," she said, in feeble tones, after another interval of a few moments. "I will be myself directly; but that ruffian did frighten me."

"No wonder, Margaret, no wonder. But are you sure you are not hurt? Who fired that shot?"

"Look in the road, Aaron. I told you I was sure of one; but before I could draw the other pistol, that man seized my arm. Bless you, Aaron, dear Aaron!" she added, as she still reclined in his arms, looking up in his face with an expression of gratitude and affection; and Major Burr, unable to control himself as he heard those words, and met that look, bent down and imprinted a kiss upon her not unwilling lips; and thus was sealed their untold pledge of mutual love.

CHAPTER VII.

THE ROYALISTS PLOTTING.

We left Corbie and Forbes closing the house of the former after the departure of the guests, and this done, Corbie filled two glasses, and drawing a chair to the table on which Forbes had already planted himself, said:

"I wonder what, in the name of all that's bad, they want of Hickey?"

"Oh, don't borrow trouble, Corbie; it will come fast enough if this is found out. I tell you it can't be anything that concerns us, or Drake never would have been so open about it. No, no; so far so well. I wonder what's the next move?"

"Perhaps we shall know to-night. Do you think the colonel will come up in such a storm?"

"Storm—why it's just the thing for him. The boat can't be seen ten feet off shore, and I don't believe the sentinels care overmuch for being out in the rain. Not a bit of it; they are hid away in some of the groves along the shore, and the rain and wind together would drown any ordinary sound; besides, the boat's oars are always muffled."

"How many have we now, Forbes?" said Corbie, lowering his voice almost to a whisper.

"Besides our own people, not over three score; and I don't think they'll be worth the money I've paid for them, except Hickey. He's worth the whole of 'em put together."

"As how, Forbes?"

"Why, he sees and hears everything that goes on yonder," and he pointed with his thumb over his shoulder toward the location of the commander-in-chief's head-quarters; "and he ain't afraid to tell it, either."

"We want some more of them fellows," continued Corbie, sipping his liquor, and laying down the glass with an air of satisfaction.

"We'll have them yet, never fear. Five guineas down, and the two hundred acres, is rather too much for men who haven't seen a hard dollar for three months, and ain't likely to see one for as many to come. Blanchard is on the lookout, too, and he'll pick out the right men, I'll warrant you."

"I'd like to get hold of that Gray, the cursed rebel," said Corbie, placing his hand to his throat in evident remembrance of the gripe he had felt there a few moments before, "I'd pay him off, or my name's not Corbie;" and as if aroused to some desperate resolve by the recollection, he swallowed the remaining contents of his glass at one gulp, an example which was followed by his companion, who, placing his glass on the table, with an emphatic gesture, added:

"I want to see the whole troop of infernal rebels strung up at once. I'd dance over their graves with pleasure. Hark!"

A low rap at the side door of the room in which they were seated was distinctly heard, and when thrice repeated, Corbie went to the door, and without parley or hesitation, opened it, saying, as he did so, "Walk in—all clear," a summons which was answered by the entrance of a short, but well-knit man of some forty summers, dressed in dark blue sailor clothes from head to foot, and with a countenance so swarthy, he might, without offence, have been taken for a mulatto, or more probably some sun-burnt sea-faring man, which last impression was fully warranted by his attire.

It was Colonel Fanning, who, by dint of hard service in India, under its broiling sun, had won his colonelcy and the liver complaint, and was now sent out to this country to win fresher laurels or a soldier's grave. His regiment was stationed on Staten Island, but he had been selected by Governor Tryon, then on board the "Duchess of Gordon," the flag-ship of the British fleet then lying opposite the island, as the most competent officer to whom he might intrust the weighty matters then in hand between himself and the royalists in the city, in furtherance of the measures which, if successful, it was conceived would put a sudden end to the war, and crush out the rebellion.

"Good evening, colonel," said the landlord, touching his forehead with a military salute, which, as well as a similar movement on the part of Forbes, he acknowledged by a slight bow, and a smile which showed, in striking contrast to his swarthy face, his pearly teeth.

"It is a shocking night for some people, but fine weather for his majesty."

The door was quickly locked and barred, and the colonel, motioning Forbes to a chair, threw himself into one himself.

"You are wet through, colonel; let me give you something to drive the cold out of you—I have some glorious old south side, you know," said Corbie. "May I venture to offer you a suit of dry clothes," he added, respectfully, almost reverentially.

"No, thank you, for I must return immediately." said the colonel, with a wave of his hand; "but I won't refuse your south side, for I know it is good;" and the loyal landlord, taking one of the candles from the table, went behind the bar, and opening a secret trap which led to the cellar, descended to procure the highly-praised wine for the drenched and tired officer.

"Well, Forbes, how goes it?" he inquired, as he drew from his breast pocket a packet of papers, the outer envelope of which was nearly destroyed by the rain which had been pouring down in torrents for so long a time. "This for the excellent mayor, and"—as he spoke, he drew forth a smaller letter directed to Forbes himself—"this for you."

Forbes, with a low bow, took the extended letter with an air of unbounded respect, and, without waiting for excuses, tore it open hastily and devoured its contents eagerly.

It ran thus:

"On Board Duchess of Gordon,
"*June 3d*, 1776.

"My Trusty Friend:

"I am exceeding pleased at the success which has attended your efforts and those of the friends to the cause of His Most Gracious Majesty in the City of New York, and which I shall take pleasure in communicating to Lord Germaine, and I have no doubt he will embrace the earliest opportunity of expressing his satisfaction with your conduct. The package herewith must reach the honorable mayor without delay. It is essential that we should secure the services of some party near the person of General Putnam, now that General Washington is in Philadelphia; and we hereby intrust you with full power to render such service to our glorious cause. Colonel Fanning will hand you the one hundred and fifty guineas, for which you called in your last, and for which you will receipt.

"Mr. Corbie's services are duly appreciated; but I wish you to caution him against permitting the assemblage of too many of our friends at his house, as it may excite suspicion and defeat our plans, which God forbid, for the sake of our most gracious King.

"William Tryon."

By the time Forbes had finished the perusal of this letter, which had occupied him some minutes, for Governor Tryon was a notoriously bad penman and Forbes a worse scholar, Corbie had returned from the cellar, bearing in one hand a bottle covered with dust, and in the other the light, which had enabled him to drag it from its hiding-place.

"That's the same seal, colonel," he said, laying both on the table, and, producing a cork-screw, he drew the cork, and placing a glass before his guest, turned to Forbes, who still held Governor Tryon's letter in his hand.

"That's partly for you, Corbie—read it," said Forbes, his face glowing with pleasure, and he thrust the letter into the hands of the burly landlord, who commenced its perusal with a very wry face, for he was even more illiterate than Forbes; and while he was thus engaged, Colonel Fanning had managed to get down three or four glasses of the generous wine which had been placed before him, and which was, indeed, worthy of all the praise Corbie had bestowed on it.

"God bless his majesty and prosper his cause," said Corbie, earnestly, for he was as thoroughly loyal as any king could wish. "Halloa!" he exclaimed, "what's that?" as the sound of a body falling heavily was heard in the next room. "Who, in the devil's name's there?" and, snatching a light, he started for the door, but was withheld by a forcible grasp from Colonel Fanning, who had seized his arm and held him back.

"Hist—wait a moment," he said, "I must be off first. Here, Forbes," and he handed the gunsmith a small bag; "his excellency requested me to hand that to you. Have you nothing to send?"

"Nothing for his excellency, to-day, colonel; everything is going on well," and, holding up the bag which contained the promised guineas, which was to pay for treason and desertion, he said: "With this we can do anything. There's something in that sound," and he shook them till they jingled again and again, as if the very sound conferred happiness, "which these half-starved and poorly-paid rebels can't resist. Say to his excellency, if you please, that we shall not relax any effort to carry out every operation he may devise, nor hesitate at any cost to prove our devotion to his most glorious majesty."

"Now, then, I'm off. Corbie, my fine fellow, that's glorious wine," said the colonel, rising from the table.

"Finish it, colonel—finish it; you have a long pull and a stormy night before you. God bless his majesty and give him many more faithful servants like your honor," said Corbie, enthusiastically, for he was, indeed, a most devoted loyalist.

"Amen," said the colonel, draining glass after glass, until he had emptied the bottle; "and now, then, good-night all. I don't know when I shall return; but when I do, I hope to hear good news from our trusty friends here;" and seizing his cap, the gallant colonel strode forth into the storm, and the door was again securely barred and bolted by the loyal landlord.

CHAPTER VIII.

A NEW RECRUIT.

"Now, then," said Corbie, seizing one of the candles which stood on the table, and proceeding toward the door whence the sound issued which had disturbed them a few moments before, "let us see what this means;" and followed by Forbes, he opened the door which led into the adjoining apartment.

"Come, who's here?" exclaimed Corbie, holding the light over his head, so that its beams illumined the whole apartment.

"Hang it, don't stop to ask questions," said Forbes, advancing to the centre of the room, and peering about with his keen, grey eyes. "Ah! there he is," and advancing toward a large mahogany table which stood between the windows, under a large mahogany-framed mirror, he raised one of the leaves, and, sure enough, *there he was.*

"Come out of that, my fine fellow, and let us see who you are," and, as he spoke, he put his hand down, and seizing a huge booted leg, which half projected from the table, drew forth a stalwart man, dressed in the uniform of the Life-guards, who, as soon as his body was free from the table, sprang to his feet, and stood gazing about him in amazement.

"Well, Barnes," said Corbie, who knew the man well, for he was one of his regular customers, "what on earth took you in there?" and, as he spoke, he turned toward Forbes with an anxious glance of inquiry, which almost said, "I wonder if he has overheard us; if he has, I'll cut his throat."

"Fact is, Corbie," said the soldier, now released from the grasp of the gunsmith, and stepping backward with an unsteady motion, "I drank a leetle too much, and I thought I would hide away, and sleep it off afore tattoo. Has it beat yet?"

"More than an hour ago," said Corbie, who saw, at a glance, the advantage he had over his man, and who was so familiar with all phases of drunkenness, he knew there was no pretence in his case. "Everybody's gone long ago. You're in for thirty-six, sure as as your name's Barnes."

"Sure enough," replied the soldier, and he rubbed his shoulders, as if he already felt the lashes on his quivering flesh. "Well, what can't be cured must be endured, and I suppose I must take 'em, as many better men have done before me."

"Do you know the sergeant was here, about an hour ago, looking for you?" asked Corbie, desirous of trying the effect upon Barnes of such a statement.

"Sure?" asked the soldier, now thoroughly sobered, and conscious of the position in which he had placed himself.

"Sure as your name's Barnes."

"You didn't tell him I was here, did you, Corbie?" he asked, half anxiously, half sullenly.

"I told him you had been here, but I thought you had gone back to the barracks, and so he left."

"Thank you for that, anyhow. Thirty-six! I swow that's too bad for a small offence like this. Why don't they hang a fellow at once, and have it all done with."

"Yes, and well laid on at that," added Corbie, pursuing his advantage. "You know Green is no baby when he gets the cat in his hand, and I rather guess he was made drummer especially for that."

"Well, I might as well make up my mind to it. I see it's got to come; but it's cursed hard anyhow. I wonder if your side treats men so."

"Not a bit of it. What! tie a man up and whip him, in the presence of his comrades, for a little spree! Why, it would raise a mutiny at once, and half the men would desert. Oh, no—they don't do things in that way on our side, and that's the reason our men never desert. Plenty to eat and drink, and sure pay, and sure promotion when it is earned. A day or two in the guard-house, and low diet, is quite cure enough for a small drunk · but the idea of whipping a grown man like you. I'm blessed if I wouldn't kill the fellow that dared to put the lash on me!"

"I'm cursed if any lash touches my back, anyhow, now mark my words. I know just what I shall get when I go back to barracks; but when they whip me, it will do Green good. I'll clear out, and take my chances outside. If they catch me, they can but shoot me, and that will be better than being flogged."

"Why, man, you can't leave the island. You are crazy; every inch of the shore is guarded, and a boat can't even land without permission."

"Sure enough, and I ain't got no boat. Come, Corbie, give us some more rum, and I'll go in and give myself up."

"I can tell you an easier way than that," said Forbes, with earnestness, and he looked meaningly in Barnes' face.

"As how, Gilbert?" queried the now thoroughly sobered guardsman, for he knew the gunsmith very well.

"Perhaps you know what these are," and the gunsmith held before the eyes of the guardsman a handful of guineas, which he rattled one against the other.

"I have seen such things before," replied Barnes, his eyes fairly glistening at the sight of so much money—more than he had ever seen at once in his life-time.

"Five of them for bounty, sure pay, plenty to eat,

and no flogging for a little spree; and besides that, two hundred acres of land, when the war is over, for every man, one hundred, if he's married, for his wife, and fifty for every child. Eh, what do you think of that? and you haven't seen ten silver dollars since you 'listed."

"Give me them guineas," exclaimed the guardsman, stretching out his hand, for while his manhood shrunk at the idea of being publicly flogged, his sense of honor was not so strong as to prevent him from desiring to escape that degrading punishment by the more disgraceful one of desertion and treason. "I'd serve the devil sooner than be stripped and flogged before the whole corps. So hand over, and I'm your man."

"Softly, Barnes; you are almost too willing," replied Forbes, who, though now sure of his man, was determined to test him thoroughly. "You know, if you 'list with us, and are caught"——

"Why, they'll hang or shoot me; anything you choose but a flogging. I never was flogged, and I never will be, so help me"——

"You will be, if you go to the barracks to-night or to-morrow."

"I don't mean to go there, boys. I'll take to the woods, and stand my chances, if you don't want me; but I'm d—d if I'm going to be flogged because I drank a glass too much."

"Well, then, Barnes, if you will join us I'm ready with your bounty," and he jingled the guineas, which sounded temptingly in the ear of the poorly paid guardsman, now thoroughly aroused to any deed, no matter how dark or desperate, so he escaped the dreaded flogging. "We don't want you to desert, but if you choose you can join us, and I'll guarantee you shan't be flogged."

"I'll join the devil, I tell you, sooner than be flogged," and to add emphasis to his words, he brought his huge fist on the table with a force which made the room ring again.

"Then take the oath I shall give you, and the guineas are yours."

"Out with it," said Barnes, doggedly. "I'm ready for anything but a flogging."

Being thus assured, Corbie, at Forbes' request, produced a Bible, and Barnes was sworn by the most solemn and terrible oath, not to reveal any secret intrusted to him, on pain of having his tongue cut from his mouth, but to aid those whom he had joined in any manner which might be demanded of him, at all times and under any circumstances, and without regard to consequences.

"Now, then, Barnes, you belong to us," said Forbes. "Here is your bounty," and he placed the price of his treason in his hands. "You are under full pay from to-night. Ten shillings a week, you know, and when this cursed rebellion is crushed, two hundred acres of land are yours, anywhere you choose to select."

"But how about that flogging; I must go back to the barracks," said Barnes, putting the price of his treason in his pocket.

"Go, stand out in the rain a few minutes, till you get wet through," said Forbes, moving toward the bar-room; and at a sign from him, Corbie opened the door through which the colonel had passed, and Barnes stepped out, as he was commanded.

A very few moments sufficed to drench him thoroughly, and he reëntered the room, dripping like a water dog.

"Now, then, what next?" he asked, as he stood there, the water fairly running from him.

"A glass of rum is next, I think," said Corbie, laughing, as he went behind the bar, and pouring a tumbler two-thirds full of rum, handed it to the new recruit, who tossed it off with evident relish, and without making a single wry face.

"Now, then, for the rest."

"Just take me by the collar, and drag me to the guard-house," said Corbie. "Say, that after everybody had left, you saw me go out and start down toward the water; that you followed me, and heard a boat approach the shore, and that when you challenged, it went back again, and you arrested me."

"And what are you going to say?" queried the

guardsman, who liked this part of the arrangement well enough, but could not discover how it would benefit him, or save him from the much-dreaded flogging.

"Leave that to me; nothing to compromise either of us; let me alone for that."

Barnes did as he was bid. and appeared before the officer of the guard, on duty, with his prisoner, narrating the adventure precisely as he had been instructed.

"I thought it very strange, Barnes, that you did not come at tattoo, but you have done well. Now, Corbie, what is this?" asked the lieutenant on duty for the night.

"Only a little bit of a smuggle," he said, doffing his cap as soon as Barnes loosed his hold on his collar. "You see, I have been expecting a lot of prime Jamaica, ever so long, from—no matter where—but as I knew that your friends wouldn't let it come, without taking toll, I made arrangements to shove it; and if it hadn't been for that 'ere spooney," and he looked at Barnes as if he would annihilate him, "I'd a had it long ago; but he must go and poke his nose in what don't concern him. It was real prime, too, I tell you, lieutenant," added Corbie, with a very slight wink; for he knew his man, who was one of his best, though sly, customers, and was fond of the "prime article" as any man in the corps.

"Well, Corbie, you had better go home, and try and get your Jamaica like an honest man. It won't do you any harm to try a little honest dealing, by the way of variety. Barnes," he said, turning to the guardsman —whose delight at this unexpected termination of his anticipated troubles could scarcely be concealed—"you acted perfectly right; but, I guess Corbie was not doing anything worse than that."

"On my honor, no, lieutenant," said the wily landlord, who saw that his wink had been rightly interpreted, laying his brawny hand over the place where the heart was supposed to be, and as he spoke, he made a low bow.

"You can go, then," said the officer, condescendingly.

"I told you so, you blasted fool," said Corbie, turning angrily to Barnes, but with a glance which seemed to say, "I told you I would save you from a flogging, and I have done it."

"Well, you did," replied the traitor, glad enough at his relief from a flogging, to forget the means by which he had escaped from well-merited punishment.

"All right," said Corbie, barring and locking the door, as he reëntered his house, and was greeted by the impatient Forbes, with the emphatic inquiry: "Well!"

"There's another good one. We've got him as fast as oaths and fears can secure him; and a few more like him, down there at old Putnam's, would make short work of the whole matter. Who the devil can I get at down there? The colonel says his excellency wants some one there, and he must be found."

CHAPTER IX.

MARGARET MONCRIEFFE AT HOME.

"You are wounded," said Margaret, rising from the arms of Major Burr, as she heard the sound of approaching horses' feet, and perceived the blood-stain on his leg.

"Oh, it's nothing--a mere scratch! it does not even pain me; and if it did, I should forget the pain in my happiness at seeing you unharmed."

"Thanks to you, major," she said, smiling sweetly "But come, let us proceed; who knows what we may meet next? One moment," and she advanced toward Selim, who had remained standing still from the moment Margaret had been dragged from her seat. As she moved toward him, she was obliged to pass the body of the man who had met his death at her hands, as it lay weltering in a pool of blood; and as she did so, she stopped for an instant, and, gazing at the frightful wound made in his throat by her ball, turned with a triumphant expression to the major, and said: "It wasn't a bad shot for a frightened girl, was it, major?"

"It was good for a brave man, Margaret. You are worthy of a better fate than I"——

"There, now—please don't," she interrupted; "you have said enough for to-day, and I have said much more than I ought. Let me load my pistol," she added, stopping to pick up the weapon which she had dropped when she had fired it, and, feeling in the pocket of her riding-dress, she drew forth a small flask of powder. The pistol was carefully loaded and primed, and, having placed it in the holster, she turned to the major, who had watched her movements with looks of affectionate interest, and said: "Come, help me to mount—I am ready."

While she had been thus engaged, the escort had rejoined their leader, and stood around watching the brave and beautiful girl with admiring eyes, commenting upon her courage and beauty in whispered tones.

"I am sure I am gratefully obliged to all of you," she said, looking around the group and smiling sweetly; "I did the best I could," and she pointed to the corpse lying in the road.

The men looked at her and each other in amazement, for until now, they knew not the part she had taken in the action, or, rather, skirmish; and from that moment they looked upon her almost with veneration.

She was assisted into the saddle by Major Burr. One of the two wounded men having been placed before, on a horse in front of one of his comrades, and Hickey declaring himself perfectly able to do more fighting for such a brave little woman, mounting his own horse, the party moved on in the same order as they had started, leaving the dead to take care of the dead, and the wounded to get along as they best could.

Paulus Hook was reached without any further adventure, and without a recurrence on the part of Major Burr or Margaret to the topic which most closely interested both; for her request was command to the young and enamored soldier.

Only once, and that was as he was handing her on board the bateau which was to convey the horses and their riders across the river, did he allude to the subject of their new-born love, and only then because he thought he perceived a shade of sadness on the beautiful face of his companion.

"You do not repent having said what you have, Margaret?" he asked, tenderly, looking in her lustrous eyes, whose expression was now wonderfully softened.

"Oh, no, no!" she replied, with deep earnestness, "I am very, very happy, and you" ——

"I cannot describe my feelings. I can only from my heart say I thank and bless you, my own dear, best, and only beloved."

It was nearly dark when Major Burr, having dismissed his escort at the New York side of the ferry, conducted Margaret into the presence of General Putnam and his family, who had just risen from their evening meal, and she was received by the ladies with an honest warmth and cordiality, which actually brought tears to her eyes; and with the impulse so natural to her, and which she could not control, she threw herself into a high-backed chair, and gave vent to her overcharged feelings in a burst of hearty tears.

"Come, come, child!" said the blunt old general, approaching and taking one of her hands within his own, while he placed the other on her head, "don't fret about it—it is the fortune of war. Your father I know to be a gallant gentleman and an honorable soldier, and you may feel just as much at home in my house as if you were with him. Mayn't she, ma?" and he turned to his wife, who had marked the advent of this new member of her family with decided interest, for there was that in her youth, beauty, and isolated situation, which commended her to that sympathy which woman never withholds from any one in distress.

"Be sure, what a question to ask. Come, child, wipe your eyes, you won't feel lonesome in a day or two. My daughters here will find something for you to do, and that will keep you from thinking. Why, Major Burr, what on earth is the matter with your leg? See, girls, it's all bloody."

"What's all this, Burr?" exclaimed the general, now for the first time noticing that which had attracted his wife's attention, and he pointed to the blood-stained clothes of his handsome young aid, to whom he had already grown strongly attached.

"Only a little skirmish with those rascally Cow-boys," was the reply of Major Burr, who, in the excitement of the journey, had quite forgotten his wound. "Graham and Hickey were slightly hurt; but we beat them off, and left five dead, and as for the rest, I am afraid they stand a poor chance for a very long life. But, general," and his eye kindled as he turned to Margaret, who was trying to dry her tears, an operation in which she was materially assisted by the general's daughters, who, kneeling on either side of her, with true girlish sympathy, were speaking low words of hope and comfort, "you ought to have seen Miss Moncrieffe then. She brought down one of the villains with a ball through his throat, as neatly and coolly as you could have done it yourself."

"She!" echoed mother and daughters, while the general turned to Margaret and gazed upon her for an instant with an expression of admiration, for he did honor to true courage whether in man or woman. "She shot a man, major?"

"Yes; and if she could have reached her other pistol in time, she would have shot two of them."

"How did it happen? Where? When?" the trio of females exclaimed in a breath.

"Some other time I will tell you; or, perhaps, you nad better ask Miss Moncrieffe herself."

"Miss Moncrieffe, can only say," said Margaret, rising, and wiping the tears from her eyes, "that she owes her life, and more than her life, to the promptness and courage of Major Burr, and he knows how grateful she is."

These latter words were accompanied with a look which spoke volumes to the young soldier, who turning away to conceal the color which her words, and her expression, as she uttered them, had called to his face, asked if Doctor Haxton was in his room, and without waiting for a reply, left the apartment, in search of the surgeon to dress his wound, which was as he said, truly, quite slight.

In three days from her first introduction into the family of the worthy old general, Margaret Moncrieffe had won all hearts, by her vivacity, her endless sallies of wit and humor, her unfailing store of anecdote, incident and adventure, her reckless, free, frank, open-hearted speech and manners, combined with an artlessness and simplicity, which rendered her perfectly irresistible.

General Putnam had been christened "grandpa," to which he submitted with a bad grace, at first, but eventually, with a smile which he could not conceal. Mrs. Putnam was "my lady," and the girls were "cousins Bell, and Mattie."

She managed to have her own way in everything. As for spinning, the daily occupation of the family, she had never learned it, and she was too old now (at fifteen) to begin. She could embroider, and she would, if "grandpa" should ask her very politely, sew on buttons. She would sit in the room with the family for hours, with her embroidery frame on her lap, and keep them in a continued strain of laughter, by her wit, her anecdotes, or her actions; in the latter of which she was a perfect romping child, when unrestrained by the forms of society.

She had coaxed the general to let her give Selim an airing every day, "as the poor brute would suffer," she pleaded, pathetically, "if he did not have his regular exercise;" and then by the way of added inducement, she promised he should have the occasional use of him, if he would pledge his word he should not be shot in action.

There was no resisting her! She fairly carried all hearts by storm; and already, as rumors of an invasion began to fly thick and fast, they were thinking of the possibility of losing her charming society, which had almost changed the character of their home.

Favored by the permission granted by General Putnam, she rode out on the fourth day of her arrival in the city, in company with Major Burr, who had been ordered to make a tour of inspection of the works in progress in various parts of the island; and as there was, on that occasion, no ban upon the topic of the ride from Elizabethtown, it was renewed by both, and with an earnestness and freedom, which showed how deeply the hearts of both were engrossed by their mutual love.

Margaret appeared to be deeply interested in the operations of the men on the breastworks, which they visited in the course of their ride; and once or twice, she drew upon her a searching glance from her companion, by the singularity and pertinency of the questions she asked. She saw everything, noted every thing; and on their return, she locked herself in the apartment occupied by her, and amused herself by noting down carefully, and accurately, in detail, all she had seen and heard during the ride; except such portion of the conversation as was directly connected with herself. These were recorded in ineffaceable characters on the tablet of her heart.

As aid to the commander-in-chief (for General Washington had not, as yet, returned from Philadelphia, and General Putnam was in full command), Major Burr was, of course, a personage of high importance, and his movements were watched with close scrutiny, by all the officers in the city. His companion, whose first appearance had that day been made in public, had been noticed by many, on this first ride, and particularly by Colonel Shee, commanding one of the four Pennsylvania battalions, who embraced the first opportunity to inquire of Major Burr, who she was, and where, on earth, he had discovered such a lovely girl.

"A Miss Moncrieffe," was the reply; "daughter of a British officer, now camped on Staten Island; and for the present, a member of General Putnam's family."

"Burr, bring her to our ball to-morrow night; she will be the brightest star there. Do, that's a good fellow! You know we're awfully short of pretty girls, and the whole corps will send you a vote of thanks."

"I am sure I shall be proud to escort her," said the young aid, laughing, "but some of your dashing youngsters will be losing their hearts. She is as witty and polished as she is beautiful, but she is an awful little Royalist."

"Royalist be hanged! She's a woman, and a pretty one, at that; so bring her along, and if she insists upon it, she shall drink the king's health; we are not fighting with women. The general's daughters are coming; two of our fellows engaged them a week ago. So do you bring your little Tory; will you, Burr?"

"If she will come, surely, and with pleasure; but I warn you, she will speak just as she thinks."

"Let her speak what she chooses, so long as she looks so sweetly on me, as she did—— Faith, no, I won't finish that sentence. Burr, you are a lucky dog; I wish I was old Put's aid for a little while."

"Well. give me your commission, colonel," said the

major, laughing, "and you may have mine, and my position with it."

"What, and your chances with the handsome little Tory?"

"Of course! I want more active service," replied the major, for he could not say anything else without committing himself; though, as he spoke, his heart smote him for allowing Margaret to be spoken of in such a trifling manner, and he turned away to conceal the flush which had been called to his cheeks by this conversation.

CHAPTER X.

AN OLD FRIEND.

THE threatened invasion of the British, by land and sea, concerning which rumors had been flying thick and fast for many weeks, had driven from the city most of the best families, and, in consequence, the wives of the generals and other officers quartered there were constrained to rely on each other for society and such amusement as they could invent, for the time passed heavily on them.

Among the troops quartered in the city, were four battalions of troops from Pennsylvania, commanded by Colonels Shee, McGaw, St. Clair, and Wayne, and officered by scions of the most wealthy and aristocratic families of the commonwealth. They had joined the army from motives of the purest patriotism, and without a thought as to any merely personal benefit, save such as might accrue to the whole country from a recognition of its independence from Great Britain.

While, therefore, ever ready for any duty, and equally ready to meet any foe, they felt that the time could be passed much more pleasantly than by watching and waiting for an enemy. They had accordingly arranged a series of balls and entertainments, which were given alternately at the head-quarters of the different colonels, who were all men of high position and large wealth, and every lady in the city was anxious to be invited on those occasions.

The generals, anxious to propitiate the troops from every section, made it a point of honor to attend each ball or party with their families, and these weekly reunions were looked upon by all as a most agreeable means of dispelling the *ennui* attendant upon garrison life.

It was to the ball given by Colonel Shee to which Major Burr had been requested to invite Margaret, an invitation which she accepted most joyfully, for when she heard the general's daughters talking about it, and saw them arranging the little details of their modest toilettes for the occasion, she had wished that she might not be left alone. The invitation, therefore, from him whom her heart acknowledged as its master, was joyfully accepted, and her pleasure was heightened by the fact that he was to be her escort.

Colonel Shee, at that period, occupied a large mansion on Broadway, near the spot where the Astor House now stands. The lower part of the building, on this occasion, was devoted to dancing, the second floor to card-playing and the punch-room—and without an attempt at going into details, it is sufficient to say that everything which lavish expenditure could procure, in view of the means at hand, for luxuries were rather rare, was provided to contribute to the pleasure of the guests.

The entrance of Margaret, leaning on the arm of her handsome escort, who was dressed in full uniform, was greeted with a buzz of admiration from the gentlemen (for Colonel Shee had boasted so much of her beauty, every one was anxious to test his judgment by his own standard) and by looks of jealousy from the ladies, for she was incomparably the most lovely woman or girl in the room.

Robed in simple white, without one single ornament, her glossy hair flowing in graceful ringlets over her snowy neck and shoulders, her countenance faultlessly beautiful, animated as well by the scene as by the presence of him to whom she had given her first affections, she might well challenge the admiration which she commanded.

Colonel Shee was among the first to notice her entrance, and apologizing to a group of ladies with whom he had been conversing, he hurried toward the youthful couple on whom all eyes were directed. The formality of an introduction was soon accomplished, and offering his arm, the colonel gallantly said:

"Major, you must allow me to rob you of your fair charge for a short time, so many are anxious to know her, and I claim, as host, the privilege of presenting her. Allow me the honor, Miss Moncrieffe," and he bowed low as she took his proffered arm, not, however, without casting a glance at Major Burr, whose meaning he rightly interpreted, and young as he was, he was too shrewd to say or do anything by which either might be compromised.

Colonel Shee led his lovely guest toward a bevy of officers who had, from her first entrance, eyed her with looks of deep admiration, and still retaining her arm within his own, introduced her to them severally. For each she had some pleasant or witty remark, the piquancy of which was enhanced by her manner, and at once she was completely surrounded, each one striving to outvie the other in the fulsomeness of the compliments he wished to pay. For each she had some happy reply, and if her beauty had failed to conquer, her wit accomplished what that had left undone.

"I declare, colonel," she said, pointing to a far corner of the room, "I am sure I see a familiar face."

"Indeed, and where?" inquired the colonel, turning to the quarter toward which her eyes were directed. "How on earth can any face here be familiar to you?"

"That tall gentleman in plain clothes," she replied, pointing to the person of whom she spoke.

"Ah, yes—that is Captain Blanchard, one of your people, by the way. He is a prisoner on parole; but he is a noble, high-spirited gentleman, and a great favorite with all of us, for we are on the most friendly terms."

"Do bring him here, colonel," she said, eagerly. "Perhaps he has seen my father lately."

"Scarcely lately, Miss Moncrieffe," replied the colonel, with a faint smile, "he has been with us over three months. But if you desire, I will bring him to you."

"No, I will go to him. Oh, how pleasant it is to see a familiar face, even where all else are so kind," she added, with a smile so bright and winning, the gallant colonel forgot the first portion of her sentence.

Making way through the crowd of admirers who thronged around her, Margaret, leaning upon the colonel's arm, was escorted to that portion of the apartment where stood the gentleman who had attracted her attention, and whose face she claimed as familiar to her.

He was reclining moodily against one of the folding doors, surveying the gay scene with emotions of anything but pleasure, for though he had been treated with the most boundless courtesy and hospitality since his capture, he longed to be among friends with whom he had closer sympathies than those who surrounded him. At the approach of Colonel Shee, he raised himself from his leaning position, and, as his eye caught sight of his companion, his countenance lighted up in an instant, and a new life seemed to be infused in him.

Advancing with outstretched hand he exclaimed, "You here, Miss Moncrieffe?"

"Yes, captain, as you see," she added, gaily, dropping the colonel's arm, and grasping his extended hand "and you are here too, I see."

"Even so," he said, as a shade of sadness crossed his features; "the chances of war have placed me here, but I won't blame them, since I am permitted to see the loveliest"——

"There, don't finish that sentence, captain; Colonel Shee, here, can say much prettier things than that, I am sure. Can't you, colonel?" and she looked archly at the colonel.

"I can feel them, if I cannot say them, Miss Moncrieffe," gallantly replied the colonel, with a bow.

"Now, colonel, please to give me a proof of your sincerity, by letting me have my own way for—let me see—just five minutes. Of course, you must dance with me; I shall be honored by the preference," and she courtesied gracefully, at the same time giving him a glance which almost bewitched the colonel, whose admiration for the fair stranger was really sincere. "Then, of course, others will claim the same privilege, and as you are the host, you may dispose of me as you choose for the evening; of course, with the consent of my escort."

"If I could dispose of you as I choose, you would only have one partner this evening," and another bow testified the colonel's gallantry.

"There, Captain Blanchard," she said, placing her

arm within his own, "how prettily that was said. Why don't you take pattern after the colonel, and pay your compliments more delicately? I don't want to be admired, and told so as you would speak of a horse."

Captain Blanchard bit his lip, to conceal the rising laugh, while Colonel Shee turned red with vexation, for he saw the young vixen was amusing herself at his expense.

"Come, colonel," she said, seeing the change in his countenance, "let me have Captain Blanchard five minutes, and you may have control of me the whole of the rest of the evening—of course, Major Burr consenting."

"I agree to that," said the colonel, gaily, pulling out his watch. "Captain, you have just five minutes, so make the most of them," and replacing his watch in his fob, he moved away, leaving Margaret and Captain Blanchard alone.

"What are you doing here?" queried the captain, in tones so low, they reached no ears save those for whom they were intended.

"I am residing with General Putnam, a member of his family at present. You are on parole, Colonel Shee says."

"He speaks the truth, I am sorry to say."

"Are you doing anything for the king?" she asked earnestly, looking him full in the face as she spoke.

"How can I? situated as I am, Miss Margaret!"

"That's no answer to my question. Time is precious, and opportunity rare; are you doing anything for your king's cause?"

"That's a very singular question for a girl to ask a soldier."

"And that is a very ridiculous answer from a soldier to the loyal daughter of a loyal subject."

Captain Blanchard looked steadily at the beautiful, but singular being who hung upon his arm, but she bore his gaze unshrinkingly. At length, seeming to read in her eyes something more than her words had made intelligible, he answered emphatically, but in the same low tones:

"I am."

"I have no time to converse with you now; there are too many eyes watching us; you must call on me, at the general's. You have that privilege, I suppose," she continued, inquiringly.

"Of course," was his reply; "unless you or I are suspected of being" ——

"Hush!" she said, hurriedly, pressing his arm, seeing a bevy of young officers approaching them. "Call on me to-morrow. I ride out every day, now, by permission of General Putnam. I shall ride out alone whenever I can. You must manage to see me whenever you possibly can. I leave that to you. Ah! gentlemen," she continued, in gay tones, as the party approached, "time is up, eh! Well, captain, I am glad to have seen an old friend. Call on me, will you, please! You know where to find me, I suppose. Gentlemen," and she turned to the group of admirers who surrounded her, "there's no harm in my receiving a visit from an old friend, I hope, though we are both sound Royalists."

"Of course not," said Colonel Shee, who had approached unperceived, from another quarter, "because we expect to convert you to our cause soon, and if we can gain you over to our side, we shall feel secure of victory."

"Upon my word, colonel," replied Margaret, gaily, moving toward him, and placing her arm within his own, "I don't know how I shall thank you for your appreciation of my worth. Come, I cannot reply to your compliments, but I will dance with you; will that do?" and again the colonel met that fascinating smile.

"I am more than honored," replied the gallant colonel, as he ventured a gentle pressure upon the arm which hung upon his own.

He did not perceive the slight curl which for an instant rested upon the lip of the vivacious beauty, or he might not have marched off with his prize so proudly and happily as he did.

CHAPTER XI.

MARGARET AND HER CONQUESTS.

MARGARET had mixed with the gay assemblage at least two hours, and had been surrounded from first to last by a bevy of admirers and flatterers. During all that time she had only caught an occasional glimpse of Major Burr, who had stationed himself among the elderly ladies, and who seemed to be pleased as well in this society as though he had joined in the giddy throng which filled the spacious apartments.

Several times she caught his look fixed upon her with an expression which she well knew how to interpret, and when, pleading with absolute truth, downright inability to dance any more, for the present, she was conducted to the coterie among which the major had established himself, she took his proffered arm with a feeling of real pleasure, which she had not experienced during the whole evening, and which she testified by a gentle pressure of the arm which held her own.

"Do, Major Burr, take me where I can get some air," she said, beseechingly; "I am almost suffocated with the heat, and absolutely wearied with dancing."

The young soldier, with a gallant bow, was about

moving toward a door which led upon a broad piazza, when, as he turned, he found himself confronted by a corps of general officers, who were approaching him from the direction of the door. General Greene led the van, arm in arm with the gallant Lord Stirling, and the rear was brought up by Generals Heath, Sullivan, Mifflin, and Spencer. They had evidently been engaged in private converse, for even as they approached, their words were uttered to each other in whispered tones.

"How now, major?" said Lord Stirling, dropping the arm of General Greene, and, advancing with his most courtly bow, "who have we here?"

"A desperate little Tory, my lord," replied Major Burr, releasing, as he spoke, Margaret's arm from his own. "Miss Moncrieffe, the daughter of"——

"Oh, yes; I know your father well, my child," he interrupted, smiling as he spoke, and he extended his hand cordially. "It was my fortune once to make a prisoner of him, and I can say, with truth, I was very sorry when he was exchanged. Pray who has captured you?"

"I believe I belong to General Putnam," she added, as she saw the old soldier advancing toward the circle by which she was surrounded, and as room was made for him, she added, "don't I, general?" and she smiled naïvely as she spoke.

Now, General Putnam, with all his well-known

courage, so often and so severely tested, was particularly sensitive to ridicule, and when he observed Margaret standing in the midst of the circle of general officers, he feared that she had been speaking of him by the pet name which she had conferred upon him, and which he had permitted because he could not help himself, and the perspiration actually stood on the soldier's brow as he approached, dreading lest he should hear himself addressed in presence of his compeers by his new title. But Margaret was too well bred to use such familiarity under such circumstances as now surrounded her, and as he caught the last words of her sentence only, he answered promptly:

"Of course you do;" for he was so glad to be freed from his apprehensions he scarcely thought what he said.

"Really, Miss Moncrieffe," said the gallant Mifflin, "I should like to enlist you in our cause. To judge by the havoc you made to-night, you must be a perfect Mars, or more likely the Goddess of Victory. What bounty shall we pay you to enlist?"

"Let me have my choice," she said, in the same gay strain.

"Oh, you need not ask his permission for that, young lady," said General Greene. "Please to look around and make your own selection—yours may be the only difficulty."

Margaret, glad to have an opportunity of turning upon themselves the badinage thus addressed to her by the generals, turned her head very leisurely around, as if taking a survey of the company present, and as she did so, her eyes met those of Major Burr, fixed upon her with anxious scrutiny, for he really feared she might say or do something offensive. She returned his glance with a look which said, as plain as words could speak, "My choice is made," and that look reassured him, for it told him she was only gaining time to make a suitable reply.

He replied by a glance of equal meaning with her own, and, after scanning the assembled company for some moments, she turned suddenly to General Putnam, and, putting her arm within his own, said, gaily: "I don't see any one here I prefer to my kind friend and host, so I will choose him."

The good old general actually blushed, as Margaret thus took him by surprise; but his astonishment was heightened, and the laughter of the circle raised to the highest pitch, as she added, "Come, general, one gavotte with me."

"You little vixen," he said, in low tones, bringing his mouth close to her ear; "I'll put you on bread and water for this for three days, and keep you locked up," and, raising his voice, he said aloud, "Me dance!" and the burly soldier laughed till the tears ran down his face at the idea—"Me dance, my child! I weigh nearly two hundred pounds, and am over sixty. No, no, I do such things by proxy, as the lawyers say. Here, Burr," and he beckoned his handsome aid, who sprang gaily to his side, "this young lady wants to dance."

"Thank you, General Putnam," she said, with well affected hauteur, as Major Burr advanced; "I did not ask you to choose a partner for me—I can do that myself. Nothing less than a general officer can get me on the floor again this evening;" and, as she spoke, Lord Stirling, the gallant, high-bred gentleman, stepped forward, and, with a low bow, said:

"General, Lord Stirling requests the honor of your hand for the next gavotte."

"Miss Moncrieffe is honored by Lord Stirling's choice," she said, with a courtesy absolutely as courteous as his bow, and with a quick, meaning glance at Major Burr, who had watched her with an interest excelled only by his admiration of her perfect self-possession, she took the arm of the gallant nobleman, and was led away by him.

"Faith, that is the greatest vixen I have seen in many a day, Burr," said General Putnam, turning to his aid, who stood by his side. "She had the impudence to ask me to dance the gavotte. I believe I will ask her to storm a battery with me some day."

"She won't refuse, general, I can promise you," replied Major Burr, laughingly, as he noticed how seriously the good old general took to heart the playful badinage of Margaret. "I don't believe she knows what fear is, any more than you do."

This well-timed and well-merited compliment soothed the old general, and joining the coterie, he was soon employed in discussing with them, but in low tones, the probabilities and possibilities which the next few weeks might bring forth, for it was generally believed that Lord Howe, who had left Virginia with his fleet, intended to make New York the centre of his operations for the next campaign.

Major Burr sauntered carelessly away, and joined a group of young officers, who stood watching the motions of Lord Stirling and Margaret, as they moved through the stately and graceful gavotte, the favorite dance of that period. Leaning against a column which stood near the folding doors, in the room in which they were dancing, he feasted his eyes in silent contemplation of her to whom he had given his whole heart and soul, envying the noble old general even the poor privilege of one dance.

Lord Stirling having concluded the gavotte with Margaret, led her again to the coterie of general officers, who, by this time, had been surrounded by a large corps of younger officers and ladies, and again she proved the centre of attraction.

Her wit was so pungent, her satire so good-natured, and her vivacity so perfectly natural, she carried all hearts by storm, and the daughter of the Royalist officer, who a few days before had been glad to find shelter and protection with her natural enemies (for as such she looked upon all Americans), was the cynosure of all eyes, and the great centre of attraction to all.

It was not until the close of the entertainment that Major Burr had an opportunity of being alone with her for one moment, and it was then only effected at her earnest request, that she should be conducted to him, and on her positive assurance she would not dance any more during the night.

"Oh, Aaron," she said, as taking his ready arm, they moved away from the throng which had surrounded her, "how I hate and despise these compliments and flatteries, meaning nothing. Do you know what I have been thinking the whole evening?" and she looked fondly in his face as she spoke.

"I know *who* I have been thinking of," he said, with a smile full of meaning.

"And so do I, Aaron. I was thinking how meaningless and hollow all their compliments and flatteries were, when I compared them with the look I met when you held me in your arms after having rescued me from that ruffian," and she clung closer to his side, as if the memory of the peril she had passed was so vivid that she dreaded its recurrence, and clung to him for protection.

"Were you, indeed, Margaret?" asked the young

officer, eagerly, as they stepped upon the balcony which fronted on Broadway.

"Indeed, Aaron, I was. Believe me, though I am young, and seem giddy, thoughtless and reckless, my feelings are warm, deep, and very earnest. You have them all. Don't heed how I act with others; I must act as I have done from policy. Remember, Aaron, I am only here by courtesy of our enemies."

"Oh, don't say enemies, Margaret," exclaimed Major Burr, impetuously. "Do not let that word come between us."

"It never can interpose between us, Aaron," and she laid her hand on his. "I have acted toward you rashly, impulsively, but only as my heart dictated Do not think less of me, that I have been so frank?"

"Dear, dearest Margaret, do what you will, say what you will, act as you will; the consciousness that I possess your love is all I ask to render my happiness on earth complete. But oh! what is to be our future?" and he sighed deeply as he spoke.

"Love, happiness, Aaron. You love me, don't you?" she asked, turning upon him her eyes, beaming with the deep feeling which prompted the question.

"Better than anything on earth, Margaret," was the earnest reply, delivered with a warmth and depth of manner which alone would have convinced any woman of his sincerity.

"I know, I felt it, and have perfect faith in your

love. So do not let us borrow trouble; it will come without our aid, and heaven only knows how soon."

"You have been very much admired to-night, Margaret," he said, half inquiringly, half reproachfully.

"Yes," she replied, laughingly, "I believe I have made several conquests. Colonel St. Clair has declared that he never will forgive me if I do not attend the ball of his battalion next week."

"And what did you say?" he inquired, with a searching look.

"Oh, I referred him to General Putnam, and if he gains his permission, I promised you should take me there."

"The dear, good old general can't refuse you anything, so of course you will go."

"And you?"

"Of course, by your permission. You know I surrendered to you, and consider myself under your orders."

The conversation was pursued in this strain for a few moments longer, the lovers leaning on the balcony on which they stood, and speaking in almost whispered tones, when it was interrupted by the appearance of a sudden flash of light, which shot up from a house apparently not far distant from the one in which they were standing.

"There is a fire, Margaret. I must go and see where and what it may be, for we have so many Tories among us, we have to be unceasingly vigilant. You must go home with General Putnam, and I will see you in the morning. I have to ride a long distance to-morrow," and these last words were uttered in tones which said, "Would you like to accompany me?"

"So much the better, Aaron. We shall have a better opportunity for conversation, for I shall manage to join you. You see I am bold, but love has made me so."

"Thank you a thousand times, my own Margaret," exclaimed the young officer, enthusiastically, as he drew her arm within his own, and leading her back into the room where the company were still assembled, consigned her to the care of the good old general, to whom he had reported the fact of the fire, and announced his intention of going to the scene in order to ascertain, if possible, whether it was an accident or the result of design on the part of some of the turbulent Tories who were permitted to remain in the city, though only upon giving bonds for their behavior.

"She will go home with me, major," he said, as Margaret drew close to his side. "Go and see what it is, and report when you return. I shall not retire until you come back. Oh, you need not fear for Miss Moncrieffe," said the old soldier, gaily, as he caught his aid stealing a glance at Margaret. "If I don't take good care of her, there are a hundred here ready to take my place. She will be safe enough, I will warrant."

Major Burr made no reply to his general, but with a low bow, took his leave, and proceeded toward the scene of the fire.

The conflagration was very trifling, and the flames being soon extinguished, the young aid retired to his own quarters, where he found General Putnam in the parlor, surrounded by his family, Margaret, of course, included, and having made his report, he was about retiring for the night, when the general arrested him by saying:

"By the way, major," and as Major Burr turned to receive his command, he continued sternly: "I wish you would send some discreet officer to-morrow night, to Corbie's, and report what he sees and hears. It is our belief that his pestilent den is the resort of the most dangerous characters, who are eternally plotting treason; and if we discover any cause, we are determined to break his house up at once, and send him out of the city. Pick out some one not likely to be known, and let him make any pretence he chooses, to find out what is really going on there, but it must be some brave, cool-headed, intelligent man."

"I have one in my eye now, general," replied the aid, "a young fellow from Elizabeth. He is the son of an old lady, with whom I am well acquainted, and with whom I have passed many a happy hour; a sharp, keen, quick-witted fellow, brave as a lion, and if there is anything wrong going on, I will guarantee he wil. find it out."

While this conversation was going on, between the general and his aid, Margaret seemed an attentive listener to the prattle of the general's daughters concerning the ball and their beaux (for in those days, young ladies were just as fond of the ball and beau, as they are at present), but she had heard and remembered every word which he had uttered.

In a few minutes after the aid had retired, she pleaded a severe headache, for leaving such pleasant company, and withdrew to her own room, and seating herself at a table, drew forth a small slip of paper, and hastily wrote a few lines in pencil. This she folded up in a very small compass, and placed in her pocket; and she then proceeded to note down the incidents and occurrences of the day and night, as, indeed, she had done since the first day she rode out with Major Burr.

CHAPTER XII.

THE BROTHERS' MEETING.

On the following morning, General Putnam's presented the appearance of a levee. Officers of every grade poured in, with kind inquiries after the health of the Misses Putnam, who had the penetration, however, to discover that this remarkable anxiety for their health, was but a pretext for seeing Miss Moncrieffe; and while slightly piqued, they had the discretion and good sense to make the best of it. Indeed, one of them, taking a moment when the parlor was empty of visitors, said to Margaret, with an arch look; "it's well you can't marry more than one, Margaret, there's some chance for us, after you have taken your choice."

"Keep them all, cousin Bell," she said, gaily. "I am too good a loyalist for any of them, and they know it, for I have spoken my mind very freely."

At this juncture another visitor was announced, one who was a stranger to the general's family, and who had inquired for Miss Moncrieffe.

It was Captain Blanchard, of the Royalist army; and as his name was announced, Margaret sprang forward, and as she did so, she hastily thrust her right hand into the pocket of her dress, and as she advanced, she drew it forth and extended both hands, which were warmly grasped by the gallant, but unfortunate officer, who, as an old friend of Major Moncrieffe, was warmly attached to his daughter.

"An old friend of mine, ladies," she said, drawing him forward, and retaining one of his hands in her own; one of my father's best friends—Captain Blanchard, of the royal army."

The Misses Putnam bowed to the salutation of the captain, but his reception was much less cordial than that of the provincial officers—for the general's daughters were ardent patriots. This was felt by the captain, who, however, only exhibited his perception of it, by directing the most of his conversation to Margaret; and the advent of two or three young officers enabled him for a few moments, to converse with her alone. She inquired after old friends, spoke about home and dear old England, with the honest enthusiasm of her heart, and, for the moment, forgot their position—he, a prisoner on parole; she, the protégée of a rebel general, glad of the protection which he had so courteously proffered, and which was so hospitably secured to her.

A few moments only, however, were allowed them for private conversation—if, indeed, that could be called private, which was overheard by all present—for the visitors soon turned it into a more general channel; and Captain Blanchard having, by his manly, polished bearing, worn away the impression which his first appearance had made, solely on account of his position, rose to withdraw, and received from the Misses Putnam, as well as from Margaret, a pressing invitation to call again, whenever he found it pleasant to do so, an invitation of which he promised to avail himself at an early day.

Margaret escorted him to the door of the parlor, where a look full of meaning was exchanged between them, and he took his leave, with a hearty shake of the hand.

Proceeding up Broadway, he stopped at the shop of Forbes, the gunsmith, and found him alone.

"Are my pistols finished yet?" he asked, after the salutation of the morning had passed between them.

"Not quite, captain," was the reply. "Won't you walk into the back room and rest a bit?"

"No, I thank you, Forbes. Are any of your boys about?"

"No, I am entirely alone," and as he spoke, the captain drew from his pocket a scrap of paper, rolled into a very small compass, saying to Forbes, as he unfolded it: "Keep your eyes wide open," and proceeded to read it. It ran briefly thus:

"I don't know who Corbie is; but a party is going to his house to-night in disguise, to see and hear what he can. If Corbie is one of *our* friends put him on his guard."

"Bravo!" he said, as he rolled the paper up and put it in his mouth. "Now, Forbes, can you see Corbie to-day?"

"Of course, if it is necessary, captain, I can do anything for his most gracious majesty's cause."

"It is of the utmost importance," said Captain Blanchard, earnestly. "You must see him or send word by some trusty friend that a person is coming to his house to-night, in disguise, probably to watch what is said and done. So tell him that if any stranger comes there, to be careful. He knows all of our friends, does he not?"

"Of course he does. But to make matters sure, I will be there myself. Oh, captain, there's the very man, Hickey," and, advancing toward the door, he hailed the guardsman, who at that moment was passing by on the other side of the street toward the lower end of the city, and who, on hearing Forbes' voice, immediately crossed over and entered the shop, which he could well do without exciting any suspicions, as it was frequented by officers and soldiers of all parties, although Forbes was a noted Royalist.

"Hickey, you must see Corbie as soon as possible, and tell him that there will be a spy at the house this evening," and as he spoke he looked at Captain Blanchard, whose face was crimsoned as he heard that word; for to him, a prisoner on parole, received and treated as a gentleman, that word emphatically belonged.

"I know where it comes from," said Hickey, with a meaning smile; "I wish there was more like" ——

"Go along, sir," said Captain Blanchard, sternly, and he gave the guardsman a look which said, as plain as words could speak, "don't name her."

Touching his cap, the guardsman left the shop, and, as he crossed the street, Forbes said to the captain:

"That fellow has brought us nearly a dozen first-rate fellows. We've got a captain in McDougal's regiment, too—a fine young fellow, who, I think, you'll like."

"No great gain, I am afraid," replied the captain, to whom the well-merited character of the regiment, for insubordination and general inefficiency, was quite familiar; "when is the boat coming again?"

"We never know; it has not been up now in three nights. I shouldn't wonder if it came to-night."

"It must not land on any account," continued the captain.

"Of course not—Corbie has that arranged. When there's any danger about, he always puts a light in the end window. Those in the boat can see it long before they reach the cove, and of course they won't attempt to land. He'll look out for that."

"Well, Forbes, be careful. You know how much depends upon silence and discretion. I am going on the island to-day for a ride. What shall I say to Mathews?"

"Say I want a hundred guineas. Hickey has got two more of the guardsmen, and I must have the subsistence money for those we've got. Prompt pay will keep them safer than oaths."

"True," replied the captain, musingly, and at that moment a couple of officers from Smallwood's command entered the shop to inquire after some repairs which they had ordered made to their weapons, and, as they had often met Captain Blanchard in social intercourse, and were well acquainted with him, they soon entered into a friendly conversation, which, turning on shooting, was terminated by a challenge from the senior of the trio, Captain Blanchard, to a trial of skill at pistols, to come off at once, in the rear of Forbes's house, and with any pistols at hand.

"My own are here, Captain Barnum," said the Royalist; "but rather out of order. However, they are better than most you will find, and we'll use them if you have no objections. Forbes, hurry and get them ready for us. What shall it be? A bottle of wine, of course," he added, gaily, "and we'll drink it at my rooms."

"A bottle apiece, captain," said Lieutenant Symmes, the other of the continental officers; to which, of course, Captain Blanchard assented.

Forbes produced the weapons belonging to Captain

Blanchard, which were handled and admired by the young Southerners with evident delight, for they were really superb specimens of workmanship, and evidently made for use.

"Why, Captain Blanchard," exclaimed Captain Barnum, "this is very singular."

"And pray what is very singular?" said Captain Blanchard, with an inquiring look.

"Why, this coat of arms on your pistols. Look here," and he drew forth his massive gold watch, to which was appended a large carnelian seal, exquisitely cut. "See," and he held the seal close to that engraved on the butt of the pistols.

Captain Blanchard looked, and a single glance sufficed to show that one was the counterpart of the other. He looked at the seal—he looked at Captain Barnum—and he looked at the seal again. But the look afforded no explanation except that they were precisely alike.

"These are my mother's arms," said Captain Barnum, pointing to his seal. "She was a Blanchard."

"And her name?" asked the Royalist, as the perspiration started to his brow.

"Mary, from Hertford County."

Captain Blanchard, without saying one word, took the pistol from the hand of the continental officer, and placed it gently in the case, then taking off his cap, he wiped the perspiration which stood in heavy beads on his forehead, and said slowly, and with deep emotion:

"She was my aunt—my favorite aunt—and we are cousins, Captain Barnum;" and, as he spoke, he extended his hand, adding, "Come, captain, we may shake hands as relations, at least; God put an end to this cruel war, which brings us into such mortal conflict with even our blood."

For an instant Captain Barnum stood mute. There could be no doubt that what had been said was true, and he, too, felt bitterly the necessity which compelled him to view as an enemy one to whom he was united by such close ties of consanguinity. But he hesitated only a moment; then grasping the hand of his royalist cousin, forgot, for a time, the position in which they were placed, in the pleasure, not unmixed with pain, of this singular meeting. Both seemed boys again. Captain Blanchard was the senior of his cousin some twelve years, but remembered him well when he was an infant, at the time he embarked with his parents for the Colony of Virginia. Nothing was heard from them for years; but at length a letter was received from Mary, picturing in glowing terms the loveliness of the country, the healthfulness of the climate, and the happiness by which she was surrounded. Indeed, her description of life in Virginia was painted in such glowing *couleurs de rose*, Mr. Blanchard's youngest son, Edmund asked and obtained permission to join his aunt in their new home, and came out to seek his own fortune in the new world—a permission the more readily granted, as the old man had a large family dependent upon him, and an income far from corresponding to the demands which they necessarily made upon it.

Edmund Blanchard wrote occasionally to his parents, but at length all communication between the families ceased, and Mr. Blanchard and his wife sank into the grave, ignorant whether their youngest and favorite child was living or dead.

Questions were asked and answered by either with marvellous rapidity, and as they continued to converse, their interest in each other grew stronger, until at length Captain Barnum put an end to the conversation by placing his arm within that of his cousin, and saying:

"Suppose we postpone our match for to-day. Come to my quarters, and I will tell you something that will surprise you more than anything you have heard yet. Come, Symmes, some other time we will shoot for the wine; you will, I am sure, excuse us now, under such circumstances;" and arm in arm, the trio proceeded up Broadway a short distance, when Lieutenant Symmes, rightly thinking that the cousins, so long separated, would have many personal and purely private matters to speak of, made some excuse for not joining them, and left them to pursue their way to Captain Barnum's quarters alone.

The captain, in company with other officers of the same command, had rented a commodious house, which stood a little back from the street now known as Chambers street, not far distant from the Battery, which extended from the corner of Warren and Greenwich streets almost to the old Vauxhall Garden.

Several officers were in the room into which Captain Blanchard was conducted, to whom he was introduced, and as all had heard him ever named with high praises, with the courtesy and gallantry characteristic of soldiers and gentlemen, they gave him a cordial welcome. Captain Barnum whispered a few words to one of the young officers, who retired almost immediately, and wine having been ordered and brought, the party were soon engaged in lively conversation. By common consent, any language which could pain or wound the feelings of the captured officer was carefully avoided, and he was soon made to feel as much at home as if he had been at his own mess-table, for he was in the society of high-toned gentlemen, who, having espoused the cause of their country from principle, were disposed to admit that those who differed with them might be actuated by motives equally commendable.

Captain Blanchard, in the company of the several southerners, soon felt at home, and the story, jest, and witticism passed freely about without fear of giving offence to any.

As the seni r officer, Captain Barnum presided over

their matutinal revel, and his presence seemed to operate as a check upon the conviviality of his compeers, who, as ready for fighting as for feasting, had turned many looks toward him, wondering at the seriousness of his manner.

But even in the midst of that hilarity, he was serious—deeply, thoughtfully so; and when he was awakened from a reverie into which he had fallen, by the return of the young officer who had before retired at his bidding, an expression of actual pain crossed his features, as he arose and said:

"Gentlemen, pray excuse my friend, Captain Blanchard, and myself, for a few moments," and at these words Captain Blanchard arose, followed by his host, and left the room, wondering, however, what could be the purpose of this summons.

"I promised you a surprise, Captain Blanchard," said the provincial officer, with a smile of actual sadness. "I know you will excuse the manner in which I fulfill my promise, in consideration of my motives; pray, come to my quarters," and he ascended to the second story, followed by the wondering royalist.

On entering the apartment, they found seated there, an officer dressed in the uniform of Colonel McDougal's regiment; a fine, stalwart looking man, who had probably seen some thirty summers. He was engaged in perusing "Rivington's Gazette," the only one published in the city a' that period; as the door was opened, he dropped his paper, and advanced to meet Captain Barnum, with whom he was on terms of familiarity, at the same time greeting Captain Blanchard with a courteous bow.

"Well, captain, you see I am a minute man," he said, gaily. "What is it? Love or war!"

"A little of both, captain," was the reply of the Marylander, and as he spoke, Captain Blanchard and the continental officer advanced close to his side.

"You do not seem to know each other," he said, turning from one to the other, with a smile.

"I cannot say I remember ever having the pleasure of seeing this gentleman, before," said Captain Blanchard, the Royalist, really lost in amazement at his host's conduct, and gazing steadily at his namesake.

"Well, then, I must refresh your memory. Captain Blanchard, of the royalist army, let me introduce to you, Captain Blanchard, of the continental army—Col. McDougal's regiment."

For an instant the two captains stood eyeing each other, as if striving to recall something either had forgotten; but nature, at length, asserted her sway, and with an exclamation of joy, they sprung forward, and as they stood clasped in each other's arms, "brother Edmund," and "brother Arthur," testified that the brothers, separated for more than fifteen years, had met again.

CHAPTER XIII.

A SPY IN THE CAMP.

It was scarcely dusk, when Gilbert Forbes, dressed in his best clothes, and looking as unlike a workman as he could make himself appear, entered the tap-room of Corbie's house, where he found some half-dozen of the soldiers, from various regiments, assembled, discussing the affairs of the nation, and making themselves ridiculous, as rapidly as they could, by swallowing glass after glass of the "real Jamaica," or the "real schnapps," set before them. With these, were present, also, as many well-known and marked royalists, who were similarly engaged.

Forbes advanced to the bar, behind which Corbie was standing, and as he called for some of the best Jamaica, a glance of intelligence passed between them and then the former was satisfied that Hickey had faithfully delivered his message.

"Come, boys," said Forbes, seating himself at the table already occupied by the half score, who moved around to make room for the jolly gunsmith, for he was known to almost the entire army, "let's have a game of cards. Corbie, have you any cards?"

"I don't know, but I can find a pack, somewhere;" and he commenced a search in the drawers of the bar, which proving unsuccessful, he lighted a candle, and left the room to search for them. He soon reappeared, bearing in his hand the articles demanded, and a well-worn, greasy looking checkerboard. "Here, you can't all play cards; here's dominoes, here's cards, and here's the checkerboard," and he placed them severally on the table, as he spoke.

Parties were soon formed, and the various games were commenced, interrupted at occasional intervals by the arrival of some habitual frequenter of the house, who, after having partaken of his drink, retreated from the bar to the table, around which the guests were seated, and amused themselves by looking over the games of the various players engaged.

It was nearly eight o'clock. Many glasses had been drank. Many of the inmates were fast approaching a condition, which, so far as the soldiers were concerned, would unfit them for appearance at their quarters, with out the risk of passing the night in the guard house, and the certainty of a flogging in the morning, and, perhaps, a diet of bread and water for a week, in addition.

Hickey was not present, as he was on duty ; but the stalwart Barnes, who had saved his back from the stripes, at the expense of his honor and manhood, was among them, having received his cue from his fellow-guardsman, and fellow traitor, Hickey.

The evening wore on. Drinking, card-playing, and the narration of marvellous adventures, helped to wile away the time, and when it lacked less than half an hour of tattoo, which was beat off at nine o'clock, Corbie and Forbes exchanged significant glances. Thus far there had been no one present, with whom both were unacquainted, for Corbie had a very regular run of customers, and each was congratulating himself, inwardly, upon having escaped the snare spread for them, when the door of the tap-room was opened, and a tall, country-looking youth, attired in a dress which defies description—for it was a motley mixture of the country farm-boy, and the aspiring soldier——entered, and with a hurried glance around the room, and scanning its inmates, unnoticed, however, by any save Corbie and his fellow Loyalist, Forbes, stepped up to the bar and demanded some liquor, at the same time laying down a continental bill of one dollar to pay for it.

Corbie knew his man at once, for that simple movement had betrayed him, as the refusal to receive the continental money at par, at that time, was, by special act of Congress, made a crime, which was most severely punished.

The liquor was poured out, and the full change handed over, which the stranger took up without remark; but he stole a hasty glance at Corbie, as he pretended to be looking over the counter at the cards in the hands of one of the players, who sat with his back toward him.

"You have nice quarters here," he said, leaning on the bar, and sipping his liquor.

"You ain't the only one who thinks so," said the landlord, with a wink and a smile, nodding toward the group of soldiers gathered around his table. "I keep a quiet, orderly house, and serve the best of liquors to anybody who will pay for them. Everybody who comes in here is a friend as long as he behaves like a man and pays his scot, and proves himself one."

"And how may that be done?" asked the stranger.

"By not talking war or politics. General Washington allows me to keep the house, right by his quarters, you see, because he knows I never meddle with what don't concern me. But I say, young man, where are you from? I never saw you before."

"Oh! I'm from Jersey."

"Yes; but where are your quarters?"

"Oh! a thundering ways off, and I'm afraid I shall get in some cursed trouble; I don't believe I can get in by tattoo; let me see," and he looked at the old clock which ornamented one corner of the bar-room—"almost nine. By hookey! I shall catch it! I say, landlord, can't I stay here to-night? and I'll make up some lie in the morning. I couldn't get through the sentries now, and I don't want to be punished for nothing. You see, I went down into the city to see a girl, and" ——

"How far have you to go?" interrupted Corbie, with an appearance of interest, as if he felt sorry for the predicament of the youthful soldier.

"Oh! 'way over to Badlam's Battery," and he named the works erected at what is now the intersection of Market and Madison streets, and distant more than two miles from Corbie's, across lots and swamps between the two points.

Corbie did not choose to ask him how he got so far out of his way; he knew that well enough; but, turning to Forbes, said:

"I say, Gilbert, you know I haven't got but one spare bed, and, as you're out so late, of course you're going to stay. Will you share with this young man?"

"Oh, of course; anything to oblige, Corbie," and, rising from the table, as he finished his game of checkers, he approached the bar, and addressing the new comer, said: "I'll go halves with you, young man, if you will promise not to quarrel; you know they call me a Royalist."

"No—be you, though?" said the youth, looking intently at the gunsmith. "Well," and he lowered his voice to a whisper, almost, as he spoke, "there ain't much danger of our quarrelling on that score," and he gave the cunning gunsmith a knowing wink.

"My name's Adams," continued the young man, emptying his glass. "What may yours be?"

"Forbes—Gilbert Forbes."

"What! Forbes, down there in Broadway? You don't say."

"The same," replied Forbes, ready to laugh at the idea of he or Corbie being taken in by such a man.

"Oh, I'm mighty glad to see you, I can tell you. It was a lucky chance as brought me here to-night. We shan't quarrel, I know. Come, as we've got to bundle in together, let's have a drink," and he threw down on the counter a Spanish shilling, part of the change which Corbie had paid him, calling for some "more Jamaiky," at the same time bidding the gunsmith to order what he chose; and as he spoke, he turned toward the group still seated around the table, and scanned them with eager looks.

While his back was turned, Corbie and Forbes exchanged glances; they knew their man, and he had already shown them how to treat him.

"Come, Mr. Forbes; I don't care whether you are a Loyalist or a Royalist, I kind o' like you, and I drink your health;" and he touched his lips to his glass.

"I drink yours in a full glass," said Forbes, laughingly, emptying his glass without taking it from his mouth.

"Come, sir," he added, drawing a long breath, "you can't do anything less than I have done."

"Of course not," said the young soldier; and he tossed off his glass of Jamaica which Corbie had poured for him, filling the tumbler nearly two-thirds full.

It lacked now only five minutes of nine, and, as the company prepared to go, Corbie went around to collect his glasses from the table; and while thus engaged, Forbes and young Adams were employed in an animated conversation.

Adams pretended to feel the effects of the liquor he had drank; but Forbes was too cunning to be caught so easily, for he had noticed that a portion of the young soldier's last glass had gone down outside his throat.

"I say, Forbes, they won't kill a fellow, will they, for being out all night?"

"Oh, no; you can make up some good lie for morning. Perhaps they'll give you two or three days on bread and water; that won't amount to much, you know."

"Not so bad as a flogging. But I say," and he dropped his voice to a whisper, "ain't these fellows going pretty soon?"

"Yes, they must go in a few moments, or the guard-house will bring them up. Why do you ask?"

"Oh, 'cause I want to talk to you a bit. I've heard of you afore, Forbes, I have;" and he leered, with a half drunken expression, at the gunsmith.

"Me, sir," said Forbes, coolly; "everybody in York knows me. Some on 'em are down on me, 'cause they say I'm a d—d Tory; but I mind my own business, and doesn't trouble anybody. They can't get any hold on me, as I doesn't meddle with anything as doesn't concern me." Forbes, who was quite able to converse in much better language, adopted this style to draw out young Adams.

While this conversation was going on, the guests had gradually departed, and the bar-room was deserted by all save Corbie, Forbes, and the young Jerseyman.

Corbie was busily engaged in locking and barring the doors and windows, talking the while to Forbes and the young soldier, the latter of whom, acting partial drunkenness, called for some more liquor, and insisted that the landlord should join them.

Corbie readily assented to this, as, to use his own words, "They had the night before them;" and pouring out three glasses of liquor, he placed them on the table, and seating himself, as did his companions, said:

"Come, young man, you must not go to bed without drinking our toast. You need not drink it unless you wish;" and raising his glass to his lips, he said: "Here's to the king—God bless him."

"Here's to the king—God bless him!" echoed Adams, emptying his glass, for the first glass he had drank, and the portion of the second, had so inflamed his appetite, he made no attempt to resist the craving thus aroused, and its effects were seemingly almost immediately perceptible.

"I say, boys," he said, lowering his voice almost to a whisper, "do they flog a fellow in your service?"

"Oh, yes," replied Forbes, constituting himself spokesman; "three dozen for being out of quarters at night, and twice as much for getting drunk."

"You don't say!" exclaimed the astonished youth.

"True as gospel. Why, Corbie, here, deserted to save his back, because the court-martial sentenced him to a hundred lashes for getting on a little spree and outstaying his time."

"Whew!" exclaimed the now really half intoxicated soldier; "you don't say!" drawing out the words to a terrible length.

"Yes, there's fifty pounds reward offered for him now, and if they get him on board the ship, or on the island, I wouldn't be in his place for twice fifty pounds."

Adams looked at Corbie, as if for confirmation of these assertions, and the landlord, setting down his glass just finished, said, with a half sigh:

"Yes, it's so. I wouldn't get in their hands again for all I've got in this house. But come, boys, you must turn in now; if the guard see any light about the house when they go the rounds, you will wish you were somewhere else—the guard-house would bring both of you up for the night, and I wouldn't answer for to-morrow. Come, Forbes, take a light, you know the way. Adams, you go with him; I want to take care of the bar. Good night," and handing a light to the gunsmith, he led the way up a small flight of stairs, to the room on the second story appropriated to the lodgers.

"Curse it," he said to himself, when alone, "I don't believe it's worth while to warn 'em off to-night. Every day is a day now, and we can manage that youngster anyhow;" and he went on cleaning his glasses, and transferring the money from his till to a buckskin bag which he drew from his pocket.

While he was thus engaged, Forbes and his young friend were preparing to retire to rest for the night. Adams seemed to be partially affected by the liquor he had drank, but Forbes, who was not only an old toper, but as cunning as a fox, found little difficulty in detecting the simulation, and was, therefore, on his guard.

In a few moments both were disrobed, and lying side by side. Forbes soon, to all appearance, settled himself for a night's rest, and commenced a snore which would have satisfied the most skeptical that he worshipped at the shrine of Bacchus, and was now paying penalty to Morpheus.

Young Adams, whose head was proof against even the quantity of "old Jamaiky" he had imbibed, and who had been selected for this hazardous mission as well on account of that peculiar qualification as for his natural snrewdness, heard his companion snoring, and after a few moments of patient, or rather impatient, waiting, to assure himself that he was sleeping, rose quietly, and stole noiselessly to the door leading to the stairs which they had ascended.

This he opened cautiously, and descending to the other door, which led into the tap-room, and which opened inwardly, he planted himself upon the steps, and with his ear close to the door, prepared to listen to anything that might transpire.

He had not been there many minutes when he heard three raps at the rear window, and the opening and closing of a door assured him that some persons had been admitted.

"Well, Corbie, what is the word now?" said Colonel Fanning, as he entered the bar-room, dressed as before.

"Hist!" said Corbie, in a whisper, pointing to the door which led to the second story.

"What is it?" asked the colonel, with an air of anxiety, but in subdued tones.

"We heard to-day, I don't know how, except that it came through Captain Blanchard, that a spy would be here to-night. He's here now, upstairs," and he pointed again to the door; "he's more than two-thirds drunk, so I thought I wouldn't set the signal."

"Right, Corbie. Now, have you seen Yates?"

"No; no one of that name has been here yet, as I know of."

"Well, he will come at any hour; treat him well, and send him aboard as soon as possible. We want to move up as soon as we can."

"Who is he? Who is Yates?"

"A fellow who has promised to pilot us as far as the Spuytenduyvel; that will answer our purpose, you know."

"But how am I to know him among so many who come here?" asked Corbie, earnestly. "I wouldn't make a mistake for a fortune."

"True. Here," and he produced a packet of letters, and, looking over them, he selected one which he handed to Corbie, for it was addressed to him. "He will ask if 'any news has been heard of the fleet.' Remember, 'any news of the fleet'—any one who comes with that password is safe."

"I understand," said Corbie, opening, as he spoke, the letter addressed to him, and striving to master its contents—a difficult task, indeed; for the writer, Governor Tryon, as has been said, was the worst of penmen, and Corbie far from being a scholar.

"Here are letters for Blanchard, Matthews, Forbes—and, let me see—and here is one for Miss Moncrieffe. Who is she, Corbie?"

"Why, that young girl at General Putnam's. She came here a few days ago from Elizabeth, and is staying with him."

"Well, that must be delivered with the greatest secrecy. How can you manage that?"

"I will see Captain Blanchard to-morrow; he can go where I cannot."

"And how do you get on, Corbie?" asked the messenger, seating himself at the table so recently vacated by the soldiers and Loyalists who had surrounded it, at the same time placing in an inner pocket of his jacket a packet which Corbie handed to him, with his finger on his lips, as if cautioning him to speak in lower tones, though all of the conversation just narrated had been carried on almost in a whisper.

"Oh, excellently. We've got four of the guards now, one of the captains of McDougal's regiment, and I don't know how many others—Forbes, you know, has the management of that."

"Well, we can't do anything without Yates. I expected to have found him here," said the colonel, with an air of disappointment and vexation combined.

"I am sorry for the sake of the righteous cause," said Corbie. "But come, colonel," and, approaching nearer to him, he whispered something in his ear, and withdrawing behind the bar, soon disappeared beneath the trap which led to the cellar, where he kept his famous "old south side."

A low, peculiar whistle from the colonel, who had advanced to the window, which he had unbarred and thrown open, was answered by a similar signal, apparently from the river, and, before Corbie had returned from the cellar, half a dozen sturdy seamen, dressed in the blue of the royal navy, were at the door, awaiting admission, for that signal had called them there.

"Here it is, colonel," said Corbie, in low tones, as he emerged from the cellar, cautiously and noiselessly closing the trap door after him, and he laid upon the table a bottle with the familiar and highly-prized seal.

The colonel made no reply; but placing his finger on his lips, pointed to the door, a sign seemingly well understood by the landlord, for he proceeded cautiously to unlock and unbar it, admitting the stalwart fellows who stood there awaiting entrance.

"Give them something," said the colonel, in low tones, as he proceeded to decant the generous wine which Corbie had set before him, and the ready landlord, going behind the bar, produced glasses for each, and, without asking what they would have, poured for them each a tumbler nearly full of the "old Jamaica."

They were in the act of gulping it down, and the colonel had just raised his third glass to his lips, when a sound was heard on the stairs which led to the second story, as of scuffling; an oath or two was uttered by the parties, whoever they were; but before any one had time to rise and seek the cause of the commotion, the door leading into the bar was burst open, and two figures rolled upon the floor.

One was Gilbert Forbes, in a state almost of nudity;

the other was the young soldier, his bedfellow ; but his head was completely enveloped in a sheet, and only his person was visible, as he writhed and tossed on the floor to which they had rolled, in his frantic endeavors to free himself from the grasp of his brawny opponent, and from the covering which enshrouded his head.

CHAPTER XIV.

GOVERNOR TRYON ON BOARD SHIP.

In an instant the young soldier was seized in the ready arms of the boatmen who had entered the room in obedience to the signal from Colonel Fanning, and one of them, taking his cravat, bound his arms securely behind. The sheet was then removed from his head, and before he had time to utter a word, and scarcely to think, another of the seamen had drawn a handkerchief into his mouth, and, fastening it behind his neck, he was as thoroughly prevented from making any noise as though a "regulation" gag had been put in his mouth.

Being thus effectually secured, he was released from the arms of his captors, and for an instant glared about him, his eyes actually flashing with rage. But he was fairly trapped, and knowing that resistance against such odds, even if he was at liberty to make any, would be sheer folly, he seated himself quietly in a chair, or, rather, on the edge of a chair, for the position of his arms pinioned behind him, prevented him from occupying the seat.

"That's right my fine fellow," said the colonel,

looking ironically on his helpless prisoner, "make the best of a bad bargain. You see what you get by meddling with what don't concern you," and, seating himself again at the table, he proceeded to finish the bottle which Corbie had placed before him.

"Now, then, Corbie," he said, as he drained his last glass, "you know what to do. That letter for the" ——; but he checked himself suddenly, as if feeling that he had no right to pronounce Margaret's name in such company. "Oh, the captain—he'll manage that, I'll warrant. Forbes said he was going out to see Mathews to-day, eh?" and he turned to the gunsmith, who was standing at the bar, quietly sipping some liquor to which he had helped himself while the seamen were securing young Adams.

"Yes," he replied, "he said so; but I don't hardly think he got away. I saw him just before sundown, as I was coming along in company with one of Smallwood's officers and that captain from McDougal's regiment—the one as belongs to us."

"Somebody must go out to-morrow. We expect the fleet almost every day, and we want to get everything in readiness, so as to act as soon as Lord Howe arrives. But what are we to do with this smart young man?" continued the colonel, turning to Adams, who sat silent, of course, but almost bursting with rage and shame at being so securely trapped in his own net.

"A few days or weeks on board the "Duchess" won't

hurt him, I'm thinking," replied Forbes, "He will have excellent company there—there's lots of his kind aboard. His excellency, I know, will treat him very well."

"Come, then, my worthy rebel, will you go quietly, or shall my fellows here help you? Take your choice."

Adams knew well what sort of assistance he might expect to receive from the sailors, so he nodded his head in acquiescence of the first part of the colonel's proposition, and Corbie having poured out another glass apiece for the sailors, which was tossed off with a bow and a scrape, the party started to leave the house, two men taking each an arm of the young soldier and leading him forward, the others following behind.

In this order they reached the boat, a large man-of-war cutter, manned by eight men; and Adams having been stowed in the stern-sheets, within reach of Colonel Fanning's arm, it was shoved off silently, and the crew pulled away very gently at first—so gently that even the dipping of the oars (which were muffled,) in the water, was scarcely heard by the prisoner.

"Now, my fine fellow," said the colonel, when the boat had reached nearly the middle of the stream, until which time not a word had been spoken, "if you make the least noise, or attempt to move, I shall have you pitched overboard as sure as you are there, now. You understand, of course?"

Adams nodded his head sullenly, for he had no other choice, and, at a sign from the colonel, the men gave way in long, steady strokes, which sent the boat fairly flying through the water. A hard pull of two hours brought them alongside the "Duchess of Gordon," the flag-ship, on board which Governor Tryon had his head-quarters, then lying off the present quarantine landing, and the hail of the sentry having been duly answered by Colonel Fanning, the party ascended her side, and the gag having been removed from Adams' mouth, and his arms set at liberty, he was directed to follow them, an order with which he complied, but of course with sullen reluctance. As he landed on the deck of the ship, Colonel Fanning, turning to the officer of the watch, said: "Give this man in charge of the master-at-arms. Let him be well treated, but well watched," and, striding aft, his arrival on board was announced by the sentry at the cabin door, to the captain and Governor Tryon, who were seated within.

The governor was in the very highest spirits, for a vessel had arrived that very day which had brought to him a letter from Lord Germaine, thanking him in the warmest terms, in the name of his majesty, for the efficient aid he had rendered to the cause, and hinting at the probability of much more substantial evidence of the king's approbation.

"Ah! colonel—returned, I see," he said, rising, his countenance flushed with the wine he had been drinking—for he was noted for his devotion to the best things of this life. "What news from the infernal rebels? Are they ready to lay down their arms and submit to the clemency of our gracious sovereign?"

"Hardly yet, your excellency, I fear," said the colonel, with a quiet smile, "though I learn from our trusty friends in the city, that a great disaffection exists among the troops. Their pay is never punctually given, and their provisions of the poorest kind, with a scarcity even of that, and they are kept at work day and night. There are, I am sure, many hundreds who will join our forces as soon as we effect a landing; at least, such is the information I gather from Forbes and Corbie.

"But how as to the other matter? What progress is making in that? You know, colonel, that is my scheme, and I place great reliance upon the result, should we succeed."

"Several of the life-guards of Mr. Washington have joined us, and when a few more are secured, the first favorable opportunity will be seized to carry your excellency's plan into operation. If successful, that will crush the rebellion without doubt, and your excellency will reap the well-earned reward of your devotion to his majesty.

"Aye, aye," replied the governor, half musingly, rubbing his hands together; for visions of stars and orders were dancing before him, as the possibility of success in his great undertaking crossed his mind. "Have you brought any dispatches?"

"Yes, your excellency," replied the colonel, drawing from his pocket the packet of papers delivered to him by Corbie. "I have brought a prisoner, on board, captain," he said, turning to Captain Chiffney, who, while this conversation had been going on, was seated quietly sipping his wine.

"A prisoner, colonel," said the governor, inquiringly.

"Yes," replied the colonel, laughing; "he set a trap for us, and fell into it himself," and he proceeded to narrate the circumstances connected with the capture of young Adams.

"I wonder how Corbie found it out?" said the general, musingly, but looking at Colonel Fanning, as he spoke.

"The notice came through Captain Blanchard, from some person in General Putnam's house."

"Margaret, by ——!" profanely exclaimed the governor, bringing his fist on the table, near which he was standing, with a force which made the glasses jingle. "That girl is worth twenty common men; she deserves to be a duchess;" and turning to the captain, he said: "Captain Chiffney, will you be pleased to order the prisoner to be brought into the cabin, and meanwhile, I will read what our friends have to say," and seating himself, he proceeded to open the package brought by Colonel Fanning, saying, as he did so: "Colonel, your faithful and arduous services are fully appreciated, and shall be reported to Lord Germaine. His majesty, I am confident, will feel it a privilege to testify his appreciation of such a faithful servant;" and Colonel Fanning, knowing that this meant "good night, I wish to be alone," bowed himself out of the cabin, and retired to the ward-room, among the lieutenants, where a state-room had been appropriated to him. While Governor Tryon, the master spirit of the daring and most infamous plot which was ever conceived among civilized men, engaged in honorable warfare, commenced a perusal of the dispatches which the colonel had brought.

They were from Matthews, the well-known tory mayor, who, through the assistance of Corbie and Forbes, was the main and most reliable agent in forwarding the desperate plot conceived by Governor Tryon, upon the result of which he relied for a speedy termination of the war.

There was, too, a letter from Captain Blanchard, containing important information which he had gathered from every conceivable source, during his social intercourse with the provincial officers, who, knowing him only as an officer on parole, and believing him to be a gentleman, were less guarded in their conversation than they would have been, had they known his true position.

A postscript to this officer's letter, attracted specially the attention of the governor. It was dated several hours after the main part was written, and spoke of his meeting his brother, whom he had not seen for many years, and who, to his sorrow, he learned, had enlisted with the rebels, and was an officer in Colonel McDougal's regiment. The pain of the discovery, however, had been mitigated by a meeting, as unexpected as it was pleasing, with Miss Moncrieffe, the daughter of the well-known Major Moncrieffe, now with the troops on Staten Island; and he added, that as the governor knew the young lady well, he need not say, that she possessed shrewdness, discretion and intelligence to a very remarkable degree, and as she was a most faithful and devoted subject, he was confident she would be enabled to render infinite service to the cause of his gracious majesty. It was owing to information imparted by her, the writer added, that they received the warning, without which, all their well-laid plans might been defeated.

"By Jove, she shall be a duchess!" exclaimed the governor, as he finished the perusal of this letter, which had been written, of course, without the knowledge of what had transpired at Corbie's on that evening, and evidently in the confident assurance, that as Corbie had been forewarned, he was forearmed against any treachery, and was prepared to disarm any suspicion.

As he spoke, the cabin door was opened, and the sentry ushered in Seth Adams, who took his station in front of the general, and who stood scowling sullenly, alternately at the gov𝒟nor and Captain Chiffney, until the sentry had retired.

"Well, my young rebel," said the governor, as he proceeded leisurely to fold up the letters which lay before him on the table.

"I am no rebel, sir," said Adams, advancing close to the table, and looking haughtily upon the treacherous governor.

"Ah, indeed!" and he smiled sarcastically; "perhaps you will tell me what you call yourself?"

"A continental soldier, ready to fight against tyranny, oppression and wrong," he replied, proudly.

"Very prettily said," continued the governor; and as he spoke, Seth cast his eyes upon the letter of Captain Blanchard, which lay open before him, and as his quick eye caught the signature, he knew the writer at once, but nothing on his countenance betrayed the emotion which this discovery, so important, had excited, and already he was ruminating upon the possibility of making his escape, and communicating the information just acquired, to the friends of the cause of liberty within the city.

"Well, it is likely to be some time before you will have an opportunity of fighting against your king, I'm thinking," said Tryon, with a sneer.

"He is not my king," haughtily and sharply said Adams, interrupting the governor, "God forbid."

"It is not polite, young man," said Governor Tryon,

with an expression of the most sarcastic politeness, "to interrupt a gentleman when he is speaking. I was about to say, that as it would, in all human probability, be a long time before you would have an opportunity of gratifying your propensity for fighting against his most gracious majesty, suppose you enlist to fight *for* him. You know what liberal terms he offers. Five guineas bounty, and two hundred acres of land at the close of the war."

"I think his most gracious majesty," replied Seth, with a tone quite as sarcastic as the govereor's, "had better keep his guineas for better purposes; and perhaps, it would look a little more honest, if he was to own the land before he offers to give it away."

"You won't enlist, then?" asked the governor, his countenance turning black with anger.

"Not for all you expect to get for betraying those who trust in you," proudly replied the undaunted youth, and as he spoke, the governor colored deeply, and said, in angry tones:

"You are a fool, and will live to repent your rebellious conduct toward the kindest and best of masters. You can retire now, unless you change your mind, and choose to give me some information as to what is going on in the rebel army."

"I only know that orders have been issued to erect a gallows for Governor Tryon, when they catch him," was the reply, delivered slowly by the undaunted soldier, accompanied by a gaze, which brought the now enraged governor to his feet.

"You insolent hound!" he exclaimed, "I'll have you flogged to death if you utter another such impertinent, treasonable word."

"That would suit you exactly. Go on, sir, and have me flogged. Do you think I should love his most gracious majesty any the more for it? Try it, sir;" and the bold youth looked undauntedly at the governor, who stood before him, actually trembling with rage.

He made no reply; but touching a bell on the table, said to the sentry who entered: "Take this young rebel below, and see that he is properly secured."

"You'd better have it well done, governor; for I shall escape if I can. I won't give my word of honor, as that precious scoundrel has"—and he pointed to Captain Blanchard's letter—"and then break it;" and as he spoke, he turned away, and followed the sentry from the cabin, and was conducted below, where he was taken charge of by the master-at-arms, and his hands and feet being securely manacled, he was left in the "brig"* to mourn his misfortunes.

"That young rebel knows too much, Captain Chiffney," said the governor, seating himself, and wiping the perspiration from his ruddy face. "He must be

* The "brig," on board men-of-war, is a space near the foremast, allotted to prisoners who are ordered in irons for any offence.

closely guarded, for if he should escape, all our plans would be foiled."

"He shall be well guarded," replied the captain; and the governor having passed to him the letters which he had received through Colonel Fanning, he commenced their perusal, while the latter renewed his devotions to the bottle.

CHAPTER XV.

THE BROTHERS IN COUNCIL.

"EDMUND, my dear, dear brother," exclaimed the Royalist captain, as, still pushing him off at arm's length, he peered lovingly in his brother's face—"how strange that we should meet here, and under such circumstances. Captain Barnum!" and he turned to the spot where the gallant Maryland captain had stood but a few seconds before; but with true Southern chivalry and nobility, he had left the apartment the moment he saw that the brothers, so long severed, had recognized each other.

"My dear Edmund," said Arthur Blanchard, turning again to his brother, "how is it I find you here? You, the son of a gallant and honored officer, serving against your king and country!"

"Oh, never mind king and country now," said the younger of the twain, loosing himself from his brother's grasp. "Tell me of home—dear father and mother—Lucy?—is she alive?"

"My dear boy," the elder brother replied, placing his hand on his shoulder as he spoke, "we are alone in the world. Father, mother, Alice, and Lucy have passed away, and I" ——

"And you are the elder brother, and of course the heir" ——

"Dear Edmund, don't speak of that; my only inheritance is my sword. Everything which became mine when I felt I was alone in the world—for you know it is many years since any tidings have been heard of you—was sold to purchase my commission as a cornet. I have fought my way from a cornetcy to a captain's commission, and—but you, Edmund" ——

"Oh, never mind me, Arthur. Father, mother, sisters—all dead," repeated the young man, mournfully, as, withdrawing his hand from that of his brother, he placed it across his eyes, to conceal the tears which moistened them.

"But how is it, Edmund, that I find you here? You, the son of a brave and loyal subject as ever lived, in arms against his sovereign. I ask and demand an answer."

"Ask me no questions, Arthur," responded the younger of the twain, with an expression of sadness.

"I must ask you—I will ask you—and, as your elder brother, I am entitled to an answer. Do not let me blush in the reflection that a Blanchard has thus disgraced his name."

"Arthur, I am not what I seem to be; I have not forgotten my father nor his loyalty; I have not forgotten that I was born a subject of the best of sovereigns—yes, Arthur, I did forget it once. Carried away by the enthusiasm which pervaded all classes, I suffered myself to be drawn into" ——

"An act of rebellion," interrupted the Loyalist, sternly. "Edmund Blanchard, I did not think I should live to blush for my own brother."

"Oh, Arthur, do not reproach me; the sight of you, after the lapse of so many years, brings back so many memories, I would not have them marred by harsh words from you. Spare my feelings now, but" ——

"Feelings, Edmund! You are nearly thirty years of age, if I recollect aright; and surely the son of Miles Blanchard ought, at that age, to know what is his duty to his king and country."

"Arthur"—and Edmund approached close to his elder brother, bending his head so as to bring his mouth close to his brother's ear, and speaking in whispered tones—"I am not what I seem to be."

"As how?" coolly inquired the Royalist.

"I am with you, for you, with all my heart and soul."

"And still wearing that uniform?" and he pointed to the dress of the speaker, the uniform of Colonel McDougal's regiment.

"Yes, and still wearing this uniform, Arthur, my brother. I committed a great wrong when I forgot my father and his people; and I committed a greater wrong when I joined those who war against a gracious sovereign; but," and he looked exultingly as he spoke, "I have repaired all those wrongs."

The Royalist looked searchingly at his brother, but made no reply, and he continued:

"I have joined the king's party here," and he looked in his brother's face for approbation.

"Are you, then," he asked, scanning Edmund from head to foot, "the captain in McDougal's regiment, who, it is asserted, has been won over to the king's cause?"

"I do not know, Arthur, what you mean."

"Simply, that I know everything which transpires in the city, Edmund. I am more than sorry that you ever so far forgot what was due to your name and family, as to forsake the allegiance you owed to your rightful sovereign, but I am proud to welcome you back to the cause of truth and justice. These rebellious scoundrels must be crushed; and, Edmund, every one who has taken part in restoring to the crown the colonies which are rightfully its dependencies, will not be forgotten. You have made me very happy by what you have said, and now I will tell you"——

But his sentence was interrupted by the entrance of Captain Barnum, who, thinking that the brothers had enjoyed ample opportunity of exchanging fraternal greetings, had opened the door, and addressing them, said:

"Well, gentlemen, if you have finished your self-introduction, may I come in?"

"By all means," exclaimed the brothers, in a breath; and the Royalist advancing with extended hand, which was promptly grasped by the warm-hearted southerner, said: "Captain Barnum, I hope I shall one day be enabled to thank you for the delicate and courteous treatment I have received at your hands this day, and for the kind and considerate manner in which you have brought me face to face with my wayward brother."

"Don't call him wayward," said Captain Barnum, smiling. "He is a perfect martinet. You know his regiment does not bear the best reputation for discipline or efficiency, and he has made himself terribly unpopular by trying to redeem its character, so far as his company is concerned. He is a thorough disciplinarian, I assure you. But come, now, drop all ceremony, and do the pair of you honor us by dining with our mess, to-day. Remember, however," and he turned, with an arch look, to either brother, "we don't allow any discussion of religious, political or military subjects."

"It seems to me," said the royalist captain, with a meaning smile, "that you rather circumscribe your guests in their range of discussion."

"Well, on these occasions we do, even between brothers. Come, what do you say; will you dine with us?"

"With all my heart," said the Royalist. "But for the kind courtesy of my enemies" ——

"Not your enemies, captain," interrupted Captain Barnum; "we are only the enemies to the principles you advocate and support. No one who knows you, could be *your* enemy."

The Royalist captain bowed low to this compliment, and the color on his bronzed cheeks was heightened as he heard these words, for his conscience told him, that he did not deserve such courtesy and such confidence from his host.

"It will afford me great pleasure to accept your hospitality," replied the Royalist Blanchard; and Captain Barnum who had noticed the flush which had come to his face, and who thought that it had been called there by his words, which might imply something of a taunt, as well as a compliment, hastily said:

"My dear captain, don't mind what I say, for you must be conscious I had no intention of wounding your feelings. Dine with us, to-day, and we will try and make you forget the misfortunes which the chances of war have brought upon you."

"I ought hardly to call it a misfortune which has thrown me into such company, and led to such an unexpected pleasure," and he turned to his younger brother, with a look of deep affection.

"Come, Edmund," he continued, addressing his brother, we will take a stroll, and return in time to accept our kind friend's hospitality," and with courteous greetings, the brothers took their leave, strolling up Broadway, arm-in-arm.

"Now let me finish the sentence which was interrupted by the entrance of Captain Barnum. I was going to tell you that I have been in direct communication with his excellency, Governor Tryon, and his honor, our loyal Mayor Matthews, ever since I arrived in the city. I must see Matthews to-day, or send word to him, by some means. Everything goes on to our heart's content, and there is every reason to believe that thousands will eagerly join our forces as soon as a landing has been effected; and if the other part of the plot, now in progress from day-to-day, is carried to consummation, the war will be ended before six weeks are over."

"The other part of the plot!" echoed the younger of the twain, looking at his brother with an expression of surprise.

"Yes, Edmund, the other part which, if carried to successful consummation, will stem this torrent of rebellion, terminate the war at once, bring these rebellious Colonies again to their allegiance, and restore them to their rightful sovereign. It is not ripe enough yet even for you to know, Edmund; but, if as you say, you are heart and soul with us, you will not hesitate to lend your aid if you should be called upon."

"Anything to prove my loyalty, and make amends for having forgotten my name and my duty."

"Edmund, you can call on Miss Moncrieffe with less suspicion than myself, as you belong to the other side," and he smiled meaningly.

"What, that young girl who has turned the head of every officer who saw her last night? I have heard nothing this morning but Miss Moncrieffe, and as for Shee's boys, I don't know but there will be fighting yet among them about her."

"So much the better. You don't know her?"

"I have never seen her; but must confess my curiosity is excited concerning her. Is she so very beautiful?"

"Very beautiful, very fascinating, and very witty but above all, shrewd and observing, far beyond her years. Why, it was only this morning she gave me information that Corbie's house was to be visited tonight by a provincial in disguise, to discover what was going on. I have caused him to be put on his guard, though there won't be much made of it, I'm thinking."

"How, in the name of goodness, did she find it out?"

"Oh, she is an inmate of General Putnam's family—a general favorite—and, being unsuspected, everything is spoken of before her with perfect freedom. To-morrow I will introduce her to you, and let her know how you stand affected. Now, Edmund, remember—in company, be more than guarded; for the world, don't let a breath of suspicion attach to either of us. Now let us talk of old times," and the conversation was turned into topics of home, parents, friends, and relatives, and thus the time was beguiled until the approach of the hour which was fixed for their dinner at Captain Barnum's quarters.

CHAPTER XVI.

MARGARET AND HER LOVER AT HOME.

On the morning after the call made by Captain Blanchard on Margaret, and which had led to such important results, so far at least as the safety of those who were conspiring against the provincials was concerned, Major Burr was seated in the apartment set apart by General Putnam for the transaction of all official business and the reception of reports.

His chair was drawn up before a large circular table, filled with letters, reports, and a miscellaneous collection of documents, from an application from some loyalist for permission to cross the river to Long Island, to a complaint (anonymous of course) against some one of the same stamp for some offence, either by word or deed, against the strict orders promulgated by the bluff old general, on receiving command of the city during the absence of General Washington. It was his duty to open these—to note their contents on their backs (when worthy such attention), and to receive and execute the orders of the general respecting them. He knew his commander so well, he rarely waited for instructions; but, in most instances, had his replies prepared before he made his appearance, and they were invariably signed after the briefest possible glance at their contents; such was the general's confidence in the activity, integrity, and capability of his youthful aid.

He was about commencing the duties of the morning, when a gentle tap at the door aroused him, and in answer to his gruff "Come in," uttered as if he was ordering a charge of infantry, it was opened very softly, and a voice, whose tones thrilled through every fibre of his frame, uttered quietly, "May I come in?"

Springing from his seat as those dear and familiar tones met his ear, he advanced toward the door, and, grasping the extended hand of the intruder, led her to a seat at the table.

It was Margaret, who, throwing herself languidly and half pettishly into a chair, said: "I really beg pardon, Major Burr; but" —— and here she paused as she met his glance, for it seemed to say:

"We are alone, and why do you call me Major Burr?"

"Aaron," she said, stretching her hand across the table, "I do beg your pardon—I did not mean to disturb you; but I was so very lonesome. Cousin Belle is in the kitchen, Cousin Martha is somewhere else, and Lady Putnam is knitting. I can't spin—I won't knit, and so I am here. May I stay?"

"Dear Margaret," replied the young soldier, his very soul beaming in his eyes, and, seizing the extended hand of his beautiful and loved visitor—"how can you ask? Stay here—only stay forever, and"——

"There, Aaron," she interrupted, "that will do for Colonel Shee or his gallant officers. I don't want such language as that from you."

"Then stay as long as you choose, dear Margaret, and make me happy."

"I will do anything to make you happy, Aaron, and so I will stay," and, withdrawing her hand—not, however, until it had been awfully squeezed and several kisses imprinted upon it—she continued: "but you must not be quite so ceremonious."

"Well, I won't," he replied, and rising, as if for the purpose of searching for some papers, he approached her, and leaning over, imprinted a kiss upon her snowy brow, and, encouraged by her passiveness, for she made no resistance to him, a second was implanted directly on her tempting lips.

"There, that will do, Aaron," she said, pushing him gently away. "I came here to work—may I help you?"

"Oh, yes, sit here and look at me; I want no better help than that. But Margaret, if you really wish to stay here, I must impose one condition on you. Look here," and he pointed to a mass of papers strewed over the table, "these must all be opened and attended to before the general comes, and if I am to do it, you must maintain profound silence."

"Oh, very well," she said, with a mischievous pout, which more than half tempted the young aid to repeat his salutations to her lips, "I suppose you think I can't be silent. Come, sir, give me some paper and lend me one of your pens. I can amuse myself if I can't entertain you."

"You are a tormenting little vixen," said the major, as he pushed the paper toward her, and tendered to her a pen, whose nib he had just clipped, for steel pens were then unknown.

Margaret made no reply, but commenced writing, or seeming to write, while Major Burr, with a tremendous effort, strove to forget her presence, and resumed the duties which her entrance had interrupted.

He was soon, apparently, immersed in an examination of a mass of papers which lay before him, while Margaret, having appropriated the paper placed before her, was soon as apparently engrossed in the letter which she proposed to write.

For a few moments, either pen wandered over the paper with wonderful rapidity; at length, there seemed to be a pause, by mutual consent; the motions of the pens grew less rapid; then they ceased entirely, and as each raised their eyes to discover the cause of this remarkable unanimity of purpose, their glances encountered each other.

Margaret threw down her pen, with a merry, hearty laugh, which fairly rang through the room; indeed, it was so loud and so earnest, Major Burr, fearing she would arouse the household, arose, and approaching her, stopped her mouth with his own, a proceeding against which she offered no resistance; probably, because she had been so weakened by her laughter, she was incapable of any.

"Dear Margaret," said the young soldier, as he stood by her side, one of her hands clasped in his own, gazing into her beautiful face with an expression of the most intense love, "how I do love you!"

"I need not say how I love you, Aaron," she said, returning his gaze with a warmth equal to his own; "but oh, what will come of it?" and burying her face in her hands, she gave way to thoughts that seemed to overpower her.

"Dear, darling, what" —— but he had no time to finish his sentence, for well-known steps ascending the stairs which led to the office, warned him of the approach of General Putnam, and hastily snatching another kiss, he sprang back to his seat, and commenced looking over the mass of papers before him, while Margaret, brushing away a tear which had gathered in her eye, returned to her pen, and before the door was opened, was again deeply engrossed in the composition of her letter, as was Major Burr in the perusal of the documents which it was his duty to overlook.

"Young lady," said the bluff old general, as he entered the room, and saw the posture of affairs, "how long since you have been my aid?"

"Ever since you have been my grandpa," she replied, rising, and approaching him, with extended hand, which, in very spite of himself, he took. "Fact is, grandpa," she continued, with a bewitching smile, "I can't spin, and I won't knit, so I came down here, and Major Burr was so kind as to let me sit at his table and write a few letters, I was so lonesome upstairs."

"Well, well," he said, smilingly, though he tried to look dignified and stern, "write away; there, sit down," he added.

Margaret thanked him with a graceful courtesy, and a smile whose power was almost irresistible.

"Now, major, what is the report from Corbie's?" he added, as Margaret, seating herself, resumed her pen.

"I declare," replied the aid, pulling out his watch, "it's ten o'clock. I ordered Adams to report by nine, and he is a man on whom I can rely, as I can upon myself."

"Not here yet, Major Burr!" continued the general, with military sternness. "Nine o'clock means nine o'clock, sir. Why has he not been here, if you ordered him to report at that hour?"

"I will send and ascertain at once, sir;" and without further remark, he went to the door, and summoning an orderly, directed him to have word sent to Badlam's

Battery, where he was stationed, for Seth Adams to report himself immediately, at head-quarters.

General Putnam appeared to be very much vexed at the failure of the man to report at the time specified, and seating himself, commenced a series of characteristic grumblings, to which Major Burr, thoroughly familiar with his character and humors, replied only by a quiet smile, as he kept on overlooking the papers before him.

"There, general," he said, handing another letter to his general, "that is in the same hand-writing as the one we received a few days ago."

"Oh, yes," replied the old soldier, glancing at the letter, and throwing it down on the table, so that it lay directly in front of Margaret, who, apparently without raising her eyes from her own letter, perused its contents. The letter was brief, and evidently written in a disguised hand, and ran as follows:

"I have warned you before—I warn you again. There are spies about, of whom you little dream. Trust no one, but watch for yourself. A FRIEND TO THE TRUE CAUSE."

"How are the works going on, major?" he said, apparently forgetting the trifling annoyance which had aroused his ire a few moments before.

"Oh, bravely, sir, bravely. The line is almost completed on both sides of the island, and a few days more of such work will render a landing impossible, for I be lieve no point is left unguarded. The works on Richmond Hill have not been pushed forward so rapidly as the others nearer the river, as Colonel Putnam did not deem them to be of so much immediate importance."

"Well, major, get through those papers as soon as possible, and then ride out to the Hill, and order those works completed immediately; General Washington will return from Philadelphia in a few days, and I wish to have everything completed before he arrives. I am going now to General Mifflin's quarters. There is to be a council at eleven o'clock, and when I return, I shall hope to receive the report of your man. Good day, major—good morning, Miss Aid," he added, turning to Margaret, who appeared to be so deeply engrossed in her writing, as not to notice his remark, and it was therefore repeated in louder tones: "Good morning, Miss Aid; I think you had better retire, for I am afraid the major won't accomplish much if you remain here."

"Do I disturb you, Major Burr?" she asked with a mischievous glance, which he alone caught and interpreted.

"Not at all, so long as you keep your promise not to talk."

"Not to talk!" said the old general, with a loud guffaw; "a girl not talk! Well, major, if you can make her do that, I give up to you."

"Good morning, grandpa," said Margaret, demurely, rising, and making a low courtesy.

"Major, you had better turn that girl out of the room," said the general, good-naturedly, as he strode toward the door. "I shall be back between twelve and one o'clock," and as the door closed upon the retreating form, Margaret and the young aid exchanged glances full of meaning, for they said, as looks would say, "I am glad we are alone again."

"Come, Aaron, go on with your work, and don't disturb me again," said Margaret, maliciously, resuming her pen, and bending again to her task. "Remember what the general said, and we will see whose fault it is if the work is not done."

Major Burr looked for an instant at his tormentress, but her head was bent over her paper, and he could not catch her eyes. For a moment or two he indulged in this profitless occupation, then, with a deep sigh, took up a letter which lay nearest to him, and opened it mechanically.

Perhaps the contents were very interesting; perhaps he was engrossed in his own thoughts; perhaps anything the reader chooses; but before he was aware of it, a pair of soft arms were around his neck, and a pair of very soft lips were pressed on his forehead; and as he felt this touch, he dropped his pen as if struck by an electric shock, and turning his face upward, met the ardent, passionate, loving gaze of Margaret.

CHAPTER XVII.

THE FIRST TEMPTATION.

"You love me, Aaron?" she murmured, as she suffered his arms to clasp her waist, and met his burning glances fixed upon her.

"Better than my life—my soul—my all."

"Oh, Aaron," murmured Margaret, and she seated herself, while her eyes were half filled with tears, "where is this to end?"

"End, Margaret? Why, darling, it has not begun yet," he replied, with a bright, happy smile.

"Oh, yes; but, Aaron, I have thought very much since yesterday—yes, ever since I came here—where is this to end?"

"I really don't know what you mean, Margaret," said the young soldier, leaning back in his chair, and gazing at his companion in amazement. "Are you already sorry for what you have said or heard?"

"Oh, no, no—not sorry, Aaron," she hastily interrupted, bending upon him a look full of love. "But think (for we *must* think), why did we ever meet? Why did I ever act and speak as I have done? Oh,

Aaron, what must you think of me—what must I—what ought I to think of myself?"

"Surely, Miss Moncrieffe," said Major Burr, rising, with an appearance of coolness in his manner. But Margaret did not permit him to finish his sentence, for springing forward, she threw herself upon his neck, and murmured:

"Dear Aaron, don't speak so coldly." He was vanquished a second time. "No, Aaron, I only feared for the future. Think—you are engaged against those with whom I am connected by every tie of honor, duty, and affection. How can it be that we ever shall be happy under such circumstances?"

"Would not my Margaret make any sacrifice for him she loves?"

"I would consider nothing a sacrifice, Aaron. But how can it be? My family are proud, haughty, and wealthy, and they would disown and spurn me if I should unite myself with one of a nation whom they have learned to look on as traitors and rebels. Nay, Aaron, do not frown on me so, for it is not Margaret who says it. I am ready to say, and thus prove my sincerity, 'thy home shall be my home, and thy God my God.'"

"Thanks, thanks, my dearest Margaret," replied the impassioned lover, gazing with enamored looks upon the beautiful and animated girl who stood before him. "I trust not to demand any such sacrifice of you, for this unnatural war cannot endure much longer. I feel confident in the success of our arms, and though your family may be proud, haughty, and wealthy, I shall be enabled to place you in a position which will make you the equal of any in this country."

"I ask no position higher than to be yours—nothing but your love and your presence to make me supremely happy. Look you, Aaron," and she gazed at her lover with an earnestness which fairly fascinated him, "situated as we are now, one of us must make a great sacrifice, or we must part."

"Part, Margaret!" and the young aid started; "part. And what does this sudden change portend?"

"Do not say change, Aaron. I cannot change," and she looked half-sadly, half lovingly at him. "I cannot change. I am yours, and only yours; do with me as you please. But listen to me," and approaching him, she lowered her voice almost to a whisper, "I am rich, highly connected, and, through my family, possess boundless influence, and what, Aaron, have you?"

"A patrimony which I am spending freely in my country's cause, my sword, and my determination to make for myself a name and fame of which even you shall be proud."

"In neither can you fail. But listen, Aaron; do not reproach me if I venture to speak as my heart dictates. I am young—very young for the sad experiences through which I have passed; but I am old enough to know my own feelings, though perhaps not old enough to control my impulses. You possess every thought and feeling which I am capable of giving; there is no sacrifice on earth I am not ready to make, to prove my love for you, if proof be needed. But, Aaron, how are you placed? You, siding with a cause which you believe to be right—nay, which you feel to be right," she added, seeing a cloud gather on the young soldier's brow, "and the success of that cause is very far from being certain, for with undisciplined troops—with men deprived even of their promised pay (you see I know all these things), poorly fed, and worse clad—men who have enlisted only because every other means of employment was debarred them"——

"Margaret, stay—you wrong my countrymen. Poorly fed, worse clad, and compelled to endure unlooked-for hardships, as they are and have been, they are animated by a feeling which makes them superior to the hirelings who compose the arms of your countrymen. Each man has a stake in this issue, and each man is prepared to stand or fall by the result of the conflict in which we are engaged."

"And you, Aaron?"

"Me—oh, well, I don't think of myself. My mistress is glory. I mean to make a name—to leave my mark on the page of history—and if I can do that, I shall depart satisfied."

"And that to me, Aaron," said Margaret, with tearful eyes, as she gazed upon the young enthusiast before her, "that to me, who have said that there is nothing I could deem a sacrifice if I could serve you. But this contest, I am confident, will prove fruitless. So far as your countrymen are concerned, there can only be one termination to it. England, with men and money at her command to an unlimited extent, will, if needed, overrun this country with troops—brave, loyal, disciplined troops. Within two months, this very city will be in our possession, and where will you be then?"

"Margaret, you talk wildly," said the major, affecting an offended air.

"I do not talk wildly, Aaron; and even while you say so, you do not believe it. I know more, much more than you think I do; but I know nothing half so precious as that you love me," and approaching, she took his unresisting hand.

"Margaret—Margaret Moncrieffe," exclaimed Major Burr, looking at her as if he would read her very soul, "what do you mean?—what do your words import?"

"What I would, as I am able to do, prove my love for you. I mean that if you have the courage to make a small sacrifice for me, I am prepared to make a greater one for you."

"I do not understand you, Margaret," said the

major, abstractedly, looking at her with an expression of inquiry.

"I must give up the certainty of wealth, rank, station, and the high position to which I was born, and to which I can raise you, or you must give up your prospects, founded upon the possible success of the rebellion," she continued, as she saw the brow of the young aid darkened by a frown; "I know no other word for it. You *hope* for a bright future. I can make ours *certain.* My ancestors have fought for their king and country from the days of the glorious Black Prince, and I have inherited their loyalty and spirit. Come, Aaron, don't make me choose," and approaching, she leaned on his shoulder, looking him affectionately in the face. "I can do all I say," she continued, in a low, soft, winning tone. "You hope to accomplish all you desire; if I must choose, my choice is already made, and you know it. But oh, Aaron! if you do love me, let me prove my love for you, and add to my happiness by the consciousness that I have served you."

"What do you mean, Margaret?" exclaimed the major, holding her off at arm's length. "In God's name, what do you mean? I dare not understand you."

"Only this, Aaron," she replied calmly, "that one of us must yield; for, without a concession on either side, we must part. I have told you what you well know now, dear Aaron, that I am ready to make it on my part—but I do implore you to pause before you compel me to a step which you may hereafter repent—I love you with all the strength and fervor of a woman's first love, and" ——

"I worship you, Margaret," exclaimed the young soldier, overpowered by her enthusiasm, and carried away by his passionate devotion to this singular and fascinating being, with whom he had been so strangely brought in contact. "Do with me as you please, only love me and be mine."

"I do love you, and will be only yours, Aaron," replied Margaret, and a glance of mingled love and triumph shot from her eyes as she spoke. "*Colonel* Burr, there is my hand—you know you have my heart," and she extended to him that hand, for the possession of which he had declared himself ready to sacrifice honor and duty.

"Colonel Burr!" he echoed.

"Yes," said Margaret, with a meaning smile, "you shall see that, young and reckless as I appear to be, I have not spoken without a purpose. But mark you, Aaron, I shall ask no aid, direct or indirect, from you. I shall neither do nor say anything which may by any possibility, however remote, compromise you. I say only this, that in three days, or four at the furthest, I will prove to you that I can accomplish all I have said. Again I say, COLONEL BURR, there is my hand—will you take it on these conditions?"

"There are no conditions on earth to which I would not submit to possess it," he said, with enthusiasm, grasping her proffered hand and pressing it to his heart.

"Now, then, we understand each other," said Margaret, with a meaning look.

"I am yours; do with me as you please," he replied, with an earnestness and warmth which showed how truly every thought and feeling had been brought into subjection by his fair enchantress.

"In four days at the furthest, Colonel Burr," she repeated significantly, "you shall see that I have made no promises which I cannot fulfill."

"But Margaret, how can I remain here?—here in the very family circle of my good old general; hearing everything—seeing everything—knowing everything?"

"But saying nothing and doing nothing, Aaron. No, no—I respect your feelings—nay, I honor your love for me too much for that; for I feel you have granted to that love for me, what nothing else on earth could have wrung from you. No, be as you are—do as you are doing—and, by the boundless love I bear to you, Aaron, no slur shall ever come upon your name. Can you not trust me?"

"With my very soul, Margaret," replied the young major, warmly; and he was about to prove the intensity of his assertion by something more palpable than words, when the sounds of heavy footsteps ascending the stairs, startled the happy pair, and each sprang to the seat from which they had arisen, and, in an instant, were as deeply engrossed, seemingly, in their respective occupations as they had been on the departure of General Putnam.

The loud rap at the door was answered by the major, and the orderly in waiting entering, with the customary military salute, announced the return of the man who had been dispatched to inquire into the cause of the non-appearance of Seth Adams at the hour appointed.

CHAPTER XVIII.

MAJOR BURR ENSLAVED.

"WELL, what is it?" queried the major, with an air of impatience, turning from the table at which he was seated, toward the person whose entrance had been announced, and who proved to be a sergeant from the Badlam barracks, to which Adams was attached.

"Adams did not return last night, and has not been to the quarters this morning sir."

"Not returned to his quarters?" said Major Burr, rising from his seat and confronting the soldier.

"No, sir," he replied, with another military salute, "and here's a letter from Major Gibbs."

"What, of the Life-guards?"

"Yes, sir. He gave it to me himself, and told me to be sure that you got it."

"Wait, then, until I see what this means;" and the young aid, forgetting in the moment everything save the impulses of duty, hastily tore open the missive which the sergeant had handed to him, and which he perused with eager rapidity, fairly devouring its contents.

"It's all right, sergeant; I have no time to reply now

to Major Gibbs. Say that I will see him as soon as General Putnam returns from the council;" and the sergeant, with a third salute, withdrew.

"Now, what on earth does this mean?" he said, soliloquizing, and forgetting the presence of Margaret. "I know Seth as well as I know myself, and he never could prove false. By Heavens! there has been some foul play here, and I will find it out, or —— O, Margaret, I beg your pardon, I quite forgot" ——

"That there was such a person in existence, as Margaret," she said, with a sad smile, interrupting him. "I don't blame you, Major Burr, only spare me; I am only a girl—a fond, foolish girl—but I throw myself upon your honor, as a soldier and a gentleman."

"Margaret, what do you mean? What have I said, what done, that you should so reproach me? What do you wish me to do?"

"Nothing, Major Burr, but to forget those words you spoke a few minutes since, and in forgetting them, cease to remember me."

"Oh, Margaret! dear, dear Margaret, forgive me. I did not know what I was saying. I know not what I have said to pain or wound you. Tell me, Margaret, what I have done; for on my life I do not know? What earthly connection can you have in this matter?" and he pointed to the letter of Major Gibbs, which he still held in his hand.

"Aaron Burr," said Margaret, and as she spoke, she

advanced toward him and placed her fair, white hand upon his arm, "it was but a few moments since, and you promised—do you remember what?"

"To be yours, and yours, only, and forever."

"And did I not make a promise, too?"

"You?" he said, earnestly.

"Even I. Did I not say, that in nothing, by word or deed, should you be compromised by me?"

"I remember that," he said, thoughtfully.

"Then let me keep my word; and do you be a man as you are a soldier. Once for all, Aaron Burr, is it me, or is it" ——

"Oh, do not ask that, Margaret. Who, what on earth is it? What can it be but you, and you only? Dear Margaret forgive me, if I have said aught to wound your feelings."

"You have not, Aaron," and she suffered him to retain the hand which he had grasped as he spoke. "But your interest for that man, and the cause in which he has engaged, seemed so much stronger than your love for me, my faith in your pledges began to waver."

"Margaret, you speak in riddles; what do you mean?" and as he spoke, Major Burr dropped her hand, and facing her, looked steadily in her eye.

"Nothing, Major Burr," she said, with a cold, majestic air. "I shall keep my pledge, though you may desire to forget yours."

"Even now, I know not what you mean. Tell me,

Margaret, for Heaven's sake, tell me, and do not let me do or say anything which may make you think less of me."

"Ask no questions, Aaron, save those from whom you have the right to ask them. If you repeat the words you spoke but just now, if you believe Margaret Moncrieffe is unable to fulfill the pledge she has made, if in saluting you as Colonel Burr, she" ——

"Ah, I see. I did forget; Margaret forgive me. My position is so new, so strange, so perfectly marvellous even to myself, I scarcely know what I say or do. The force of habit, you know, Margaret," and he smiled faintly, as he spoke, "is very strong."

"With me, the power of love is stronger," she replied, with something of pride in her tones. "You have once made your choice; do you wish to abide by it?"

"Margaret, and Margaret, only," enthusiastically replied the young soldier, again completely bewildered.

"Then ask no questions. Pursue your own investigations and learn what you can."

"I shall gladly take lessons from you."

"Not very gladly, Aaron," she said, sadly.

"Oh, do not reproach me. Remember, Margaret, how brief has been" ——

"Our intercourse," she interrupted; "and would you reproach me with that? Would you reproach me because I have said that there was nothing on earth I would not sacrifice to prove, if proof was needed, my love for you? Oh, Aaron! you either do not know yourself, or you do not know me."

"Margaret, what shall I do?"

"Have I not said but now, do nothing so far as I am concerned? You have your report there; act upon it. Is it necessary that I should know your official business, even if I am Miss Aid?" and she quoted, with an arch smile, the general's appellation.

"I see, I see," said the major, half musingly. "Margaret, I yield the palm to you. Teach me, for I will gladly learn from you."

"And for the future?"

"Count me yours, and yours only. Your cause is mine—your quarrel mine. Only, Margaret," and he spoke despondingly, "I would not have it known here how I have fallen."

"Fallen, Aaron! Risen, rather—risen say," and she stood erect before him a very Pythoness. "Risen, I say, Aaron; for your elevation is as sure as that of the daily sun, and it will be as glorious," and, as she spoke, she threw herself into his arms with a sob of joy. "Now, Aaron," she continued, rising from his embrace, "ask me no questions and I shall have nothing to answer hereafter. When I fulfill my pledge to you, then I shall ask you to think and act with me Until then, we know nothing of each other's movements. Oh, yes, Aaron," she added, as she saw a shade of sadness come over his face, " one thing we do know—one thing—whatever fate may bring for us, we can never forget our love."

" Never, Margaret—never; and I can give no better proof of mine than I have done by sacrificing honor, duty, morality, and all, to love—I do so love you, Margaret," he added, with an expression amounting to intensity of earnestness.

" And I do know and feel it," she responded.

" And pray, Miss Moncrieffe, what may that be which you know and feel," inquired General Putnam, who, unheard and unannounced, had entered the room while Margaret and the major were thus earnestly conversing, but had only caught her last words.

"I was saying how deeply I should feel the loss of my daily exercise, grandpa," she said, turning to him with a countenance as free from emotion as that of a marble statue. " Major Burr was saying he did not think I ought to ride so much about the works, for fear I should make some improper use of the privilege, and " ——

" Major Burr is a very cautious officer," replied the general, sententiously, at the same time taking a huge pinch of snuff. "If he will not trust you I will, and assume the responsibility of any mischief you may do except among our officers."

"Thank you, grandpa," and she turned, with a

meaning look, to the young aid, who by this time was again poring over his files of documents.

"May I go now?"

"Go now—yes, go when you choose and where you choose, and stay as long as you choose; but mark you, Miss Impudence" ——

"Margaret, sir, is my name," she said, very demurely, with a low courtesy.

"Well, Miss Impudence Margaret, if I catch you at any capers, I'll hang you as high as Haman."

"As high as who, grandpa?" she asked, with an arch smile; and as she saw a cloud gathering on the old general's brow, she hurried from the room, and in less than five minutes was cantering through Broadway, mounted on Selim, who pranced and curvetted, as if proud of his lovely burden.

CHAPTER XIX.

MARGARET AND THE ROYALIST CAPTAIN.

As she was riding along, attracting the attention of all beholders, as well by her splendid horsemanship as by the ease and grace with which she managed the impatient Selim, she perceived, at some distance ahead, the well-remembered form and face of Captain Blanchard, walking arm-in-arm with an officer in the Provincial uniform, and reining in the impatient Selim, she moved along slowly until they met, when, checking her horse so suddenly that he almost went on his haunches, Captain Blanchard advanced toward her, and, with a courteous salute, inquired how it chanced that she was out alone.

"Because I hoped to meet you, captain," she said, meaningly.

"It is a fortunate meeting," he said; "for I was on the road to pay you a call. I have something for you."

"From his Excellency the Governor?" she inquired, eagerly.

"Even so, Miss Margaret," and, looking cautiously around, to see whether he was observed or not, he hurriedly thrust into her hand a letter which he had crumpled into the smallest possible space, and which Margaret as quickly thrust into the pocket of her riding-dress, but without interrupting the conversation; for she continued, in unchanged tones: "Who is your friend who seems to watch your movements so intently?" and she eyed the young Continental officer with a scrutinizing glance.

"You will be surprised when I introduce him to you, and more surprised when I tell you that he is one of us."

"Indeed!" she exclaimed, her countenance lighting with an expression of pleasure; for she had recognized the uniform of McDougal's corps as she again fastened her gaze upon the officer, who stood there, carelessly kicking his heels on the pavement, as if quite unconscious of the presence of any parties, but stealing occasional glances of admiration at the beautiful creature who had burst so suddenly on his sight.

"You have heard, I suppose, for you seem to learn everything, that a captain in McDougal's regiment has joined the cause of his majesty?"

Margaret nodded assent, but made no verbal reply.

"Edmund," he said, turning to his brother, for it was he who was his companion, and at the word the young Provincial advanced with unwonted alacrity.

"Miss Moncrieffe, Captain Blanchard, my younger brother."

"Your brother, Captain Blanchard!" exclaimed Margaret, turning from one to the other, with looks of unrestrained amazement.

"My only living brother, and only relative on earth, Miss Margaret," replied Arthur, with a low bow.

"I am truly glad to make your acquaintance, captain," she said, extending her hand cordially, "the more so that I find in you the brother of my father's dearest friend; and I am doubly glad to learn from your brother that." ——

"Hush, Miss Margaret," said the Royalist, "there are persons turning that corner who may overhear our conversation. You may repose as much confidence in him as you would in myself. It will be much more easy to communicate through him than through me, and everything intrusted to him will reach the proper quarter. I vouch for his sincerity and truth."

Margaret gazed earnestly into the face of the young Provincial, now all aglow at finding himself so suddenly placed on terms of confidential intercourse with one of whom he had heard so much, and whose appearance, he felt, fully justified the lavish encomiums passed upon her.

"Captain," and she addressed the Royalist, "I have no time or opportunity to write to-day, and if I had I might not be able to dispatch it. Do you write to Governor Tryon, and say that I desire him to send to me—mind, to *me*, captain—a colonel's commission in blank."

The Royalist captain looked astounded at this request, while the Provincial officer, who construed her words at once as an intention to secure to him a reward for his treason, could scarcely conceal the smile of gratification and triumph, which her words had called to his face.

Margaret noticed the expression, and the slightest possible curl of contempt was perceptible on her pretty mouth; but it passed as quickly as it had come, and she continued:

"Yes, a colonel's commission—write that. He must not deny me—I scarcely think he will. Tell him that orders were given to-day to strengthen the defences in the vicinity of Richmond Hill, and that General Washington is expected to return in a few days. What was done with that man who was sent to Corbie's last night?"

"I really don't know. The letter you have was brought to me this morning by a messenger from Corbie, but he said nothing to me of anything having occurred last night."

"Something has evidently gone wrong, I am afraid. The man who was sent there, and who was to have reported this morning, has not been seen since, and there will be much trouble about it, for he was a great favorite; so tell any one concerned to be on his guard. Mind, captain, don't fail to write by the first opportunity for that commission," and as she spoke, she fastened her lustrous eyes again on the young Provincial, who had remained a silent but deeply interested listener to this conversation. "You will call on me, will you not? I shall be exceedingly happy to see you at any time," she said, addressing him.

"With more pleasure than I have words to express," he replied, with an earnestness scarcely called for by this simple invitation, for the beauty and fascinations of Margaret had already done their work, and the glance with which she accompanied her words, had completely carried him away.

"Upon my word, captain," she said, laughing, but at the same time regarding him with a speaking glance, "I do believe you have been taking lessons from Colonel Shee."

"Surely I do not require teaching to admire Miss Moncrieffe," said the young soldier, with a low bow, and placing his hand on his heart as he spoke.

"There, that will do; get a new speech ready for to-morrow, captain," she said, smiling, at the same time touching Selim with her riding-whip, and as he sprang forward with a bound, she kissed her hand gaily to the twain, and had only time to say, "Don't forget the commission," with another meaning glance at the younger, ere she was out of speaking distance.

"What a lovely girl," said Edmund to his brother, as he followed her receding form with admiring eyes.

"What—already, Edmund?" said his brother.

"I don't wonder at anything I have heard now. But I say, Arthur, for whom do you suppose she intends that commission?"

"I can't guess," replied the brother, drily, for he had, in the question, read his brother's thoughts. "Can you?" he asked, smiling maliciously.

"Me? Oh, no," replied Edmund, confusedly, and blushing as he spoke. "No matter; I don't care for whom it is intended. She is a lovely girl, and may do as she chooses."

"She generally does; and you would have thought so, on the night of the ball, if you had seen her surrounded by a suite as large as that of a queen. But come, I must go to my rooms and do this beauty's bidding. She is too important to our cause to be neglected; besides, the information which she gives is of the highest importance to our plot."

"I wish, Arthur, you would not use that word again, unless you explain yourself."

"Well, then, Edmund," and locking arms, the Royalist proceeded to detail to his brother the plot which was fast maturing, upon the success or failure of which depended, as was believed, the continuation or the sudden termination of the war. Edmund listened in rapt silence, and as his brother concluded his disclosure, exclaimed:

"By heavens! that is wonderfully conceived."

"Yes, and if carried to a successful termination, every party concerned in it, you may rest assured, will be remembered by a grateful sovereign."

"I believe I am the only commissioned officer yet enlisted," said Edmund, half musingly.

"Still harping on my daughter, Edmund," said the brother, laughing, for he well knew that the colonel's commission was running through his busy brain.

"Well, I can't help it, Arthur, and if I can do anything to earn it, I will, you may rest assured."

"Earn what?" asked his brother, pretending not to understand his meaning.

"Oh, pshaw! I suppose I was talking to myself, Arthur. Those terrible eyes of Miss Moncrieffe have quite unnerved me."

"And that parchment, with the great seal attached, is required to restore you," said Arthur, laughing. "I hope you will get it, for I know you are able to earn it now," and the conversation which turned upon the prospects of the Royalists, and which is not necessary to repeat, was carried on almost in whispered tones, until the brothers reached the quarters of the Royalist, where they parted, the one to indite his letter to Governor Tryon, in obedience to Margaret's behests; the other to gather all the information he could which might be of any service to the cause he had espoused at the sacrifice of manhood and honor.

Margaret rode on slowly, meeting at almost every hundred yards some one of her conquests at the ball. For each she had some pleasant greeting, and each one received one of those bright sunny smiles which were so irresistible. She reached her home while General Putnam and Major Burr were still engaged in conversation, not only as to the singular conduct of young Adams, who was nowhere to be found, but as to the conclusions reached by the Council of Generals which had been that day convened, and from which the general had just returned when Margaret started for her morning ride.

Retiring to her own room, she locked the door without waiting to disrobe herself, threw herself into a chair, and, drawing forth the crumpled letter which Captain Blanchard had handed to her, commenced its perusal. As she read, a smile of triumph lighted her beautiful face; and when she closed, she leaned back in her chair, and burying her dimpled chin in one hand, sat for several moments mute and motionless; but that pleasant thoughts were running through her busy brain, was evidenced by the expression of her countenance, which spoke of love and happiness.

"Oh! how happy I shall be when I show him how promptly I have kept my pledge to him. Oh, *Aaron, Aaron!* do you love me as I love you?" and again she sank into a fit of musing, from which she was aroused by a gentle tap at the door. Hastily thrusting the letter of Governor Tryon back into her pocket, she opened it, to admit the general's eldest daughter—a bright, sprightly girl, who had quite sense enough not to be jealous of Margaret's superior attractions, and also the wisdom to admire, and acknowledge her admiration for the beautiful and fascinating stranger.

"I declare, Margaret," she said, as she took a seat, "I never saw you look so perfectly lovely!" and she gazed with earnest admiration upon Margaret, whose color, heightened by the ride and the occurrences which had transpired during it, and whose eyes were actually dancing with happiness, fully justified her assertion.

"Really, I am afraid I shall begin to be very vain if everybody tells me I am so handsome. I am sure, Belle, I don't think of my beauty at all, though I know I have my share."

"I really believe you don't, Margaret," said Belle; "and that is the reason why every one admires you. What is that, Margaret?" and she stooped to pick up a piece of paper which lay at the young girl's feet, half hidden by the long trail of her riding-dress.

It was the letter which Margaret had just received from Governor Tryon, and which she thought she had thrust into her pocket, whereas it had only been laid between the heavy folds of her dress. Margaret intuitively knew what it was; but without exhibiting the least surprise or emotion, said, coolly:

"Pick it up; that's a dear girl. I am so tired, I am sure if I should stoop I couldn't get straight again;" and Miss Putnam, laughing at what she deemed to be Margaret's affectation, picked up the letter and handed it to her.

"Come, now, Margaret, what is it?" she asked, as Margaret proceeded leisurely to open the letter, and commenced its perusal with a face as free from expression as a marble statue—"some love-letter, I'll wager."

"You would not be far out of the way, Cousin Belle," said Margaret, gaily; "you know I made several conquests on the night of the ball."

"Is it a declaration? Come, read it to me. I don't care for the names; but I do want to hear a genuine love-letter. I never had one myself."

"You won't say anything?"

"'Pon honor, not a word."

"You won't tell grandpa?"

"No I won't tell grandpa, nor Lady Putnam, nor even Mattie. Come, read—that's a good girl; I want to hear how a man writes when he is in love."

"Oh, then, you have heard a man talk love?—eh, Cousin Belle?" and she looked quizzically at the young lady, thus beseechingly addressed, who colored to the very roots of her hair."

"Oh, go along, Margaret, you little torment. Come, read the letter, and perhaps I'll tell you something afterward."

Thus appealed to, Margaret, holding the letter up, pretended to read its contents, and she proceeded to recite a string of nothings—of fulsome compliments, absurd flatteries and declarations of intense passion. As she had to invent as she went along, she halted occasionally; but she excused herself for this by abusing the penmanship, as she closed, and expressed the hope that her lover, whoever he might be, would employ a secretary for his next effusion, a suggestion which drew from Belle a burst of such uproarious laughter, that her sister came running into the room to learn the cause, and seeing Margaret standing with the open letter in her hand, her curiosity was also awakened, and she insisted upon knowing the cause of her sister's mirth.

It would have puzzled Margaret to repeat verbatim the string of nonsense she had just put together to satisfy the curiosity of Belle; so drawing herself up with a mock dignity, which brought a merry laugh from Mattie, she folded the letter up very deliberately, and as she placed it this time very securely in her pocket, she said: "I don't think you are quite old enough, Cousin Mattie, to understand such things;" and Mattie now joined her sister in the boisterous mirth, which, considering that she was nearly four years the senior of Margaret, was fully warranted. Margaret managed very readily and adroitly to turn the conversation into topics more interesting to her new cousins than a love-letter addressed to her, and in a few moments the occurrence was quite forgotten.

"Come, children," she said with a demure look, and again their noisy laughter rang through the room, "I wish to change my attire, and I will thank you to retire," and she courtesied very reverently at them.

"Oh, certainly, my lady," they replied, in a breath, and in the same strain, and moving backward to the door, they saluted her with another courtesy as dignified as her own, and once more she was alone.

Hastily locking the door, she drew the letter which had so nearly been discovered, from her pocket, and seating herself, with a pair of scissors commenced cutting it into pieces so minute, it would have been impossible to reunite them. This done, she chewed the pieces until recognition of their original shape or purport was out of the question, and threw them out of the window. Having completed this important work of destruction, she changed her riding-habit for a becoming morning dress, and in a few moments was seated in the room with Mrs. Putnam and her daughters, as unconcernedly as if she had not just escaped being hung "as high as Haman," in accordance with the general's threat.

Of the contents of this most important letter, it is

only necessary to say, that the governor warmly thanked her for the proffer of her valuable aid. He instructed her to communicate as often and fully as possible with him, designating Captain Blanchard, her father's intimate friend, as the safest medium; and he urged her, if possible, to secure the coöperation of some officer of position and influence, possessing means of correct information, as the success of the measures in which they were engaged, depended upon the first blow. In conclusion, he assured her that any promise made by her, to secure the aid of such an officer or officers as might be required, would be faithfully carried out by him, and he referred her to Captain Blanchard for full particulars as to the intentions to which his letter alluded.

And this was the love-letter which had excited such mirth on the part of Cousin Belle, and which Cousin Mattie was too young to understand.

CHAPTER XX.

NEW CHARACTER INTRODUCED.

I HAVE said, in a previous chapter, that at the time when the rumors of the intended or expected invasion of New York reached the city, all the best families had fled, and sought refuge and safety in distant quarters.

Many, however, remained. Some from choice, for they were strongly attached to the cause in which the Provincial troops were engaged, and were willing to prove their loyalty by their presence, and by sharing the dangers and privations of those who governed the city. Many, again, remained from necessity, not having the means to leave the scene of threatened danger; or if they had, they knew not where to find shelter.

Among the latter class was one family, consisting of a mother, a daughter aged about nineteen, and a son, twenty-two.

Mrs. Brainard was a widow—the widow of a soldier who had sacrificed himself on his country's altar in one of the earliest contests which commenced the quarrel between the colonies and the mother country—and she was as deeply imbued with a spirit of patriotism, as had been her husband, when he left home and family to volunteer for his country's defence.

Lizzie, as she was familiarly called, the daughter, was about nineteen, and was the unfortunate possessor of two qualities which in all ages have subjected their owners more or less to temptation, and often insult. She was very beautiful and very poor.

Albert, the son, a fine, stalwart youth of twenty-two, who had been brought up to the trade of a cooper, was anxious to avenge his father's death, and with full consent of his truly Spartan mother, had enlisted in Colonel McDougal's regiment, and was assigned to Captain Blanchard's company.

Mrs. Brainard, on the arrival of the troops ordered to the defence of New York, had opened a small shop in what is now known as John street, where she managed, with the aid of Lizzie, to earn a comfortable living by making up linen for the officers of the various corps who occupied the city. As the daughter was assigned to the charge of the shop, the fame of her beauty and attractions soon spread abroad, and customers flocked thither more to enjoy a few moments converse with her, than from any real need of her services as a seamstress; and many were the fulsome compliments and the broad innuendoes to which she had been compelled to listen, from these roystering young men, more than half of whom had received commissions with the sole view of conciliating their families, or securing their influence, and not from any military or civic qualifications.

More than once she had, with crimsoned cheeks and flashing eyes, been forced to listen to proposals more dishonorable to those who claimed to be men, than to her, whose necessities compelled her to hear them in silence; but the pure, truthful glance of her clear blue eye, and her firm, though modest demeanor, invariably drove them from her, with a feeling of self-abasement known only to the truly guilty.

At length there came one whose admiration was so truthfully expressed—whose conduct in all things was so irreproachable—who was so polite, so courteous, so attentive, she dared to hope that at length she had found one in whom she might confide, the more so, as he had been brought there by her own and only brother.

Captain Edmund Blanchard had heard much of the beauty and fascinations of Lizzie, and knowing that her brother Albert was one of his company, had incidentally (to all appearance) hinted his desire of having some linen made up, and Albert, anxious at once to propitiate his commanding officer, and to serve his mother and sister, had offered to introduce him to the house.

The reader will please to remember, *en parenthèse*, that in those days many of the commanding officers were no more than the equals of those under him, and that such a thing as a strictly military discipline was almost unknown throughout the entire army of nearly thirteen thousand men who garrisoned the city, except when in actual service, and often then it was grievously neglected or not attended to.

Albert Brainard was but too happy to introduce his captain to his beautiful sister, of whom he was justly proud, and whom he loved with more than a brother's devotion.

Captain Blanchard was more than pleased with the beautiful girl—he was fascinated, and he embraced every opportunity, and made many almost impossible ones, for visiting the humble shop over which she presided. The sequel need hardly be told, for every reader can imagine it. He was polite, kind, courteous; and as he showed in a thousand little ways the feelings with which she had inspired him, she could not, unless she had been less than a woman, fail to perceive the impression she had made on him.

She began to draw comparisons between Captain Blanchard and the other officers who visited the shop; she contrasted his quiet, modest, yet pointedly attentive behavior, with the roystering and often insulting conduct and language of others; and as the comparison always ended in his favor, she gradually began to think him worthy of the feelings he had sought to win, and the result was, she gave them to him, in all the truth, and strength, and purity, of a virtuous woman's first love.

It is a cruel thing to have to narrate, but the truth must be told, and that a sad truth, that Lizzie Brainard, whose whole heart, and soul, and feelings had been won by the handsome and gallant young captain, in an evil hour trusted to his honorable vows of intended marriage, which was only postponed on account of the uncertainty of his future, and gave to him that which, once given, could never be recalled.

To say that Edmund Blanchard did not love Lizzie, would be to tell a foul falsehood, for he did, as much as he then thought he was capable of loving anything, and the poor trusting fool, but too happy in that love, had scarce a regret for that sacrifice which she had made, for every feeling of her heart prompted her to repose the most implicit faith and trust in him, and that he would fulfill his promise was no more a subject of doubt to her, than that she was alive; and in that faith and trust, and in his love daily evinced, and as yet showing no change, she found her happiness.

Each day only seemed to strengthen the ties which bound them together, and Albert, who saw the current of affairs, was but too happy to think he had been the means of introducing to his sister one who was so evidently calculated to make her happy. Captain Blanchard, as an evidence of his love for Lizzie, had promoted her brother to the rank of sergeant, soon after the first introduction to the family, and held out to him the promise of further promotion on the occasion of the first vacancy in the company—a promise which he soon afterward succeeded in redeeming, and Albert Brainard received his commission as a lieutenant, in the place of an officer dismissed for insulting and striking a woman. For this kindness, brother and sister were equally grateful, and he was looked upon by either almost as an idol.

Such was the position of matters at the period when Edmund Blanchard was first introduced by his brother to Margaret Moncrieffe. On that occasion he had been completely bewitched by her beauty, by her fascinating manners, and, above all, by the prospect which, with her speaking eyes, she had held out to him of a colonelcy, in reward for his treason. She had, even in that single brief interview, effaced almost completely the image of the injured Lizzie, and when he parted from her, he found his greatest pleasure in dwelling upon her bewitching loveliness, her fascinating smile, and the prospective commission. It was, with every thought thus engrossed, he found himself almost unconsciously at the door of Mrs. Brainard's shop, for it had, of late, been his daily habit to call there on some pretext or other, though pretext was scarcely necessary, for Mrs. Brainard looked upon him as her future son-in-law, and Lizzie felt that he was to be her husband, for had she not his promise?

He was received by Lizzie as he ever had been, from the day when she first acknowledged to her heart her own feelings for him, with a quiet but meaning smile, which spoke more than volumes of mere words could have done.

But he scarcely noticed her smile, nor returned her words of friendly greeting, for when there was a possibility of being overheard, she confined herself to these. Visions of Margaret, of her matchless beauty, her bewitching smile, and that commission, were floating before him, and throwing his cap on one chair, he took a seat on another, with a moody, abstracted air, which she had never before witnessed.

"Are you sick, Edmund?" she asked in low tones, but every word breathed the deep affection which prompted them.

"No, not sick, Lizzie, not sick. I am a little tired; I have had a long walk, and something has occurred which has excited me very much, to-day."

"May I know it?" she asked, in tones which seemed to convey the impression that she was touching on something which did not concern her.

"Oh, surely," he replied. "By some chance, for which I have not yet learned to account, I met to-day my only and elder brother, Arthur. I think you must have seen him here with some of our officers. He is a captain in the king's army, on parole; we have not seen each other for fifteen years."

"Oh, I know him very well; he has often been here. And he—is that your brother?" she asked, eagerly.

"My only living relative on earth," he replied, sadly.

"How bad it must have made you feel, Edmund, to meet your brother under such circumstances, fighting against each other. Oh, Edmund! it is awful to think of; suppose you and he should ever be in battle; just think—brother against brother; why don't you talk to him, and show him how unjust the king is acting toward us? Do, Edmund, do talk to him, and make him feel—for I know you can—how deeply we are wronged."

"You talk like a little fool," replied the soldier, half-angrily; and as he spoke, his face fairly crimsoned, for her words cut him to the heart—him, who had sold himself for gold, and for gold was ready to betray his country.

"Please don't speak so, Edmund," said Lizzie, the tears gathering in her eyes at his words. "Don't make me feel that you think I have acted like a fool."

"I do beg your pardon, Lizzie," said the captain, recalled to himself by these words, and gazing upon the beautiful and trusting girl with his wonted look of affection. "I did not mean that; but when you spoke of asking him to join" ——

"Oh, I see now; the idea of asking him to join our cause would have been about as sensible as to ask you to join his. Of course, I forgive you, Edmund; I did not mean anything wrong by my foolish words."

"Come, Lizzie, never mind that," he said, again col oring deeply, for her words had cut him to the quick "We won't talk of that any more; what have you heard to-day?"

"Oh, not much; there have been half a dozen here to-day, but they don't seem to know much of what is going on. Everybody thinks that Lord Howe is coming here to sack and burn the city. For my part, I don't believe any such thing; do you, Edmund?"

"No," he answered, half abstractedly, for he dared not make any other reply lest he should commit himself. "Suppose, Lizzie, they should come and land troops all around us, and hem us in, and offer terms."

"I'd die, for one," she interrupted, "before I would surrender; no, no, Edmund, no terms for me; death or liberty!" and her eyes fairly flashed with the enthusiasm which animated her.

"You did not hear me out, Lizzie," said Edmund, almost shamed into honor by this noble girl. "Suppose we found it impossible to hold the city, and Lord Howe offered not only pardon, but rewards to those who would return to their allegiance to the king."

"I don't think I heard you rightly, Edmund," she said, and he repeated his sentence.

"Well, go on."

"Suppose he was to offer me a colonel's commission?" he continued.

"Shall I tell you what I would do?"

"Of course; I asked for the purpose of learning your opinion."

"I would tear it up and throw it in his face," exclaimed the enthusiastic patriot, "and tell him that twenty commissions could not purchase my freedom, nor could he quench my love of liberty with all the gold his master owned."

Edmund Blanchard fairly quailed and cowered beneath her glance, as Lizzie spoke. As yet, he had not dared to confide to her his treason, for he had hoped to win her to his views, and through her, her brother; but these words effectually crushed all such hopes, and with a deep sigh, his head sank upon his breast, and for a few moments he sat mute and motionless.

"And what is the matter, Edmund?" asked Lizzie, as she noticed his changed appearance and manners.

"Nothing," he said, with an appearance of carelessness which his looks belied, as he raised his head, "I was only thinking."

"Well, I don't think of such things. When we can't hold the city we can leave it, and if no one else will do it, I will volunteer to set it on fire, before the king's troops shall hold it one hour. No, no, Captain Blanchard, you will always find me as you first knew me; and when I change from my love and devotion to my country, I will give you leave to find another if you can, who," and she sank her voice to a low whisper, "will love you as I have done."

Poor Lizzie! she was cutting slowly but surely, by such words, the cord which bound her lover to her. Every word she had uttered, expressing the deep love she bore for her country, and her determination to sacrifice even her life for its welfare, was a severance of some slender thread; for he was so completely wrapped up in the idea which Margaret had not in reality held out to him, but which he had construed as he wished, of promotion in the cause which he had espoused, and so wholly engrossed was he by her beauty and the bright smile which gleamed on him (even now in Lizzie's presence), that the words of Lizzie sounded like reproaches to him, and because he knew he deserved them, he felt them the more keenly.

He was glad, therefore, when Lizzie changed the conversation, and turned it into the channel in which her own thoughts were running, namely, her love for Edmund, and the hope of speedily becoming his own. In this he joined with his usual apparent cheerfulness; but, in spite of himself, there was an air of constraint about him which the eye of love readily perceived, and which his very efforts to conceal made only the more palpable.

When he took his leave, she retired to her post behind the little counter, resuming her work; but, as she did so, she heard a deep sigh. It was the echo from her own heart, and that foreboded, in very spite of herself, some sorrow, sadness, or trouble; for, "coming events cast their shadows before."

CHAPTER XXI.

MAJOR BURR, AND CORBIE THE TORY.

We left General Putnam in close consultation with his aid as to the extraordinary disappearance of Seth Adams.

The old general was perfectly furious when the report was made to him that no tidings had been received of the young Jerseyman. He denounced him as a traitor. He would offer a reward for his restoration, dead or alive. If dead, he would have his body hung in chains, as a terror to any who might feel inclined to follow in his footsteps; if alive, he would have him whipped to death.

Major Burr suffered the passionate old general to exhaust his wrath on his suppositions; and when he had recovered a little composure, he ventured to suggest that it might be as well to institute an investigation. As for Adams, he knew him so well, he would stake his life on his fidelity; and acquainted as he was with his coolness and shrewdness, he was perfectly confident that something had occurred beyond the power of man to control, or he would have made his report at the hour specified.

"It's all very well to talk, major—all very well to talk," and the general treated his nose to an extraordinary quantity of snuff; "but there's the fact. He went, and he hasn't come back. Now, sir, explain that."

"I cannot, general, until I make some inquiries. Major Gibbs, you see, reports," and he pointed to the letter from the commander of the Life Guard, "that Adams was seen at Corbie's at half-past eight."

"D—n that Corbie! D—n the whole of his infernal tribe! I have a great mind to hang every man of them, and report to the general when he comes back that they have been hung as spies. Yes," he continued, his anger again getting the better of him, "and I would commence with that infernal scoundrel, Forbes—he's the worst of all."

"Suppose I investigate the matter, general?" suggested the aid.

"Suppose we hang 'em first, Burr, and investigate afterward. I don't believe any one would find much fault."

"But they might not like it," replied the major, suggestively; and the idea so pleased the old general, he broke into a loud laugh, and, directing the major to act as he thought proper, left the room to prepare for dinner; for he was as simple in his habits as he was brave, generous, and confiding, and did not disdain to confess to hunger at noon, especially when he had been on active duty since six in the morning.

Major Burr hurried through the remainder of the papers which required attention; and having ordered his horse to be brought up, prepared to start for Corbie's house, with the intention of learning for himself, so far as he could, the probable fate of the young soldier who had been intrusted by him with a duty at once so delicate and so hazardous.

As he was buckling on his sword, the door of the apartment was gently opened, and the well-known face of her to whom he had sold his very soul, in exchange for her love and smiles, peered in.

"May I come in?"

"Yes, for I am going out," was the reply of the major; but uttered in playful tones.

"Well, that is certainly an inducement to enter," she said, in a similar strain. "Pray, are you going to battle?" and she looked inquiringly at his sword.

"I hardly know what I may meet, Margaret," he said. "I am going to that infernal scoundrel, Corbie, to learn, if I can, what has become of poor Seth."

"And pray, who is poor Seth?" she inquired.

"Oh, I forgot! The fact is, between love and war I am getting a little confused, I am afraid."

"I hope your memory will not desert you entirely," she said, playfully but meaningly.

Major Burr caught the full import of her words, and as he met her ardent, loving gaze, he forgot everything again, but her and her love.

"Fear not, Margaret; the prize offered is too great for human resistance. Seth is a young Jerseyman, a cousin of Patsy, by the way, who was with me. Why Margaret, what have I said?" he exclaimed, as she turned from him with moistened eyes.

"Oh, nothing, Aaron, nothing. I see that your memory has not failed you, for Patsy's cousin can make you" ——

"Good Heavens, Margaret!" he interrupted, "how can you be so unreasonable? It is not because he is Patsy's cousin, but because he has been my trusty follower through every hardship. I sent him on a mission last night of great delicacy. He has not returned, and I am really anxious for his safety."

"Because he is Patsy's cousin?" asked Margaret, looking sadly but tenderly in his face.

"Because I love the young man for his courage, devotion and fidelity, and only therefore, Margaret. Do not be silly or unreasonable. If you do not know me, learn to know me now. I have no thought, or hope, or wish disconnected from you, but I have duties to discharge."

"True, Aaron," said Margaret, her countenance brightening at his words, "I was selfish, and I am afraid," she added, looking lovingly into his face, "I was a little jealous; you will forgive me, won't you?"

"I forgive everything, Margaret, but a suspicion of my devotion to you. I am yours, and yours only."

"But who is this Corbie, and what is he?"

"Oh, a pestilent, turbulent fellow, who keeps a low drinking-house near Richmond Hill. I wonder the commander-in-chief allows it. We think the house is the head-quarters of" —— but he checked himself, and did not finish his sentence, for he remembered he, too, had been bought with a price. "But come, I cannot stop to discuss such matters with you now," he continued, "I must be off. Shall I see you again, to-day?"

"I am not afraid to walk in the garden," she replied, with a demure look, "and if you choose to see that I am not interrupted, I shall be obliged to you. I love to walk on moonlight nights, and think or"—and she bent her head close to his own—"talk, as the case may be. I never walk before nine or ten o'clock at night."

"You shall be secure from any disagreeable intrusion," said the major, and imprinting a kiss upon her hand, he left the room, and Margaret was alone.

A sharp ride of some fifteen minutes brought him to Corbie's house, where he dismounted, and giving his horse in charge to an orderly who had followed him, entered the place.

He was received by Corbie, who was alone (for at that hour of the day the soldiers were at dinner, and the loyalists who frequented his house rarely came there in the day-time), with a profusion of bows and scrapes, and expressions of gratification at the honor conferred upon him by this visit, from an officer of such distinction as Major Burr.

"You need not take any great credit to yourself, Corbie, for this visit, and perhaps you won't think it much of an honor before I leave you. Sit down, Corbie, and answer my questions."

"I couldn't think of sitting down, major, in your presence, but I will answer any questions your honor may ask. Won't your honor permit me to offer you some old Southside? There ain't its equal, I know, in New York; at least Colonel Fanning says so, and he's a first-rate judge."

"Colonel Fanning! and who is Colonel Fanning, Corbie?"

"Oh, bless you, sir, don't you know Colonel Fanning?" replied the landlord, whose face would have flushed if it could, through the roseate hues that dyed his cheeks at this slip of the tongue. "Oh, sir, he belongs to the regular army, and he used to come over here with his friends on purpose to drink some of that. S'pose you try a glass major, I do assure you" ——

"No matter just now, Corbie. There was a young man here last night, named Adams,"

"I know him, major; a tall, sandy-haired, rather well-favored young man," replied the host, who had now fully recovered his composure. "He said he was from Jersey."

"The very man; you seem to know him pretty well."

"And I ought to remember him. He came in soon after eight and had three stiff glasses right atop of one another, and then his tongue began to wag, and he told me who he was."

"Well, go on."

"He said he wanted to 'list with the king's troops, and I told him he'd come to the wrong place for that. I told him I was under heavy bonds, and that I wouldn't abuse the general's confidence by no manner of means. Fact is, major, he was desperately drunk."

"Well, and what then?" inquired the major, with an air of apparent concern, for Corbie's air and manner were so truthful, Major Burr could find no reason to doubt him.

"Why, he staid and staid till there was nobody here but Forbes and me. You see, major, Forbes lives away down in the city, and when he gets belated, I always give him a bed, cause you know we're old countrymen. So, as I said, he staid and staid, and I couldn't get him away, and the first thing I knew, we heard tattoo, and then I swore he should go, 'cause if he was found here at that time of night, it would be worse for me than him; and so Forbes and I put him out and shut the house up 'cording to orders. I try to keep my house quiet and orderly, but, major, there's some desperate hard drinkers as comes here, and I'm afraid they will give me a deal of trouble yet."

Major Burr mused a moment, and turning to Corbie, or rather looking him full in the face, he said:

"And no one but Forbes and yourself were in the house when he left?"

"He didn't leave," replied the wily publican, who saw through the question in an instant. "Forbes and I put him out."

"Ah, yes, I remember. Well, I will see Forbes; but, Corbie, you had better be careful. You know your house is suspected as being the head-quarters of all the mischief going on, and if General Putnam catches you at anything wrong, he will relieve your bondsman and put you—you know where," and the young officer looked at the landlord very meaningly.

Now these words might have been interpreted as a caution or a threat, and they were intended to be ambiguous, but the speaker well knew that the impression in either case would be the same.

"Major, I've heard that before; but I tell you I do all I can to keep a quiet house, and I make it a rule never to allow any one to talk on subjects which might occasion trouble. General Putnam will never catch me at anything wrong," and it was the landlord's turn to look meaningly at the officer, for his words also would bear two constructions.

Major Burr turned quietly away, and saying, "I will see Forbes myself," was about taking his leave, when the host, starting forward, said eagerly:

"But, major, won't you try some of that old Southside? I do assure you, there ain't anything like it in New York."

"No, thank you, Corbie," was the major's reply, still moving toward the door, and without turning round, continued: "Mind, Corbie, be careful, and don't get caught in any trouble."

"I won't, I promise you, major. I'm sorry you won't try my Southside. Perhaps you'd let me send you a case?"

"By no means," hastily replied the major, turning round and facing the landlord, and he spoke so eagerly and quickly that a faint, meaning smile crossed the Tory's face. In another moment he was alone, and as the door closed upon the receding form of the officer, he muttered:

"I wonder what the devil that fellow means! No matter; I thank him for his caution, or threat, as it may be. He'll see Forbes, will he? Much good may it do him!" and he chuckled to himself with evident satisfaction.

Major Burr, after stopping a few moments to pay a call on the commander of the Life Guard, Major Gibbs, rode down Broadway, and reined up in front of Forbes' door. The shop was half filled with customers, or rather visitors, among whom were several Provincial customers, and the brothers Blanchard, of whose relationship, however, he was as yet ignorant. As he entered the shop, he saluted the younger of the two with great cordiality, and complimented him upon the appearance and discipline of his company, which, he said (and he spoke in the name of General Putnam), any captain might be proud to command, and he only wished the rest of the regiment was like it.

Captain Blanchard colored, and looked pleased at this official praise, for although Major Burr was his junior by many years, his rank and well-earned reputation rendered even his praises pleasing, and begged to introduce his brother, the Royalist.

"Ah, yes, captain, I have often seen you," he said cordially extending his hand. "I remember meeting you at Colonel Shee's ball. You seemed to know Miss Moncrieffe very well."

"Ever since she was born, sir. Her father and myself have been friends from boyhood. She is a very lovely girl."

"Very lovely," replied Major Burr, hurriedly, for he felt the color was coming to his cheeks, and hastily excusing himself for a few moments, he went to the rear of the shop, where Forbes was engaged, and requested, or rather commanded, him to retire to the back room for a few minutes.

Forbes was fain to comply, and when the door was closed, he was submitted to an examination similar to that which Corbie had undergone, but there was no variance in their narratives, and Major Burr felt that, as they were the only witnesses who could shed any light upon the occurrences of the evening, whatever they might have been, it would be useless to pursue the investigation further, and with a caution to the gunsmith not to meddle with what did not concern him, he returned to the store and joined the group of officers assembled there. A few moments were passed in social chat, when he took his leave, and rode directly to his quarters, where he reported to General Putnam the result of the inquiries he had just made, and he was about closing with an expression of his confidence in the integrity of Seth Adams, when the old general broke forth in a perfect tornado of denunciation and invective.

"Adams, he knew, was a deserter—had been bought over to the enemy, and, curse him, he'd have him hung if a hundred pounds could accomplish it!"

Major Burr listened, of course, without interruption, for he might as well have attempted to stem the torrent of Niagara as soothe the old general's wrath when once aroused.

When he had exhausted himself, he closed by a threat to have every one of those infernal Tory hot-houses of treason closed, and their keepers either imprisoned or hung, and wound up, as he took a tremendous pinch of snuff, by directing his aid to go to the office and prepare a reply to a communication from the commander-in-chief, who had written for certain information on behalf of the committee of Congress.

He was soon immersed in his work, but if he could have been watched, an observer might have noticed that he often laid his pen upon the table, and gave way to fits of musing. At times his thoughts were evidently troubled, and again his countenance was lighted up by a smile of almost rapturous happiness.

Was he thinking of his treason, or Margaret's love, or both?

CHAPTER XXII.

MARGARET FINDS A NEW LOVER.

THE brothers Blanchard were seated in the apartments occupied by the Royalist, and over a bottle of wine had been discussing not only their present prospects, but had enjoyed a long talk over old times.

"By the way, Edmund," said the elder, "you have called, I find, very often on Miss Moncrieffe. Now don't make a fool of yourself there. Pardon me," he said, as he noticed his brother's heightened color, "but I speak only for your good. She is a desperate flirt and coquette. I have known her almost from infancy, and I know what I say. As a devoted Royalist, she is of infinite service to us, and is esteemed accordingly; but I know her thoroughly. Mark my words, Edmund, she does not care any more for you than for the orderly who waits on you. She will use you to her heart's content—lead you on surely, and then laugh at your folly. You had better wait until this infernal war is over, and when we reach home you will find some one to appreciate you and make you happy. You have your captain's commission now?"

"Oh, yes! Governor Tryon sent that to me at

once, with my pay, and I receive my subsistence money regularly every week."

"Then be content for the present. I have no doubt you will earn and receive promotion in due time."

"Do you think," interrupted Edmund, "that commission Miss Moncrieffe asked for, was for me?"

"I don't know what to think of her conduct in that affair. You are the only commissioned officer at present engaged with us, and it may be that she has—well, I don't know—I can't say," he continued, interrupting his own sentence. "She is a queer, unmanageable girl, and may have taken a sudden fancy"——

"To me?" asked Edmund, eagerly. "Do you think so?"

"To you! No, Edmund; don't be so foolish. I meant to say that she might have taken a fancy to show an appreciation of your services, or rather what she expects of you. But look out for her; she will lead you a chase, and then hide from you at the last moment."

"Well," said Edmund, rising, with something of a sigh, "I must return to my quarters; it is nearly the hour for drill."

"I will walk with you part of the way. I have to stop at Mrs. Brainard's and see about some shirts she is making up for me," and the young Provincial turned away to conceal a blush which the mention of this name had called to his face. He had not dared to confide to his brother the fact of his acquaintance and connection with that family, and dreaded lest he should discover it. For an instant he hesitated whether or not he should disclose it to him, but for very fear he decided not to do so, trusting to chance it might pass unknown, and hoping that Lizzie would not avail herself of the information he had imparted as to his relationship to the Royalist officer.

These thoughts ran through his brain while he was buckling on his sword, which, on his entrance, he had laid aside, and turning to his brother with an air of well-assumed composure, he declared his readiness to accompany him as far as their roads led together.

Arm in arm, they proceeded up Broadway, until they reached John street, when, with the promise of soon seeing each other again, they separated, the one to join the company which he did not intend to lead to battle in his country's defence, the other to visit the humble shop of the widow Brainard.

Since the conversation with Edmund, Lizzie had been anxiously looking for the Royalist captain; for, in the guilelessness of her own heart, she felt that her lover must of course have made known to his brother their position; not the sacrifice she had made for him, but the promise he had made to her. When, therefore, she perceived him entering the little shop, she greeted him with a smile and blush, both of which were so unwonted with her, they attracted his attention; for Lizzie, since she had acquired sad experience by intercourse with the gay and dissolute Provincial officers, had ever been noted for her reserved manner.

"Walk in, captain," she said, rising from her seat behind the counter; "take a seat. Mother, Edmund's brother is here for his —— Oh! I beg your pardon, sir," she said, crimsoning as she turned again to him—"we call him Edmund here always. Captain Blanchard, I mean."

"And pray, Miss Lizzie, why should you beg my pardon?" asked the Royalist, whose interest was excited by this little episode, and who, thinking there might be more behind than he had dreamed of, determined to ascertain the truth.

"Oh! really, captain, I spoke hastily, and I beg your pardon; but he was here a day or two ago, and he told me he met his brother whom he had not seen in ever so many years, and when he told me who it was, I knew it was you, and—and" ——

"And that is why you begged my pardon?" he asked, with an arch look.

"Oh, no, sir! but I did not mean to use his name so familiarly in your presence."

"Oh, yes, I see. You are on very familiar terms with him; but you did not wish me to know it."

"Not at all, sir," said Lizzie, blushing again. "Please, sir, if you will walk in the back room, mother is just putting up your things;" and the captain, whose interest and curiosity were now excited, gladly availed himself of her invitation, and he entered the little back room off the shop, where he found Mrs. Brainard, as Lizzie had said, putting up "his things."

"Captain, I am very glad to see you," said Mrs. Brainard, a fine, matronly woman, who had, perhaps, seen fifty summers. "Lizzie was saying the other day that Edmund had found a brother whom he had not seen for many years, and we were right glad to know it was you."

"Edmund again," thought the captain; but he said: "Yes, Mrs. Brainard, it was a very pleasant meeting, after an absence of fifteen years. I only remembered Edmund as a little boy, and, to meet him as I did, was a great surprise, you may well imagine."

"We think all the world of him here, captain," continued the old lady; "and, as for Lizzie, why she thinks him about perfection."

"Ah! that accounts for it," thought the captain, as he recalled the smile and the blush which greeted his entrance; but he said: "Yes, I know; and of course he thinks as much of her?"

"I hope he does," said Mrs. Brainard, looking up from the work she was smoothing down, preparatory to tying it up. "If he don't, he's told a good many—lies, I suppose I must call 'em," and she gave him a meaning glance.

"Oh, Edmund would not tell lies, I am sure; and I

don't blame him for thinking much of your daughter; for she is certainly a very lovely and a very modest, well-behaved girl."

"She is a good girl, captain, and that's better than being lovely; and she'll make him a good wife, I know. She would make a good wife for any man."

Captain Blanchard was a thorough man of the world, an old soldier, and a campaigner, and it was a rare thing for him to be taken by surprise; but these words of the simple-hearted widow did make him start. She did not observe it, however, for, as she finished her sentence, she bent her head again to her work.

"Yes, madam, she would make a good wife for any man; but Edmund did not tell me when it was to come off. When does she expect to be married?"

"Oh, as soon as this war is over. He calculates it can't last much longer, and then" ——

Her sentence was interrupted by the arrival of some half dozen officers, who, under pretext of giving orders for work, and examining the small stock of goods in the shop, sought the opportunity of chatting with Lizzie.

Captain Blanchard listened to their silly prattle for a few minutes, and, while he was disgusted with them, he was perfectly delighted with the modest and correct deportment and language of Lizzie. She listened to their fulsome compliments, for she had no choice but to listen; but her replies were so worded as to convey the unmistakable impression that she fully understood and appreciated their promptings, and never for a single instant did she forget her self-respect.

Finding themselves foiled at every point, the officers took their leave, each one as he went out saluting her with some compliment which was meant to be expressive of his own personal admiration; but Lizzie listened in silence, and gently courtesied them out.

Captain Blanchard had overheard every word that had passed during the interview; had noticed the perfect propriety of Lizzie's conduct and language, and taking up the bundle which Mrs. Brainard had put up for him, he reëntered the shop, and as he again met the bright smile and blush of the young girl, he took off his cap with an air of respect, and said, with deep earnestness: "I think with your mother, Miss Lizzie, that you will make a good wife for any man;" and, with a courteous bow, he left the shop.

Lizzie's heart beat with fearful rapidity as she heard these words, for they told her that she had been the subject of conversation between the captain and her mother.

"Oh, mother, what have you been saying?" she exclaimed, entering the room where her mother was seated, plying her busy needle.

"Well, daughter, I don't know what you mean by such a question."

"What have you been saying about me to Captain Blanchard?"

"Why, I don't know as I said anything very particular. I told him you and Edmund was going to be married as soon as the war was over, and he said as how you'd make—no, I said as how you'd make a good wife for any man."

"Oh, mother, how could you?" asked the blushing girl.

"How could I! ain't he Edmund's brother, and ain't you going to be married?"

"Yes, but, mother"——

"Well, what, mother? A good daughter will make a good wife, I know, and I'm sure you've been a good daughter to me."

At these words, which brought home to poor Lizzie the consciousness of her own guilt, she blushed crimson; but the fond, doting mother, not dreaming of the cause, attributed her blushes to the fact of her having spoken so plainly of her expected marriage to the brother of her betrothed, and said, with an apologetic air: "Oh, Lizzie, dear, I didn't mean to make you feel so bad about it, but he seemed to know all, and so I spoke freely with him."

"Did he, really?" asked Lizzie, earnestly.

"Oh, yes; when I spoke about it, he said he knew, only Edmund hadn't told him when it was to come off; and so I told him. I am sure there was no harm in that."

"No, nothing;" said Lizzie, half musingly, but she

was thinking of the words which the captain uttered as he was leaving, and she was happy. "I am sure I'll try to be a good wife, mother, as good as I know how to be. Dear, dear Edmund!" she murmured, as, leaving her mother at her work, she resumed her place behind the counter of her little shop.

CHAPTER XXIII.

MARGARET RECEIVES A PROPOSAL.

EDMUND BLANCHARD could not, because he would not, believe what his more experienced brother had said concerning Margaret, and he determined to ascertain how far he had spoken correctly, little thinking how recklessly he was exposing himself to the most imminent danger.

The next morning, therefore, after the interview with his brother, found him at General Putnam's house, and the family being engaged in their usual avocations, his heart bounded with delight when he found he was permitted an interview with Margaret, alone. He had fully prepared himself (mentally) for this interview, but to say his heart failed him when she entered the room, radiant with beauty, and wearing her most fascinating smile, would be but feeble truth; he actually trembled as she approached and held out her hand, which he grasped with a force which made the fair girl wince, but which, young as she was, let her into his secret.

"Well, captain," she said, as in obedience to her motion, he seated himself, and she drew her chair near to him, "what word have you?"

"Nothing, Miss Moncrieffe, of any special importance. Nothing, at all events, worth communicating to our friends. And you?"

"Oh, matters go on with me pleasantly and happily as usual, though I must confess I am tired of being cooped up here. By the way, where is your brother, and why is he not with you? When did you see him last?"

"We dined together yesterday, but he said nothing of coming to see you."

"He does well to leave that to you," said Margaret, with a meaning smile, which he entirely misinterpreted; for in speaking to him, she had but one purpose in view, the accomplishment of the project in which she had volunteered her services, and in the success of which she felt a truly deep interest.

"My brother is very kind to deprive himself of the privilege he allows me," he replied, with a low inclination of the head, accompanied by a glance which the shrewd coquette rightly read.

"And do you really esteem it a privilege, Captain Blanchard?" she added, bending on him a look which went to his very soul.

"I know no higher privilege, and surely no greater pleasure, than is permitted me in seeing Miss Moncrieffe," and the young soldier blushed as he spoke, for Margaret's eyes were fixed upon him with an intensity of expression which thrilled through him.

"I hope you have not been taking lessons of your brother," she added, half averting her face.

"I need no teacher, Miss Moncrieffe, save my own heart, to enable me to tell you how solely, how truly, and how devotedly I am yours."

"Really, Captain Blanchard, you must not speak so earnestly, or I shall be more than half inclined to believe what you say."

"Mean, Miss Moncrieffe! Oh! could you read my heart—could you but see how indelibly your image was impressed there from the moment you crossed my path—could you but know how I have dreamed of you—aye, even dared to hope of you—you would at least do me the justice to believe me sincere in what I say."

"I do believe you, Captain Blanchard," said Margaret, with well affected hesitancy, and stooping her head until the color came (a trick she had learned from reading of a French abbé, who, whenever he wished to blush, bent down his head and held his breath for a moment), she raised her eyes to his; her face was suffused with a deep blush, her eyes wore a softened expression, and there was an outward indication that she had appreciated the fervor of the young soldier's feelings, and reciprocated them. "I do not know what you mean," she said, confusedly, turning toward the door, as if fearful of interruption.

"Oh, then let me say," exclaimed the impassioned young man, "that since the moment I saw you your image has haunted me. I see nothing, hear nothing, know nothing, care for nothing, but you."

"You must not speak so, Captain Blanchard. I am young—very young, and very inexperienced. My position here is one of peculiar difficulty; do not let me think you would take advantage of it."

"For the world, no. On my honor as a man and gentleman, I am true, honest, and sincere. Speak one word to me—say that you have known my devotion for you—say that you know"——

"I can say nothing, Captain Blanchard," she said, interrupting him, and continuing, with an appearance of deep emotion, "I have no right to say anything. My father is not here to counsel me, and when we may meet, heaven only knows. Do not ask me now," and again she averted her head, as if to conceal her blushes.

"Give me one word of hope—one single word, and I am your slave," he exclaimed, passionately; "only one word, Miss Moncrieffe."

"Captain Blanchard, I am too young to listen to such words from any man, and you ought to respect my position more than to urge them upon me. What can I say to you? What ought I say to you? Go on in the course you have marked out for yourself, and --and," she continued, hesitatingly, "hope for your reward."

Captain Blanchard was so blinded by his desperate

passion for Margaret, he could put only one interpretation on her words, and that was favorable to his aspirations; and as he listened to them, his eyes kindled, his cheeks flushed, and rising, he said, with an energy which almost startled the self-possession of Margaret:

"Thanks, thanks—ten thousand thanks. I will go on—I will prove myself worthy even of you, and make you proud of the love I bear you."

"Please don't say any more, Captain Blanchard," said Margaret, deprecatingly. "It is wrong in you to speak so, and more than wrong in me to listen."

"Your words are law, Miss Moncrieffe," he said, with an air almost of reverence, and bowing as he spoke, for he felt now secure, at least in the right to hope, and he was but too happy to prove his devotion by his obedience.

Fortunately for Margaret, whose dexterity had been taxed to the utmost by this interview, the door of the parlor was at this moment opened, and Major Gibbs, the commander of the Life Guard, entered, having been summoned thither by a special summons from General Putnam, and after dispatching his business, stepped in the parlor to pay a call on the ladies of the family. He either did not, or affected not to notice the agitated manner and flushed cheeks of the young captain, but, with the blunt gallantry for which he was so conspicuous, proceeded to pay Margaret some home compliments upon the conquests she had made during her brief stay in the city.

She repelled them with well assumed sincerity of language and manner, and occasionally, as she spoke, she stole a glance at Captain Blanchard, which, in his infatuation, he chose to read as saying, "I am satisfied with one."

The latter soon afterward took his leave, in a perfect state of ecstasy, having received a gentle pressure of the hand from his new idol as they parted, and wended his way to his quarters, scarce knowing whether he was on his head or his heels, but quite confident that Margaret reciprocated his feelings, for had she not said, "hope for your reward," and what reward could he hope for—what could he care for, but her love?

Even the coveted commission of colonel was forgotten, dimmed by the brightness of Margaret's eyes, and obscured by the fascination of her smile.

When Edmund Blanchard reached his quarters, he was somewhat surprised to find his brother there, awaiting him, and the brother was scarcely less surprised at the air of exultation, and the smile of triumph which lighted the face of the young Provincialist.

"Well, Arthur," said the younger, throwing his cap on the bed, and turning to his brother, with a bright, buoyant smile, "I am glad to see you; but," and he paused a moment, and gazed at his brother, before he spoke, "what makes you look so confounded glum?"

"Sit down, Edmund, and tell me what makes you look so confounded happy? to quote your own expression."

"Oh, the easiest thing in the world," replied Edmund, throwing himself into a chair; and, stretching his legs out to their fullest length, he thrust his thumbs into the arm-holes of his vest, and looked his brother steadily in the eye.

"Well, out with it; I'd like to know your secret."

"I can't tell you my secret, brother Arthur; but I will tell you, that there never was a man so mistaken in his life as you have been."

"And you have seen her?" asked Arthur, with a little of sternness in his manner, for he well knew what his brother meant, and with full information of his promises to Lizzie, could not refrain from some exhibition of his displeasure.

Edmund bristled up a little at his question, more, however, at the manner in which it was put; but recalling his brother's words concerning Margaret, and knowing that he alluded again to her, he replied: "I have; and what then?"

"And what then?" continued the Royalist, coolly.

"That is for me to know, Arthur," replied his brother, with an air of exultation.

"And pray, young gentleman, what is to become of

Lizzie Brainard?" and the Royalist looked at his brother with an expression as if he would read his very soul. "Yes, sir, I repeat, what is to become of Lizzie Brainard? I have something to do with the honor of our name, Edmund, and I ask you again, what is to become of Lizzie Brainard?"

"Why?" replied Edmund, with a forced laugh, "you can have her if you choose."

"I don't understand you," said the Royalist, with a tremendous effort to restrain his anger at this unmanly remark. "What do you mean?"

"I really don't think you have the right, even as my elder brother, to call me to account for my little escapades. I do know Lizzie Brainard, and what of that?"

"Have you never promised her marriage?"

"And what if I have? Have you never done the same, most gallant brother, and forgotten it whenever it was convenient to do so?"

Captain Blanchard bit his lips until the blood almost started from them; but still he restrained himself, and continued, with a coolness perfectly marvellous under the circumstances: "I never did, thank God; such a sin lies not on my conscience."

"Really, brother Arthur, I should like to know why you take such an interest in Lizzie?"

"Because I believe her to be a truthful, pure-minded, noble-hearted girl, and"—

A loud, contemptuous laugh from Edmund interrupted this sentence, and for a moment the Royalist looked at his brother with an expression of the most unutterable contempt.

It was returned by Edmund, who, with a cynical smile, replied to this look by saying: "Why, Arthur, you don't think I was such a cursed fool as to marry a girl like that?"

"Did you never promise to marry her, Edmund? was the question I asked, Edmund; and I hope for a plain, straightforward answer, such as becomes a man."

"And what if I did. Perhaps I am not the only one who has promised the same thing."

"And has she not trusted to your promise?"

"Well," and the young soldier stroked his beard complacently, "perhaps she has."

"And have you not wronged her, Edmund?"

"I don't know what you mean by wronged, Arthur. I certainly have received abundant proof of her love."

"And given because she believed you loved her, and trusted to your love and honor."

"Possible," was the cool reply.

"And you have been to see Miss Moncrieffe, and have dared to offer your love to her?"

"There is a vast difference in their positions."

"Only one difference, sir; Lizzie Brainard is beautiful and poor—Margaret Moncrieffe is wealthy as well as beautiful. I ask you, Edmund, in honest sincerity—I ask you as your elder brother—as the rightful representative of our name and the guardian of its honor, as yet unstained, have you brought this foul wrong on a loving, trusting girl?"

"I don't know what you call a wrong; I repeat I have received from Lizzie every proof of her love I could ask. What more do you require?"

"Nothing more from you, sir. Henceforth we are no longer brothers. I will not raise my hand against you, nor will I provoke you to raise your own against me; for I consider you so far beneath the contempt of an honorable man you could not insult me. Edmund Blanchard, I blush for you and I despise you, for you are no man."

"Sir—Arthur—brother, what does this mean? How dare you use this language to me?"

"How dare you ask that question, sir? How dare you, who have confessed to a crime which ought to shut you out from the society of every honorable man, ask such a question of me? I tell you, Edmund Blanchard, you will rue the day you have proved so false to everything that belongs to a gentleman and honorable man. Under the plea of an honorable promise, you have deceived and betrayed a fond, loving, trusting, virtuous girl. Oh, shame! shame! But, mark me, sir," and, hat in hand, he strode close up to his brother, who, conscious of guilt, was perfectly astounded at such a rebuke from a quarter so unexpected—"that girl is not without friends. I believe and shall believe, until I have better evidence than your assertion, that until she knew you, she was as true and pure in heart as an angel; and, sir, if you ever again show your face within the house that holds her, the consequences rest on your own head, unless you go there to fulfill your promise to her."

"Now go to Miss Moncrieffe; I shall go there too; but I shall not betray you; for, coquette as she may be—reckless, heedless, impulsive as she is—she would spurn you as I do now, if she knew half your vileness. Your sure punishment will find you, so truly as there is an avenging God. Farewell, sir. Henceforth we are strangers!" and before Edmund Blanchard could recover from the effects of this terrible denunciation, or utter one word in reply, he was alone.

No, not alone; for even then, with his brother's words—almost curses—hissing in his ear, and burning into his very heart, with the recollection of the irreparable wrong he had inflicted upon the loving, trusting Lizzie, Margaret Moncrieffe was with him; and, in the remembrance of her cheering smiles, which bade him "hope for his reward," he was content to forget the world beside; and, throwing himself into a chair, when the door closed upon the retreating form of his brother, gave away to a reverie of which Margaret formed the only component part. Poor Lizzie Brainard!

CHAPTER XXIV.

SETH ADAMS A PRISONER.

Seth Adams threw himself on the deck of the ship, and strove to penetrate the darkness and gloom which surrounded him; but for a long time it was vain, as the berth deck in which the "brig" was located, was lighted by only one lantern, hung well forward, near the berth occupied by the master-at-arms, and where the sentry was stationed who watched over the prisoners. At length his eyes became accustomed to the dim light, and he was enabled to perceive that the hammocks were slung fore and aft, and that he was surrounded by some half dozen men, prisoners like himself, but who were buried in sleep. In vain he attempted to scan their countenances, but he could not distinguish the features of either; so, composing himself with perfect *sang froid*, he gave way to the thoughts which his position naturally called up.

He was, then, a prisoner on board a king's ship, and under circumstances which rendered his detention of the utmost consequence; for he was the possessor of a secret of the deepest importance, as well to his country as to its enemies. That some infernal plot and treachery was in contemplation he knew; for, as has been seen, when he was secured at Corbie's house, Colonel Fanning and Corbie had conversed with perfect freedom as to the plans of the Royalists. For an instant he regretted that he had not dissembled with Governor Tryon, and, by manifesting a readiness to serve the enemies of his country, secured the opportunity of serving her interests; but he felt his cheek mantle with the blush of shame at the very idea, and the thought was as quickly dispelled as it was born in his mind—not his heart.

His only possible chance now was to pretend that he was at least content with his position, and gather all the information he could with reference to the movement in which the Royalists were engaged, and, having learned all he could, to escape if possible; if not, to lose his life in the attempt; for, as to serving against his country, that he never would do. He would lie, or deceive, or do anything to gain his ends, and having comforted himself with the reflection that "what can't be cured must be endured," he closed his eyes, and was soon lost in a slumber, whose peacefulness could only be enjoyed by one whose conscience was at rest.

At daylight he was aroused by the customary morning gun, and in a few minutes the berth deck was cleared of all its occupants, save those like himself, in the "brig."

"Come out of that, you rebel dog!" was his first

salutation, accompanied by a smart blow from a ratan on the place where, in some natures, the seat of honor is located. The voice, which was a very gruff one, belonged to the master-at-arms, and it was he who held the ratan which had inflicted the first blow Seth Adams had received since he was a boy.

Manacled as he was, he could not resent the insult, for such he deemed it, quite forgetting that he was a prisoner in the power of an enemy; but as he sprung up to his full height at one bound, he fastened a glance upon the petty tyrant, which spoke as plainly as words could speak, "if I ever do catch you, that will be the last blow you will ever strike."

"Come out of that, on deck with you, and air yourself," and the ratan was again raised, but Adams said:

"Don't strike me again; tell me what you want me to do."

"On deck, you scoundrel," and the ratan fell, this time on the young man's shoulders.

Tears started to his eyes, but they were tears of shame and mortification; he obeyed, however, in silence, and ascending the ladder which led to the upper deck, he found himself surrounded by a crowd of sailors and soldiers, the former making preparations to wash down and holy-stone the deck, the latter striving to get out of the way as much as possible, for they well knew the antipathy which sailors bear to soldiers.

He had no time to look about, for he was conducted

at once to the forecastle with his fellow-prisoners, and bidden to stand still there until he was ordered below. He gladly embraced the opportunity thus afforded, and the strangeness of the sight for a time made him forget his position; any one who has been on board a man-of-war at that hour, for the first time, could well appreciate his sensations. All was bustle and activity, but there was no noise or confusion, for every man had his station and knew his duty, and perfect silence prevailed, broken only by the whistle of the boatswain's mates, or the gruff orders of the officers of the deck.

While engaged in watching this novel scene, he was accosted by a voice which seemed familiar, and turning he saw before him, dressed in the garb of a seaman, a young man, Paul Babcock, a neighbor and a friend of his own at Elizabeth, who had early left home to follow the sea, and had not been heard from for three or four years.

"What on earth are you doing here with them 'ere bracelets on?" he asked, pointing to the manacles on Seth's wrists.

"And what are you doing here?" was the reply.

"I belong to the forecastle, Seth; I was pressed in Liverpool, nigh on three years ago, and I've been aboard this bloody craft ever since. But I say, what do them mean?" and he looked at the irons.

"I am a prisoner, you see, Paul," said Seth, and he held up his hands with a shrug of his shoulders, which yet smarted under the blow of the brutal master-at-arms.

"And so am I, only worse, for they make me serve when I don't want to, and fight agin my own flesh and blood. Hush! I'll get a chance to see you before long. I'll look out for you as well as I can—only mind me, Seth, you hear?"

Seth nodded assent, feeling but too grateful to have found an acquaintance among the crowd of foreign faces which surrounded him.

It is not necessary for the purpose of this work to narrate the incidents connected with the brief captivity of Adams, for it was briefer than his captors had intended by many months. Seth Adams in no wise belied the character Major Burr had given him, as being shrewd, cool, determined, and cunning as a fox. He listened to everything, treasured up everything, and submitted without complaint to every indignity which the brutality of the master-at-arms, who had sole charge of him, could inflict. He had gathered from hints and expressions of the Royalist sailors and soldiers, aided often by direct communications from Paul, information of the highest importance to the commander-in-chief—information which, if the country was to be saved, must be communicated to him at the earliest possible moment at all hazards, and he determined to risk his life in the attempt to impart it in person, for by no other possible means could it be conveyed to head-quarters.

By careful watching he had learned much of life and habits on ship-board, and he determined to avail himself of the information thus acquired, and if possible to effect his escape. To facilitate this, he had practised on his manacles at every conceivable opportunity, and by patient and constant effort had succeeded in so loosening the key which united them, he could withdraw and replace it with his teeth. To illustrate the possibility of this, it is only necessary to say that ship's "irons" are entirely different from those used on shore, keyed only at one end, and very roughly manufactured. There is a place on board the ship which every seafaring man knows as the "head," the purposes of which it is not necessary to explain; but Seth had determined to make use of his knowledge of this place to effect his escape, and awaited only what he deemed a fitting opportunity. He learned with dismay that the whole British fleet, with thousands of hired troops on board, was daily expected, and knowing that the consummation of the infamous plot, whose particulars he had gleaned from every conceivable source, only awaited their arrival, he determined to *make* the long desired opportunity.

The night chosen for his perilous undertaking was pitchy dark, and the rain was pouring down in torrents, so that every man, whether sailor or soldier, was stowed away in every possible spot where shelter might be afforded Every soul on the berth-deck was asleep, except Seth, and the sentry, who was seated on a mess-chest near the lamp burning on the forward part of the ship, straining his eyes to decipher the words of some book he held in his hand.

Seth arose, and stooping so as to avoid the hammocks, whose inmates were sound asleep, he approached the sentinel, and said, in a disguised voice:

"Please, Mr. Soldier, I want to go to 'the head?'"

The sentry looked up from his book, and not noticing who it was, thought it was one of the prisoners of the ship's crew, who were not in irons, as the light of his lamp was too dim to enable him to distinguish anything, for it was not a necessary consequence of being in the "brig" that a prisoner should be in irons, but Seth had earned his distinction by his insolence to Governor Tryon, who, sooth to say, had entirely forgotten the young man, and did not remember he was on board.

"Go and be d—d," was the gruff reply of the sentry, who, hearing the rain pattering on the deck above him, and whose duty it was to accompany his prisoner to the head, and return with him to the lower deck, had no idea of going on deck to be soaked through for the accommodation of any prisoner, for he would have to sit the remainder of the watch with wet clothes on, and to save himself from this, he gave Seth permission to go unattended.

Seth made no reply, lest his identity should be discovered, but turning away, he silently moved toward the hatchway which led to the deck, and as he passed along, gently withdrew the key which secured his manacles. Sliding them off, he put them in the bosom of his shirt, and ascended the companion way, and for the first time since he had been on board, he trod the deck a free man, for even in this step he felt a consciousness of freedom. The darkness was so impenetrable, he could not see one step before him, nor could he perceive a single human being. He knew the way, however, to the "head," and moving cautiously along, he reached unnoticed the steps which led to the top-gallant forecastle, where the "head" is located.

There was a sentry posted there, but as it was no unusual matter for the men to go to the "head" at all times of day or night, he paid no attention to Seth, but stood with his back to the wind, and his face buried up to his eyes in his coat-collar. Another moment, and Seth was in the "head," where, unnoticed, he divested himself of his coat, and everything but his pantaloons, and wrapping them up, with the irons inclosed, he dropped them overboard. The pantaloons he tied about his neck by the legs, in such a shape they would afford as little resistance to the water as possible. Silently but fervently he commended himself and his purpose to God, and sliding down, he managed to reach the martingale guys, and thence glided to the martingale. With one more brief prayer, he dropped into the water, a distance of only about three feet, and fortunately the noise of the wind and the violence of the rain drowned the sound made by his body as it cut the water.

Rising from the plunge, he looked around, and seeing the lights on Staten Island, suffered himself to float noiselessly up with the tide, which was running then strong flood, his intention being to wait until he got out of possible hearing, and then make for the Jersey shore, which, from the spot where the ship lay, near the entrance to the "kills," was distant about three miles. When he had reached a sufficient distance from the ship, he struck out, noiselessly and slowly, so as not to fatigue himself, for he had a long swim even for so strong and bold a swimmer as he was. But he was animated, first by the sense of freedom, and next by the hope of thwarting the enemies of his country, by imparting to the commander-in-chief the important information he had acquired.

He had swam perhaps two or three hundred yards, when some hard substance struck his chest with such force as to cause him great pain, and on reaching his hand forward to discover what it might be, he found it was a piece of board about ten or twelve feet long, and a foot in width, which had probably been dropped by some vessel. Blessing providence for this most welcome and timely aid, he at once seized hold of it, and for a while suffered himself to float along with the tide, so as to gain strength, and by watching the lights on the shore, he perceived that he was drifting up the "Kills" at a very rapid rate, for the tide runs there with much greater force than in the open bay.

Seth was glad of this, and determining not to weary himself unnecessarily, lest when exertion should be needed he would be incapable of making any, he held quietly to his plank, and floated on, occasionally giving a few strokes to aid his progress. Of course he suffered much from the coldness of the water, but his sufferings were diminished much by the recollection that he was free, and he bore them in silent patience. It was nearly midnight when Seth escaped from the ship, and how long he had floated he knew not; but he hailed with delight a streak of grey dawn which broke out in the east, for he knew that ere long he would be able to discover where he was. The rain had gradually moderated, and, about the time day was breaking, had ceased entirely, the clouds, at the same time, beginning to break away. He could only hope that he had gone through the "Kills;" but whether he had kept in them, or floated into Newark bay, he could not tell, and his joy may be imagined when daylight permitted him to discover his position, he found himself about a mile above the present site of Elizabethport. He knew every inch of the shore, for he had fished and clammed it for years, and when he made this discovery, a new life seemed to be given to him. Heading his plank toward the shore, he now struck out manfully, and, in the course of half an hour, was safe on land, wearied, cold and exhausted, it was true, but he was *free.*

Entering the woods which skirted the shore, he wrung out his pantaloons, and drawing them on, threw himself on the leaves, panting and worn out, and his first thought was an ejaculation of thankfulness to God for his escape. He lay there a very few minutes, for he knew how important it was that his information should be instantly conveyed to the city, and rising, stretched his benumbed and aching limbs, and started forward.

Seth had providentially landed within two miles, or a little more, from the house of Mrs. Adams, his aunt, by whom he had been brought up from boyhood, and he pushed on with cheerfulness, though every step gave him pain, so terribly had he been affected by his long immersion in the water. But he had a sacred duty to perform, and scorning pain, he kept on his weary road, and after two hours of painful struggling through the woods, his naked flesh and feet torn by the bushes and briers through which he had to force his path, he came in sight of the house, which was just across the road from the woods through which he had worked his toilsome, weary way.

The sight of his well-remembered home revived him; and panting, bleeding, yet never faltering in the courage which had thus far animated him, he crossed the woods, passed through the fence, and reaching the door of the kitchen, sank exhausted on the step, absolutely unable to make his presence known by the slightest noise, so completely was he worn down by his tremendous efforts.

How long he lay there he knew not, but at length the door was opened, and a loud scream from Mrs. Adams, who had discovered the bleeding and half-naked form lying there, and hastily closing the door, ran back into the house, assured him he had been seen. Her screams brought Patsy from her room, her simple toilet half finished, but her mother could only point to the door; she was too much frightened to utter a word.

Patsy boldly approached the door, and as she did so, Seth, who had managed to raise himself on one elbow, met her searching glance of pity. For an instant she gazed inquiringly at him; her breath came thicker and faster, and at length, with a scream of mingled joy and pity, she sprang out and raising his head, exclaimed: "Seth, in God's name what does this mean?" for she had recognized, half-naked, scarred and bleeding as he was, her cousin, the playmate of her earliest years, him whom she had ever looked on as a brother.

"Mother, mother!" she fairly screamed, "come here, it's Seth—quick, mother!" and stooping down, she placed her arms under his own, and with a tremendous effort raised him to his feet. Mrs. Adams, as she heard her daughter's exclamation, came out as quickly as she had hurried away, and raising her hands in pity and horror at the sight, sprang forward to assist Patsy in her labor of love, exclaiming, as they bore him into the house, "Massy me, what on airth is all this?"

Seth was placed in the large rocking-chair, his head sinking wearily on Mrs. Adams' shoulder, while Patsy sprang into the other room, and returned as quick as thought, bearing a bottle which she placed to his mouth, and of which he eagerly drank.

A few swallows revived him so that he was able to sit up, and looking in Patsy's face, with eyes beaming with fraternal love, he said, "Thank God, I am free!"

CHAPTER XXV.

THE TEMPTRESS CONQUERS.

THE moon ought to have shone on that night, but it did not; the almanac declared that it was a full moon, but the clouds belied the almanac, for the moon could not be seen through the heavy veil which they had thrown over her.

Every member of General Putnam's family was fast asleep, and if ladies ever snore, was snoring long before ten o'clock. The general, wearied down with the work of the day, for he was actively and personally engaged in superintending the fortification of the island against the probable and almost certain advent of the British, had retired early, and his family had followed his example.

The quarters of General Putnam, as history has informed us, were at that time located at No. 1 Broadway, and the garden extended to the river, then bounded by Greenwich street. The house, built by Captain Kennedy, a Royalist officer of wealth, had been selected by him as the most eligible spot on the Island, and little dreaming of what a few years of future might bring forth for him, he had adorned the place in the most tasteful and expensive manner. The grounds extended down as far as the lower side of Greenwich street, and at that time were filled with trees, flowers, and shrubbery of all kinds.

Fort George, then the principal fortification of the Island, was located on what is now known as the "Battery," and in the rear of the general's quarters, was located "Oyster Battery." Of course, in each of these, sentinels were posted to prevent the approach of any one from the river side, but no thought was taken of that portion of the city inland. As a consequence, the garden of General Putnam's quarters was never intruded upon, and the only precaution taken to guard the approach to his quarters, was from the seaward, or rather river side.

As has been said, the moon, according to the almanac, ought to have shone that night, but she could not; the clouds were too thick and too heavy even for her penetration, and in consequence, a deep gloom, amounting almost to darkness, prevailed.

It was between nine and ten o'clock at night (hours most unseasonable for that period, for every one not on duty was presumed to be in bed and asleep), that a form attired in dark clothes might have been seen (if the moon had permitted sight to be available) pacing to and fro in the broad walk which ran parallel with the river and the house, and which was so shaded by the trees that no one in the house or on the river could have perceived anything, even with the aid of the moon.

It was Margaret, who was taking the walk to which she had declared herself accustomed, and in which, by implication, she had invited her lover to join her. She was pacing the gravelled walk impatiently, half-angrily, and perhaps was wondering whether she had not better return to the house, when a well-known voice, close by her side, uttered the simple word, "Margaret;" it was enough:

> "'Twas his own voice—she could not err,
> Throughout the breathing world's extent,
> There was but one such voice for her,
> So kind, so soft, so eloquent."

In another moment she was clasped in the arms of him to whom she had given her virgin affections; him, for whom she would have sacrificed her very soul; him, whom meaning to serve, she had betrayed and purchased with the price of her love.

"Margaret, my own Margaret!" murmured the young soldier, as she returned his warm embrace, and permitted the ardent kiss with which he expressed his happiness.

"I was afraid I might be intruded upon," said Margaret, meaningly.

"And I—shall I say I fear I have intruded upon you?"

"Say what you choose, Aaron, now you are here,"

she said, placing her arm within his own, and pressing it warmly. "But come, we must not waste these precious moments. You know me now, and you have said you did not despise me for the unsought acknowledgment of my love."

"Unsought, Margaret? Did not my first glance disclose to you the love which sprang full-born into my heart? Did not my first words testify how solely I was yours? Did not the first kiss I dared to impress upon your lips, when my heart was gladdened by the assurance of your safety, carry to your heart the conviction of the boundless love I bore you?"

"Yes, yes, Aaron. Fate, chance, or destiny has thrown us together strangely. God only knows what will be the end or where we may land; but, whatever may be your fate, I will share it with you."

"My own Margaret—my heart's best treasure!" exclaimed the enthusiastic lover, "what can I do to prove my devotion to you?"

"Be faithful, only, Aaron; be faithful, for my love's sake. You are engaged in a cause which cannot within the range of human possibility command success. I know it—I feel it. May I tell you what I know? Remember, I have said I will not do or say anything by which you may be compromised until the proper time; nor would I ask you to do or say anything which could conflict with the duties you now owe those with whom you are associated."

"Do you mean, Margaret, that I am to make my choice?"

"I thought you had made it," responded Margaret, with an air of coldness, half withdrawing her arm from that of her companion; but this was prevented by her companion, who, seizing her hand, drew it again within his own, and said:

"And have I not? I know no one—I know no tie—I know no allegiance save that which binds me to you. To call you mine—to know that you are mine—is the dearest wish of my heart, and I ask you only to teach me how I may soonest compass that."

"I am yours, Aaron, come weal, come woe; I love you with all the strength and ardor of first love. I have told you that I was ready to make any sacrifice rather than be separated from you, and I am still prepared to do it; but," and she spoke with deep earnestness, "I told you at the same time that if I was called upon to make the sacrifice which would keep us united, you would be the first to regret it. Do you remember that?"

"Well, Margaret, perfectly; and I did not make my choice."

"You did; but you act at times as if you had regretted it."

"Margaret!" exclaimed the major.

"I repeat, you act as if you regretted it. Now, Aaron, I shall put you to the test; I am ready to prove my love for you as I said; I am prepared to forsake father, family, friends, name, wealth, standing, for your sake; I am equally prepared to confer on you all I promised. Make your choice now and forever, and ever after abide by it."

"Margaret, and Margaret alone—I care only for you. Do with me as you choose."

"Will you accept the title I gave you this morning?"

"Not without you, Margaret; I would not accept a throne without you."

"In a few days, I cannot say how many, you shall have the proof of my sincerity and of my power. Aaron," and she spoke almost solemnly, "we are both young, but both have seen much of the world. I do not believe that two like ourselves were thus strangely brought together merely to meet and part. Our hearts sprang to each other from the first; did they not, Aaron?"

"Indeed and indeed they did," was the ardent response of the young officer, as he raised the hand which lay on his arm, and imprinted a fervent kiss upon it.

Now listen to me, Aaron, for I am going to give you my very soul."

Major Burr turned as if he would read the countenance of his companion; but the darkness forbade that, and he could only press her arm in acknowledgment of the confidence he was prepared to receive.

"I shall tell you all frankly, Aaron, because I know you will not betray *me*, at least. I am in constant communication with those whom you have been taught to look on as enemies; but who, for my sake, dearest, are henceforth your friends. Are they not?"

For an instant Major Burr was silent. He, of course surmised; nay, knew, from what she had previously said, that she was so strongly attached to the interests of the Royalists, she would not scruple at anything to serve that cause; but he had not known that she was so closely connected with the cause which he had learned to condemn. Indeed, until this moment, he scarcely realized his true position with regard to Margaret, and his pledges to her, so wildly, madly, blindly did he love her. The alternative was now plainly presented to him, and he either must lose her, or, in winning her, sacrifice all he had been accustomed to look upon as sacred and honorable. He must sacrifice name, position, character, reputation, and honor, but his reward would be Margaret. True, she had promised him wealth, rank, and station; but how could she, a mere girl, exercise such influence? If she could, would they restore to him the name and fame and character he must lose; and above all, the consciousness that he had proved faithless to his country's cause? These, and a hundred similar thoughts flashed through his brain in the few moments of silence which followed the last words uttered by Margaret, and his mind was not fixed upon anything definite, nor had he brought himself to resolve on any particular course of action, when he was aroused from his reverie by a gentle pressure of the arm which lay within his own, and at the same time he heard a gentle sigh.

These recalled him to himself, and seizing the hand which hung over his arm, he raised it to his lips, and murmured: "Dear Margaret, do with me as you choose; but do not tell me more now—do not insist that I shall so soon forget the ties which have hitherto bound me to those with whom I am associated now."

"I do not ask you, Aaron, to say, or do, nor even to think, anything by which you may be compromised or your fair name tarnished. I only ask that when the hour for action arrives, and it will soon come, you will act with us. Shall that be so?"

"By my love for you, yes," and he sealed his pledge with a kiss upon her fair hand.

"Now, Aaron, all I ask is, that you forget what I have told you for the present. I do not need aid from you, for I have means of information as correct as yourself. A very few days will decide which party is to be victorious."

"A very few days?" echoed the major, inquiringly.

"Yes, Aaron, a very few days. Even now the whole of his majesty's fleet is close at hand, bearing with it thousands of hardy, tried, and disciplined troops. If the blow which it is contemplated to strike first shall fail, those troops will be landed, and you know how poor a chance your undisciplined and half-clad men would stand against such an army as is already close at hand. I tell you, Aaron," and a glance of pride and triumph crossed her features as she spoke, "this war will be ended in less than three months; the rebellious colonists will be dealt severely with, while those who have remained true to their king, and, above all, those who have abjured or forsaken their errors, will be nobly rewarded. As for you, a few days will suffice to prove that Margaret Moncrieffe has promised nothing which she cannot perform."

"But, Margaret," inquired the major, almost in a whisper, "it is evident that some plot is hatching—some conspiracy breeding; do you count the consequences of an ultimate discovery, in case it should be ascertained that you were implicated?"

"My friends here will make every preparation for my security, and at the first alarm we would fly—would we not, Aaron—would you not go with me?"

"To the end of the world, Margaret. Everything for you—nothing without you. I will not ask, for I do not wish to know, what the plot is; it is better I should not. But I have given my word to you, and no matter what it may be, when the hour for action comes, you will find me ready."

"Do you know this young Blanchard, of McDougal's regiment?"

"I was only introduced to him this morning by his brother. What of him?"

"Nothing especial, only I desire unrestrained communication with him."

"So far as I can aid in that, no one shall prevent it."

"I am playing a little game with him."

"Surely, Margaret, you do not expect to buy him over to your side?"

"Our side, Aaron. No, that is already done. Gold has done that for him long ago. He had his price, and it was paid."

"Well, I must confess I am surprised. Are there others of"——

"Do not ask too much. Nothing is said or done in this city which is not known to Governor Tryon within twelve hours—not an order given which is not reported to him; and his plans are so well laid, and so many have pledged themselves to aid him in carrying them to consummation, that success is certain, and cannot be prevented except by an untimely discovery. Come, now, let us talk of other things," and Margaret, who possessed powers of conversation really fascinating, soon drew her lover from himself, by her vivid description of her beautiful home in England, of the wealth and luxury by which they would be surrounded, when at the close of the war, they could retire thither, and pass their days in the peaceful repose of domestic happiness. She told him of the court and its splendors; charmed him by the brilliant picture she drew of his future career in their new home, and when they parted, almost at midnight, with an ardent embrace, Major Burr was so completely enchanted, he would have enlisted under the banners of Beelzebub, provided Margaret belonged to the corps.

CHAPTER XXVI.

A DINNER PARTY AND A QUARREL.

AMONG the notabilities of New York, at the period of which this narration treats, none was more conspicuous than Major Smallwood, who commanded the Maryland battalion, which was distinguished as well for its splendid uniform (described in another chapter) as for the strict discipline which he preserved, despite the great license granted by other commanders. The major was a gallant southerner—a chivalrous, high-toned gentleman. Possessing in his own right an ample fortune, he had devoted that, as he had dedicated his life, to the cause of his country.

It was his practice to have a regular weekly mess-dinner, to which all the officers of his battalion were invited, and as many friends as his quarters would accommodate.

On the day after the last interview between the Blanchard brothers, his weekly dinner was given, and having heard, through Captain Barnum, of their relationship, and of the singular manner in which it had been discovered, both had been invited and accepted his invitation, but of course unknown to each other, as from the occasion of the interview before detailed, Arthur had studiously avoided all places where he might meet his brother.

Chance, or providence, or destiny, placed the brothers far apart at the table. Captain Arthur, the Royalist, was seated next to Captain Edwards, of the battalion, while Edmund had been assigned a seat near Major Smallwood, a compliment intentionally paid in view of the high state of discipline to which he had brought his corps.

The dinner passed off pleasantly. Wit and jest had flown freely around, and every one seemed to be on the best possible terms with everybody else. The cloth was removed, and the wines being duly placed on the table, the guests were called on severally for their toasts, and all, knowing the peculiar position of Captain Arthur Blanchard, were particular to avoid anything which might be construed into a possible intention to affront him.

It came at length to the turn of Edmund Blanchard to propose a toast, and as he rose, it was evident he had been indulging too freely in the generous wines which had been set before him.

When called upon, he arose, and leaning one hand on the table to steady himself, he proposed, "the Ninon d'Enclos of New York—Lizzie Brainard."

Truth compels me to say, that out of all that company present, there were very few who had ever heard or read of "Ninon d'Enclos," and fewer still who could appreciate the allusion conveyed in the toast. Most of them heard only the name of "Lizzie Brainard," and tossed off their glasses, thinking they were toasting her; while others, only half conscious of what they were doing, drank the toast, presuming that it was some special compliment to her.

There were, however, three present whose glasses remained untouched; Major Smallwood, Captain Edwards, and the Royalist Blanchard.

As Edmund Blanchard, already affected by the wine he had drank, tossed off his glass, he turned and glanced around the assemblage; his eye fell first on Captain Edwards, and he said with an asperity of manner excusable only from his condition, "I see you do not drink to my toast, Captain Edwards."

"I could not, sir," was the reply, coldly delivered.

"And why not, pray?" asked the young officer, now half aroused to anger, for he had drank just enough to take offence at the slightest cause.

"I will not insult any woman whom I believe to be honest, truthful and virtuous, by drinking to a sentiment which connects her name with so much infamy."

At these words many of the young officers who had drank the toast, hearing only Lizzie Brainard's name, pricked up their ears and looked at each other, as if wondering what they had done.

"You are mighty sensitive, sir," said the young officer, again filling his glass. Perhaps you did not hear the toast; let me repeat it."

"No, sir," responded Captain Edwards, arising, "you need not repeat it; I *will* not drink it."

"You will not?" asked Edmund, with a flushed face and flashing eyes.

"I have said so, sir," quietly responded Captain Edwards. "I will not insult any woman for whom I cherish so much respect as I do for Miss Brainard, by drinking such a toast."

"That is personal, sir," exclaimed Captain Blanchard, rising.

"I am content to have it so," coolly replied Captain Edwards, toying with his wine-glass, yet full.

"You will compel me to feel that you intend to insult me, Captain Edwards."

"I would rather have you think so, sir, than feel that I could be so base as to drag the name of a virtuous girl into such a connection."

"Virtuous!" laughed Captain Blanchard. "Oh, very well, sir, if you are her champion, I have no more to say, so you need not drink my toast. You know her, I suppose, as well as I do," and he spoke sneeringly.

"Gentlemen," said Major Smallwood, "this must stop," and he held up his own glass, yet untouched. "I would not drink to that toast, myself. Captain Edwards, I thank you for caring for the honor of our corps."

"Thank you, major," responded the captain, and as he spoke, he turned his wine upon the floor, with a glance of contempt at Edmund Blanchard.

"I understand you, sir," said the young Provincial, with a meaning look, "we can settle this hereafter. Major Smallwood, I ask your pardon for having proposed a sentiment which does not seem acceptable to Captain Edwards."

"Nor to me, sir," coolly said Major Smallwood, interrupting him.

"Oh, very well, one at a time. Captain Edwards, I drink my respects to you, and our speedy meeting."

Everybody present knew well what this meant, and no one was surprised when Captain Edwards, who had refilled his glass, turned it off, with a courteous bow to the young Provincial.

"Come, gentlemen," said Major Smallwood, who had been pained by this interruption to the harmony at the festive board, "allow me to propose a toast, and I scarcely think any gentleman will refuse to join me. If he does, I certainly shall not quarrel with him; I propose the belle of New York—Miss Moncrieffe."

The toast was responded to, not only by the prompt emptying of every glass, but was hailed with uproarious cheers; for every officer present had either seen Margaret, or had heard marvellous accounts of her matchless beauty and irresistible powers of fascination.

The harmony of the evening was completely destroyed by the rash conduct of Edmund Blanchard, and the guests departed at a much earlier hour than had been their wont on such occasions. Captain Edwards, as the door was reached, sought for, and took the arm of Captain Arthur Blanchard, and said, as they moved onward: "I suppose I shall have to fight that drunken fool."

"Yes," replied the captain, "I am afraid you will."

"Oh, you need not be afraid on my account. I was bred to honor and respect women, and when I heard the name of an honest, virtuous girl brought in such infamous contact, my manhood would not allow me to pass it unnoticed."

"From your remark, Captain Edwards," said the Royalist, "I surmise that you require the services of a friend."

"You have guessed rightly," was the response.

"Are you aware of the relationship existing between the officer who insulted you so grossly, and myself?"

"Assuredly not. I only know that you bear the same name—surely not an uncommon occurrence in a city garrisoned by thirteen thousand soldiers from every quarter of this widespread land."

"He is my younger brother—my only living relative—and when I say this, I am sure I have said enough to justify you in pardoning me for not offering my services at this moment."

"You surprise and distress me, Captain Blanchard," said Captain Edwards, with an expression of pain.

"Oh, do not feel distressed on my account. I am free to admit that he deserves no mercy at the hands of any gentleman; for a man who would thus ruthlessly drag a woman's name so publicly before a crowd of men, and darken her fair fame by such a foul insinuation, scarcely deserves the honor you intend according to him. But come, leaving her out of the question, how else can I serve you?"

"Find some one who will act as my friend in this matter; there are plenty in our battalion who would gladly serve me, but I ought not to ask them."

"I will see you to-morrow before seven o'clock, and bring with me one on whom you can rely. I shall be *with* you, but not *for* you, Captain Edwards," he added, sadly.

"I understand you, captain, and am the more grateful for your present kindness. At seven to-morrow?"

"At seven, Captain Edwards, you may rely upon me," and as they reached the corner of John street, the friends shook hands; the one to return to his quarters which he had just left, the other wended his way to the house occupied by Mrs. Brainard, for the hou. was not too late for a visit there, the dinner-party hav ng been broken up two hours before the usual time, by the rash and inconsiderate conduct of Edmund Blanchard.

The shop was closed; but the light streaming through the shutters, showed that the family had not retired. His rap at the door was answered, contrary to his expectations, but much to his pleasure, by a gruff, manly voice demanding who was there, and, at the announcement of his name, the door was instantly thrown open, and the captain found himself face to face with a fine, stalwart, hearty-looking young fellow, wearing the uniform of McDougal's regiment.

"Are you Lieutenant Brainard?" he asked, in a low voice, as he caught sight of the young officer.

"I am so called," was the reply, civilly returned, as the young soldier surveyed the visitor. "Will you not walk in, Captain Blanchard?"

"No, I thank you, not just now. Please put on your hat, and walk with me a few steps. Make any excuse to get away from your mother and sister. I wish very much to speak with you in private."

At this moment Lizzie, who had also heard the knock at the door, and whose heart, ever prompting her to think of Edmund, led her to hope it was himself, approached the door, and seeing the Royalist, pushed past her brother, and, extending her hand, said: "Oh, come in, captain; do come in."

"Thank you, no. This is your brother, I believe."

"Oh, I beg your pardon. Brother Albert, this is

Captain Blanchard, Edmund's brother, I have so often spoken of to you."

"Yes, Lizzie, he gave me his name before I opened the door; but he has declined to come in. He has some message for me. I will walk a little way with him, and return soon. Bring my hat, Lizzie; and as his sister went back into the house, Captain Blanchard whispered, "Don't answer any of her questions." Contrary to the usual custom of women, Lizzie brought her brother's hat, and actually suffered them to depart without asking a single question.

"Well, captain, and in what can I serve you?" asked the young officer, as they moved away from the house, arm in arm.

"You love your sister very much?" asked Arthur.

"That is a very singular question to ask me—her brother."

"She is worthy of your love, my young friend. But now to business. Her name has been most grossly misused to-night, and a friend of mine has taken it up for her. A challenge must follow. Will you serve the gentleman who has taken your sister's part?"

"No, by heavens!" exclaimed the young officer, firmly, "I will take his place."

"No, sir, that cannot possibly be. My peculiar position forbids that I should act for him, much as I approve his course. You will know all the circumstances to-morrow. Will you act in my stead, as the friend to him who has rescued your sister's name from infamous insinuations?"

"In any stead, sir, and thank you for the privilege You are very kind, Captain Blanchard, to grant me this favor. But who is the scoundrel who has dared to connect my sister's name with anything of wrong?"

"You will know in due time, and when you learn his name, you will not wonder that I have asked some one to take the place which I ought to have claimed. Now listen to me," and, linking arms with the young captain, he proceeded to narrate the occurrences of the dinner-table, concealing the name, however, of the offending party.

"And you will act for him?" he asked, when he had closed his narrative.

"With all my heart, though I would rather take his place. Captain, I am not used to anything of this kind. I must ask you to give me some instructions."

"Come, then, and share my quarters for the night, and I will put you in the way of serving your sister's friend. I am sorry to say I have been in many similar affairs. Return home now. Make any excuse you choose, and come around to my rooms as soon as you can get away; but be cautious, and do not say anything to alarm Lizzie or your mother."

The next morning before Captain Blanchard had finished his breakfast, Captain Edwards was at his rooms, and with a smile, handed him the missive he had just received.

"Captain Edwards," said Arthur, as he took the note, "this is Lieutenant Brainard, the brother of the young lady whose name and reputation you so promptly defended last night, and surely no one has a better right to act for you than himself."

The captain greeted the young soldier warmly, and a very few minutes sufficed to place him in possession of the circumstances which had led to this call for satisfaction.

The rage and shame of Albert Brainard, when he learned the name of him who had traduced his sister, were indescribable. He begged and implored the captain to let him take his place; but that was, of course, out of the question, and the preliminaries having been arranged between them, it was settled that the meeting should take place in the Bowery lane (now at the junction of the Third and Fourth Avenues), at an early hour on the following morning, and everything was left to Captain Blanchard and the young Provincial.

When Captain Edwards had left, Captain Blanchard gradually, but kindly, communicated to him his brother's desertion of Lizzie, and his sudden attachment to Miss Moncrieffe, but he did not dare to tell him all he had heard—that would come to him soon enough, no matter what might be the result of the meeting between the two officers.

Everything being arranged, Albert Brainard returned to his mother's home with a weight upon his heart, such as he had never known before. He dreaded to make known to his sister what he had heard as to the infidelity of Captain Blanchard, to whom he knew she was strongly attached, and whom they had looked upon as her future husband. When he reached the house, he was not sorry to find his mother absent, and taking a seat opposite his sister, in their little parlor, which commanded a full view of the shop, he looked at her as she sat there, the personation of youth, health and innocent beauty, and his heart ached as he dwelt upon the blow which he was about to inflict; and as she raised her eyes from her work and fixed them upon him with looks of sisterly affection, tears gathered in his own. Lizzie perceived the tears coursing down her brother's cheeks, and hastily dropping her work, arose and placing one hand on his shoulder, inquired, soothingly, what ailed him.

"I have heard some very unpleasant news this morning, Lizzie."

"I am sorry for you, Albert," she said, smoothing down his hair as she spoke. "Can I do anything to cheer you?"

"Poor Lizzie!" he said, "you need comfort more than I shall. My news concerns you as deeply as myself."

"Concerns me, Albert," she exclaimed, with a start, and as she spoke, the color deserted her cheeks.

"You have heard, of course, of this young lady at General Putnam's—Miss Moncrieffe—everybody is talking about her."

Lizzie could not reply with words; a choking sensation about the throat prevented her utterance, but she nodded her head affirmatively.

"Have you heard her name mentioned in connection with that of any officer in the city?"

Dark forebodings crossed Lizzie's mind, as her brother spoke thus, for her heart half divined what he hesitated to say.

"How does that concern me, Albert?" she asked, in tones of deep emotion.

"Edmund Blanchard has forgotten his honor, manhood, and truth, and"——

"Oh, don't say that, brother!" Lizzie exclaimed, in tones of agony, and as she spoke a shudder ran through her frame.

"Lizzie, dear, my darling sister, remember who you are, and what you owe to yourself. Edmund Blanchard is unworthy the love of any virtuous woman"——

Before he could finish the sentence, the hapless girl, through whose busy brain ran with lightning speed the memory of her past, and the prospect of her dark, dismal future; the sacrifices she had made for him who had now proved faithless; the terrible consequences which must result from a discovery of her shame—a mother broken-hearted, a brother disgraced--and, for herself, the scorn and contempt of the world—all flashed across her mind, and with one deep sob, she made an effort to approach her brother, but ere she could reach him, sank heavily upon the floor in a death-like swoon.

Albert Brainard had expected tears and reproaches, but he had not looked for such a demonstration of feeling, and, affrighted, he sprang forward and lifting the helpless girl, laid her upon a couch which stood on one side of the room.

Fortunately, during this scene, no person had entered the shop, and Albert had, therefore, ample opportunity to attend to his helpless sister, and was enabled to avoid the answering of any questions. In a few minutes, by the aid of water and the application of such simple restoratives as he could lay his hands on, Lizzie recovered her consciousness; and when she languidly opened her eyes, she met those of her brother fixed upon her with an expression of love and pity.

A deep sigh broke from her lips, a shudder ran through her frame, and as she closed her eyes again, her brother perceived tears trickling through the closed lids.

"Oh, Lizzie!" he murmured, bending over her, "did you so love that worthless villain?"

Lizzie made no reply, but shook her head languidly and mournfully, conveying an impression deeper than any which mere words could express.

"No matter, my dear sister, he will have his punishment soon. He insulted Captain Edwards last night and he has been challenged. They meet to-morrow, and if Captain Edwards does not shoot him, I will."

Still Lizzie made no reply; but as she heard these words, her tears flowed more freely, and her whole frame was convulsed with indescribable emotion. What booted his death to her? Would it restore her honor sacrificed on the altar of her trusting love? Would it screen her from the scorn of the world? These and similar thoughts crossed her, and as her brother finished speaking, she arose from her recumbent position slowly, and fixing her eyes, still running over with tears, on him, said: "I hardly know if I have heard you rightly, Albert; were you saying that Edmund Blanchard had proved false to me?"

"False to you, and faithless to every sentiment of honor, truth, or manhood. Miss Moncrieffe, it seems, has so completely" ——

"Miss Moncrieffe!" exclaimed Lizzie, actually dashing away the tears from her eyes; "and he has deserted me for her? Brother, I must see that woman."

"Woman, Lizzie! she is hardly more than a child."

"Be she what she may, I must and will see her. She shall know, at least, his faithlessness and my wrongs."

"It would be folly, Lizzie—it would be worse than folly—besides, it would only bring on you remarks which now will never be made; for no one but ourselves know of the affair."

"The whole city will ring with it ere long, Albert," she replied, sadly, though he little dreamed of the full import of her words. "Yes, my dear brother, the city will know it all in time," and she shuddered as she spoke; for the thoughts of the certain infamy which would be entailed on her, and the misery which would be brought on those who loved her so dearly, flashed through her brain. "No, Albert, I must see Miss Moncrieffe—I *will* see her, and you must not try to prevent me. I do not believe that she, whatever she may be, would receive the attentions of a man like Edmund Blanchard when she knows the truth. Come, brother, I am better," and she wiped the tears from her eyes; and with a great effort, regained her composure, at least to outward appearances.

"I think you do yourself a great wrong, in humbling yourself before Miss Moncrieffe or any other woman."

"I shall not humble myself, rest assured. I cannot forget the respect I owe to myself or my family; so, dear brother, have no fears for me on that score. I only desire that Miss Moncrieffe shall know my position with regard to Edmund Blanchard, and then she may take her own course."

"I suppose you feel that you are acting right; but I cannot agree with you—so act at your own pleasure.

I must go and finish my preparations for the meeting which is to take place to-morrow morning."

The entrance of Mrs. Brainard at this moment put an end to the conversation on this subject; for, by tacit consent, brother and sister agreed not to distress her by communicating intelligence which they knew would cause her so much wretchedness.

Albert soon took his leave, with a meaning glance at his sister, which was returned, and in a few minutes, Lizzie, making some pretence for her absence, put on her hat and shawl and left the house.

CHAPTER XXVII.

MARGARET AND LIZZIE BRAINARD.

MISS MONCRIEFFE was seated in her own room; her sewing lay unnoticed in her lap, and, from the expression of her countenance, it was evident that she was engrossed in pleasant thoughts.

"A young woman to see you," said Belle Putnam, gently opening the door, without waiting for an answer to her summons.

Margaret started from her reverie, and, hastily passing her hand across her forehead, as if to collect her wandering thoughts, said, with an expression of surprise: "A young woman, Belle, to see me?"

"Yes, my lady," replied Belle, with an affectation of profound respect; for, since the little escapade of the letter from Governor Tryon, so skillfully misinterpreted, Belle had made a confidant of Margaret, and had intrusted to her the secret of her own heart. "Your ladyship, I suppose, expected" ——

"My ladyship didn't expect anything or anybody," said Margaret, with a smile. "But really, I can't imagine what any young woman can want with me; I don't know half a dozen ladies in the city, and they would not feel flattered to hear Miss Belle Putnam call them young women! But no matter, I will see her here if you have no objections. There may be somebody in the parlor, and perhaps she desires to see me in private," and as she spoke, the thought crossed her mind that the visitor might be some emissary from her Royalist friends, who had found it necessary to communicate with her through such a medium.

In a very few moments the door was closed upon a young and certainly very handsome woman, a stranger to Margaret, who, scanning her hastily, and perceiving she was neatly dressed, invited her to take a seat; and as the stranger sank into a chair, Margaret, with another hasty glance, discovered she was pale, was trembling excessively, and that her eyes bore traces of recent tears.

"What can I do for you?" she asked, in kind and earnest tones.

For an instant her visitor, Lizzie Brainard, could not speak. Sobs were rising in her throat, which she choked down with a strong effort, and tears were coming from her eyes, which she vainly strove to force back.

Margaret noticed her excessive agitation, and paused a moment to allow her to recover her composure.

"Come, young lady," she repeated at length, "in what can I serve you?"

"In all—in everything—and you alone can serve me," replied Lizzie, clasping her hands, and looking up to Margaret with streaming eyes.

"Then I will, most assuredly," said Margaret, whose interest was already awakened in the young stranger, for as the reader has already discovered, she was one of those impulsive creatures who act always on the first promptings of her feelings.

"Oh, thank and bless you," said Lizzie, striving to dry her tears.

"Never mind thanks yet. Now what can I do?"

"Captain Blanchard," said Lizzie. "You know him?"

"Oh, yes," said Margaret, for the instant thrown off her guard, supposing Lizzie was a messenger from the Royalist captain; "he has known me ever since I was a child; he is a very dear friend of my father's."

"I did not know you had ever met before," said Lizzie, her countenance expressing the disappointment she experienced at these words. "Edmund never mentioned your name to me."

"Oh, Captain Edmund, you mean," said Margaret, glad that she had not committed herself, yet wondering what could have brought this strange girl to her with that name on her lips.

"Yes, Miss Moncrieffe, that is the one I mean. I do not know his brother; I never saw him but once, to know them as brothers. I am speaking of Captain Edmund Blanchard."

"You speak very familiarly of him," said Margaret, eyeing her visitor with a keen, scrutinizing glance.

"I have a right to do so, Miss Moncrieffe."

"But in what can I serve you, so far as he is concerned?" and Margaret looked at Lizzie with an air of surprise.

"In what can you serve me? Why, Miss Moncrieffe, are you not engaged to him?—I do not mean exactly that," she interrupted herself, seeing the heightened color on Margaret's cheeks. "Is he not paying attention to you?"

"Pray tell me, young woman, first what is your name? I can converse with you perhaps, with more freedom when I know it."

'Lizzie Brainard."

"Then, Lizzie, pray tell me what earthly reason you have for asking me such an absurd, such a ridiculous, question? I won't call it impertinent, for I think I can interpret the motive of your visit, and I will ease your mind at once. I never saw Captain Blanchard—your captain—more than half a dozen times in my life, and have no more thoughts of him than a score of others, who find amusement in paying compliments and flatteries to me."

"And is he not paying attention to you? Oh, do excuse my freedom, miss, but I am very unhappy. I only heard this morning that he was paying attentions to you, and that he had spoken slightingly of me, and it made me very unhappy to hear it, I assure you."

"If Captain Blanchard has said anything by which

any one might connect my name with his own, he has uttered a willful, malicious falsehood. I have never given him reason to think that I would receive his attentions, and certainly, knowing what I now do, I would not, on any consideration. So take heart, Lizzie, and believe me, I do not care a pin's head for your captain, nor do I believe he does for me, except that he has seen a new face, though I am sure yours is pretty enough for any one," and she gazed earnestly at Lizzie, whose countenance, while Margaret was speaking, had been gradually lighted up with pleasure. "But is there anything else in which I can serve you?"

"Oh, yes, Miss Moncrieffe. You are here at head-quarters—do have that duel stopped. I have heard that you can do almost anything with General Putnam."

"Duel, child! I do not know what you are talking about. You have not said anything about a duel."

"Yes, miss, last night Edmund and Captain Edwards, of Major Smallwood's corps, quarrelled, and they are to fight to-morrow morning. Oh, do stop it, Miss Moncrieffe."

"What was the cause of this quarrel? No matter what was the cause; for your sake Lizzie, as you have come to me, I will stop it; so you may rest quiet on that score."

"Thank you, again and again, Miss Moncrieffe. You have made me very happy."

"And you love Captain Blanchard so much?"

"Oh, better than my life, miss—better than words can tell."

"And he was deserting you on my account?"

"So I heard from my brother."

"Well, well—set your heart at rest. The duel shall not come off, and, I pledge you my word, your captain shall never see me but once more."

After a further short conversation, in the course of which Margaret reassured poor Lizzie of the interest she took in her, she took leave of Margaret with a light heart, for she felt that once Edmund was without the pale of Margaret's charms, she could win back his waning love.

Margaret was prompt to act as to speak, and before three hours had passed, Captains Blanchard and Edwards were summoned to General Putnam's quarters.

"Gentlemen," said the bluff old general, when they stood before him, "the enemy is expected here daily, and no one knows when our city may be attacked. Our country needs every man for its defence, and you have no right to throw away, in a private quarrel, lives which belong to your country."

The captains looked at each other in amazement, for they could not imagine how the matter had come to the general's ears, but they bowed an acquiescence to his remarks.

"Unless," continued the general, "you pledge to me your words as gentlemen to pursue this no further, for the present, at least, I shall put you both under arrest, and keep you there until after the battle, which we will have soon to fight, is decided. You are both brave men, I know, and I think this might be arranged. Come, tell me what it is all about?"

"I beg your pardon, general," said Captain Edwards, "I leave that to Captain Blanchard."

"General Putnam," said the officer thus applied to, "I was wrong; I acted rashly and foolishly. Captain Edwards, if I had not been drinking, I should not have said what I did, nor acted as I did. I am really sorry for it, and ask your pardon."

"That's right—that's manly," fairly shouted the general. "Captain Edwards give him your hand. There; I like that," he continued, as the late foes shook hands. "Captain Edwards, will you do me the favor to say to Major Smallwood I wish very much to see him;" and the captain, with a cool salute to Captain Blanchard, bowed himself out.

"Captain Blanchard," said the general, "Miss Moncrieffe has intrusted me with a request to see you; you will find her in the parlor;" and with a very distant salute, he pointed to the door of the parlor, which adjoined the office in which they had been seated.

Captain Blanchard entered the room with a feeling of apprehension for which he could not account, and his heart fairly sunk within him as he saw Margaret seated there.

Closing the door, he approached her, but she did not rise or invite him to take a seat, but gazed upon him with a look of sternness and contempt, strangely blended.

"Captain Blanchard," she said, with a cold, stern expression, as he stood before her, unable to bear the gaze of her piercing eyes, "I have heard that you have been taking most unwarrantable liberties with my name."

"Oh, Margaret!" —— he exclaimed.

But she hastily interrupted him, by saying: "Miss Moncrieffe, sir. You will please to remember, Captain Blanchard, that a few harmless pleasantries passed between a lady and a gentleman," and she placed a terrible emphasis on that word, "do not give him the privilege of boasting of a conquest, nor using her name in such close connection with his own, as I have heard that you have done with mine. I wish you good morning, sir;" and before the astounded officer could reply, she arose with the grace and dignity of a queen, and moving toward the door, turned to him and added, "you had better go and ask pardon of one who has much greater cause of complaint than I have, against you. It was for her sake, sir, and not for yours, and I have to tell you this, for fear you might boast of my interest in you, that I have interfered to stop this meet ing. Good morning, captain," and before he could recover from his stupefaction, Captain Blanchard was alone.

He did not dare face General Putnam, for he knew that Margaret had communicated everything to him, but stole quietly out of the house and moved moodily toward his quarters, cursing himself, Margaret, and more and deeper than all, poor, disgraced Lizzie, whom he conjectured, though he knew not why, was at the bottom of the whole.

Captain Edwards, ignorant, of course, of the cause which had interfered with the meeting, retired to his quarters, where he found Lieutenant Brainard awaiting him, to whom he communicated the affair which had just transpired, and he at once made known to his friend, his belief that his sister and Miss Moncrieffe had outwitted the whole of them. He then communicated to the captain his position and that of his sister, with reference to Captain Blanchard, and expressed a determination to seek the earliest opportunity of insulting him so grossly that no apology could be received. Captain Edwards of course proffered his services, which were accepted, and after a glass of wine the friends parted.

CHAPTER XXVIII.

CONSEQUENCES OF SETH'S ESCAPE.

THE attempt to send a spy among the Royalists who were in the habit of frequenting Corbie's house, and its failure, had shown to the conspirators that they were watched, because suspected, and it was therefore resolved no more assemblages should be held there for especial purposes, but that henceforth their head-quarters should be at the tavern of Thomas Mason, also a devoted Royalist, which being situated directly opposite General Putnam's residence, would be less liable to suspicion; for it was very natural to suppose that the general would not think of looking for a nest of conspirators at his very door.

Mason's house, which was known by the sign of the "Highlanders," was therefore the place whence all communications would emanate for the future.

Corbie's (from its proximity to the river, and the facility which its situation afforded for landing of a boat without fear of discovery) was still the depot for the receipt of the letters and messages so constantly passing between Governor Tryon and Mayor Matthews (then at Flatbush) and the Tory residents of the city who had joined the ranks of the conspirators.

Forbes and Corbie took upon themselves to inform the leaders in the city of the occurrences narrated in a previous chapter, and to give the necessary caution as to their future watchfulness; for a discovery now, would not only foil all their plans, but would probably send many of them to the gallows; a fate which, however merited, they were not yet prepared to meet.

A few days after the disappearance of Seth Adams, General Washington returned to the city from his official visit to Philadelphia, and a council of generals being convened, he communicated to them the certain information that the fleet under Admiral Howe, with a very large body of troops, including several thousand Hessian soldiers all under the command of Lord Howe, were even now on the voyage to New York, which would be the first point of attack, and who might be expected daily.

Orders were given for the strengthening of all the fortifications on the island which would present any point of attack to the invaders, and Long Island, within the circuit of several miles from the city, was directed to be fortified and occupied, as a landing would most probably be first attempted there.

The most stringent rules were promulgated for the government of the Tory residents of the city; many were sent out of the city; others, who had given bonds for their good behavior, and pledged themselves not to take side against the colonists, were imprisoned, on information that they had violated their parole by too free speech, as well as by their actions, among which was the refusal to take Continental money at par. The houses of Corbie, Mason, Houndling, and of Forbes, the noted gunsmith, all devoted Royalists, were put under strict surveillance, and the difficulty of communication between the conspirators on board the Duchess of Gordon, and those in the city, was very much augmented by the measures thus adopted.

Every officer and soldier was now more constantly and busily engaged than ever, in carrying out the orders of the commander-in-chief, and Major Burr found few opportunities of private conversation with Margaret; but even in the moments which they managed to steal unnoticed, their vows of mutual love and fidelity were again and again renewed, and Margaret comforted her lover by the assurance that the hour for action was near at hand, and that their future would be all sunlight and happiness.

On one occasion she found time to say to him, while a bright smile illumined her face, "I told you, Colonel Burr, I would keep my promise."

"So you really meant it, Margaret?" he asked, eagerly.

"Did I ever deceive you, Aaron?"

"Never, Margaret, never."

"I have in my apartment, at this moment, the commission of a colonel in the army of King George, in blank, which awaits only the insertion of your name by me, to confer upon you the rank and title which I promised should be yours."

"How little worth would that be without you," he said, gazing with looks of fond devotion upon the lovely speaker who had so enslaved him.

And she spoke the truth. Governor Tryon, who could not but acknowledge the valuable and most important services she was constantly rendering to the king's cause, could not, and did not deny her request, but dispatched to her the commission she had desired, in blank, leaving her to insert such name as she might select, receiving however, her assurance that it was intended for one of whom the Royal army might be proud, and who, young as he was, had won a name and reputation excelled by none in the army, for every quality which goes to make up the soldier; one, whose name, however, from prudential reasons, she thought proper not to disclose at the present time. Governor Tryon had already received such abundant evidence of her discretion, that he was perfectly willing to trust her to any extent, and therefore his readiness to confide to her such an important document in blank.

The gaieties of the city were nearly suspended by the

necessity for making preparations to receive the enemy; but the wives and families of such officers as were on the island continued to visit each other, and, of course, on these occasions the posture of affairs was freely canvassed.

What Margaret did not hear in person, she was sure to hear through Belle or Mattie, who were glad enough to escape from the spinning-wheel, and steal a gossipping chat with Margaret.

Everything she heard—everything she saw—was immediately made known to Governor Tryon, through the Royalist Blanchard, who had said with truth, and it might be escaped any taint of suspicion, that no one in the city had rendered such essential service to the cause of the Royalists, as did Margaret Moncrieffe.

The sentry who was in charge of the "brig," had quite forgotten all about his prisoner's request, and his own gruff reply; for he had resumed the attempt to read as soon as Seth had turned away, and was thus occupied when his relief came to take his place. With a yawn, and a few curses upon the weather, he gave up his post, and retired to his hammock, entirely unmindful of what had transpired, and never once cast his eyes toward the prisoners over whom he had been placed in charge. The other marine, of course, knew nothing of what had occurred before he went on his post, and, taking up the book which his companion had thrown down on the mess-chest, he was very soon as deeply absorbed in its pages as his comrade had been.

This neglect on the part of the marine was most fortunate for Seth; for he was a prisoner of so much importance, and was in possession of such weighty secrets (though it was thought that he knew nothing beyond what he had heard at Corbie's, while he lay gagged and bound), his safe keeping was most essential, and instant pursuit in every direction would have followed the information that he was missing.

It was not until daylight, when all hands were turned out, and the master-at-arms came, as usual, to resume his charge of the prisoners, that he was missed, and the information was at once communicated to Governor Tryon and Captain Chiffney. Great was the trouble and confusion incident upon this revelation. A thorough and strict search was made in every part of the ship, and every spot not half large enough to have held a boy of ten years of age, much less the stalwart young soldier, was ransacked; but, as may be imagined, the search was unavailing. The sentries in charge of the "brig" during the night (four in number), were called up and examined. Each swore through thick and thin that the prisoners were all secured when they took post, and they swore to what they really believed; but this did not save them. A prisoner, and a most important one, had escaped from one of them, and as the guilty one could not be found out, all were treated alike.

The formality of a court-martial was not necessary, and within two hours after the discovery that Seth Adams had escaped, each of them had received three dozen with the cat well laid on, and were permitted to groan and writhe upon the berth deck, until the condition of their lacerated backs might enable them to return to their duty.

Governor Tryon held a consultation with Captain Chiffney and the principal naval and army officers on board, upon this occasion. As all the evidence went to show that the prisoner, when last seen, was securely ironed, it was deemed impossible that he could have escaped alive if he had fallen or jumped overboard. Even had his hands been free, it was deemed equally impossible that he could have reached the shore on such a night; but, to make matters more sure, a boat was dispatched to Staten Island to ascertain if any person had landed within range of any of the sentries which lined the shore during the night.

The assurance being given that no one had been seen, the presumption seemed fair that he had fallen or jumped overboard in an insane attempt to escape, and had been drowned, and the majesty of the law "martial" having been vindicated by the punishment of the offending marines, nothing more was said about it. But Colonel Fanning was instructed, on the occasion of his next visit to Corbie's with dispatches, to notify him of the circumstances, at the same time, however, intimating the impression of the governor as to the impossibility of Seth's escape.

CHAPTER XXIX.

THE PATRIOT GIRL.

THE stringent orders issued by the commander-in-chief, on resuming his command, rendered, as has been said, communication between the conspirators more than usually hazardous. But the stake was too great to be lost sight of, and the boat continued to ply between the "Duchess of Gordon," the head-quarters of Governor Tryon, and the city, a set of signals having been arranged, by which due warning of danger was given. Corbie had been, in accordance with the instructions of Governor Tryon, informed of the loss or escape of Seth Adams, a matter, however, which he treated so lightly, that he had mentioned it in jest to Forbes and one or two of his intimates, and they agreed with the governor as to the impossibility of his having escaped alive.

They therefore continued to send and receive messages as usual, though with more than the ordinary caution, for as the crisis approached, they realized not only their own personal danger, but feared for the success of the important enterprise in which they were embarked. Thus far everything had prospered as well as could be desired. More than five hundred men were enlisted with them, many bound to the cause by ties of loyalty which nothing could shake, others bought over by gold and promises of future grandeur. They awaited now only the arrival of the fleet bearing Lord Howe, and the mine laid with such consummate skill and caution was ready to be sprung, and while they are reposing in this fancied security, let us turn to Seth Adams.

"Seth, dear Seth," said the old lady, as he gave signs of returning animation, after swallowing the rum Patsy had brought him, "what on airth does this mean?"

"Wait a little, aunty," said Seth, in a feeble voice, for he was weakened almost to helplessness. "Patsy, give me some more," and the bottle was again handed to him, from which he drew another hearty pull. "Now, aunty," he said, straightening himself up. "Oh, Patsy! I forgot—bring me something," and he pointed to his naked and bleeding body. "Never mind them, they are only scratches," and as he spoke, Patsy had run into the adjoining room, and returned almost immediately with some of her late father's clothes. "There, that will do—that's enough for the present, Patsy," he said, as he slipped a shirt over his bleeding shoulders. "I have no time now for ceremony. Patsy, you or aunt must go to the city to-day."

"Go to the city!" they exclaimed in a breath, but

before they could say more, he interrupted them, saying:

"Yes, to the city, and that immediately. Now listen to me. I am too weak, too exhausted, to attempt it, and it is absolutely necessary that some one should go—nay, must go."

"My dear Seth," said Patsy, smoothing down his tangled, matted hair, "you are not yourself—you are wild; wait—rest a while; get some sleep, and then you can say what you wish, and"——

"Patsy," exclaimed Seth, rising from his chair with a great effort, for he was really almost exhausted by his long immersion in the water, and his subsequent journey through the woods, "listen to me. The safety of General Washington—perhaps the fate of our country—depends on you or me being in the city to-night. I am willing to go, but I know I never could reach it alive, and you"——

"Oh, Seth, Seth, what do you mean?" exclaimed Patsy, whose patriotic soul had been fired by these words.

"Listen to me a few moments," he said, sinking languidly back in his chair, for he was too weak to stand longer; "I was taken prisoner ten days ago in New York; I've been on board the 'Duchess of Gordon' a prisoner until last night, when, by God's help, I escaped. Now, Patsy, even if I was strong enough to reach the city, as a man I might be over taken and captured by some one, for no one would believe what I have to tell. Will you go to the city?"

"Anything, Seth. I will crawl there on my hands and knees, if I can serve the dear, good General Washington."

"Then, Patsy, you must go, if you have to walk every step of the way. Now hearken to me, for time is precious. You must go directly to Major Burr," and as he uttered that name, Patsy colored deeply, for with true maidenly modesty, she shrank from seeking one toward whom she was so peculiarly situated. "Yes, Patsy," he continued, noticing her heightened color, "go directly to Major Burr, for he got me into this infernal scrape, and I suppose he thinks I have deserted. Tell him I was seized, bound and gagged at Corbie's on the night he sent me there; that I have been on board the 'Duchess of Gordon' ever since, and only escaped last night by swimming ashore. Say to him that a plot is on foot, which, if not stopped now, will result in ruin to our cause. The city is full of conspirators; I can't name all of them, for I have not heard the names, but a boat goes up almost every night to Corbie's house from the ship. I know that a Captain Blanchard is one of them, and there was said something about a woman, who gave them every information. Corbie, to whose house the major sent me, and Forbes, the gunsmith, are mixed up with it. Tell nim that, as soon as the British fleet comes in, it is their plan to sail up either river; that the Tories in the city, and the men whom they have bought over, intend to make an attack on General Washington's quarters, take him prisoner, blow up the magazines, and destroy King's Bridge, and that their hope is, when Washington is secured, the rebels, as they call us, hemmed in on the island, will be glad to come to terms at once. I have picked this up on board the ship. I know—I feel it is true. Will you, Patsy, make it known to him?"

"Will I, Seth? What a question to ask. I'll go this very hour."

"Yes, Patsy, delay now might be fatal to the country. Tell Major Burr that as soon as I can stir I shall be at my post."

"Did you ever see that young girl who was staying with us, Seth?" and Patsy colored as she spoke.

"I have never seen her; but I have heard of her almost every day. She is quite a character in the city, and is invited everywhere. Come, Patsy, get your breakfast and be off. You will have a long ride."

"I am to have a long walk, Seth," she replied, with a quiet but meaning smile; and the young soldier looked in her face for an explanation, for he knew they owned a horse.

"Old grey was stolen a couple of weeks since; but no matter, I may find some one going to the city, and get a ride a part of the way. But, ride or walk, General Washington shall know what you have told me before I sleep to-night."

"God bless you, brave Patsy!" said Seth, warmly; "you deserve to be a soldier's wife, and I hope you'll get a good one for a husband."

"Go along," she said, coloring deeply; for she knew he was aware of her attachment to Major Burr, and, moving away, she commenced preparations for the morning meal.

Rest and the generous liquor which he had swallowed, had already so far restored Seth, he sat up and joined in the conversation of the family. Once or twice he arose, and essayed to move across the floor; but his limbs were so sore and stiffened by their long immersion in the water, and by his tremendous efforts to force his way through the woods, the attempt proved futile, and he sunk back in his seat with a heavy sigh and groan.

"There, Seth; don't try," said Patsy, as she hurried to and fro, preparing the frugal meal; "it will only keep you back, and I know how anxious you are to return to your post and pay off the score you owe the Royalists. Suppose I can't find Major Burr, shall I go directly to General Washington?" she asked, pausing in the middle of her work, and addressing the young soldier.

"Of course, Patsy—of course; the information con

cerns him directly. By the way, I remember now I heard the name of a man named Hickey as one of the conspirators. There is a guardsman of that name, but it can't be him. I wonder who that woman can be?" he said, half to himself, and evidently striving to recall something he had forgotten. "No matter; don't forget the names I have told you already."

"Never fear, Seth," replied Patsy, her eye kindling with pleasure as she spoke, at the thought of the important service it was to be her privilege to render to the cause of her country.

"Come, let me draw you up, Seth," she said, approaching the soldier; but, to her surprise, he made no reply, and, on looking closely at him, she discovered that his exhausted nature had succumbed, and even while listening to her, sleep had overcome him.

"Hush, mother!" she said, softly, placing one hand on her lips, and with the other pointing to the sleeping youth.

"Poor Seth! he has had a terrible time of it; just think, Patsy, of his being in the water so long, and then walking through them woods after all that. Poor fellow! how he must have suffered."

"Come, mother, sit down; I must be off as soon as possible—let me see," and she turned to a large, old-fashioned clock, which stood in one corner of the kitchen—"it's now half-past six. By smart walking, I ought to be there before twelve. Perhaps I may get a ride—who knows?—no matter. Now," she continued, between the mouthfuls, "don't be frightened if I am not at home to-night. If I have to walk all the way, I am sure I shan't be back to-day; so be easy. Seth will be with you. Now my hat," and hastily swallowing the remainder of her cup of coffee, went to her room, and returned in a few moments attired for her journey.

"There, good bye mother, till I see you again," she said, as the tears gathered in her eyes, and she held up her mouth for the mother's kiss; but her mother, rising from her chair, approached, and, placing a hand on either shoulder, said, with an air of solemnity:

"May the Lord bless and keep my dear, brave daughter on her journey of duty. Go, Patsy, and God grant you a safe return." Then flinging herself on her daughter's neck, she gave away to the emotions she had long struggled to keep down.

For a moment or two, mother and daughter mingled their tears; and at length, with a long kiss of love, Patsy withdrew from her parent's embrace, and, with one lingering look, in which her glance took in everything in the room, she boldly stepped from the door, and started alone and unprotected on her perilous but most important mission.

CHAPTER XXX.

THE PLOT DISCLOSED.

Margaret Moncrieffe was walking in the garden of General Putnam's house, which, as has been said, at that period ran nearly down to the water's edge, and which was beautifully laid out with trees and shrubbery and flowers. It was in full sight of Fort George, the site of the present Battery, and commanded also a fine view of the spot where the periaguas and other boats which were plying to and from Paulus Hook, landed their passengers.

It was a little past noon, and as a fresh breeze was blowing from the southwest, the air was refreshingly cool, coming as it did over such an expanse of water.

Margaret always chose the garden as her resort when she wished to meditate, and many a brief but important communication had been made to her over the fence which separated the garden from the road which led to the ferry-landing, now known as Battery Place.

She was walking in the garden, evidently in high good humor with herself and everybody else. Her star was now in the ascendant; she loved with all the depth and intensity of her passionate nature, and was beloved in return, and if anything could have endeared her lover more to her, it was the fact that he had for her sake, joined the cause in which every feeling of her heart was enlisted.

She had rendered essential service to that cause, and had received her reward, not only in the high commendations and warm thanks of Governor Tryon, but in the commission which she had been enabled to procure for her betrothed. Her active, busy brain was at work still, for as long as there was work to be done, she must keep in motion. Everything thus far had gone on swimmingly; the plans of Governor Tryon had succeeded to his entire satisfaction. He had not only many hundreds of devoted Royalists in the city ready to act at the proper moment, but many valuable acquisitions had been made to their ranks from the Continental troops. The mine was constructed, the fuse laid, and on the signal from the proper source it was ready to be lighted, and death and destruction scattered abroad by the explosion.

While meditating upon her possible future when the war should be over, and she should be united to her heart's master, surrounded in her own country by all the appliances of wealth and luxury, and blessed with his companionship, she chanced to turn her eyes toward the river, and perceived a periagua which plied regularly between the city and Paulus Hook, approaching the landing.

She went to the fence which skirted the garden, and shaded by a cherry-tree which was near by, stood watching its approach, and the persons who were passengers, of whom there seemed to be quite a number.

There were farmers with produce for the city, some soldiers from the breast-works at Paulus Hook, and three females. As they landed from the boat, they passed near the spot where she was standing, one by one, and when nearly all were gone, she turned to resume her walking and thinking.

At that moment one of the females approached close to the spot where she was standing, and instantly Margaret's attention was attracted to her; for a casual glance at the dusty, travel-worn, flushed and heated woman, disclosed a familiar face—that of Patsy Adams, who, somewhat rested after her long and toilsome walk, by her sail across the bay, for she had walked the entire distance, was moving slowly along, ever and anon casting glances at the house occupied by General Putnam.

"Patsy," exclaimed Margaret, as she caught sight of the well-remembered face; and Patsy turned to the place whence the voice proceeded. At first she did not discover any one, and thinking that her ears must have deceived her, was turning away, when Margaret, in louder tones, repeated her name, and added: "Here, Patsy, it's Margaret; don't you see me?"

For an instant Patsy looked again in the direction of the voice, and this time she discovered Margaret's face peering over the fence, and as she approached, Margaret addressed her in kind tones, saying:

"Why, Patsy, how very hot and tired you look. Where did you come from?"

"From home, and on foot. But how well you look, Margaret," and she gazed with a pang at the beautiful girl, for she had not forgotten that he whom she loved, and had breathed vows of love to her, had been under the influence of such charms since they had parted.

"Oh, I am well enough. But what on earth could have induced you to walk such a distance on such a day?"

"Oh, that's a secret," said Patsy, with a quiet smile. "I want to see Major Burr; can you tell me where he is now?"

"Oh, I suppose," replied Margaret, carelessly, though she understood the point of Patsy's question, "he's in the office. Did you come all the way on foot on such a day to see him, Patsy?" and Margaret looked searchingly at the young girl.

"I did," was the reply, and as she spoke, Patsy drew herself up, with an expression on her countenance which conveyed to Margaret the well-merited rebuke she intended. "I have urgent business with him, and I must see him immediately."

"I will show you his office. Here, Patsy, you can come in by this gate;" and, moving on a few steps, she opened a small gate which led into the road, and invited Patsy to enter the house by that way.

"No, thank you, Miss Margaret; I am on important business, and don't see any necessity why I should enter the house privately."

"Oh, yours is public business, then," said Margaret, with an ill-concealed expression of interest.

"Whether public or private, it is very urgent, and I am sorry to leave you so soon. I hope you have enjoyed yourself here."

"Oh, wonderfully," she replied, with a malicious smile. "Aaron and I ride out almost every day, and then we have parties, and all kinds of gaieties."

Margaret spoke thus purposely. She suspected Patsy's attachment for Major Burr, and her heightened color and expression of sadness, as she heard these words, indicating such close intimacy, confirmed her suspicions. In truth, she had cut Patsy to the heart. Her familiarity in calling him Aaron, convinced Patsy that her charms had already done their work, and that she had won him from her. But even in that moment of deep grief and sadness, she did not forget her high mission, and bowing her head, as if to say adieu, but in reality to conceal the tears which gathered in her eyes, she moved on, and Margaret was left to conjecture what could be the nature of that business which had induced a young girl like Patsy to walk so great a distance on such a day.

She did not, however, pause long for thought, but acting upon one of her impulses, with which the reader is already acquainted, she ran through one of the pathways of the garden into the house, and had gained the office where Major Burr was seated, long before Patsy had turned the corner of the road which led into Broadway.

Her hurried rap at the door was answered by him, and as she entered, she glanced around hastily, and was rejoiced to find he was alone. On her entrance, Major Burr threw down the pen with which he had been writing as she knocked, and rising, with an expression of pleasure on his face, was about to spring forward with extended hands to greet her, when she placed her fingers on her lips, as if cautioning him to be silent, and ere he had found time to ask any questions, she approached him and said, in tones which showed she was unusually moved:

"Something has gone wrong, I am afraid. Patsy has just crossed the river, and will be here in a few moments. She has walked all the way from her mother's, and she says she has business of great importance with you. Be on your guard, Aaron, and if anything should transpire which might demand action on my part, let me know at once."

"What on earth can this mean," said the major, and as he spoke the color rose to his cheeks.

"You will find out soon enough. Only, Aaron,"

and as she spoke, her lips quivered, and her eyes were moistened by the rising tear, "remember."

"I never can forget that the dearest and loveliest of her sex has said she loves me, and will be mine."

"Thank you, Aaron; now sit down again to your writing. I had better go; it would not look well if Patsy saw me now, as I know she is here."

"As you choose, Margaret," he replied, and he resumed his seat, while Margaret, approaching him, bent over, and imprinting a kiss on his broad and white forehead, stole quickly and silently away.

Major Burr threw down his pen, and leaning back in his chair, mused and wondered what could be the purpose of Patsy's visit under such circumstances. That the matter which had brought her there was important, was evidenced by the fact of her having walked the entire distance to communicate with him; but before he had time to reach any probable solution as to the cause of her visit, the orderly who was on duty, entered and announced that a young woman desired to see him on important business.

"Let her come in," was the reply, as he bent his head to conceal the expression of anxiety which he felt was on his face, and in another moment Patsy was in the room, and the door was closed upon her.

"Why, Patsy!" exclaimed the young aid, rising and springing forward with extended hand, "what on earth brings you here?" and as he spoke, he seized her hand and led her to a chair.

The warmth of his greeting, his apparent pleasure at seeing her, and the manner in which he had received her, touched the feelings of the fond girl, who, for the moment, forgot that such a person as Margaret Moncrieffe lived, and felt happy in her own love

"Oh, Aaron—I beg pardon—Major Burr."

"Certainly. Major, if you please," he said, laughing, as he looked at her flushed cheeks and travel-stained clothes; "had you not better make it Colonel?"

"I wish I could make you greater than that, major."

"Come, come, Patsy, don't be silly. Call me what you choose; but answer my question: What on earth brings you here?"

"Cousin Seth"—— But she had no time to finish her sentence; for as he heard these words, Major Burr felt the hot blood crimsoning his cheek, and he hastily interrupted her, saying: "Is Seth alive?"

"Alive, Aaron!" replied Patsy, half forgetting herself, and repeating the name so dear to her. "Yes—alive, Aaron, and it is at his request I am here. He desired me to say—let me see—I am so worried with the excitement, and so wearied by my journey, I am afraid almost I shall forget my message. Oh, no!—I remember now. He bade me seek you, and say that he was seized and made a prisoner at Corbie's—I think that was the name—the night you sent him there; that he was sent on board the 'Duchess of Gordon,' where he has been ever since until yesterday, when he managed to escape. Oh, Aaron, you should have seen him, all cut and scratched and bleeding; why, he was so exhausted when he got to our house, he fell asleep while we were talking to him. He was too feeble to come to the city, so I came in his place."

"I knew Seth was true and honest," said Major Burr, who, only in Margaret's presence, forgot the high duty he owed to his country.

"Who ever doubted him?" exclaimed Patsy.

"No matter, Patsy, go on. What message did he send?"

"He bade me say the city is full of conspirators; that a plot has been formed by Governor Tryon, with the aid of Mayor Matthews, as soon as the British fleet comes in, to go up both rivers at once, to break down King's Bridge; to blow up the magazines, and to seize the commander-in-chief and make him a prisoner!"

"In heaven's name, are you crazy, Patsy?"

"Not a bit of it, Aaron; I would not have walked sixteen miles on a crazy man's errand. Seth has picked up his information on board the ship. There is a Captain Blanchard, a man named Hickey, and some woman in the plot, besides the men Corbie and Forbes, who had him bound and sent on board the vessel. As soon as the fleet arrives, the plan is to be carried out."

Major Burr listened to these disclosures with feelings which can be better imagined than described. Twice he had received an intimation that the time for action might soon arrive; but he had never dreamed of such a plot as was here developed, and he was committed to aid in carrying it to consummation. His soul shrank from it, and as he thought for an instant upon the terrible position into which he had been not unwillingly, but irresistibly drawn by his passion for Margaret, the blood rushed to his heart with such violence, that for an instant it ceased to beat, and he grew pale as marble.

Patsy noticed his emotion, and attributing it to his horror at hearing of such an infamous plot against the liberties of the country for which she would have gladly laid down her life, exclaimed: "It is horrible, is it not, Aaron?"

Her words recalled his scattered senses, and he stammered out some reply.

"Who can that woman be, Aaron? Seth was so earnest when he spoke about the woman."

"How did Seth manage to escape?"

"Really, Aaron, I never asked him, we were so glad to see him, and he was so anxious to have this known to you, we never thought a word about that. Seth loves his country too well to think of himself, and so we all do. But who is that woman?"

"Oh, never fear but we'll find her out," said the

major, who at the mention of the word, had felt the hot blood mount to his cheeks, for he well knew who *that woman* was, and the consequences of her detection flashed across his mind. "If she is in New York, we will find her out. Captain Blanchard, you say," and he commenced writing.

"A man named Hickey, and a woman; yes, and Mayor Matthews," she added: "he manages everything, Seth said, as far as he could learn;" and Major Burr added the mayor's name to his list.

"Don't forget the men who had poor Seth gagged and bound and sent on board the ship—Corbie and Forbes."

"I will see General Putnam at once, and communicate this to him. Patsy, you have rendered important service to General Washington and the country, and it will not be forgotten. You are a noble girl," he said, warmly, turning to her and grasping both her hands, "and deserve"——

"No matter what I deserve, major," she said, releasing her hands and turning to leave the room, an expression of sadness crossing her countenance, for he had not spoken one word, as yet, which reached her heart.

"No, Patsy, stay here; the family will give you refreshments, and you need rest."

"Oh, never mind, major, I have an aunt in the city, in Crown street; I will go there and stay until to-morrow, when I will return home. Shall I say anything to Seth?"

"Yes; say that I knew and felt that he would prove true and honest, and I am proud of him; and of you, too," he added, looking earnestly at her, but not with such an expression of affection as she had been wont to receive from him.

"Thank you, Aaron; I must go now," she said, half mournfully; "you will find me at Aunt Crosby's in Crown street. You will see General Washington?"

"Immediately," he replied, earnestly; for in the presence of the pure, true-hearted, patriotic girl, he felt his high enthusiasm for his country rekindled, and for an instant Margaret was forgotten; though it was but for an instant, for almost ere he had ceased speaking, her image rose before him, radiant in glorious beauty, her brown eyes beaming upon him with love and passion, and with a kind, friendly farewell, but not one word of heartfelt greeting, he suffered Patsy to leave the office.

As soon as he was alone, he threw himself into a chair, and leaning his head upon the table, gave way to the thoughts which this interview had called up, and to conjectures as to the consequences which it must entail on himself, if he permitted still the sway which Margaret had obtained over him and his actions. His reflections, whatever they were, were interrupted by a gentle pressure on the shoulder, and looking up, he saw

Margaret before him, her eyes fixed on him with an expression of the most intense anxiety. She had watched until she saw Patsy leave the house, and hurried down to the office to learn the nature of the important business which had induced a young girl to walk alone and unprotected, a distance of sixteen miles, in order to communicate it to him.

Major Burr raised his head languidly at first, for he was fairly bowed down by the weight of his thoughts, and as he met the eyes of her for whom he had promised to barter honor, name, and all a man could hold dear, fixed on him, his whole nature seemed on the moment changed; for there was a magic in her presence, a fascination in her look, which subdued him, and rendered him powerless.

For an instant he gazed in her lustrous eyes; he read there the deep love she had avowed for him; he read there the only happiness he coveted on earth, and sinking his head upon the table, he gave way to the feelings which he could not repress; and though he shed no tear, his heart was nearly bursting with the conflict of emotions which Patsy's communication and Margaret's presence had aroused.

CHAPTER XXXI.

THE TEMPTRESS TRIES HER ARTS AGAIN.

"WHAT does all this mean?" asked Margaret, approaching the table at which he was seated, and laying her hand gently on the young aid's shoulder. 'What has happened?"

Major Burr raised his head as he heard the well-known and ever welcome tones, and looked at the fair speaker with a sad, mournful expression. His countenance wore a deathly pallor; his lips were quivering with emotion, and his whole frame seemed convulsed with some terrible excitement, such as she had never before witnessed in him. He shook his head sorrowfully, and pointed to the slip of paper lying before him, and on which he had made a memorandum of the information communicated to him by Patsy.

Margaret glanced over the writing, and as she observed the names of Blanchard, Matthews, Hickey, and the other well-known Royalists, intuitively she divined the purpose of Patsy's visit, and judged rightly that her business was, as she had said, of the utmost importance. As the last words on the memorandum caught her eye, in which he had noted down the fact that there was "a woman" connected with the matter, whatever it might be, her own countenance paled, and she bit her lip to repress the exclamation she was about to utter, and which might have betrayed the emotion she did not care to acknowledge even to Major Burr.

"Well," she said, with well-assumed calmness, "I do not see even now what it means. Am I to infer from that," and she pointed to the paper, "that some one has betrayed us? Tell me all, Aaron, and you will see, if occasion should present, how well prepared I am to act, and how much a girl can accomplish, when her heart is interested."

"Simply this, Margaret," said Major Burr, speaking in low, deep, earnest tones; "young Adams, as I predicted he would, has proved true to his duty. He was seized at Corbie's on the night he went there by my orders, and was forcibly taken on board the Duchess of Gordon. From what he heard at Corbie's, and from what he managed to learn during his confinement on board the ship, he has gathered enough to satisfy me that a deep-laid plot has been in progress for some time. You, of course, know its purpose; but until communicated to me by Patsy, I never dreamed of such a thing. It passes my comprehension how, in the conduct of civilized warfare, such an atrocious scheme should have been conceived."

"It was not necessary that you should know, Aaron," said Margaret, laying her hand upon his arm, and looking earnestly at him. "I only asked that you would promise to act with us when the proper time should arrive for action, and that promise you gave me."

"Seth has, somehow, found out those names," and he nodded to the paper, "and having escaped from the ship by swimming ashore, made his way to his aunt's, where I first saw you, whence he dispatched Patsy to communicate the information which he had gathered to me, for he was too much enfeebled, by his efforts to escape, to come himself. That Patsy is a noble, glorious girl," and as he spoke, Margaret fastened her eyes on him with a singular expression, but she only said:

"It was fortunate she came to you first. If she had gone directly to head-quarters—ugh! I dread to think of it," and she fairly shuddered. "Now what does he mean by 'a woman?'"

"He did not know himself—at least so Patsy said. He had only heard that some woman was concerned in the plot, for he heard that mentioned as well at Corbie's as on board the ship."

"It is impossible that I should be suspected, for my name has never been mentioned in the city, save to the Captains Blanchard and Corbie, and I am sure Governor Tryon would never suffer my name to pass his lips, circumstanced as I am at present."

"It was evidently meant for you, Margaret. Now what do you propose to do?"

"Let me ask, rather, what do you now propose?"

"To make this known to the commander-in-chief at once. That, of course, is my first duty, the more especially after all the trouble dear Patsy took to make it known to me."

"Of course; and what then?"

"I hardly know how to act."

"It is scarcely probable that the general will be found now at his quarters, at this hour of the day."

"I know that he has gone to Long Island to examine the progress of the works there."

"And will he return before night?"

"I scarcely think he will."

"And General Putnam?"

"Oh, he will laugh at it, even if I make it known to him. He, too, is absent, riding about overlooking the works, and will not be at home for some hours."

"So much the better; those hours are infinitely precious to us. Now, Aaron, you shall see how I will act. But before I say one word, need I ask if you are prepared to act with me?" and she looked at him with a mournful, tender expression, but one mingled with intense interest, as if she almost dreaded to hear his reply.

"I will go to the end of the world with you, Margaret," exclaimed the major, in whom the deep love he bore for her had resumed its full sway, and conquered every other sentiment, as was ever the case when in her presence, for she had cast a spell over him from which he could not release himself. "I will be yours and yours only, in life or death."

"Life and happiness, Aaron," she exclaimed, her face lighted by love and enthusiasm. "Long life and boundless happiness, my own dear Aaron," she repeated, as she threw herself into his arms; and straining her to his heart, he showered kisses upon her upturned lips, and cheeks, and eyes.

"There, there," and she rose from his embrace; "come what will, I shall be happy so long as I possess you and your love. You say you love me; I know you do, and I ask no greater happiness on earth. Now, Aaron, go on with your official duties as if nothing had occurred. At four o'clock I will return and see you again, and meantime I will have every necessary arrangement made to meet the emergency which has arisen. You are sure General Washington is on the island?" she asked, with an expression of anxiety.

"I was so informed by Major Gibbs, who accompanied him to the ferry. But what do you propose to do, Margaret?" and Major Burr looked at her with a strange expression of mingled curiosity and interest.

"Fly this very night. A few hours of rowing will place us in safety and beyond the possible reach of pursuit, and then Colonel Burr shall assume the rank and station he has so nobly earned and which he is so fitted to adorn; and as she spoke, she drew herself to her full height, as if in thus saluting him, she had added the dignity of the title to herself.

"Anywhere, Margaret, so I am with you," was the enthusiastic reply.

"I must go, then, and make my preparations. I told you before you would find me ready for any emergency, and you will soon learn that I spoke the truth. This night, before midnight, we will be in safety on board the governor's ship, and then let the worst come to the worst; you shall be saved, though all else perish," and permitting another embrace, she left the apartment, and once more he was alone.

No, not alone; for his thoughts occupied him so entirely, he found it impossible to transact any of his official business; so thrusting aside his papers, he arose, and paced the room, abstractedly. The hour had arrived when he was called upon to sacrifice honor, name and reputation; to lose his very nationality, and to bring upon his name the scorn and detestation, not alone of his countrymen, but of all honorable men. He saw before him, even at his feet, the deep, dark abyss of crime into which he was about to plunge, and for the moment shrunk back aghast at the spectacle thus presented to him; but through the darkness, and gloom and despair of that void, there beamed a bright and shining light—the eyes of Margaret lighted with love; Margaret's form of matchless grace, clasped in his arms, and all his own; Margaret's glowing face pillowed on his bosom, her snowy arms clasping his neck, his lips glued to her own in the long, long kiss of youth and love—and he gazed, and gazed, till all else faded from his view, and involuntarily he exclaimed, half aloud: "Margaret, dear Margaret, you at any sacrifice;" and as he spoke, his face lighted up with an expression which seemed the reflection of her own, as he had caught it in his vision.

A few minutes more and he had resumed his composure. Calmly he proceeded to open, examine, and note the contents of the dispatches before him; and this done, he folded carefully the minutes he had made of Patsy's disclosures, which he placed in the breast pocket of his coat, and taking his hat, left the apartment, giving directions to the orderly on duty to say that he would not return before three o'clock.

He passed leisurely up Broadway, and was glad when he found himself accosted by some officers off duty, for their conversation seemed to divert his thoughts from himself. He cared only to pass the time till it was necessary for him to return to his quarters; for he had made up his mind as to the course he intended to pursue, and nothing doubted that Margaret, through means of those friends with whom she was in constant intercourse, would arrange for her flight. He placed implicit reliance on her word that his name had never been mentioned in connection with her, so far as she was implicated in the disclosures made by Seth Adams, and therefore felt perfectly at ease as to himself. He had thoroughly determined to go with Margaret under any and every circumstance, and to that his mind was now, since their last interview, irrevocably made up, as he then thought.

He passed the time in pleasant conversation, joined in the gaiety and sallies of his friends; nay, he even listened with unchanging countenance when Margaret's name was mentioned, coupled with highest commendations and flattery, no one of his companions dreaming for an instant that their listener cherished any special interest for her.

In this manner he continued to while away the time till the clock on Trinity Church sounded the hour of three, when he bade adieu to his friends, pleading an engagement at that hour, and turned down Broadway toward General Putnam's residence, moving along with as much *nonchalance* and calmness of manner as if he had not in his pocket the possible fate of the nation and its honored champion.

He reached his own quarters shortly after the hour he had designated for his return, and in answer to the question he had put to the orderly, if any one had been there for the general, was informed that only the same young woman who had been there before, had called again; but he could not say whether she had gone away nor not.

This announcement rather disturbed the major's equanimity for a moment; but for a moment only. His reliance on Margaret was implicit. He knew that General Washington was out of the city, and therefore Patsy could not have seen him, and he entered his office with as much unconcern as he had left it.

He was surprised to find Patsy seated there, awaiting his return, and on this occasion he greeted her with more than his usual warmth. In this, perhaps, he was actuated by the consciousness that Margaret was not in the house; perhaps by the remembrance of the past, for that Patsy loved him, he had abundant reason to know.

He therefore hastened up to her with extended hand, and, assuming an expression of pleasure which was but partially felt, he offered to salute her; but she repelled him, not coldly, but with a dignity and grace of manner which fairly overawed him; for it showed that she had read him.

"Well, Patsy," he said, seating himself with an air of apparent *nonchalance*, "this is the first time you ever refused me a kiss. Who has won you from me?"

He spoke in a tone of half serious gallantry, which cut the young girl to the quick, and her only reply was a look which sent the hot blood mounting to his cheeks, for he interpreted it rightly.

Well knowing that a further continuance of this conversation would only insure defeat to himself, he said, assuming an official air: "Well, Patsy, what now? What has happened?"

"Nothing, Major Burr, only I find a chance of riding home to-night; so I thought I would stop and ask if you had seen General Washington yet?"

"He is over on Long Island, Patsy, examining the works, but will be home about six o'clock. I shall see him the moment he returns, and communicate to him the important information you have brought, and I shall not forget to tell him to whom the whole country is so deeply indebted."

"Thank you, major. I am sure you are as deeply interested as I am in the success of our glorious cause, and I am happy that I had the good fortune to find you, since he is away; for the delay of a single day might lead to disastrous results. Major Burr, will you pardon me if I say something that does not properly concern me?" Patsy continued, hesitating, and a slight blush tinging her cheek.

"You cannot say anything, Patsy, requiring pardon from me or any one else. I hope it is something in which I may serve you."

"I took the liberty once of cautioning you against Miss Moncrieffe. Pardon me, major," she said, seeing that he was about to interrupt her, "not on my own account, but for my country's sake; and as I know that you are as warmly devoted to its interests as myself; I say now, I believe she is the woman to whom Seth alludes. If I had seen General Washington, I should have told him so myself. You know best whether you have seen anything to justify the suspicion of which I cannot divest myself."

"Indeed, Patsy," said the young officer, coloring to the very temples, "I think you are entirely mistaken."

"Of course, I am aware that you think so," and she spoke with an emphasis whose meaning he could not misinterpret. "But," she continued, "Seth bade me see *you*. He, as well as myself, knows your devotion to your country, and God grant that my humble services may" ——

"They will be appreciated, dear Patsy," exclaimed Major Burr, interrupting her, and anticipating, as he thought, her words; but she checked him, saying:

"You misunderstand me, major. I was going to say, I hoped my humble services would prove of some value to my country and to our beloved general. Good day, major," and she moved toward the door, with a face as pale as marble and eyes moistened with tears; for the bitter disappointment she had experienced on her first meeting with him to whom her heart was given, and who had sought her love—the certainty that Margaret had won his heart from her—had struck a blow to her very soul, from which she felt she could never recover.

"Patsy—dear Patsy!" exclaimed the major, springing forward; but again he met that look, and recoiled from it much further than he would have done from a frowning battery. In another moment he was alone with his own thoughts, and Patsy, brushing away the tears which had gathered in her eyes, and choking down the rising sob, left the house and proceeded to the ferry-boat. As she entered it, she gave one lingering look at the house, which contained all she held dear on earth, then, with a smothered sigh, seated her self in the stern-sheets, and during the entire passage dared not trust herself with another look.

CHAPTER XXXII.

THE ROYALISTS IN DANGER.

As may be supposed, the reflections of Major Burr, after the departure of Patsy, were not of the most pleasant character. He felt keenly the rebukes conveyed by her words, though, of course, none were intended by her, as she could not possibly be cognizant of his contemplated treason; and each time that she had alluded to his love for and devotion to his country, a pang shot through his heart; for he could not but reflect that he had consented to array himself with its enemies.

But his mad, blind, passionate love for Margaret had swallowed up every other feeling, and perhaps, there may be some readers who may find a partial excuse for him in his youth, his inexperience, and the invincible power of the little god, who, from the days of Adam and Eve, has ruled the world; for, as Pope has most truly said of love—

> "Kings he makes subjects, and meaner subjects kings."

He was engaged in the avocations of his office, and

pursuing them with his usual coolness, method, and system, when the door of his office was abruptly opened, and General Putnam, flushed, and evidently somewhat out of temper, entered. The general had been around the city, examining the progress of the various works for its defence, and had found great cause of complaint at the tardiness of the men at work upon them. Then, again, he had been called upon several times during the day to settle some sectional quarrels; for even with the danger of invasion threatening them, the most bitter sectional feeling prevailed throughout the city—the southern troops, who were generally well equipped, making it a point to decry the hardy sons of New York, New Jersey, and the more northern colonists, who presented a most motley array indeed, scarcely any two being armed or uniformed alike. In fact, he was generally out of humor, and, throwing his hat upon the sofa as he entered, he exclaimed:

"I wish to God some of these turbulent, quarrelsome fellows would leave the city. They seem to think that its safety depends only on them. What is going on now, major?" and as he spoke, he seated himself, and treated his nose to a pinch of snuff.

"Only a small conspiracy, general," was the reply of Major Burr, uttered as composedly as though he had no concern in it.

"Fiddle de dee!—I have heard of nothing but conspiracies since I have been quartered here. What new one is this now?" he asked, impatiently.

"Why, this looks as if it had some foundation in fact. You remember Seth Adams, whom I sent to Corbie's, general?"

"Yes, the confounded deserter! I wish I could catch him."

"He will not give you the trouble to catch him, and I am sure you won't hang him."

"The d—l I won't. Let me see him once. But what about him?"

"You remember I pledged my honor for his truth and fidelity."

"And he has deceived you."

"Not at all; on the contrary, he has rendered most important services. He was taken prisoner and sent on board the Duchess of Gordon, and managed to effect his escape only last night by swimming ashore on the Jersey side. While on board the ship he picked up information concerning a plot, which, if there be any truth in it at all, has been brewing for some time between Governor Tryon and the Royalists in the city. His information is not very full, but of the very highest importance, and certainly deserves an examination."

"And how did it reach you, major?"

"Seth was too weak and too much exhausted to come to the city, so he sent his cousin, a young girl, the daughter of the old lady where I found Miss Moncrieffe, and she has walked to-day all the way from Elizabeth to make it known to me."

"And what does it all amount to?"

"Simply this, general," and the major drew from his pocket the memorandum he had made of Patsy's disclosures. "He states that he heard there was a plot on foot in which many of the Royalists of the city were engaged, to blow up the magazines, destroy King's Bridge, and seize General Washington and carry him on board one of their ships, in the hopes of thus terminating the war. He names some parties"——

At this moment a tap at the door, which Major Burr well knew, caused him to pause, and the general in a gruff voice summoned the party to enter.

It was indeed Margaret, who entered with a countenance as composed as if she was in no wise interested in the subject of their conversation. Seeing the general, she was about to retire, when he said, in a voice half gruff, half pleasant: "Oh, come in, you little Tory; I shouldn't wonder if you had a finger in this, too. Go on, major; does he name any parties?"

"Yes, general—Captain Blanchard."

"What, that Royalist scoundrel who has been so well treated here?"

"I suppose it must be him—Corbie and Forbes."

"Those infernal Tory scoundrels. I wish I had hung them when I first proposed it. Go on."

"A man named Hickey"——

"Who the devil is he?" growled the general.

"I have no doubt it is one of the Life Guardsmen. Then he spoke of some woman."

"That's you, Miss Impudence," exclaimed the general, turning suddenly upon Margaret, with an awful frown upon his face, though she could perceive that his anger was assumed. "I am sure that's you, and I'll keep my promise, mind you."

"I am ready, sir," said Margaret, composedly, at the same time baring her snowy neck, for she well knew to what he alluded.

"Umph!" said the old general, and as he gazed upon the glorious beauty before him, his eyes fastened upon that swan-like neck, "I am afraid it would hurt you; I'll wait till I find out with more certainty. Go on, major."

"That is all, sir," replied the aid, folding up the paper from which he had been reading, and replacing it in the breast-pocket of his coat.

"Well, I don't believe there is anything in it, but I suppose it is well enough to inquire. I wish I was commander-in-chief for one hour; I would hang every Tory in the city, and investigate afterward. I suppose you will make this known to General Washington."

"Of course, general, He has gone to examine the works on Long Island, and as soon as he returns, I will communicate with him."

"Major, you had better keep a good lookout on

this young hussy. I shouldn't at all wonder if she was mixed up with it. I have a great mind, Miss Impudence, to have you put under lock and key until this is thoroughly investigated. Never mind, I won't at present. Major, keep your eyes on her," and again he put on a look of awful severity, which Margaret met with one of well assumed meekness and submission. Then taking his hat from the sofa, he strode out of the room, leaving Margaret and the young aid alone.

"You did well, Aaron," she said, "to report to the general. It will disarm all suspicion as to myself. I have kept my promise; now there is no time to waste in words; you are familiar with the island?"

"With every nook and corner of it," was the reply.

"About a quarter of a mile above Corbie's house, there is a small cove completely shaded by large trees, and with low underbrush on the edge. On the south side of that cove there will be a boat at nine o'clock this evening. I name that time, because a later hour might subject all parties to more examination than they choose to undergo. I shall be in that boat at that time. If Colonel Burr does not regret what he has said and promised, he will be there also."

"I will be there, Margaret; I have thrown the die, and I will abide by the cast. You, and you only. But how can you manage, or rather, how have you arranged it?"

"Have no fear for me; I will be there if I am alive."

"You are a noble girl," said the major, enthusiastically, as he gazed upon the beautiful temptress, who had so enchained him, "and deserve more than I can ever repay."

"You love me, don't you, Aaron?"

"Better than my soul."

"Then that is my reward, and I am well repaid. Now, we have no time for idle words; we know each other too well to need them. You will report to General Washington—when?" she asked.

"As soon as he returns—perhaps about six o'clock."

"That will give you abundant time to make any preparations you desire."

"I need none. Under such circumstances, I shall take nothing which may retard our departure."

"You will bring your pistols, major. I always carry mine when there is a prospect of having need of them. Now, Aaron, adieu, till we meet at nine o'clock. I may not have an opportunity for conversation until then, and when we meet again, it will be never to part in life," and she held out her hand, which was gladly seized, and drawing her to him, he clasped her fair form in a long, close embrace, and imprinting a kiss upon her snowy forehead, she withdrew, with the simple words, "Remember, Aaron, nine o'clock."

Major Burr had nerved himself to the act he was about to perpetrate, and was now reckless of consequences. He felt, too, a sense of security which aided him wonderfully in retaining his composure, and he was quite equal to the task of facing the commander whom he was about to betray, and to communicate to him the information imparted by Seth, with the certainty that, under any circumstances, he would never be known as an accomplice.

Shortly before six o'clock, he mounted his horse, and followed by an orderly, rode to the head-quarters of General Washington, and throwing the reins to his attendant, entered the house, and demanded an immediate interview with the general on important business.

His rank and position entitled him to attention, and in a few moments an orderly of the Life Guards appeared, and ushered him into the presence of the commander-in-chief, by whom he was received with the courtesy and amenity for which he was so famed, the more especially as having once been his aid, the general was thoroughly familiar with, and appreciated his worth and services.

"Be seated, major," said the general, waving him to a seat, and laying down the pen he had been using, prepared to receive any communication he might have to make.

"I have important information to communicate," said the major, at the same time drawing forth the memorandum he had made, and at a sign from the general, who was not accustomed to waste words, he proceeded to detail briefly and succinctly all the facts communicated by Seth Adams through Patsy.

"And why did that young woman not call at my quarters, sir?" demanded the general as the major concluded.

"Because, general, Seth Adams had directed her to report to me."

"And why to you, sir, do you suppose?"

"Because, by directions of General Putnam during your absence, I had sent him on the mission which resulted so unfortunately to him, pledging myself for his fidelity and fitness, and his orders then were to report direct to me; and further, because I am an old friend of her family."

"That is well, sir. You may leave your memorandum; I will think of this. There may be something in it; but it is not unlikely some story invented to divert our attention from more serious designs. The whole affair looks to me absurd. I thank you, major, for your attention to this, and will embrace the earliest opportunity to express my sense of the obligations I owe to that noble girl, who has taken such pains to serve her country."

Major Burr knew that the interview was closed, and with a bow he retired, glad to be free from the searching glance of the chief whom he had promised to betray.

CHAPTER XXXIII.

GENERAL WASHINGTON AND THE PLOTTERS.

MAJOR BURR had scarcely closed the door, which separated him from his chief, when the latter, rising, with a flushed countenance and eyes flashing with unwonted anger, rang the small bell which stood on his table, and the summons was answered almost before the sound had ceased to vibrate on the ear, by an orderly, who, touching his hat, awaited erect and in silence the order which had summoned him there.

"I wish to see Captain Hamilton, or Major Webb," he said, naming two of his favorite aids, and as the orderly withdrew, he commenced pacing the room with measured strides, ever and anon pausing to look at the memorandum which Major Burr had left.

Major Webb soon made his appearance, and without any waste of words, was directed to issue orders at once to the various commanders in the city. To one was intrusted the arrest of Forbes and Houndling and Mason, with every person found in either of their houses at the time of their arrest. To another he gave directions for the arrest of Corbie and all in his house; while special orders were issued to General Greene, then in command on Long Island, whose quarters were at Bedford, to detail a select party of men, and arrest Mayor Matthews, then residing at Flatbush, and particular directions were given to have the arrest made at precisely one in the morning. To Major Gibbs, in command of his Life Guard, orders were issued to put Hickey under immediate arrest, and at two o'clock in the morning to arrest Captain Arthur Blanchard and all found in his quarters; and strict orders were issued to the commanders of every battery on either river, not to allow any boat to land or to depart after sundown, under *any circumstances.*

Major Webb received his orders, of course, without a question as to their real purport, and having completed the writing which they required, they were passed to the general, who, hastily glancing over them, affixed his signature, and, without a word of explanation, dismissed his aid, with the simple injunction, delivered in very earnest tones, to have them immediately delivered to the parties to whom they were issued.

The major did wonder somewhat at the silence maintained by his chief, who was usually very communicative with his aids, in whom he reposed the most boundless confidence; but as he knew as well how to obey, as he afterward proved he knew how to fight, he merely shrugged his shoulders, and retired to execute the commands he had received.

Major Burr, on leaving the quarters of the commander-in-chief, rode leisurely down Broadway, followed by his orderly, and, as he was moving slowly along, he perceived Captain Blanchard, the Royalist, coming toward him.

His first impression or rather impulse was to accost him, and, by gently hinting at the occurrences of the day, he could possibly glean something from him, by means of which he might ascertain if Captain Blanchard was as well informed as himself. But second thoughts prevailed, and as they neared each other, the captain gracefully touched his hat, and addressed the major with the usual salutations of the day, which were as courteously responded to by the young aid. There was no appearance of coolness—none of suspicion—nothing to warrant the supposition that either knew of the other's participation in the important matters which were on the eve of transpiring; but each, without knowing why, *felt* that their positions were mutually known; for somehow, and most unaccountably, Captain Blanchard had imbibed the idea that the intimacy between the major and Margaret was entirely too close for him to be unacquainted with her movements.

With an expression of the hope that Miss Moncrieffe was well, uttered by Captain Blanchard, they separated, and each went on his way.

Major Burr, on reaching his quarters, found his

office vacant, and was glad of the opportunity of being alone; for he was on the eve of taking the most important step of his life—one which was to operate for or against him for all time, and was, therefore, pleased to have one more opportunity for reflection before he made the fatal plunge.

His return, however, had been anxiously watched for by Margaret from the window of her room, which fronted on Broadway; and he had scarcely unbuckled his sword and thrown himself into a chair, burying his face in his hands, when a gentle touch aroused him, and, as he raised his head, he met again those eyes, whose power he could not resist, if he had so desired.

With a bound and a cry of joy he sprang up, and, seizing both her hands, looked intently at her for an instant with such an earnest, mournful expression, that the tears came to her eyes in very spite of herself.

"You will always love me, Margaret? You will not despise me for my faithlessness?"

"Love you, Aaron! Love you! I never can love any one but you; and where I do not honor, I could not love. Be true to yourself for a few short hours, and you will find your reward in the brilliant future before you and in"——

"Your love, my own Margaret," interrupted the infatuated officer.

"Come now, Aaron, time is precious. Have you made your preparations?"

"I have none to make. I shall discard my uniform, and take nothing with me which may remind me of the past. Pardon me, Margaret," he said, as he saw a shade cross her countenance, " even with your love and presence to cheer me, I cannot at once forget the associations of all my life, short as it has been, and the ties which have until now bound me here."

"You do not regret their severance?" she asked, half sadly.

"I shall have no regrets when you are mine," was his reply, delivered with a depth and earnestness which found their way to her heart.

"I shall go now, and leave the tea-table early, on pretence of going out to pay some calls, and I shall say that you are to call for me at Mrs. Shee's at nine o'clock. Of course, you will be there."

"Of course," he replied, smilingly, for he well knew to what she alluded.

"Now then, Aaron, give me the countersign," and as she spoke, he started, for it was the first occasion on which he had been called on for direct action. He colored, hesitated, and stammered, for madly, blindly and wildly as he loved, nay, fairly idolized her, the idea of betraying a trust, now that it was brought to him in a palpable form, struck him as something terrible. Margaret saw his heightened color, she noticed his hesitation, and rightly divining the cause, gave him a moment's reflection, then not trusting to words, smiled tenderly on him, and he was conquered.

Approaching close to her, he whispered in her ear the parole and countersign, and then, as if ashamed of what he had done, turned suddenly away, for it was his first direct betrayal of his trust.

Margaret gazed at him with a singular expression of countenance, then turned and moved toward the door, saying as she placed her hand on the latch, "Remember, nine o'clock! I shall be there."

The last words were enough; the last struggle was over, and Aaron Burr was thenceforth to be named as a traitor and deserter.

The family assembled at the evening meal, and the subject of the information communicated by Patsy to Major Burr was made the topic of discussion, the general scoffing at it as ridiculous, but occasionally taunting Margaret, and renewing his caution to Major Burr to keep a sharp lookout on her movements, and if he caught her amiss, to hang her first and investigate afterward.

Margaret joined in the conversation with her wonted ease of manner and nonchalance, and joked the general upon his great desire to hang the Tories, which she admitted was a much easier method of getting rid of enemies than to kill them off in a fair fight, at which the general laughed good humoredly. Major Burr, who had not the self-possession of Margaret, was compelled to listen to this conversation, and as he looked at her whose neck might be, as it were, almost encircled by a halter, smiling and jesting on the very brink of such a precipice as that on which they stood, his admiration for her was, if possible, heightened.

Immediately at the close of the meal, Margaret arose from the table, and turning to General Putnam, said, with her most winning smile: "Grandpa, won't you let Major Burr come after me, this evening; I am going out to pay a call at Mrs. Shee's, and you know that if I should return alone, and any of the sentinels should challenge me, I couldn't say anything, and he might take me to the guard-house," and as she closed, she looked as demure as a nun.

"I don't know as the major will care to discharge such a duty. If he does, I have nothing to detain him. Eh, major!"

"I will wait upon Miss Moncrieffe, with pleasure," and he bowed to Margaret, who cast upon him a triumphant look, which seemed to say that all of her plans had worked thus far successfully, and with a low courtesy she withdrew

"That is a singular creature," said Mrs. Putnam to her husband, as the door closed upon Margaret's retreating form.

"Most singnlar—really a remarkable girl. By the way, major, have you thought who that woman can be?" asked the general, turning suddenly to his aid.

16

The suddenness of the question, as well as its character, destroyed for an instant the composure of the young aid, who stammered and colored and hesitated; but he was saved from a reply by the general, who bursting into a broad laugh, said: "Why, major, you blush and stammer, like a schoolboy caught in a trick. I didn't mean anything when I spoke so to Margaret."

"I have not any idea, general," responded the major, whose face at the last words of his chief had turned ashy pale.

"Well, I did not suppose that you did, major; but if there is anything in it, we will find it out, I dare say."

Major Burr murmured something which he meant to be an assent, and rising from the table, withdrew from the apartment.

"It is my private opinion," said the general, drawing back from the table, "that Major Aaron Burr and Miss Margaret Moncrieffe are a pair of love-sick children Bah! what nonsense."

CHAPTER XXXIV.

MARGARET ATTEMPTS TO ESCAPE.

The orders of the commander-in-chief were obeyed with alacrity, zeal and fidelity, though many were the expressions of wonderment as to what they portended, but of course they were executed without question.

The evening of the day so portentous in the history of our country, was bright, clear, and pleasant. The moon was in its first quarter, and detracted nothing from the brilliancy of the stars which studded the firmament.

Shortly after eight o'clock, two parties were seen wending their way past Richmond Hill, and as they walked leisurely along, with linked arms, they seemed deeply engaged in conversation—so deeply, that they at first scarcely heeded the challenge of the sentinel who paced the road which passed in front of the head-quarters of the commander-in-chief of the American forces. A second challenge, however, aroused them, and the smaller of the twain, in answer to the hail, "to advance and give the countersign," dropped his companion's arm, and approaching the soldier, gave the required word in low tones. The musket was at once restored from the charge to the shoulder, and the pair again joining arms, passed on, followed by the eyes of the soldier, who wondered what could have brought them there at such an hour, and how they had learned the countersign; but having it, he was in duty bound to permit them to pass.

How, in heaven's name, Miss Margaret, did you get the word?" asked the larger and elder of the two, when out of ear-shot, for his companion was no other than Margaret Moncrieffe, dressed in male attire, accompanied by Arthur Blanchard.

"All in good time, captain—all in good time, captain. In another hour you shall know all, or," and she shuddered as she spoke, "nothing."

"You are a wonderful girl," said the captain, pressing his companion's arm. "If you had only been a man, what wonders you would have achieved; indeed, you have already accomplished more than all of us together."

"Yes," she laughed, "if I had only been a man, I should have been nothing but a man. No, no, Captain Blanchard, I am so proud to be Margaret Moncrieffe, I would not exchange my name for any reputation manhood might bring to me."

"Ahem!" said the captain, meaningly, but intuitively both felt it was no time now for mere bantering conversation. Both were fleeing for their lives, and although one danger had been passed, others must be encountered.

Slowly they moved on, so as not to attract suspicion, and when fairly out of sight of the Richmond Hill House, and of course of the sentry, whose beat did not extend beyond the garden, Margaret turned suddenly into a lane, or rather path, which tended toward the river.

Noiselessly and cautiously they moved along in single file, Captain Blanchard taking the lead, and winding their way through the shrubbery and underbrush, the water's edge was at last reached. A low whistle from the captain was answered by some party hidden beneath the brush which concealed the water from sight, and in a few moments a man, in the garb of a sailor, made his appearance.

"Is all ready?" asked the captain, as the man approached and touched his hat.

"All right, captain," was the response, accompanied by another military salute.

"We had better get in the boat at once," said the captain to his companion, who now stood by his side. The shrubbery will conceal us beyond the possibility of discovery. Does your friend know the spot?"

"Perfectly, and he will be here, I am confident, at the appointed hour."

"Come, then," and taking her hand, he led her

down the steep bank, aided by the sailor, who had answered his summons, and in a few minutes they were seated in the stern-sheets of the boat—a small yawl, manned by four men, who, evidently aware that they were engaged in a dangerous enterprise, stood up, gazing around as well as the darkness would permit, and crouching down upon their seats at the slightest noise.

Captain Blanchard, now feeling secure from the probability of capture, strove to draw Margaret into conversation; but gently waving her hand, as if to request his silence, she said: "Please don't;" and burying her face in her hand, she gave way to her thoughts.

Leaving them thus placed, let us return to other parties. Shortly after they had passed the sentry, the officer of the guard came around, and gave strict orders that no persons were to be permitted to pass on any account whatever, whether they had the countersign or not, but to direct them to the guard-house. The sentinel's post was removed further down the road, so as to command a view of Corbie's house, and he was specially instructed to note, so far as was possible, how many entered there.

After receiving these orders, the soldier then communicated to the sergeant the fact that two persons, having the countersign, had passed shortly before. The sergeant, a keen, quick-witted soldier, who had seen much service, and who was devotedly attached to his general, questioned the man closely as to their dress, manner and appearance, so far as he could judge, and having obtained all the information which the sentinel could communicate, hastened to the barracks, and requested an instant audience of Major Gibbs, to whom he reported what he had just learned.

"Has Captain Martin reported yet?" was the inquiry of the major, after he had heard the sergeant's statement.

"There's a company just below the barracks, major; but I don't know whose it is. They came up just before I started on my rounds."

"Send the orderly here, and allow no person to pass the lines, even if he has the countersign," was all the reply which the major made, and, in a few moments after the sergeant's departure, the orderly entered the room.

"Whose company is that below the barracks?"

"One from Colonel McDougal's regiment," was the reply, accompanied by the military salute.

Major Gibbs, as commander of the Life Guards, was, of course, in the most intimate confidence of the commander-in-chief, and to him had been communicated the information brought by Major Burr, which made him cognizant of all the orders issued by General Washington, and of the reasons which had governed him. He had been informed of the disclosures made within the past few hours, and fairly worshipping his general, had received the impression that the plot thus providentially betrayed, was much more extended than had been supposed. As the custodian of the personal safety of the commander-in-chief, holding the very highest post of honor in the army, the major realized the full sense of his responsibility, and, with characteristic prudence, he resolved to act upon his own judgment. Thus far he had rigidly obeyed his orders. He had none others to act upon; but the emergency seemed to be such as to demand prompt action, and that he determined to take upon his own responsibility; and, after a few moments' reflection, feeling that he had not only the right, but, by virtue of his office, the power to do so, he resolved to act. The passage of two persons through the lines, with the countersign, might or might not be unimportant; but with the prudence of a cautious, brave, and devoted soldier, he determined at once upon his course.

"Captain Martin, major," said the orderly, interrupting the major's reverie, and ushering in the commander of the company in McDougal's regiment, who had been ordered to make the arrest at Corbie's house when the proper time had arrived.

"Captain, I am glad to see you so prompt; but I had no reason to expect anything else from you," and the captain bowed in response to the compliment, which, by the way, was hardly merited.

"You will please take your men by any route the

least noticeable, and post them on the banks of the river near Corbie's. We have reason to believe that he is in constant and direct communication with the enemy. If any boat approaches, let it land, and make the whole party prisoners."

"If any boat attempts to pass your command, and does not land when hailed, fire into it without hesitation. There is treason and treachery abroad, Captain Martin, and we must put them down. Go at once, captain, we have no time to lose," and, with a salute, the captain was about to retire, when Major Gibbs added: "By the way, you had better take the lane just north of us; it leads to the river, and you can get down by that path without trouble, and the fact of your going past Corbie's, will disarm the inmates of any suspicion as to your purposes."

In a few moments, his command, some forty men, was in motion, and he led them by the lane mentioned by Major Gibbs, which wound down to the edge of the river, and through which Margaret and Captain Blanchard had passed a few minutes previously, intending by making a detour to get in the rear of Corbie's house, and where, secured from observation by the bushes which skirted the river, everything could be seen.

CHAPTER XXXV.

AARON BURR FREE AGAIN.

WHILE matters are in this posture, let us turn to Major Burr, whom we left as he arose from the tea-table at General Putnam's. He ascended to his own apartment, and locking himself in, threw himself into a large, leather-bottomed chair which stood by the table in the centre of the room, and burying his face in his hands, he gave way to the thoughts which the occasion would naturally be supposed to excite.

Here was he—a youth just out of his teens, who had won honor, fame and distinction, such as hundreds of older officers would have been glad and proud to enjoy. His reputation as a brave, cool, skillful and accomplished officer, was not surpassed by that of any young officer in the Continental army, and by few of his seniors. He had enjoyed the confidence and regard of the commander-in-chief, who had evinced his appreciation of his worth and talents, by making him one of his aids—a position which he had abandoned voluntarily, for the reason, as he had said, that he was not content as a soldier to discharge only the clerical duties which devolved upon an aid, and desired more active service; and he was then, at his own request, backed by that of General Putnam, transferred to his staff as aid, where he had service as constant and active as his heart desired. He was the intimate friend and confidant of this brave old general, who loved him as a son, while every member of the family treated him as one of themselves.

The career before him under such a leader, gave promise of abundant active service, with the certain prospect of promotion if he should deserve it, and he felt that he could; and more than all, he was in the very presence of the enemy, for they were daily expected to arrive, and in such numbers as would call forth all the energies and courage and talents of every man in the army. Here was a chance for distinction. for new laurels, for added honors, and his defection now, at this imminent crisis, would it not be attributed to cowardice? He shrunk with a blush of shame from this thought.

Then again, the fact that Margaret had fled the city at the same time with himself, would, no doubt, make his name a very by-word of ridicule and contempt, as one who for the sake of a pair of brilliant eyes, a voluptuous form and fascinating manners, had forsaken his country in her sorest hour of trial—had forfeited his honor, and sullied a name which now bade fair to shine in the firmament of the country's history, among the brightest of the bright stars which studded it.

There was no Margaret there then to wind her snowy arms around his neck, to tempt him with languishing looks and burning kisses; reason, judgment, conscience, and the high sense of honor and patriotism which had led him to volunteer with Arnold for that trying and disastrous expedition, were rapidly regaining their sway, and freed now from the wiles of the enchantress who had ensnared him, he was fast regaining his self-control.

True, the image of Margaret did rise up before him, and he sighed as he thought of the happiness he might call his own; but the picture had lost something of its brilliancy—it was dimmed by the doubts which his thoughts had woven around it, and he could gaze upon it without a quickening of the pulse, or a brightening of the eye.

How long he had thus mused he knew not, but he was aroused by the clock of Trinity Church, which sounded the hour of eight, and as he counted the strokes, he sprang from his seat, and clenching his hands until the nails almost entered the flesh, exclaimed: "No, by the great God above, never; I love you, Margaret, but I will not sell my soul for you; I will not live, even for your love, to be branded as a traitor. She is safe; thank heaven for that, and she must learn to forget me, as I will her. If she does love me, she will feel prouder of me as I am, than as she would make me; and so farewell, Margaret!"

What more he might have said was interrupted by a

tap at his door, and on opening it, Belle Putnam stood there, and as she saw him, said, "Ma thinks you had better go now for Margaret; she ought to be home by nine o'clock, and it is a great way to Colonel Shee's quarters."

"True, Belle; I had almost forgotten it."

"What, forgotten Margaret?" she said, archly and with a mischievous look.

"Yes, Belle; I was very deeply engrossed in thought, and the time has passed without my noticing it."

"And what for your thoughts, major?"

"I was thinking what the next few days might bring forth for all of us," and he spoke with such solemnity, Belle fairly shuddered, for she, too, was in constant terror of an invasion by the British, and presumed that he alluded to that.

"Well, you had better go now, and bring her home."

"Certainly; I ought to have been away before," and seizing his chapeau, he left the room and the house, proceeding leisurely up Broadway, deeply engrossed in thought. He felt that he had seen Margaret for the last time, but derived some consolation in the reflection that she was safe, and that through his assistance.

It was near the hour of nine by the time he had reached the immediate vicinity of Richmond Hill, and a feeling which he could not define, came over him as he remembered that he had promised Margaret to be at the boat by that hour. Crossing out of the road, he leaned up against the fence, awaiting the striking of the hour which was to place Margaret in safety, and to disenthrall him from the spell which had so strangely bound him to her, in spite of every call of honor, duty, morality or patriotism.

With his face turned toward the water, he was looking over toward the Jersey shore, when he was startled by the report of one musket, followed almost instantly by a volley which seemed to come from the bushes just below Corbie's house, and a short, sharp scream, which rang through the still night air, went to his very heart, for he felt that it came from Margaret.

In another moment, and before he had time to collect his thoughts, a boat swept out from the shade of the trees, and shot directly across the river, propelled by arms which were nerved by the certainty that they were pulling for life or death.

Slowly and sadly Major Burr turned away, almost wishing that the ball which he doubted not had been fatally sped for Margaret, had found him in her stead; but now that the possibility of ever seeing her again, whether she had died thus, or escaped unharmed, was beyond peradventure, he felt a sense of relief, and a new life seemed to be infused into him.

He reached General Putnam's house long after the family had retired, and proceeding to his own apartment, passed the night in meditation, revolving in his own mind the extraordinary occurrences of the past few days—for all here narrated had transpired between the first day of June and the 28th of the same month, in the year 1776, on which day Hickey, the guardsman, was hung. But let us turn again to Margaret, whom we left seated in the boat which was lying in the cove in the rear of Corbie's house, awaiting only the arrival of Major Burr, to push off and make for the Duchess of Gordon.

CHAPTER XXXVI.

CONCLUSION.

We left Margaret and Captain Blanchard seated in the boat, awaiting the arrival of the other party, as yet unknown to the captain, but so anxiously expected by the former, and who was to share the perils and hazards of the night. Margaret had remained silent, engrossed in her thoughts so deeply she seemed almost to have forgotten where she was, or the circumstances which surrounded her, when she was startled by the hand of the captain, laid gently on her own.

"Hist!" he said, raising his finger to his lips, as if to caution her to silence, and in another moment their ears, quickened by the sense of the danger which encompassed them, detected the tread of a body of men coming directly toward the spot where the boat lay concealed beneath the underbrush.

"This way, men," was uttered in loud, commanding tones; "spread yourselves along the bank of the river, and keep both eyes wide open; we'll catch some of these infernal Tory scoundrels yet."

The men in the boat had heard the sound of the soldiers' feet as they advanced gradually toward them, and they heard, too, with terrible distinctness, the command to skirt the bank, which, if accomplished, would render escape next to impossible.

Immediate action was, of course, peremptorily necessary, and the man at the bow oar, rising, placed it against the bank and pushed the boat off from the shore, so that it swung out into the stream, but still in the shadow of the bushes.

Margaret caught a view of what had been done, and grasping Captain Blanchard's arm with a force of which her slender frame seemed incapable, whispered in hoarse, hurried tones: "For the love of heaven, captain, stop them. Do not let them go until he arrives; I know he will be here in time."

"It is impossible, Margaret. Our lives would certainly pay the forfeit of a minute's delay. Did you not hear the order to skirt the bank?"

"Then let me go ashore; I will not leave without him," and she strove to rise, with the intention of leaping on shore; but the captain threw his arms around her, and, placing his mouth close to her ear, whispered hurriedly: "Would you have our blood upon your head? You cannot, shall not go on shore;" and waving his hand to the men at the oars, the boat was pushed off boldly, and the muffled oars placed silently in the row-locks. One strong, hearty pull sent her at least ten feet from the shore, but not yet outside the shade of the trees and bushes which lined the bank;

another given as heartily, made her fairly spring from the water, and as she shot out into the river, one of the soldiers, who had poked aside the bushes with his musket, discovered the retreating boat, and at once gave the alarm, and challenged the boat, now rapidly receding from the shore.

Captain Blanchard, who held the tiller, knew that they must be discovered soon, and, with a view of presenting as small a mark as possible to the enemy, directed the course of the boat straight across the river, thus affording only a sight of the stern, a mark too small to render the danger at all imminent, especially at night, and with the distance between them increasing at every stroke of the oars, now plied with a heartiness doubled by the certainty that it was a matter of life or death to all on board.

The soldier who had discovered the boat and given the alarm, forced his way through the bushes, and gaining a stand on the water's edge, took deliberate aim at the now indistinct object on the water, and discharged his piece. The other men had by this time managed to scramble down the bank and through the bushes, and, discovering the speck on the water, sent a volley after it; but the balls fell harmless around those in the boat, but so close—for one of the oar blades was pierced—as to draw a scream from Margaret, who had crouched close to Captain Blanchard's side, and who, between her anxiety for the safety of him she loved so well, and from whom she was now perhaps forever separated, and the uncertainty of her own fate, was completely unnerved. It was this scream which had been heard on shore by Major Burr through the stillness of the night.

Fortunately for the party in the boat, there was no other boat along the shore nearer than a mile down toward the city, and their pursuit was rendered impossible, and Captain Martin, whose company had fired at the escaping party, could only report what had occurred, to which Major Gibbs replied, that he was glad to get rid of them anyhow, but would much rather have captured them, that he might have the pleasure of hanging the infernal Tories. He was a little puzzled when the captain remarked that he had heard a woman scream; but his conjectures as to who she could be, were solved on the next day, when the absence of Margaret was discovered.

The orders of the commander-in-chief for the arrest of the parties implicated in this diabolical plot, so far as they were known, were executed with zeal and promptness. Of course Captain Blanchard was not found, and the rage of General Putnam when he was compelled to feel that he had been out-generalled by a girl of fifteen, exceeded all bounds.

Great was the commotion in the city on the following day, when it was known that during the night, some forty or fifty Tories had been arrested and sent to jail.

but greater still was the surprise and indignation of the Provincials, when the existence and discovery of the plot were made known.

The Tories were handed over to the Provincial Congress for trial, while the soldiers implicated were turned over to the mercies of a court-martial, which was convened on the following day, and which terminated its labors by finding the guardsman Hickey guilty, and sentencing him to be hung—a sentence which was carried into execution on the 28th of June, 1776, near the site on which the present Tompkins Market is erected, at the junction of Fourth and Third Avenues

Margaret Moncrieffe lived many years after these events; but her career was one, the details of which would be unfit for publication, though it is only simple justice to her woman's nature to state, and she has so recorded in her published memoirs, that she never *loved* but one man, and that was Major Aaron Burr, who had won, and retained throughout her whole life, dissolute and abandoned as it was, her undying devotion.

Edmund Blanchard, who, by reason of the names of the conspirators having been sent on board the "Duchess of Gordon," had escaped arrest, returned to his sober senses, and made some reparation for his past infamy, not only by his after courage and devotion to the cause which he had once consented to betray, but by marrying Lizzie Brainard, with whom, after the war had closed, he lived for many years in unclouded happiness.

Patsy, in due time, forgot her faithless lover, and as the wife of a sturdy, thriving farmer in New Jersey, lived to hear the country ring with the praises of him she had once so loved and trusted, and unmoved, watched his upward flight, until he came within one step of reaching the highest office in the gift of a free people.

Of the after career of Aaron Burr, much has been written—much, too, that is not only contradictory in the statements, but false in particulars. The Appendix which follows, the reader will perceive, gives, under his own hand, a flat denial to one important accusation, which has been published and reiterated. To that Appendix the author refers as substantiating his claim to at least a partial historical accuracy in the story of MARGARET MONCRIEFFE AND AARON BURR.

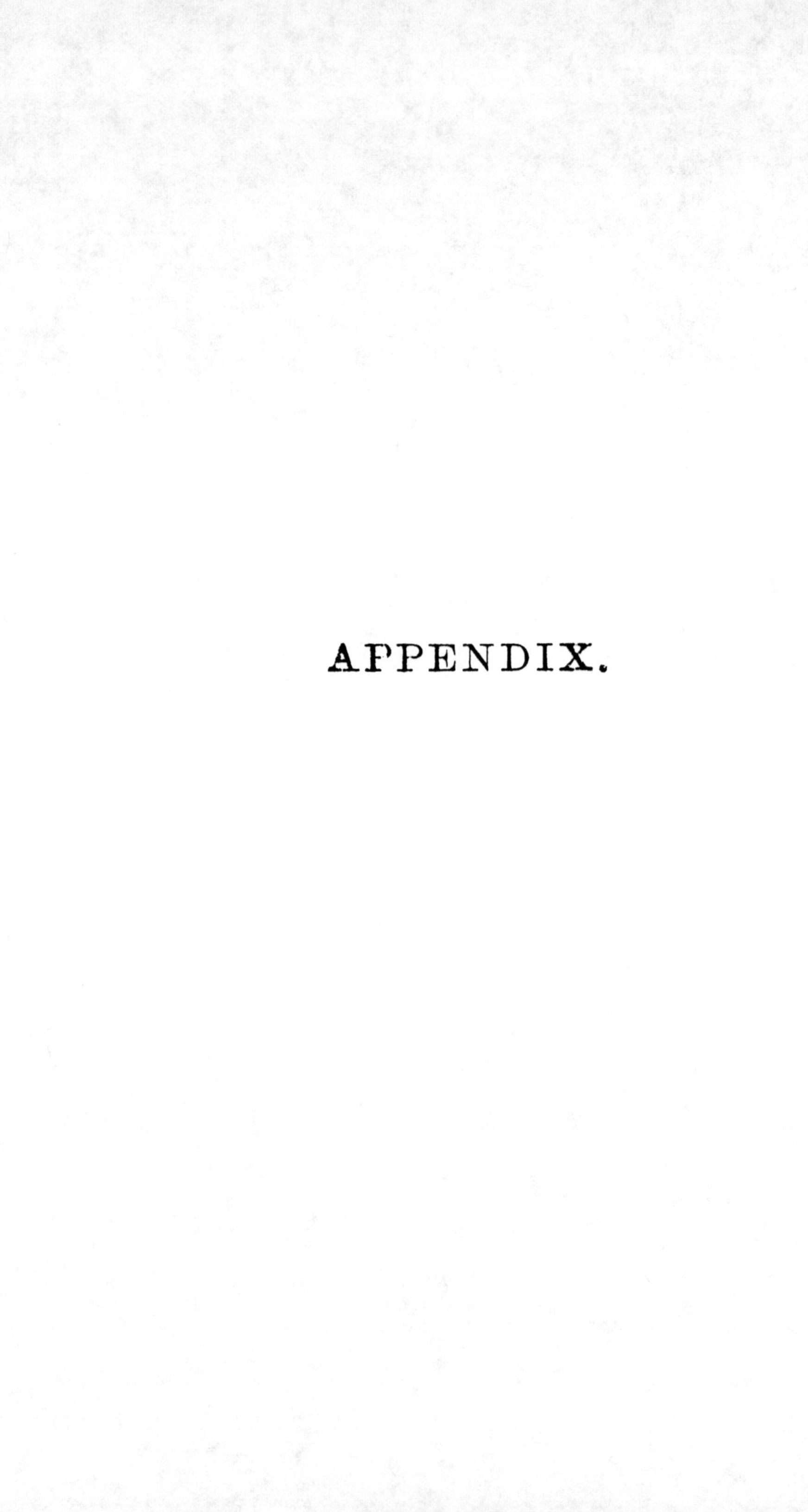

APPENDIX.

APPENDIX.

APPENDIX I.

The author having claimed for this work that it records historical circumstances, presents the following pages, copied from the "American Archives," in which the reader will find mentioned many of the names introduced to his notice in the course of the narrative. The trial of the life guardsman Thomas Hickey, for treason, and which terminated in his conviction and subsequent execution, brings the whole plot and the infamous plotters clearly to the reader's view; and it is, therefore chosen as the most appropriate, as well as the fullest record of events which transpired during the period when Margaret Moncrieffe was an inmate of General Putnam's house, received and treated as a member of his family. The documents now given are copied from Vol. VI. of "American Archives," and, apart from their direct connection with the author's fiction, may serve to interest, for the reason that the circumstances thus detailed before the court-martial, have only been alluded to in the most general and briefest terms by those who have written the history of those troublous times. The evidence is not presented in full, as it would occupy too much space; but the main and most prominent circumstances are here recorded, proving, beyond the possibility of cavil, the existence of one of the most diabolical plots ever conceived, and which was only defeated by Providential interposition. The names of the Provincials who had enlisted in this infamous plot had been sent on board the "Duchess of Gordon," so that with every effort, the court-martial was unable to fasten criminality on any save a few of the Royalists whose names are mentioned in the course of the trial. Corbie, Forbes, Mason, Houndling, and others, directly implicated, were imprisoned, and only released when the British took possession of the city after it had been evacuated by the Continental troops.

TRIAL OF HICKEY BEFORE THE COURT MARTIAL.

Col. Samuel H. Parsons, *Pres.*

Lt. Col. Wm. Sheppard,	Capt. Warham Parkes,
Major Levi Wells,	Capt. William Reed,
Capt. Jos. Hoyt,	Capt. Jos. Pettingil,
Capt. Abel Pettibone,	Capt. David Lyon,
Capt. Samuel Warren,	Capt. David Sill,
Capt. James Mellen,	Capt. Timothy Percival.

William Tudor, *Judge Advocate.*

The warrant being read, and the court, first duly sworn, proceeded to the trial of Thomas Hickey, a private sentinel in his Excellency the Commander-in-Chief's Guard, commanded by Major Gibbs, brought prisoner before the court, and accused "of exciting and joining in a mutiny and sedition, and of treacherously corresponding with, enlisting with, and receiving pay from the enemies of the United American Colonies."

The prisoner being arraigned on the above charge, pleads not guilty.

William Green sworn, deposes: That about three weeks ago, I was in company with one Gilbert Forbes, a gunsmith, who lives in Broadway, and we fell into a conversation on politics; I found Forbes' pulse beat high in the Tory scheme; I had repeated conversations with Forbes afterward, and he was always introducing politics and hinting against the impossibility of this country standing against the power of Great Britain; he invited me to dine with him one day, and a day or two afterward asked me if I would not enlist in the king's service; I asked him where the money was to come from to pay me for the service; Forbes replied the major would furnish money; I was pleased with the notion of getting some money from the Tories, and agreed to the scheme, with a view to cheat the Tories and detect their scheme; I mentioned the matter to several, and among others to Hickey, the prisoner; I told him the principle I went upon, and that we had a good opportunity of duping the Tories; Hickey agreed to the scheme, but did not receive any money, except two shillings, which I gave him; Forbes left it with me to enlist and swear the men; Forbes swore me and one Clark on the Bible to fight for the king, but I swore Hickey to fight for America; after the prisoner was engaged, I proposed to him to reveal the plot to the general, but Hickey said we had better let it alone till we had made further discoveries; all that Forbes proposed to me was that when the king's forces arrived, we should cut away King's Bridge, and then go on board a ship of war which would be in the East River to receive us; I enlisted ten or a dozen, and told them all my plan; the prisoner wrote his name upon a piece of paper, with five others, which I gave to Forbes, and this was all the enlistment that I knew of the prisoner's signing.

Gilbert Forbes: A night or two after Gen. Washington arrived in New York from Boston, Green fell into company where I was; we were drinking, and Green toasted the king's health, and I did so too; a day or two afterwards Green called upon me; said, that as I had drank his majesty's health, he supposed I was his friend, and immediately proposed to enlist some men into the king's service, and told me he could procure considerable numbers to join him; I put him off, and declined having any hand in the business; but in repeated applications from him I at last fell into the scheme; Green was to enlist the men, in which I was not to be concerned, nor have my name mentioned; in a day or two, Green gave me a list of men who had engaged, among whom was the prisoner, Hickey; soon after Hickey asked me to give him a half a dollar, which I did, and this was all the money that Hickey ever received from me; Green received eighteen dollars, and was to pay the men who enlisted, a dollar a piece, and we were to allow them ten shillings per week subsistence money; I received upward of a hundred pounds from Mr. Matthews, the mayor, to pay those who should enlist in the king's service; who, after enlisting, were to go on board the king's ships, but if they could not get there, were to play their parts when the king's forces arrived; that he knows one —— Silk; that he was left by Cap. Aidy to wait upon his wife, who lives on Long Island, somewhere near Hampstead; that he is often in town, frequently at Mrs. Oiry's and Mrs. Brandon's; has the air of a soldier; wears a short brown hunting coat, and a double-breasted jacket of the same color; that he used to wait on a Mr. Miller, who lives or lodges in Mr. Gouverneur's house, on Rotten Row; that Sergeant Graham (an old soldier, discharged from the royal artillery) was employed by Governor Tryon to speak to examinant about enlisting men for the king's service, and told this examinant from the governor, that if this examinant exerted himself in that business, and raised a number of men, he should have a company; that the said sergeant also informed him, that at the request of the governor, he had surveyed the grounds and works about the city, and on Long Island, in consequence of which he had concerted a plan for an attack, which he had given to Governor Tryon, and of which the governor approved; which was as follows, viz.: That the men-of-war should cannonade the Battery at Red Hook, and that while that was doing, a detachment of the army, with some cannon, etc., should land below or about Red Hook, and march round so as to come upon the back of the batteries near the Swedeland House; that a small part of the detachment should make a feint of marching up the road leading directly to the battery, but that the main body were to make a circuitous march so as to reach the battery while our attention was engaged by the feint aforesaid; that if they carried that battery, which they expected to take by storm, they were immediately to attack the battery on the hill near the ferry, which the sergeant said would be easily done, as no embrasures were made or cannon fixed on the back side of it; that this latter battery, when in their possession, would command the works on Gouvernour's Island, which they would keep between two fires, viz.: the battery last mentioned, on the one side, and the shipping on the other; that then the shipping, with the remainder of the army, were to divide; one division was to run up the North River and land at or near about Clarke's farm, and march directly to Enclenbergh Hall and fortify there; the other division was to run up the East River and land in such a manner as to gain Jones' Hill, from whence they expected to command and silence the battery on Bayard's Hill; that should they gain possession of the places above mentioned, their next object would be the grounds adjacent to King's Bridge, where they intended to erect strong works, so as to cut off the communication between the city and the country.

Gilbert Forbes being further examined, saith: That some time before the man-of-war removed from the town to the narrows, one Webb, a burr-millstone maker, told examinant that if he had any rifles to sell, he could get a good price for them by sending them on board the man-of-war, and that a young man who lived with James Rivington told him the same; that this examinant had then nine rifles which he made, but they were bad and would not shoot straight, and eleven smooth, narrow-bored guns; that he sent some of them to Mrs. Becks, a tavern keeper, near the Fly Market, with orders to send them on board, which she accordingly did, and that the said Webb carried the remainder; that the said Webb told this examinant that Governor Tryon would give him three guineas apiece for them; that at the same time when an exchange of prisoners took place with the man-of-war, and Tiley was, among others, exchanged, the mayor, viz., David Matthews, Esq., sent for this examinant and told him that he was going on board the governor's ship, and that he would get the money due from the governor to this examinant for the rifles aforesaid; that on his return the mayor told this examinant he would pay him in a few days; that this examinant never did receive any money from him for the said fire-arms; that this examinant told Charles Benson that he was about enlisting men, and that he told this examinant it would do.

William Welch: Between a fortnight and three weeks ago, I met the prisoner on the street; he asked me to go with him to a grog shop; when we got there he told me he had something to tell me of importance, but insisted on my being sworn before he would communicate it; I accordingly swore on the Bible to keep secret what he should tell me; he then said, that this country was sold; that the enemy would soon arrive, and that it was best for us old countrymen to make our peace before they came, or they would kill us all; that we old countrymen should join together, and that we would be known by a particular mark, and if I would agree to become one of them, he would carry me to a man who would let me have a dollar by way of encouragement; I did not relish the project and we parted.

Isaac Ketchum: Last Saturday week the prisoner was committed to jail, on suspicion of counterfeiting the Continental currency, and seeing me in jail, inquired the reason of it; I told him, because I was a Tory; on this, a conversation ensued on politics; in different conversations he informed me that the army was become damnably corrupted; that the fleet was soon expected, and that he and a number of others were in a band to turn against the American army when the king's troops should arrive, and asked me to be one of them; the plan he told me, was, some were to be sick, and others were to hire men in their room; that eight of the general's guard were concerned, but mentioned only Green by name; he further told me, that one Forbes, a tavern keeper, was to be their captain, but that the inferior officers were not yet appointed, lest the scheme should be discovered.

The prisoner here being called upon to make his defence, produces no evidence, but says "he engaged in the scheme at first for the sake of cheating the Tories, and getting some money from them, and afterward consented to have his name sent on board the man-of-war, in order that, if the enemy should arrive and defeat the army here, and he should be taken prisoner, he might be safe."

William Forbes, of Goshen Precinct, in Orange County, tanner and currier, being examined, saith: That he knows Gilbert Forbes, of the city of New York, gunsmith; that the first time he saw him was in this city, between the brick meeting and the jail; that he heard somebody call him Mr. Forbes; this examinant accosted him, and told him that his name was Forbes also; that thereupon they went into Houlding's tavern, and drank together; that he has been at the house of the said Gilbert Forbes, on an invitation from him. That he knows a sergeant in General Washington's Guards, but cannot recollect his name; that he became acquainted with him at Corby's (an inn-keeper), near General Washington's; that this examinant went to Corby's in company with one James Mason, of Ringwood, who was at work in Corby's garden; that the sergeant was a middle-sized, fair-complexioned man—an Englishman; that examinant became acquainted with James Mason at Duchess County; afterward saw him at Goshen, and from thence came in company with him to this town; that he told Mason he had been on board the man-of-war last winter, while she lay in the East River; that he never was on board the Duchess of Gordon; that he never said he was on board the Savage when she fired on Staten Island; that he had heard, and, among others, from the said Mason, that two hundred acres of land were offered by Governor Tryon to each man who would go in the king's service, and one hundred to the wife, and fifty to each child; that examinant borrowed twenty odd shillings of Mason, and promised to pay him when examinant got money from on board the man-of-war, where he had two brother's-in-law, who had promised to send him money to pay his debts; that he never had engaged with Governor Tryon, or any other person whatever, to undertake the business of enlisting soldiers for the king, nor of enticing the Continental soldiers to leave that service; that he and Mason came to town by way of Elizabethtown, and that at Warwick Mason persuaded one William Benjamin to go along with them; that he knows Peter McLean, a shoemaker, near the Exchange; that examinant applied to him to put him on board the man-of-war; that McLean answered he could not do it all, the sentries were so strict; that examinant then said to McLean that then he would enlist in the Continental service, which he has since done, in Captain Beekman's company, of Lasher's battalion; that examinant and Mason lodged, the first night they came to town, at Houlding's; that while they were there, Corby was introduced to Benjamin and Mason by Gilbert Forbes and the aforesaid sergeant of the guards. This examinant says the said sergeant and Gilbert Forbes administered oaths of secrecy to Mason and two or three soldiers; that Corby was present when the said soldiers were sworn as aforesaid. That after McLean, as aforesaid, had told this examinant that he knew not how to get on board the man-of-war, McLean recommended him to David Matthews, Esq., as a proper person to direct him how to get on board the man-of-war; that examinant accordingly went to Mr. Matthews, and told him that McLean had directed examinant to him as a proper person to tell him how he should get on board the man-of-war, and that there was a lad (meaning Mason) that had come down from Ringwood, who wanted to go along; that Mr. Matthews told him that it was too dangerous for him to say anything about it, but that he would direct him to one who could get him on board, and sent this examinant for that purpose to Gilbert Forbes; that this examinant accordingly applied to the said Gilbert Forbes, and that Forbes said he could not do anything in it till he had seen Corby; that shortly after, the said Gilbert Forbes told this examinant he had seen Corby, and that Corby said he would get examinant on board in a few days; that examinant afterward saw Corby, and that he made the like promise to examinant, but Corby afterward told him he could not, and that he had been able to send only one on board by a mulatto fellow. That this examinant knows John Clarke, and that he told this examinant that he had fifty or sixty men to go in the king's service, and that he had prevailed upon his brother, Anthony Clarke, to consent to go with them; that John Clarke was to be a captain, and that one Seeley, of Chester, in Orange County, was also to be one of the officers.

William Forbes.

Examined 23d day of July, 1776, before us:

John Jay,
Gouverneur Morris.

John Yates, of the Wallkill Precinct, in Ulster County, laborer, being sworn, saith: That early in this last spring, Absalom Bull, one of deponent's neighbors, came to him, and told him that he was but a poor man, and that if he would go with the said Bull, he would make a gentleman of this deponent; that this deponent asked him how; he replied that if this deponent would go and serve the king for three years, or to the end of the American war, if that should sooner happen, this deponent should have two hundred acres of land on the frontiers; that deponent said it was very uncertain, for he did not see how he was to get a warranty deed for it; but if he could get a warranty deed for two hundred acres of land, he did not know but he might engage; on this they parted; that for many days repeatedly after that, the said Absalom Bull, together with Isaac Waugh and Richard Bull, came to this deponent and pressed him to enter into the king's service, but the deponent put them off; that they afterward went, as they informed this deponent, on board the man-of-war, and when they returned, brought him a letter from Governor Tryon, informing this deponent that if he would come on board his ship and pilot the men-of-war up the river, he would give this deponent a dollar a day and five pounds a foot for every foot that the vessel he piloted drew more than twenty feet, and should have two hundred acres of land at the determination of the American war; and that Ireland, Scotland, and Wales had all united with England to subdue America; that this deponent had, till within a few years last past, been a seafaring man, and was well acquainted with the navigation of the North River, which was well known to his said neighbors, and, as this deponent believes, was by them made known to Governor Tryon; that this deponent afterward received two other letters of the like import from Governor Tryon; that about six weeks this deponent, together with the said Absalom Bull, Richard Bull, and Isaac Waugh, travelled from their homes down through Westchester County to Whitestone Ferry, where they crossed over to Long Island, and thence to Hempstead, and went to the house of one Simonson, a tavern-keeper in that town; that they went from thence to the house of Captain Hulet, where they all lodged; that the next morning this deponent's companions went off from Rockaway in an oyster boat that plied between that coast and the ships, and supplied them with provisions, as he was informed and believed; that they desired this deponent to go with them, but this deponent being sick and not much inclined to go on board, said he would wait at Captain Hulet's till their return; that after three days they all returned to this deponent at Captain Hulet's aforesaid, and that Colonel Fanning, the governor's secretary, came with them; that the said Colonel Fanning was well known to this deponent, he having often seen him, and this deponent having been a mariner in Captain Hunter's ship, which brought the colonel from England; that at present this deponent did not know Colonel Fanning, he being disguised in the dress of a common laboring man, but on taking this deponent aside, he made himself known to him, whereupon this deponent immediately recollected his face and person; that he asked this deponent to go on board with him; this deponent answered that he was too sick to go; that then the colonel told him that if he could not go then he must come down when the fleet arrived, and that they would send this deponent a letter informing him of it, to which this deponent agreed; that Colonel Fanning told him New York was to be the seat of war; that some of the fleet would run around into the Sound, and land troops on Long Island; that another division would land on the south side and hoist the king's standard; and that all the men that had engaged to serve the king should come to Long Island, and that there were then three field-pieces and a mortar piece under the floor of the barn of the said Simonson; the said Colonel Fanning also told this deponent that they should want him to pilot vessels of war up the North River, and that the Savage, Phœnix, and Shuldan (which he believes was formerly the Rhode Island packet) were designed for that service; that the colonel desired this deponent to bring all the provisions he could on board the ships, and that he should receive the following prices for them, viz.: five pounds a barrel for salt pork; one shilling per pound for gammons; eighteen pence per pound for butter, and a good price for fowls, eggs, etc., and then gave this deponent a paper (now delivered), with a seal on it and the letters W. T. on the back of it, and told this deponent that it would serve him as a pass to go by all the men-of-war and cruisers unmolested; that Colonel Fanning further told this deponent that Absalom Bull, aforesaid, had enlisted a great many men, and desired this deponent to do the like, but this deponent declined it; that this deponent knows John Clarke, a painter; that he saw him in this town about a fortnight ago; that he told this deponent he was going on board the ships, and requested this deponent to go with him, which this deponent refused; that he advised this deponent to engage to fight for the king, and said the Americans would be beat; that the aforesaid Absalom Bull showed this deponent, this Spring, a list of persons whom he had enlisted for the king's service; that the said Absalom told this deponent that there were two hundred names on it, which this deponent really believes to be true, but this deponent does not remember the names of any of them, except Richard Bull, Alexander Scadden, James Scadden, Isaac Waugh, John Clarke (the painter, aforesaid), Jewel Smith, and one Seeley, of a place in Orange County called Oxford; that Absalom Bull, aforesaid, was to be a captain, and had a commission for it from Governor Tryon, which he showed to this deponent, and that it was written on parchment and a great seal hanging to it, but that this deponent did not read it; the said Absalom Bull further said, that all the men so enlisted for the king's service were to join the fleet when it arrived, and that all who did not would be treated as deserters from the king's service.

his
JOHN + YATES.
mark.

Sworn the 24th June, 1776, before us,

JOHN JAY,
GOUVERNEUR MORRIS.

The court being cleared, after mature consideration, are unanimously of the opinion that the prisoner is guilty of the charge against him, and of a breach of the fifth and of the thirteenth articles of the Rules and Regulations for the Government of the Continental Forces; and the court unanimously sentence and adjudge that the prisoner, Thomas Hickey, suffer death for said crimes, by being hanged by the neck till he is dead.

SAMUEL H. PARSONS, *President.*

WARRANT FOR THE EXECUTION OF HICKEY.

BY HIS EXCELLENCY, GEORGE WASHINGTON, ESQ., GENERAL AND COMMANDER-IN-CHIEF OF THE ARMY OF THE UNITED STATES.

To the Provost Marshal of said Army:

Whereas, Thomas Hickey, a soldier enlisted in the service of the said United Colonies, has been duly convicted by a

General Court Martial of mutiny and sedition, and also with holding a treacherous correspondence with the enemies of said Colonies, contrary to the Rules and Regulations established for the government of said troops; and the said Thomas Hickey being so convicted, has been sentenced to death, by being hanged by the neck till he shall be dead, which sentence, by the unanimous advice of the general officers of the said army, I have thought proper to confirm; These are, therefore, to will and require you to execute the said sentence upon the said Thomas Hickey this day, at eleven o'clock in the forenoon, upon the ground between the encampments of the brigades of Brigadier General Spencer and Lord Stirling, and for so doing this shall be your sufficient warrant. Given under my hand this twenty-eighth day of June, in the year of our Lord, one thousand seven hundred and seventy-six.

GEORGE WASHINGTON.

HEAD-QUARTERS, NEW YORK, June 28th, 1776.

NEW YORK, June 28th, 1776.

By virtue of, and in obedience to, the foregoing warrant, I have this day, at the time and place therein ordered and directed, caused Thomas Hickey, the prisoner within mentioned, to suffer death in the way and manner therein prescribed, and accordingly return this warrant fully executed.*

WILLIAM MORONY,

Provost Marshal in the Army of the United Colonies.

* *New York, July* 1, 1776.—Last Friday was executed, in a field between the Colonels McDougal and Huntington's camp, near the Bowery Lane (in the presence of near twenty thousand spectators), a soldier belonging to his Excellency General Washington's Guards, for mutiny and conspiracy, being one of those who formed, and was soon to have put in execution, that horrid plot of assassinating the staff officers, blowing up the magazines, and securing the passes of the town, on the arrival of the hungry ministerial myrmidons. It is hoped the remainder of those miscreants, now in our possession, will meet with a punishment adequate to their crimes.

Extract of a Letter dated New York, June 24, 1776.

My last to you was by Friday's post, since which a most barbarous and infernal plot has been discovered among our Tories, the particulars of which I cannot give you, as the committee of examination consists of but three, who are sworn to secrecy. Two of Washington's guards are concerned; the third they tempted to join them made the first discovery. The general report of their design is as follows: Upon the arrival of the troops, they were to murder all the staff officers, blow up the magazines, and secure the passes of the town. Gilbert Forbes, gunsmith in the Broadway, was taken between two and three o'clock Saturday morning, and carried before our Provincial Congress, who were then sitting, but refusing to make any discovery, he was sent to jail and put in irons. Young Mr. Livingston went to see him early in the morning, and told him he was sorry to find he had been concerned, and as his time was very short, not having above three days to live, advised him to prepare himself. This had the desired effect; he asked to be carried before the Congress again, and he would discover all he knew. Several have been since taken (between twenty and thirty), among them our mayor, who are all now under confinement. It is said their party consisted of about five hundred.

I have just heard that the mayor has confessed bringing money from Ryan to pay for rifle-guns that Forbes had made.

CERTIFICATES OF THE SERVICES OF COL. AARON BURR IN THE AMERICAN REVOLUTION, FROM HIS FELLOW-SOLDIERS.

Letter from Samuel Rowland, Esq., *to* Richard V. Morris, Esq.

Fairfield, Conn., *January* 29th, 1815.

In answer to the inquiries relating to the evacuation of New York in 1776, I can only observe, but few persons who were present and eye-witnesses of the event, are now living in this part of the country; I find, however, the Rev. Dr. Ripley, a gentleman of eminent respectability, and Messrs. Wakeman and Jennings, respectable citizens of this town, now living, who belonged to the brigade of the late General Silliman, the information of which gentlemen, on any subject, can be relied on, and will be no otherwise than correct, however prejudice or other cause might occasion a reluctance in disclosing the information in their power to give; yet duty impelled their narrative, and the neglecting an opportunity to give evidence of noble acts and unrewarded worth, they consider *ingratitude.* In preference to communicate to you by way of letter, concerning transactions of so long standing as in the year 1776, I desired the inclosed certificates, which the gentlemen freely gave, in order to prevent any misconstruction by passing through a second hand, by which you'll have more correct information than possibly is in my power to give.

I am respectfully, your obedt. sevt.,

SAMUEL ROWLAND.

RICHARD VALENTINE MORRIS, ESQ.

Certificate from the REV. HEZEKIAH RIPLEY.

(COPY).

On being inquired of by Samuel Rowland, Esq., of Fairfield town and county, in the State of Connecticut, relative to my knowledge and recollection respecting the merits of Col. Aaron Burr as an officer and soldier in the late Revolutionary war between the United States and Great Britain, can certify as follows:

Hezekiah Ripley, of said Fairfield, do certify: That on or about the fifteenth day of September, 1776, I was the officiating chaplain of the brigade, then commanded by Gen. Gold S. Sullivan; from mismanagement of the commanding officer, that brigade was unfortunately left in the city of New York, and at the time before mentioned. While the brigade was in front, and myself considerably in the rear, I was met by the late Gen. Putnam, deceased, who then informed me of the landing of the enemy above us, and that I must make my escape on the west side of the island; whereupon I, on foot, crossed the lots to the west side of the island unmolested, excepting by the fire from the ships of the British, which at that time lay in the North River; how the brigade escaped, I was not an eye-witness, but well recollect, from the information I then had from Gen. Chandler (now deceased), then acting as a colonel in said brigade, that Mr. Burr's exertions, bravery and good conduct, was the principal means of saving the whole of that brigade from falling into the hands of the enemy, and whose conduct was then by all considered judicious and meritorious.

But, however, I well recollect before I had the information alluded to from General Chandler, I had seen Mr. Burr and inquired of him how the brigade had made their escape, who then told me the particulars, which were afterward confirmed by all the officers, who were all of opinion that had it not been for him they would not have effected their retreat and escape.

As to my own opinion of the management of the troops on leaving New York, I then and still suppose, as did Gen. Chandler, that Col. Burr's merits then as a young officer ought and did claim much attention, and whose official duties as an aid-de-camp on that memorable day, justly claimed the thanks of the army and his country.

(Signed) HEZEKIAH RIPLEY.

Certificate from MR. ISAAC JENNINGS *and from* MR. ANDREW WAKEMAN.

Being requested by Samuel Rowland, Esq., to give information relative to the evacuation of New York in the year 1776, by the American army, we, the subscribers, then acting, one in the capacity of a lieutenant, and the other as a private, in the brigade commanded by the late General Sullivan, now deceased, do certify: That on the fifteenth day of September (being on the Lord's day) the British landed on the east side of the island, about four miles above the city; the American troops retreated the same day to Harlem Heights; by some misapprehension of the orders, or from other causes unknown to us, our brigade was left, and was taken by General Knox to Bunkers Hill, a small fort (so called) about a mile from town; the fort was scarcely able to hold us all; we had but just got into the fort, when Aaron Burr, then aid-de-camp to General Putnam, rode up and inquired who commanded there; Gen. Knox presented himself, and Burr (then called Major Burr) asked the general what he did there, and why he did not retreat with the army; the general replied, that it was impossible to retreat, as the enemy were across the island, and that he meant to defend that fort; Major Burr ridiculed the idea of defending the place, being, as he said, without provisions or water, or bomb proof, and that with one mortar, or one howitzer, the enemy would take the place in four hours, or in some very short time, and again urged General Knox to retreat to Harlem Heights; but General Knox said it would be madness to attempt it; a smart debate ensued, the general adhering to his opinion; Burr addressed himself to the men, and told them that if they remained there, they would, before night, be all prisoners and crammed into a dungeon, or hung like dogs; he engaged to lead them off, and observed that it would be better that one-half should be killed in fighting, than all be sacrificed in that cowardly manner. The men agreed to follow him, and he led them out, he and his two attendants riding on the right flank; about four miles from town, we were fired upon by a party of the enemy; Burr galloped directly to the spot the firing came from, hallooing to the men to follow him; it proved to be only a guard of about a company of the enemy, who immediately fled; Burr and his horsemen pursued and killed several of them; while he was thus engaged, the head of a column had taken a wrong road; Burr came up and turned us to the left into a wood, and rode along the column from front to rear, encouraging the men, and led us out to the main army with very small loss.

The coolness, deliberation and valor displayed by Major Burr, in effecting a safe retreat without material loss, and his meritorious services to the army on that day, rendered him an object of peculiar respect from the troops, and the particular notice of the officers.

(Signed) ISAAC JENNINGS,
ANDREW WAKEMAN.

Letter from NATHANIEL JUDSON *to* COMMODORE R. V. MORRIS.

ALBANY, 10*th February*, 1814.

SIR: I have received your letter with the preceding statement respecting our retreat from New York Island, in September, 1776, and in compliance with your request, I have to reply, that the relation made by Mr. Wakeman and Mr. Jennings corresponds with my recollection. I was near Colonel Burr when he had the dispute with General Knox, who said it was madness to think of retreating, as we should meet the whole British army; Col. Burr did not address himself to the men but to the officers, who had most of them gathered around to hear what passed, as we considered ourselves as lost; but Col. Burr seemed so confident that he could make good a retreat, and made it clear that we were all lost if we staid there, that we all agreed to trust to his conduct and courage, though it did appear to us a most desperate undertaking; and he did not disappoint us, for he effected a retreat with the whole brigade, and I do not think we lost more than thirty men; we had several brushes with small parties of the enemy; Colonel Burr was foremost, and the most active where there was danger, and his conduct, without considering his extreme youth, was afterward a constant subject of praise and admiration and gratitude; this affair was much talked of in the army after the surrender of Fort Washington, in which a garrison of about 2,500 men was left under circumstances very similar to ours, this fort having no bomb proof; that garrison surrendered, as is well known, on the very same day our army retreated, and of those 2,500 men, not 500 men survived the imprisonment they received from the British. I have since then heard it repeated hundreds of times by the officers and men of Sullivan's brigade, that our fate would have been the same, had it not been for Col. Burr; I was a sergeant-major in

Chandler's regiment of Silliman's brigade at the time of the retreat. I am, your very humble sevt.

NATHL. JUDSON.

To R. V. MORRIS, ESQ.

Letter from COLONEL RICHARD PLATT *to* COMMODORE V. MORRIS.

(Copy).

NEW YORK, *January* 27, 1814.

VALENTINE MORRIS, ESQ.,

DEAR SIR: In reply to yours of the of November last, requesting to be informed what was the reputation and services of Colonel Burr during the Revolutionary War, I give you the following detail of facts which you may rely on, as no man was better acquainted with him and his military operation than your humble servant, who served in that war from the 28th of June, 1775, till the evacuation of our capital, on the memorable 25th November, 1783; having passed through the grades of Lieutenant, Captain, Major, Major of Brigade, Aid-de-Camp, Deputy-Adjutant-General, and Deputy-Quartermaster-General, the last of which by selection and recommendation of General Greene, McDougal, and Knox, in the most trying crisis of the Revolution, viz., the year 1780, when the Continental money ceased to pass, and there was no other fiscal resource during that campaign but what resulted from the creative genius of Timothy Pickering, then appointed successor to General Greene, the second officer of the American army, who resigned that department because there was no money in the national coffers to carry it through the campaign, declaring that he could not nor would not attempt it without adequate resources, such as he abounded in during the term of nearly three years antecedently as quartermaster-general.

In addition to the foregoing, by way of elucidation, it is to be understood by you, that so early as from the latter part of the year 1776, I was always attached to a commanding general, and in consequence, my knowledge of the officers and their merits was more general than that of almost any other in the service, and my operations were upon the extended scale from the remotest parts of Canada, wherever the American standard had waved, to the splendid theatre of Yorktown, when and where I was adjutant-general to the chosen troops of the northern army.

At the commencement of the Revolution, Colonel Burr, then about eighteen years of age, at the first sound of the trump of war (as if bred in the camp of the Great Frederick, whose maxim was: "To hold his army always in readiness to break a lance with or throw a dart against any assailant,") quit his professional studies and rushed to the camp of General Washington, at Cambridge, as a volunteer, from which he went with Colonel Arnold, on his daring enterprise against Quebec, through the wilds of Canada (which vied with Hannibal's march over the Alps), during which toilsome and hazardous march he attracted the admiration of his commander so much that he (Arnold) sent him alone to meet and hurry down General Montgomery's army from Montreal, to his assistance, and recommended him to that general, who appointed him his aid-de-camp, in which capacity he acted during the winter, till the fatal assault on Quebec, in which that gallant general, his aid, McPherson, and Captain Cheesman, commanding the forlorn hope, fell; and afterward continued as aid to Arnold, the survivor in command.

Here I must begin to draw some of the outlines of his genius and valor, which, like those of the British immortal Wolfe, who, at the age of twenty-four, and only major of the 20th regiment, serving on the continent, gave such specimens of genius and talents, as to evince his being destined for command.

At the perilous moment of Montgomery's death, when dismay and consternation universally prevailed, and the column halted, he animated the troops, and made many efforts to lead them on, and stimulated them to enter the lower town, and might have succeeded but for the positive orders of Colonel Donald Campbell, the commanding officer, for the troops to retreat. Had his plan been carried into effect, it might have saved Arnold's division from capture, which had, after our retreat, to contend with all the British force instead of a part. On this occasion I commanded the first company in the first New York regiment, at the head of Montgomery's column, so that I speak from ocular demonstration.

The next campaign, 1776, Colonel Burr was appointed aid-de-camp to Major-General Putnam, second in command under General Washington, at New York, and from my knowledge of that general's qualities and the colonel's, I am very certain that the latter directed all the movements and operations of the former.

In January, 1777, the continental establishment for the war commenced. Then Colonel Burr was appointed by General Washington a lieutenant-colonel in Malcom's regiment, in which he continued to serve until April or May, 1779, when the ill state of his health obliged him to retire from active service, to the regret of General McDougal, commanding the department, and those of the commander-in-chief, who offered to give him a furlough for any length of time, and to get permission from the British general in New York for him to go to Bermuda for his health.

This item will show his value in the estimation of Generals Washington and McDougal:

During the campaign of 1777, Malcom's regiment was with the main army, and commanded by the lieutenant-colonel. For discipline, order, and system, it was not surpassed by any in the service, and could his (the lieutenant-colonel's) and Wolfe's orderly books be produced, they would be very similar in point of military policy and instructions, and fit models for all regiments.

This regiment was also hutted at the Valley Forge in 1777 and winter of 1778, under General Washington, and composed part of his army at the battle of Monmouth, on the 28th of June, 1778, and continued with it until the close of the campaign of that year, at which time it was placed in garrison at West Point by General Gates; but upon General McDougal assuming the command of the posts in the Highlands in December, Malcom's, Spencer's, and Patten's regiments were together ordered to Haverstraw, the three colonels were permitted to go home for the winter on furlough, and Lieutenant-Colonel Burr had the command of the whole brigade at a very important advanced post.

At this period General McDougal ordered a detachment of about three hundred troops, under the command of Lieutenant-Colonel Littlefield of the Massachusetts line, to guard the lines in Westchester County, then extending from Tarrytown to Whiteplains, and from thence to Mamaroneck or Saw Pits, which last extension was guarded by Connecticut troops from Major-General Putnam's division.

In this situation of affairs, a very singular occurrence presented, viz., that neither Lieutenant-Colonel Littlefield nor any other of his grade in the two entire brigades of Massachusetts troops composing the garrison of West Point, from which the lines were to be relieved, was competent, in the general's estimation, to give security to the army above and lines below; and in consequence he was compelled to call Colonel Burr from his station at Haverstraw, to the more important command of the lines in Westchester, in which measure, unprecedented as it was, the officers acquiesced without a murmur, from a conviction of its expediency. At this time I was doing the duty of adjutant-general to General McDougal.

It was on this new and interesting theatre of war that the confidence and affections of the officers and soldiers (who now became permanent on the lines, instead of being relieved every two or three weeks as before) as well as of the inhabitants, all before unknown to Colonel Burr, were inspired with confidence by a system of consummate skill, astonishing vigilance, and extreme activity, which in like manner made such an impression on the enemy, that after an unsuccessful attack on one of his advanced posts, he never made any other attack on our lines during the winter.

His humanity and constant regard to the security of the property and persons of the inhabitants from injury and insult, were not less conspicuous than his military skill, etc. No man was insulted or disturbed; the health of the troops was perfect; not a desertion during the whole period of his command, nor a man made prisoner, though the colonel was constantly making prisoners.

A country which, for three years before, had been a scene of robbery, cruelty, and murder, became at once the abode of security and peace. Though his powers were despotic, they were exercised only for the peace, the security, and protection of the country and its inhabitants.

In the winter of 1779, the latter part of it, Major Hull, an excellent officer, then in the Massachusetts line, was sent down as second to Colonel Burr, who, after having been familiarized to his system, succeeded him for a short time in command, about the last of April, at which time Colonel Burr's health would not permit him to continue in command; but the major was soon compelled to fall back many miles, so as to be within supporting distance of the army to the Highlands.

The severity of the service, and the ardent and increasing activity with which he had devoted himself to his country's cause for more than four years, having materially impaired his health, he was compelled to leave the post and retire from active service. It was two years before he regained his health.

Major Hull has ever since borne uniformly the most honorable testimony of the exalted talents of his commander, by declaring his gratitude for being placed under an officer whose system of duty was different from that of all other commanders under whom he had served.

Having thus exhibited the colonel's line of march and his operations in service, I must now present him in contrast with his equals in rank and his superiors in command.

In September, 1777, the enemy came out on both sides of the Hudson simultaneously, in considerable force, say from two to three thousand men; on the east side (at Peekskill) was a major-general of our army, with an effective force of about two thousand men. The enemy advanced, and our general retired without engaging them; our barracks and store-houses and the whole village of Peekskill were sacked and burnt and the country pillaged.

On the west side, at the mouth of the Clove, near Suffre· was Colonel Burr, commanding Malcom's regiment, about three hundred and fifty men. On the first alarm he marched to find the enemy, and on the same night attacked and took their picket guard, rallied the country, and made such show of war that the enemy retreated the next morning, leaving behind him the cattle, horses, and sheep they had plundered.

The year following, Lieutenant-Colonel Thompson was sent to command on the same lines, in Westchester, by General Heath, and he was surprised at nine or ten o'clock in the day, and made prisoner, with a great part of his detachment.

Again, in the succeeding winter, Colonel Green, of the Rhode Island line, with his own and another Rhode Island regiment, who was a very distinguished officer, and had with these two regiments, in the year 1777, defeated Hessian grenadiers, under Count Donap, at Red Bank, on the Delaware, who was mortally wounded and taken prisoner, commanded on the lines in Westchester, there receded to Pine's Bridge, and in this position Colonel Green's troops were also surprised after breakfast and dispersed, the colonel himself and Major Flagg killed, and many soldiers made prisoners, besides killed and wounded.

On the west side of the Hudson, in the year 1780, General Wayne, the hero of Stony Point, with a large command, and field artillery, made an attack on a block house, nearly opposite Dobb's ferry, defended by Cow-boys, and was repulsed with loss; whereas Col. Burr burnt and destroyed one of a similar kind in the winter of 1779, near Delancy's Mills, with a very few men and without any loss on his part, besides capturing the garrison.

Here, my good friend, Commodore, I must drop the curtain till I see you in Albany, which will be in the first week in February; where I can and will convince you that he is the only man in America, (that is) the United States, who is fit to be a lieutenant-general, and let you and I, and all the American people look out for Mr. Madison's lieutenant-general in contrast. Adieu. I am,

Your friend and most obt. servt.,

(Signed) RICHD. PLATT.

Copy of a letter from ROBERT HUNTER, ESQ., *formerly a lieutenant in* MALCOM'S *regiment, to* GABRIEL FURMAN, ESQ., *member of Assembly.*

NEW YORK, *January 22d*, 1814.

DEAR SIR: I have understood that an application will be made to the Legislature by, or on behalf of Col. Burr, for remuneration for his military services during our Revolutionary war.

Having had the happiness to serve under him for more than two years, and having retained an unbounded respect for his talents and character, you will pardon me for asking your active support of anything which may be moved in his favor; for certainly if any officer of the army deserved recompense, it is Col. Burr.

He sacrificed his health, and underwent more fatigue and privations than any other officer of whom I had any knowledge.

If I thought it could be useful to him or amusing to you, I would enter into details; but the facts are of general notoriety, and his superiority as a military man, is, as far as my knowledge extends, universally allowed.

I will, however, detain you while I relate a single incident, because it was the first of which I was a witness: I was attached as a cadet to Col. Malcom's regiment, then stationed in the Clove, when Burr joined it as lieutenant-colonel, being in the summer of 1777; Malcolm seeing that his presence was unnecessary while Burr was there, was with his family about twenty miles distant. Early in September we heard that the enemy were out in great force; Burr gave orders for the security of the camp and of the public stores, and within one hour after news was received, marched with the choice of the regiment to find the enemy; at Paramus the militia were assembled in considerable force, but in great disorder and terror; no one could tell the force or position of the enemy; Burr assumed the command, to which they submitted cheerfully, as he alone (though but a boy in appearance) seemed to know what he was about; he arranged and encouraged them as well as time would permit, and taking a few of the most hardy of the men, continued his march toward the enemy; two or three miles this side Hackensack, we learned that we were near the enemy's advanced guard; Burr chose a convenient place for the men to repose, and went himself to examine the position of the enemy; a little before daylight he returned, waked us and ordered us to follow him; he led us silently and undiscovered within a few paces of the British guard, which we took or killed; from the prisoners we learned that the enemy were about 2,000 strong; without loss of time he sent expresses with orders to the militia, and to call out the country, and I have no doubt but he would within forty-eight hours have had an army capable of checking the progress of the enemy, and of preventing or impeding their retreat; but they retreated the day following, and with every mark of precipitation; during these two days and nights, the colonel did not lay down or take a minute's repose; thus you perceive, my dear sir, that Burr being more than thirty miles distant when he heard of the enemy, was in their camp the same night; you will agree with me that things are not done so now-a-days.

Similar instances of activity and enterprise occurred in each of the four campaigns he served, and very frequently during the winter he commanded on the lines of West Chester.

I repeat that it will afford me pleasure to relate so much of these things as came to my own knowledge, if it would be of any use.

Malcom was never a month with the regiment after Burr joined it, so that it was Burr who formed it, and it was a model for the whole army in discipline and order; he never in a single instance permitted any corporal punishment.

His attention and care of the men was such as I never saw,

nor anything approaching to it, in any other officer, though I served under many,

It would be a disgrace to the country if such a man should be denied a liberal compensation, when it is too well known that he stands in need of it.

I shall consider myself as personally obliged by your exertions in his favor, and hope your colleagues will add theirs to yours.

Please to show this letter to your colleagues, and to offer them my respects. I am, yours, etc.,

(Signed) ROBERT HUNTER.

To G. FURMAN, ESQ., *Member of Assembly, Albany,*

Copy of a letter from SAMUEL YOUNG, ESQ., *of West Chester County, lately Member of Assembly, and for many years Surrogate of the county, to* COMMODORE VALENTINE MORRIS.

MOUNT PLEASANT, *January 25th*, 1814.

DEAR SIR: Your letter of the 30th ult., asking for some account of the campaign in which I served under the command of Col. Burr during the Revolutionary War, was received some days ago, and has been constantly in my mind. I will reply to it with pleasure, but the compass of a letter will not admit of much detail.

I resided in the lines from the commencement of the Revolution until the winter of the year 1780, when my father's house was burned by order of the British general; the county of West Chester, very soon after the commencement of hostilities, became, on account of its exposed situation, a scene of the deepest distress; from the Croton to King's Bridge, every species of rapine and lawless violence prevailed; no man went to his bed but under the apprehension of having his house plundered or burned, or himself or family massacred before morning; some, under the character of Whigs, plundered the Tories, while others of the latter description plundered the Whigs; parties of marauders, assuming either character, or none, as suited their convenience, indiscriminately assailed both Whigs and Tories; so little vigilance was used on our part, that the emissaries and spies of the enemy passed and repassed without interruption.

These calamities continued undiminished until the arrival of Col. Burr, in the autumn of the year 1778; he took command of the same troops which his predecessor, Col. Littlefield, commanded; at the moment of Col. Burr's arrival, Col. Littlefield had returned from a plundering expedition (for to plunder those called Tories was then deemed lawful), and had brought up horses, cattle, bedding, clothing and other articles of easy transportation, which he had proposed to distribute among the party the next day; Col. Burr's first act of authority was to seize and secure all this plunder, and he immediately took measures for restoring it to the owners; this gave us much trouble, but it was abundantly repaid by the confidence it inspired; he then made known his determination to suppress plundering; the same day he visited all the guards, changed their position, dismissed some of the officers whom he found totally incompetent, gave new instructions; on the same day, also, he commenced a register of the names and characters of all who resided near and below his guards; distinguished by secret marks, the Whig, the timid Whig, the Tory, the horse-thief, and those concerned in, or suspected of giving information to the enemy; he also began a map of the country in the vicinity of the fort, of the roads, by-roads, paths, creeks, morasses, etc., which might become hiding-places for the disaffected, or for marauding parties; this map was made by Col Burr, himself, from such materials as he could collect on the spot, but principally from his own observation.

He raised and established a corps of horsemen from among the respectable farmers and young men of the country, of tried patriotism, fidelity, and courage; these also served as aids and confidential persons for the transmission of orders. To this corps I attached myself as a volunteer; but did not receive pay. He employed discreet and faithful persons, living near the enemy's lines, to watch their motions, and give him immediate intelligence. He employed mounted videttes for the same purpose, directing two of them to proceed together, so that one might be dispatched, if necessary, with information to the colonel, while the other might watch the enemy's movement. He established signals throughout the lines, so that whether by night or day, instant notice could be had of an attack or movement of the enemy. He enforced various regulations for concealing his positions and force from the enemy.

The laxity of discipline which had before prevailed, enabled the enemy frequently to employ their emissaries to come within the lines and to learn the precise state of our forces, supplies, etc. Colonel Burr soon put an end to these dangerous intrusions, by prohibiting all persons residing below the lines, except a few whom he selected, such as Parson Bartow, Jacob Smith, and others, whose integrity was unimpeachable, from approaching the outposts without special permission for the purpose. If any one had a complaint or request to make of the colonel, he procured one or more of the persons he had selected, to come to his quarters on his behalf; this measure prevented frivolous and vexatious applications, and the still more dangerous approach of enemies in disguise. All these measures were entirely new, and within eight or ten days the whole system appeared to be in complete operation, and the face of things was totally changed.

A few days after the colonel's arrival, the house of one Gedney was plundered in the night, and the family abused and terrified. Gedney sent his son to make a representation of it to the colonel. The young man not regarding the orders which had been issued, came to the colonel's quarters, undiscovered by the sentinels, having taken a secret path through the fields for the purpose. For this violation of orders the young man was punished. The colonel immediately took measures for the detection of the plunderers, and though they were all disguised and wholly unknown to Gedney, yet Colonel Burr, by means which were never yet disclosed, discovered the plunderers, and had them all secured within twenty-four hours.

Gedney's family, on reference to his register, appeared to be Tories, but Burr had promised that every quiet man should be protected.

He caused the robbers to be conveyed to Gedney's house, under the charge of Captain Benson, there to restore the booty they had taken; to make reparation in money for such articles as were lost or damaged, and for the alarm and abuse, the amount of which the colonel assessed; to be flogged ten lashes, and to ask pardon of the old man, all which was faithfully and immediately executed.

These measures gave universal satisfaction, and the terror they inspired effectually prevented a repetition of similar depredations. From this day plundering ceased. No further instance occurred during the time of Colonel Burr's command; for it was universally believed that Colonel Burr could tell a robber by looking in his face, or that he had supernatural means of discovering crime. Indeed I was myself inclined to these opinions. This belief was confirmed by another circumstance which had previously occurred. On the day of his arrival, after our return from visiting the posts, conversing with several of his attendants, and among others Lieutenant Drake, whom Burr had brought with him from his own regiment, he said: "Drake, that post on the North River will be attacked before morning; neither officers nor men know anything of their duty. You must go and take charge of it. Keep your eyes open, or you will have your throat cut." Drake went. The post was attacked that night by a company of horse. They were repulsed with loss. Drake returned in the morning with trophies of war, and told his story. We stared and asked one another, "How could Burr know that?" (for he had not then established any means of intelligence.)

The measures immediately adopted by him were such that it was impossible for the enemy to have passed their own lines without his having immediate knowledge, and it was these very measures which saved Major Hull, on whom the command devolved for a short time, when the state of Colonel Burr's health compelled him to retire.

These measures, together with the deportment of Colonel Burr, gained him the love and veneration of all devoted to the common cause, and conciliated even its bitterest foes. His habits were a subject of admiration: his diet was simple and spare in the extreme; seldom sleeping more than an hour at a time, and without taking off his clothes or even his boots. Between midnight and two o'clock in the morning, accompanied by two or three of his corps of horsemen, he visited the quarters of all his captains, and their picket guards, changing his route from time to time, to prevent notice of his approach. You may judge of the severity of this duty when I assure you that the distance which he thus rode every night must have been from sixteen to twenty-four miles, and that with the exception of two nights only in which he was otherwise engaged, he never omitted these excursions, even in the severest and most stormy weather; and except the short time necessarily consumed in hearing and answering commands and petitions from persons both above and below the lines, Colonel Burr was constantly with the troops.

He attended to the minutest articles of their comfort—to their lodgings, to their diet; for those off duty he invented sports, all tending to some useful end. During two or three weeks after the colonel's arrival, we had many sharp conflicts with the robbers and horse thieves, who were hunted down with unceasing industry. In many instances we encountered great superiority of numbers; but always with success. Many of them were killed and many taken.

The strictest discipline prevailed, and the army felt the fullest confidence in their commander and in themselves, and by these means became really formidable to the enemy. During the same winter Governor Tryon planned an expedition to Horseneck, for the purpose of destroying the salt-works erected there, and marched with about two thousand men. Colonel Burr received early information of their movements, and sent word to General Putnam to hold the enemy at bay for a few hours, and he (Colonel Burr) would be in their rear, and be answerable for them. By a messenger from him, Col.

Burr was informed by that general, that he had been obliged to retreat, and that the enemy were advancing into Connecticut. This information, which unfortunately was not correct, altered Colonel Burr's route toward Mamaroneck, which enabled Tryon to get the start of him. Colonel Burr then endeavored to intercept him in Eastchester, according to his first plan, and actually got within cannon shot of him. But Tryon run too fast, and in his haste left most or all of his cattle and plunder behind him, and many stragglers who were picked up.

I will mention another enterprise which proved more successful, though equally hazardous. Soon after Tryon's retreat, Colonel Delancy, who commanded the British refugees, in order to secure themselves against surprise, erected a block house on a rising ground below Delancy's Bridge. This Col. Burr resolved to destroy. I was in that expedition, and recollect the circumstances.

He procured a number of hand-grenades, also rolls of port-fire, and canteens filled with inflammable materials, with contrivances to attach them to the side of the block-house. He set out with his troops early in the evening, and arrived within a mile of the block-house by two o'clock in the morning. The colonel gave Captain Black the command of about forty volunteers, who were first to approach. Twenty of them were to carry the port-fires, etc., etc. Those who had hand-grenades had short ladders to enable them to reach the port-holes, the exact height of which Colonel Burr had ascertained. Colonel Burr gave Captain Black his instructions in the hearing of his company, assuring him of his protection if they were attacked by superior numbers; for it was expected that the enemy, who had several thousand men at and near King's Bridge, would endeavor to cut us off, as we were several miles below them. Burr directed those who carried the combustibles to march in front as silently as possible; that on being hailed, they should light the hand-grenades, etc., with a slow match provided for the purpose, and throw them into the port-holes. I was one of the party that advanced. The sentinel hailed and fired. We rushed on. The first hand-grenade that was thrown in drove the enemy from the upper story, and before they could take any measure to defend it, the block-house was on fire in several places. Some few escaped, and the rest surrendered without our having lost a single man. Though many shots were fired at us, we did not fire a gun.

During the period of Colonel Burr's command, but two attempts were made by the enemy to surprise our guards, in both of which they were defeated.

After Colonel Burr left this command, Colonel Thompson, a man of approved bravery, assumed it, and the enemy, in open day, advanced to his head-quarters, took Colonel Thompson, and took and killed all his men with the exception of about thirty.

My father's house, with all his out-houses were burnt. After these disasters, our troops never made an effort to protect that part of the country. The American lines were afterward changed and extended from Bedford to Croton Bridge, and from there, following the course of that river, to the Hudson. All the intermediate country was abandoned and unprotected, being about twenty miles in the rear of the ground which Colonel Burr had maintained.

The year after the defeat of Colonel Thompson, Colonel Green, a brave, and in many respects a valuable officer, took the command, making his head-quarters at Danfords, about a mile above the Croton. This position was well chosen; but Colonel Green omitted to inform himself of the movements of the enemy, and, consequently, was surprised. Himself, Major Flagg, and other officers were killed, and a great part of the men were either killed or taken prisoners; yet these officers had the full benefit of Colonel Burr's system.

Having perused what I have written, it does not appear to me that I have conveyed any adequate idea of Burr's military character. It may be aided a little by reviewing the effects he produced. The troops of which he took command were, at the time he took the command, undisciplined, negligent, and discontented; desertions were frequent. In a few days these very men were transformed into brave and honest defenders—orderly, contented, and cheerful, confident in their own courage, and loving to adoration their commander, whom every man considered as his personal friend. It was thought a severe punishment as well as a disgrace to be sent up to the camp, where they had nothing to do but to lounge and eat their rations.

During the whole of his command, there was not a single desertion; not a single death by sickness; not one made prisoner by the enemy; for Burr had taught us that a soldier with arms in his hand ought never, under any circumstances, to surrender; no matter if he was opposed to thousands, it was his duty to fight.

After the first ten days, there was not a single instance of robbery. The whole country under his command enjoyed security. The inhabitants, to express their gratitude, frequently brought presents of such articles as the country afforded; but Colonel Burr would accept no present. He fixed reasonable prices, and paid in cash for everything that was received, and sometimes I know that these payments were made with his own money. Whether these advances were repaid, I know not.

Colonel Simcoe, one of the most daring and active partisans in the British army, was, with Colonels Emerick and Delancy, opposed to Burr on the lines, yet they were completely held in check.

But perhaps the highest eulogy on Colonel Burr is, that no man could be found capable of executing his plans, though the example was before them.

When Burr left the lines a sadness overspread the country, and the most gloomy forebodings were too soon fulfilled, as you have seen above.

The period of Colonel Burr's command was so full of activity and of incident, that every day afforded some new lesson o instruction.

But you will expect only a general outline, and this faint one is the best in my power to give.

I am, with real esteem,
Your obedient servant,
(Signed) SAMUEL YOUNG.

MARGARET MONCRIEFFE, GENERAL PUTNAM, AND AARON BURR.

From Parton's Life of Aaron Burr, pp. 88–95.

At Kingsbridge, about the date of this letter,* Burr was engaged in an adventure little in harmony with the warlike scenes around him.

The breaking out of the Revolutionary War found a number of British officers domesticated among the colonists, and connected with them by marriage. In New York and the other garrisoned towns, officers of the army led society, as military men still do in every garrisoned town in the world. When hostilities began, and every man was ordered to his post, some of these officers left their families residing among the people; and it happened, in a few instances, that the events of war carried a father far away from his wife and children, never to rejoin them. The future Scott of America will know how to make all this very familiar to the American people by the romantic and pathetic fictions which it will suggest to him.

Margaret Moncrieffe, a girl of fourteen, but a woman in development and appetite, witty, vivacious, piquant, and beautiful, had been left at Elizabethtown, in New Jersey, by her father, Major Moncrieffe, who was then with his regiment on Staten Island, and of course cut off from communication with his daughter. Destitute of resources, and anxious to rejoin her father, she wrote to General Putnam for his advice and

* September, 1776.

assistance. General Putnam received her letter in New York about the time that Major Burr joined him, and his reply was prepared for his signature by the hand of his new aid-de-camp. The good old general declared in this letter that he was her father's enemy, indeed, as an officer, but as a man, his friend, and ready to do any good office for him or his. He invited her to come and reside in his family until arrangements could be made for sending her to Staten Island. She consented, an officer was sent to conduct her to the city, and she was at once established in General Putnam's house. There she met and became intimate with Major Burr.

What followed from their intimacy has been stated variously. Great indeed was my astonishment, on recurring to the work itself,* to find that her narrative, read in connection, not only affords no support to Mr. Davis' insinuations, but explicitly, and twice, contradicts them. It is known and conceded that the young officer whom she extols in such passionate language, and whom she miscalls "colonel," was Major Burr. Thus writes Mrs. Coughlan, *née* Moncrieffe:

"When I arrived in Broadway (a street so called), where General Putnam resided, I was received with great tenderness, both by Mrs. Putnam and her daughters, and on the following day I was introduced by them to General and Mrs. Washington, who likewise made it their study to show me every mark of regard; but I seldom was allowed to be alone, although sometimes, indeed, I found an opportunity to escape to the gallery on the top of the house, where my chief delight was to view, with a telescope, our fleet and army on Staten Island. My amusements were few; the good Mrs. Putnam employed me and her daughters constantly to spin flax for shirts for the American soldiers, indolence, in America, being totally discouraged; and I likewise worked for General Putnam, who, though not an accomplished *muscadin*, like our dilettanti of St. James' street, was certainly one of the best characters in the world, his heart being composed of those

* Memoirs of Maj'r Coughlan, published by Swords, New York.

noble materials which equally command respect and admiration.

* * * * * * * *

"Not long after this circumstance, a flag of truce arrived from Staten Island, with letters from Major Moncrieffe, demanding me, for they now considered me as a prisoner. General Washington would not acquiesce in this demand, saying 'that I should remain a hostage for my father's good behavior.' I must here observe, that when General Washington refused to deliver me up, the noble-minded Putnam, as if it were by instinct, laid his hand on his sword, and, with a violent oath, swore 'that my father's request *should* be granted.' The commander-in-chief, whose influence governed the Congress, soon prevailed on them to consider me as a person whose situation required their strict attention; and that I might not escape, they ordered me to Kingsbridge, where, in justice, I must say, that I was treated with the utmost tenderness. General Mifflin there commanded. His lady was a most accomplished, beautiful woman—a Quaker. And here my heart received its first impression—an impression that, amidst the subsequent shocks which it has received, has never been effaced, and which rendered me very unfit to admit the embraces of an unfeeling, brutish husband.

"O, may these pages one day meet the eye of him* who subdued my virgin heart, whom the immutable, unerring laws of nature had pointed out for my husband, but whose sacred decree the barbarous customs of society fatally violated. To him I plighted my virgin vow, and I shall never cease to lament that obedience to a father left it incomplete. When I reflect on my past sufferings, now that, alas! my present sorrows press heavily upon me, I cannot refrain from expatiating a little on the inevitable horrors which ever attend the frustration of natural affections: I myself, who, unpitied by the world, have endured every calamity that human nature knows, am a melancholy example of this truth; for if I know

* Col. Aaron Burr.

my own heart, it is far better calculated for the purer joys of domestic life, than for the hurricane of extravagance and dissipation in which I have been wrecked.

"Why is the will of nature so often perverted? Why is social happiness forever sacrificed at the altar of prejudice? Avarice has usurped the throne of reason, and the affections of the heart are not consulted. We cannot command our desires, and when the object of our being is unattained, misery must be necessarily our doom. Let this truth, therefore, be forever remembered: when once an affection has rooted itself in a tender, constant heart, no time, no circumstance can eradicate it. Unfortunate, then, are they who are joined, if their hearts are not matched!

"With this conqueror of my soul, how happy should I now have been! What storms and tempests should I have avoided (at least I am pleased to think so) if I had been allowed to follow the bent of my inclinations! and happier, O, ten thousand times happier should I have been with him, in the wildest desert of our native country, the woods affording us our only shelter, and their fruits our only repast, than under the canopy of costly state, with all the refinements and embellishments of courts, with the royal warrior who would fain have proved himself the conqueror of France.

"My conqueror was engaged in another cause, he was ambitious to obtain other laurels: he fought to liberate, not to enslave nations. He was a colonel in the American army, and high in the estimation of his country: his victories were never accompanied with one gloomy, relenting thought; they shone as bright as the cause which achieved them! I had communicated by letter to General Putnam the proposals of this gentleman, with my determination to accept them, and I was embarrassed by the answer which the general returned; he entreated me to remember that the person in question, from his political principles, was extremely obnoxious to my father, and concluded by observing, 'that I surely must not unite myself with a man who would not hesitate to drench his sword in the blood of my nearest relation, should he be opposed to him in battle.' Saying this, he lamented the necessity of giving advice contrary to his own sentiments, since in every other respect he considered the match as unexceptionable."

According to a story told by the late Colonel W. L. Stone (author of the "Life of Brant"), it was no other than Burr himself. Before her arrival at General Putnam's, it appears that Burr, though he was delighted with her wit and vivacity, conceived the idea that she might be a British spy; and as he was looking over her shoulder one day, while she was painting a bouquet, the suspicion darted into his mind that she was using the "language of flowers" for the purpose of conveying intelligence to the enemy. He communicated his suspicion to General Washington, who thought it only prudent to remove her a few miles further inland, to the quarters of General Mifflin; where, after the evacuation of the city, Burr met her again, and, as she says, won her virgin affections. Colonel Stone was very intimate with Burr in his later years, and had long conversations with him about Revolutionary times. He may have derived this pretty tale from Burr himself.

PARAGRAPH RELATING TO MARGARET MONCRIEFFE.

From a New York Newspaper of July, 1846.

During the Revolutionary War, there was an extraordinary lady, highly gifted and beautiful, who made a great noise at that time, by the name of Moncrieffe, who subsequently wrote her memoirs, which will be found in the City Library. While she was riding on horseback near our lines, with a servant, she was taken prisoner and brought to West Point, her father being a major in the British service, and a distinguished engineer. She was detained as a prisoner by General Putnam. An American officer of any rank, she said, would be given for her. She commenced drawing flowers for her amusement, which were executed with great taste and skill, and presented them to General Putnam. She drew some also for her own purposes. In this manner her time was occupied for several days, promenading the walks wheresoever she thought proper. Col. Burr, aid to Putnam, was absent during this period. On his return to camp, these specimens of the lady's taste and talent were shown to him. He requested the favor of being shown all that she had drawn for her own use. They were promptly produced. After being entirely satisfied that he had them all in his possession, he remarked that they were so beautiful, and so admirably executed, that he could not part with them. At or about this time, the works at West Point had undergone great improvement and repairs, under the superintendence of a French engineer. On retiring from the presence of Miss Moncrieffe, Col. Burr exhibited to General Putnam, and the other officers, who had paid no attention to the drawings, some faint lines under the flowers which the lady had painted—that those lines, when connected, was a complete draft of all the works, as recently improved, and which she intended to bear off to the camp of the enemy. Her capture was premeditated. Miss Moncrieffe was a regular spy in petticoats. She was sent down to New York, and staid at head-quarters, at the corner of Broadway and the Battery; but she was so close an observer of everything going on, that the commanding general had to send her to her father, who was with the British troops in New Jersey.

COL. BURR DENIES CLAIMING PROTECTION AS A BRITISH SUBJECT.

"New York, 28*th July*, 1812.

"Sir: When interrupted this morning, I was about to say to B—— that when abroad in whatever part of the World, I always defended and eulogized our political and municipal institutions. It was often objected to me that I myself had been a victim of Democratic rage. Is there any other Government in the World under which only one man out of 5,000,000 can complain of oppression? If not, a single instance proves nothing against the forms of Government. A reply which is more suited to silence, though perhaps without convincing the objector.

"Another rumor which has been industriously circulated, may have appeared to you more probable, to wit, that I had claimed protection as a British subject, having had some difficulty with the Home Department, (then Lord Liverpool's) about passports and permission to travel (which terminated in my imprisonment and banishment).

"It was strongly recommended to me by a man of very high consideration, enjoying an important place under Government, but hating personally Lord Liverpool, to defend myself against his persecutions, by claiming my birth-right as a British subject. It was presumed that I would cheerfully seize this mode to disengage myself from thraldom, and to mortify and if I should please, to punish Lord Liverpool.

"It became a topic of conversation, and many distinguished persons took a very lively interest in the question. A very profound, and learned argument of 60 octavo pages, tracing the law from the time of William the Conqueror to the then present day (1808) was drawn up *for the occasion* by one of the ablest and most celebrated Lawyers in the British dominions, and put into my hands. My rights were Demonstrated beyond a doubt. *I refused to suffer myself to be called a British subject, for a single day; for any purpose, under any circumstances; nor did I at any moment swerve from this determination.*"

The letter from which the above is extracted, was addressed to his tried and intimate friend, Erie Bolman, Esq., of Philadelphia, and has been very strangely overlooked by **M. L. Davis, and Parton.**

APPENDIX II.

LETTERS OF COL. BURR TO "KATE."

AND so my dear Kate has come a little nearer. I do think I shall call one of these days and take a dish of tea with you, and be off again in half an hour; in the meantime I want to be a little better acquainted with you and the brats; tell me their ages and what they are like, and be a little more communicative about your pretty self; have you grown fat or lean, or neither? *Est ce que tu es toujours belle? je veux que ma nièce soit toujours belle;* now if you dare grow ugly, Lord, how I will hate you?

21*st, August*, 1812.

MY DEAR KATE: While I read your letter, I seem to hear the sound of that soft voice which has so often charmed me. How I wish you were near me to help me dispel this gloom that threatens to subdue my soul; indeed my dear creature, I am fit for nothing.

Your offer of a refuge for a victim of despair, is kind and considerate, but alas, I fear the subject of it will smile under the weight of his afflictions.

Excuse me, my lovely friend; in a few days I will write you more.

7*th February*, 1813.

MY DEAR KATE: I have received your letter of yesterday, but not in season to answer by return of mail.

Theodosia sailed from Georgetown, S. C., on the 30th, Dec., being thirty-eight days ago, in the pilot boat schooner, the Patriot, Capt. Soustocks; since that day nothing has been heard of her, nor of the vessel, and I am filled with the most gloomy apprehensions; my hope is, that the vessel may have been taken and carried into Bermuda, where, I have every reason to believe, she would be treated with respect and hospitality; but indeed I am wretched, and the utter impossibility of doing anything for her relief or my own, makes me still more so. When or how this dreadful suspense will terminate, God only knows.

LETTER OF COL. BURR TO ELIZA.

Your little letter of the 16th, my dear Eliza, is full of consolation and goodness, and now you are away, God knows where; Julia condescended to seek me; she won't do at all; sense without refinement—passion without sentiment—*point de tact* —the acquaintance is dropped; my two most useful and most intimate friends are sexagénaires.

I have seen our little coz., Cora, a fine, plump, rosy-cheeked, black-eyed girl, very pretty, and what the men would call desirable; plays and sings well, and is graceful in her manner; *plus anglaise que française;* she has neither money nor protection to undertake the journey proposed, yet she would suit that market; *Mille choses à notre chère cousine.*

The last letter of Min distracts me, yet I augur some good from your visit, it was very, very kind; alas! my sister, I find nothing here like you; the more I compare you with the best I see (and I see *the best*) the more I prize you; our brother writes me that your affairs have been neglected since the absence of your friend; curse their hollow hearts and treacherous promises; but persevere, and let me have the happiness to know that two dear friends are happy.

October the 4th.

LETTER FROM LEONORA TO AARON BURR.

In a postscript to Gov. Alston, the night before the duel with Gen. Hamilton, Burr says: "If you can pardon and indulge a folly, I would suggest that Madame ——, too well known under the name of 'Leonora,' has claims on my recollection. She is now with her husband at St. Jago, of Cuba."

The following letter is from "Leonora" to A. Burr, the orthography of which is strictly adhered to:

CAPE FRANCOIS, HAYTI, *May 6th*, 1818.

I have so much to relate of all that I have seen, heard, and done since my arrival in this country, that I am at a loss where to begin, finding myself in a world where the customs, language, dress & manners were so different from that which I had left. I was at first dazzled & bewildered, but on a nearer view I beheld the passing scene with a cooler eye & I almost despis'd—not the climate, oh no, this charming climate where smiling spring & laughing summer dance their eternal round. I cannot describe the effect it has on me, the nights in particular, love-inspiring nights!—but love was never known in this desolated country, perhaps no one was ever so sensible of this truth as myself—but more of this anon.

Almost a year has passed since I arrived here, during which time I have been coop'd up in the hollow bason in which the town is built, for there is no means of going a mile in any direction beyond it without I chose to make a sortie on the brigands which I have not yet determined on—when I was on the point of leaving the continent, do you recollect having told me, that order would be established here in less than three weeks after my arrival—alas we have beheld months after months passing away & we are still far from that tranquility so much desired—when Toussaint was arrested it was suppos'd the war was finish'd & it would have been had vigorous measures been immediately pursued, but general le Clerc was without energy—tormented by jealousy for his wife, deceived by his officers, impos'd on by the black chiefs with whom he was alway in conference, he saw himself on the point of being made prisoner by the Negroes, & in the danger which his own imprudence had occasion'd, incapable of forming any project of defence, he only thought of saving himself by evacuating the place—this he was prevented doing by the admiral la touche & the efforts of the garde national which had been organiz'd but a few days before, repelled the Negroes & saved the Cape—

the next day he gave a dinner to the officers of the garde national, made them a long speech (they say he was eloquent) and then died of a fever two or three days after. it was the best thing he could do, for if he had continued alive he would have liv'd dishonor'd—

I was presented to his wife a few days before the attack she's small, with a common, laughing face, that announces neither dignity, nor wit, and I who have always thought that people in superior situations should be superior to common people, was surpris'd to find nothing extraordinary in the sister of Bonaparte—I gave her the Medal of Jefferson which I suppose will figure in the collection of Medals at Paris—I saw her but once for she received nobody living retired at a plantation on the mountain—that is she received no ladies, foul mouth'd fame says she was far from cruel to Gen'l Boyer and all the etat major,—however when her husband died, she cut off her hair (which was very beautiful) to put in his coffin & play'd so well the part of a disconsolate widow, that she made every body laugh—after having had him embalm'd she embark'd with his lov'd remains for france, where she is (as I suppose you know) arriv'd—

general Rochambau, who was then commandant at port au prince, was sent for to take the command here, till a captain general should be nam'd,—he came, and here commences the adventures of Clara—do you recollect her? that Clara you once lov'd—She came to St domingo about the time I did, and at first liv'd tranquilly enough with her husband—but you know she never lov'd him & he was jealous, and sometimes render'd her miserable—but the general arriv'd and the scene was chang'd—

Apropos of Clara, you would not know her, positively not, the climate has had on her an effect quite miraculous, she has acquired a degree of enbonpoint that renders her charming, she has grown fairer and her black hair arrang'd a la greque gives her an air truly interesting her person even in your land of beauty was found passable but here it is regarded as a model of perfection—the general soon after his arrival gave a ball, Clara was invited and went, but in the crowd she attracted general notice without attracting the notice of the general—the week following the admiral la touche gave a ball on board his Vessel, Clara was there & there began her empire like that of Venus rising from the waves—the Ball was superb the whole length of the vessel was levell'd with a false floor and cover'd with a painted awning, ornamented with wreaths of natural flowers, with glasses & with lights beyond number—the seats were enclosed by beautiful palisades & the orchestra was plac'd in a gallery surrounding the main mast—you must observe that the creole women have no taste for dress, they cover themselves from head to foot, & the very few French women that are here, have follow'd the army & know very little of taste or fashion—

here then was the Theatre on which Clara exhibited for the first time, where she distanc'd all her rivals. Dressed with a licence which can be authoriz'd only by the heat (for she was almost naked) she was led round the room by an officer, where as a belle-femme and a stranger her vanity was fully gratified by the buzzes of admiration, her husband delighted by the splendor of what he deem'd his property follow'd her at a small distance, at length she was seated, but rous'd from her contemplation of surrounding objects by a flourish of music she turn'd her eyes to the door & saw the general who enter'd at that moment, this moment was decisive, he caught her eye, and saw for that night nothing but herself—when the first dance was finish'd, which she did not join (she walk'd again) her husband following as before, the general stopp'd him and ask'd who is that Lady—Madame ——— replied he—is she not a stranger?—yes an american—she's a charming creature (continued the general) but where's her husband? they say he's very jealous, and bien sot (?)—Monsieur le viola (answer'd the husband) & the general was a little disconcerted—as this conversation finish'd the walse began, he who has not seen Clara walse, knows not half her charms—dance delightful but dance dangerous from a woman fond of walsing, an adroit partner will gain all he wishes—but while she display'd in the mazes of the dance all the voluptuous graces of which her person is susceptible, her eye sought & fix'd that of the general, he alone fill'd her imagination—before the desire of securing that conquest, every other consideration faded, yet 'twas vanity alone that led her to desire it—the general resembles in his person Dr. Brown, rather shorter—and fat you know was always her aversion, but in this country above all things, 'tis dreadful. he has a face agreeable enough, a pretty laughing mouth, but nothing, *nothing* extraordinary, the bitise he had made with her husband, render'd it difficult to approach her & had a fatal influence on the sequel of their acquaintance. at the dawn of day the ball broke up & the company return'd to their homes,—the general had in his suite an officer who was formerly intimate with the husband—the friendship was renew'd and the officer went to the house to reconnoitre,—it is that Duquesne that was in America during the last war, & as he says an ardent admirer of Miss Sally Shippen (now Mrs. Lee)—this Duquesne informed Clara of what she knew as well as himself, that the general was smitten, but he told her also something which she did not know, among which was that a grand ball was preparing at which he was expected to figure, she was invited, she went, and there large as is her portion of vanity, it was amply gratified by seeing the general at her feet, and all the women bursting with envy. The taste of of the general influenc'd that of the company, & all the men offer'd their hommage at the samo shrine, the eye of the husband saw what pass'd—he saw & trembled, proud of possessing an object that excited universal admiration, he trembled lest that object should be wrested from him, he knew that the adoring general was a military despot, he knew also that the heart of his wife had never been his, but it was now too late, he had himself placed her on the scene, & it was not in his power to withdraw her.

Suffer me again to repeat that she was guided by vanity alone, & that not one feeling of her heart was interested, there was fifty young men in the room, whose persons, whose manners, could have interested her highly, some of them *had* almost show'd her tenderest favors, but 'twas power, 'twas place she aim'd at, and had she not been thwarted, she would have rul'd St. Domingue; at present she has sunk back to her original nothingness, because she has a husband who would neither shut his eyes and profit by her powers, nor open them and join her to secure & it this husband she owes to you. To return—the acquaintance here formed, was cultivated with indescribable ardor. Breakfasts, (which the french give delightfully), parties, balls, concerts, all succeeded rapidly, & the penchant of the chief was generally known; here admire the inconsistency of the French character, those who before scarcely noticed Clara since her marriage, now sought her with the utmost impressment, & those who pass'd without saluting her, now that she was almost the declar'd mistress of the general, show'd her the politest attention; the train of amusements was interrupted by an insurrection in the southern part of the colony—the general went to port-au-prince where he staid sometime, but at his return it was again commenc'd; a ball was announc'd for the third day after his arrival, where some interesting affairs were to be discuss'd; when lo! on the morning of that third day the brigands attack'd the town in three different directions, at three o'clock in the morning; they had taken the advanc'd posts by surprise, kill'd the officers, their wives, and the soldiers, and advanc'd upon the town; had they been wise enough to have done this without firing (which they might have done) we had been all lost; imagine our position—the cape is open on one side to the sea, the three others are surrounded by high mountains; on the tops of these mountains the negroes were encamp'd and all the country on the other side is in their power; their plan of attack was good, but it was badly executed, for one of the divisions advancing too precipitately spread the alarm; they were repell'd with great slaughter; all the troops that march'd, as well garde national as troops of the line, were order'd to remain on the frontiers; the general did not go out; he sent word to Clara, whose husband had march'd, to tell her not to be afraid, or if she was, to come to his house, & he'd send her on board the admiral's vessel; this she dar'd not do, having receiv'd orders from her husband, not to stir from the house; but towards evening, after repeated messages from him, she determined to go & to learn the fate of her husband, who had been all day, and still was, expos'd to the fire of the enemy. She went, accompanied by her little friend, & after a visit of half an hour, return'd; this was the only time he saw her except in crowded assemblages, and in the presence of another he could say very little; perhaps there was a piano, perhaps a library, but of this I am not certain; perhaps, also, Clara can say with Mrs. Coughlan,* if he is no better in the fields of Mars than in the groves of Venus, —— etc.

the ball was deferr'd till the next day, and the husband was to be kept at his post till it was over; but the next day news arriv'd from a small island near this place, call'd la tortue, that the negroes had pass'd an arm of the sea that divides it from the main land, & kill'd all the Pick, amounting to five thousand, and burn'd all the hospitals & plantations; this was another hindrance to the ball, and the garde national was permitted to descend; you know that the lives of any number of citizens is a very trifling consideration when the commander-in-chief wishes to remove an incommode husband, & on this occasion they were wantonly trifled with; from

* *Née* Moncrieffe.

this moment the structure of Clara's good fortune was abolish'd; her husband had an infernal old servant who told him as soon as he enter'd, that Madame had gone with a servant of the general's to his house, accompanied by Mademoiselle, that the same servant had often brought letters, which Madame had answered (this, by the bye, was true); this, join'd to the fatigue he had been expos'd to unnecessarily, and the jokes that the officers (who all suspected the cause), pass'd on him, render'd him furious; he went to his wife's chamber, told her that all her conduct was known to him, & demanded the letters she had receiv'd; she denied having receiv'd them, and in short denied the whole affair; enraged at being unable to draw anything from her, he lock'd her up, and went to the general's house; he was receiv'd with great cordiality; but without paying any attention to the general's civility, he told him he had not come on a visit of friendship, but to reproach him with having attempted to seduce his wife, and with having seiz'd the occasion of the last attack, to expose to imminent danger him and the company he commanded, in order to be more at liberty to gratify his desires; the general, astonish'd, assur'd him that he was mistaken; but the husband listen'd not, he told him that if he was any other than the general-in-chief he'd have his life; it rests with you to forget that distinction and consider me as your equal, was the reply; this, however, was impossible; after having vented his wrath in a long speech, representing how abominable it was for a person who should be the father of the colony, and the protection of it's inhabitants, to seek to trouble the repose and destroy the peace of family's, he went off; the officers in the antechamber heard the altercation, and the story flew like wildfire through the town; the husband return'd to the house and prepar'd to embark his wife for Philadelphia; passeports were granted as a great favor for Clara and her suite, but the husband was not suffer'd to go; this leads to another observation; when the attachment was first suspected, the husband had arrang'd his affairs to go to Charleston; this did not please Clara; she inform'd the general, and an order was immediately issued that no officer of the garde national could leave his post during four months; & thus you see she had still some influence in public affairs; but the season was so bad at the time the eclat was made, that every body persuaded him not to send her, & the vessel on which she was to have embark'd, perish'd almost in view of the cape.

shortly after another ball was announced; the gen'ral sent Duquesne to the husband of Clara, begging him to accompany him to it, saying it was the only way to stop the storys that were in circulation; but the husband return'd the billet of invitation, requesting that another might never be sent; the ball had been, and such was the effect of Clara's adventure, that in those rooms which on similar occasions were crowded to suffocation, there was that night but fourteen ladies.

to account for this, you must be told that the inhabitants of this Island, that is, the creoles, regard the french army with more horror than the revolted Negroes, & with great reason. They are oppress'd beyond measure, and see daily the wreck of their fortunes torn from them by those who come to restore their property. The citizens are expos'd on every occasion to the fire of the enemy, while the troops of the line rest quietly in their forts. The people of france regard st. domingo as their peru, and each individual that embarks for it becomes fully determined to make his fortune at all events, & thus the war has been & will be continued for an indefinite time. They were irritated by these and many other vexations, of which they dar'd not complain; but a grief of a new kind was that of troubling a *menage*, not that fidelity was ever known or thought of here; but it was a novelty to see a husband concern himself about such an affair, & it was at least as great a one to see a simple individual propose a challenge to a general-in-chief. Every body expected to see the rash mortal imprisoned, embarked for france, or perhaps hanged; but as the general suffered it to pass, every one join'd the cry, & the people were astonished to find one of their commonest customs made a wonder of. One consideration which, perhaps, had great weight with the general.

was his having written very often and very explicitly to Clara. The letters had been destroyed; but the husband said he had them.

the general lost much of his popularity, and went shortly after to fix his government at port-au-prince, & thus ends the adventure of Clara, who, though she was disappointed in her ambitious aims, has been made so much the object of public attention, that she never appears without fixing every regard; for myself, I live retir'd, applying, with unceasing attention, to learn french, & as a proof of my progress, I send you a page written in that language.

Miss Sansay is so near being married that—to-day is Wednesday—and on Saturday the ceremony will be performed. Since our arrival here, her temperament has declared itself, etc., etc. on that subject, one day or other, I intend exciting your regret. should the story of Clara, with many incidents which I have omitted, and some observations on all that is passing here, be written in a pretty light style, could it be printed in America in a tolerable pamphlet in french and english, & a few numbers sent here? If it could I should be delighted, & know one who would undertake to write it. Answer me. I think this long letter deserves an answer. There's certainly matter enough in it to form a romance; but whose life has afforded so many subjects for romance as that of its writer? I hear sometimes indistinct accounts of the United States, but nothing satisfactory. Have you seen many Swiss emigrants? Have you raised an army to hinder the french taking possession of Louisiana? All this I might learn from the papers, but I don't get them. Adieu. Remember, write to me. Apropos—the lady who takes charge of this paquet is driven from this country by fear—in the last attack she made a vow to the blessed Virgin to throw herself into the sea if the brigands entered the town, so great was her fear that her person should be exposed to their lascivious desires. This was a rash vow, considering she is only sixty-four years old—there's nothing so diverting as the pretensions of the old women here. One of seventy has vowed to wear neither rouge nor lace, nor trinkets till the revolution is finished; giving for reason that ornaments are useless when the people don't enjoy the blessings of tranquillity, and that, perhaps, she might be deranged in the midst of her toilette by a hostile incursion. Do tell me if I write frenchified english, I dread that, of all things; it has so much the air of affectation, which I always abhorr'd. Couldn't answer the letter addressed to my Mentor—he might find himself indisposed to write, or for some other reason. I should prefer it infinitely.

Adieu, je vous embrasse.

LEONORA.

THE END.

MEMOIRS OF THE QUEENS OF FRANCE. Written in France, carefully compiled from researches made there, commended by the press generally, and published from the Tenth London Edition. It is a truly valuable work for the reader and student of history. By MRS. FORBES BUSH. 2 vols. in one. Cloth. Price $1 75.

MEMOIRS OF THE LIFE OF ANNE BOLEYN, QUEEN OF HENRY VIII. In the records of biography there is no character that more forcibly exemplifies the vanity of human ambition, or more thoroughly enlists the attention of the reader than this—the Seventh American, and from the Third London Edition. By MISS BENGER. With portrait on steel. Cloth. $1 75.

HEROIC WOMEN OF HISTORY. Containing the most extraordinary examples of female courage of ancient and modern times, and set before the wives, sisters, and daughters of the country, in the hope that it may make them even more renowned for resolution, fortitude, and self-sacrifice than the Spartan females of old. By HENRY C. WATSON. With Illustrations. Cloth. $1 75.

PUBLIC AND PRIVATE HISTORY OF LOUIS NAPOLEON, EMPEROR OF THE FRENCH. An impartial view of the public and private career of this extraordinary man, giving full information in regard to his most distinguished ministers, generals, relatives and favorites. By SAMUEL M. SCHMUCKER, LL. D. With portraits on Steel. Cloth. $1 75.

LIFE AND REIGN OF NICHOLAS I., EMPEROR OF RUSSIA. The only complete history of this great personage that has appeared in the English language, and furnishes interesting facts in connection with Russian society and government of great practical value to the attentive reader. By SAMUEL M. SCHMUCKER, LL. D. With Illustrations. Cloth. $1 75.

LIFE AND TIMES OF GEORGE WASHINGTON. A concise and condensed narrative of Washington's career, especially adapted to the popular reader, and presented as the best matter upon this immortal theme—one especially worthy the attention and admiration of every American. By SAMUEL M. SCHMUCKER, LL. D. With Portrait on steel. Cloth. $1 75.

Life and Times of Alexander Hamilton. Incidents of a career that will never lose its singular power to attract and instruct, while giving impressive lessons of the brightest elements of character, surrounded and assailed by the basest. By Samuel M. Schmucker, LL. D. With Portrait on steel. Cloth. $1 75.

Life and Times of Thomas Jefferson. In which the author has presented both the merits and defects of this great representative hero in their true light, and has studiously avoided indiscriminate praise or wholesale censure. By Samuel M. Schmucker, LL. D. With Portrait. Cloth. $1 75.

Life of Benjamin Franklin. Furnishing a superior and comprehensive record of this celebrated Statesman and Philosopher—rich beyond parallel in lessons of wisdom for every age, calling and condition in life, public and private. By O. L. Holley. With Portrait on steel and Illustrations on wood. Cloth. $1 75.

Public and Private Life of Daniel Webster. The most copious and attractive collection of personal memorials concerning the great Statesman that has hitherto been published, and by one whose intimate and confidential relations with him afford a guarantee for their authenticity. By Gen. S. P. Lyman. With Illustrations. Cloth. $1 75.

Life and Times of Henry Clay. An impartial biography, presenting, by bold and simple strokes of the historic pencil, a portraiture of the illustrious theme which no one should fail to read, and no library be without. By Samuel M. Schmucker, LL. D. With Portrait on steel. Cloth. $1 75.

Life and Public Services of Stephen A. Douglas. A true and faithful exposition of the leading incidents of his brilliant career arranged so as to instruct the reader and produce the careful study which the life of so great a man deserves. By H. M. Flint. With Portrait on steel. Cloth. $1 75.

LIFE AND PUBLIC SERVICES OF ABRAHAM LINCOLN. (In both the English and German languages.) As a record of this great man it is a most desirable work, admirably arranged for reference, with an index over each page, from which the reader can familiarize himself with the contents by glancing through it. By FRANK CROSBY, of the Philadelphia Bar. With Portrait on steel. Cloth. $1 75.

LIFE OF DANIEL BOONE, THE GREAT WESTERN HUNTER AND PIONEER. Comprising graphic and authentic accounts of his daring, thrilling adventures, wonderful skill, coolness and sagacity under the most hazardous circumstances, with an autobiography dictated by himself. By CECIL B. HARTLEY. With Illustrations. Cloth. $1 75.

LIFE OF COLONEL DAVID CROCKET, THE ORIGINAL HUMORIST AND IRREPRESSIBLE BACKWOODSMAN. Showing his strong will and indomitable spirit, his bear hunting, his military services, his career in Congress, and his triumphal tour through the States—written by himself; to which is added the account of his glorious death at the Alamo. With Illustrations. Cloth. $1 75.

LIFE OF KIT CARSON, THE GREAT WESTERN HUNTER AND GUIDE. An exciting volume of wild and romantic exploits, thrilling adventures, hair-breadth escapes, daring coolness, moral and physical courage, and invaluable services—such as rarely transpire in the history of the world. By CHARLES BURDETT. With Illustrations. Cloth. $1 75.

LIFE OF CAPTAIN JOHN SMITH, THE FOUNDER OF VIRGINIA. The adventures contained herein serve to denote the more noble and daring events of a period distinguished by its spirit, its courage, and its passion, and challenges the attention of the American people. By W. GILMORE SIMMS. With Illustrations. Price $1 75.

LIFE OF GENERAL FRANCIS MARION, THE CELEBRATED PARTISAN HERO OF THE REVOLUTION. This was one of the most distinguished men who figured on the grand theatre of war during the times that "tried men's souls," and his brilliant career has scarcely a parallel in history. By CECIL B. HARTLEY. With Illustrations. Cloth. $1 75.

Life of General Andrew Jackson, the Celebrated Patriot and Statesman. The character here shown as firm in will, clear in judgment, rapid in decision and decidedly pronounced, sprung from comparative obscurity to the highest gift within the power of the American people, and is prolific in interest. By Alexander Walker. $1 75.

Life and Times of General Sam Houston, the Hunter, Patriot, and Statesman. It reminds one of the story of Romulus—who was nurtured by the beasts of the forest till he planted the foundations of a mighty empire—and stands alone as an authentic memoir. With Maps, Portrait, and Illustrations. Cloth. $1 75.

Lives of the Three Mrs. Judsons, the Celebrated Female Missionaries. The domestic lives and individual labors of these three bright stars in the galaxy of American heroines, who in ministering to the souls of heathens, experienced much of persecution. By Cecil B. Hartley. With steel Portraits. Cloth. $1 75.

Life of Elisha Kent Kane, and of Other Distinguished American Explorers. A narrative of the discoverers who possess the strongest hold upon public interest and attention, and one of the few deeply interesting volumes of distinguished Americans of this class. By Samuel M. Schmucker, LL. D. With Portrait on steel. Cloth. $1 75.

The Life and Adventures of Pauline Cushman, the Celebrated Union Spy and Scout. Stirring details from the lips of the subject herself, whose courage, heroism, and devotion to the old flag, endeared her to the Army of the Southwest. By F. L. Sarmiento, Esq., Member of the Philadelphia Bar. With Portrait on steel and Illustrations on wood. Cloth. $1 75.

Jefferson Davis and Stonewall Jackson: The Life and Public Services of Each. Truths from the lives of these men, both of whom served their country before the war, and afterwards threw themselves into the cause of the South with unbounded zeal—affording valuable historic facts for all, North and South. With Illustrations. Cloth. $1 75.

CORSICA, AND THE EARLY LIFE OF NAPOLEON. Delicately drawn idyllic descriptions of the Island, yielding new light to political history, exciting much attention in Germany and England, and altogether making a book of rare character and value. Translated by Hon. E. JOY MORRIS. With Portrait on steel. Cloth. $1 75.

THE HORSE AND HIS DISEASES: EMBRACING HIS HISTORY AND VARIETIES, BREEDING AND MANAGEMENT, AND VICES. A splendid, complete, and reliable book—the work of more than fifteen years' careful study—pointing out diseases accurately, and recommending remedies that have stood the test of actual trial. To which is added "RAREY'S METHOD OF TRAINING HORSES." By ROBERT JENNINGS, V. S. With nearly one hundred Illustrations. Cloth. $1 75.

SHEEP, SWINE, AND POULTRY. Enumerating their varieties and histories; the best modes of breeding, feeding, and managing; the diseases to which they are subject; the best remedies—and offering the best practical treatise of its kind now published. By ROBERT JENNINGS, V. S. With numerous Illustrations. Cloth. $1 75.

CATTLE AND THEIR DISEASES. Giving their history and breeds, crossing and breeding, feeding and management; with the diseases to which they are subject, and the remedies best adapted to their cure; to which is added a list of remedies used in treating cattle. By ROBERT JENNINGS, V. S. With numerous Illustrations. Cloth. $1 75.

HORSE TRAINING MADE EASY. A new and practical system of Teaching and Educating the Horse, including whip training and thorough instructions in regard to shoeing—full of information of a useful and well-tested character. By ROBERT JENNINGS, V. S. With numerous Illustrations. Cloth. $1 25.

600 RECEIPTS WORTH THEIR WEIGHT IN GOLD. An unequalled variety in kind, the collection and testing of which have extended through a period of thirty years—a number of them having never before appeared in print, while all are simple, plain, and highly meritorious. By JOHN MARQUART, of Lebanon, Pa. Cloth. $1 75.

EXPLORATIONS AND DISCOVERIES DURING FOUR YEARS' WANDERINGS IN THE WILDS OF SOUTHWESTERN AFRICA. Importan' and exciting experiences, full of wild adventure and instructive facts, whic. seem to possess a mysterious charm for every mind, and in which the spiri' o. intelligent and adventurous curiosity is everywhere prominent. By CHARLE' JOHN ANDERSON. With Illustrations. Cloth. $1 75.

LIVINGSTONE'S TRAVELS AND RESEARCHES IN SOUTH AFRICA. Given in the pleasing language of Dr. Livingstone, and rich in the personal adventures and hair-breadth escapes of that most indefatigable discoverer and interesting Christian gentleman—making a work of special value. By DAVID LIVINGSTONE, LL. D., D. C. S. Profusely Illustrated. Cloth. $1 75.

TRAVELS AND DISCOVERIES IN NORTH AND CENTRAL AFRICA. Recounting an expedition undertaken under the auspices o. H. B. M.'s Government, exhibiting the most remarkable courage, perseverance, presence of mind, and contempt of danger and death, and immensely important as a work of information. By HENRY BARTH, Ph. D., D. C. L., etc. With Illustrations. Cloth. $1 75.

ELLIS' THREE VISITS TO MADAGASCAR. Written in Madagascar, while on a visit to the queen and people, in which is carefully described the singularly beautiful country and the manners and customs of its people, and from which an unusual amount of information is obtainable. By Rev. WILLIAM ELLIS, F. H. S. Profusely Illustrated. Cloth. $1 75.

ORIENTAL AND WESTERN SIBERIA. A Stirring narrative of seven years' explorations in Siberia, Mongolia, the Kirghes' Steppes, Chinese Tartary, and part of Central Asia, revealing extraordinary facts, showing much of hunger, thirst, and perilous adventure, and forming a work o. rare attractiveness for every reader. By THOMAS WILLIAM ATKINSON. With numerous Illustrations. Cloth. $1 75.

HUNTING SCENES IN THE WILDS OF AFRICA. Thrilling adventures of daring hunters—Cummings, Harris, and others—amon; the Lions, Elephants, Giraffes, Buffaloes, and other animals—than which few, if any works, are more exciting. With numerous Illustrations. Cloth. $1 75.

HUNTING ADVENTURES IN THE NORTHERN WILDS. A tramp in the Chateaugay Woods, over hills, lakes and forest streams, at a time when millions of acres lay in a perfect wilderness, affording incidents, descriptions, and adventures of extraordinary interest. By S. H. HAMMOND. With Illustrations. Cloth. $1 75.

WILD NORTHERN SCENES; OR, SPORTING ADVENTURES WITH THE RIFLE AND THE ROD. Affording remarkably interesting experiences in a section where the howl of the Wolf, the scream of the Panther, and the hoarse bellow of the Moose could be heard—presenting a racy book. By S. H. HAMMOND. With Illustrations. Cloth. $1 75.

PERILS AND PLEASURES OF A HUNTER'S LIFE; OR, THE ROMANCE OF HUNTING. Replete with thrilling incidents and hair-breadth escapes, and fascinating in the extreme, while depicting the romance of hunting. By PEREGRINE HERNE. With Illustrations. Cloth. $1 75.

HUNTING SPORTS IN THE WEST. An amount of novelty and variety, of bold enterprise and noble hardihood, of heroic daring and fierce encounters, which seem to be much more entertaining by the quiet fireside than they would be to the one going through them in the forest or field. By CECIL B. HARTLEY. With numerous Illustrations. Cloth. $1 75.

FANNY HUNTER'S WESTERN ADVENTURES. Vividly portraying the stirring scenes enacted in Kansas and Missouri during a sojourn of several years on the Western Border, and fully representing social and domestic affairs in frontier life—containing curious pictures of character. With Illustrations. Cloth. $1 75.

WONDERFUL ADVENTURES, BY LAND AND SEA, OF THE SEVEN QUEER TRAVELLERS WHO MET AT AN INN. Revelations of a singular and unusually entertaining character, in which the most terrible circumstances and mysterious occurrences are faithfully and forcibly placed before the reader. By JOSIAH BARNES. Cloth. $1 75.

NICARAGUA; PAST, PRESENT, AND FUTURE.

Setting forth its history, the manners and customs of its inhabitants, its mines, its minerals, and other productions, and throwing light upon a subject of very great importance to the masses of our people. By PETER F. STOUT, Esq., late U. S. Vice-Consul. Cloth. $1 75.

FEMALE LIFE AMONG THE MORMONS; OR,

MARIA WARD'S DISCLOSURES. Romantic Incidents, bordering or the marvelous, which show the evils, horrors, and abominations of the Mormon system—the degradation of its females, and the consequent vices of its society. By MARIA WARD, the Wife of a Mormon Elder. With Illustrations. 40,000 copies sold. Cloth. $1 75.

MALE LIFE AMONG THE MORMONS. Detailing

sights and scenes among the Mormons, with important remarks on their moral and social economy; being a true transcript of events, viewing Mormonism from a man's standpoint, and forming a companion to the preceding volume. By AUSTIN N. WARD. Edited by MARIA WARD. With Illustrations. Cloth. $1 75.

PIONEER LIFE IN THE WEST. Describing the

adventures of Boone, Kenton, Brady, Clark, the Whetzels, the Johnsons, and others, in their fierce encounters with the Indians, and making up a work of the most entertaining and instructive character for those who delight in history and adventure. With numerous Illustrations. Cloth. $1 75.

THRILLING STORIES OF THE GREAT REBEL-

LION. Fearful adventures of soldiers, scouts, spies, and refugees; daring exploits of smugglers, guerillas, desperadoes, and others; tales of loyal and disloyal women; stories of the negro, and incidents of fun and merriment in camp and field. By Lieut. CHARLES S. GREENE, late of the U. S. Army. With Illustrations in Oil. Cloth. $1 75.

HISTORY OF THE WAR IN INDIA. FURNISHING

the complete history of British India, together with interesting and thrilling details which have scarcely a parallel in the world's history, to which is added a memoir of General Sir HENRY HAVELOCK. By HENRY FREDERICK MALCOLM. Illustrated with numerous Engravings. Cloth. $1 75.

www.ingramcontent.com/pod-product-compliance
Lightning Source LLC
LaVergne TN
LVHW021135110826
845150LV00005B/1033

* 9 7 8 1 4 2 5 5 4 9 6 0 2 *